ZOMBIE
FAIRY TALES

KEVIN RICHEY

To summon the author, please send incantations to info@zombiefairytales.com.

Cover design by David Gardner.

www.zombiefairytales.com

First Edition

ISBN: 149429804X
ISBN-13: 978-1494298043

For David.

ACKNOWLEDGEMENTS

This series would not exist without the input, time, and support of many remarkable individuals. I'd like to thank, first and foremost, my husband David: for being my first reader; for the wonderful covers; for his never-ending encouragement throughout the many drafts and long nights that each story required; and for always reminding me that it's okay to be dark, and better yet to be darker. I'd like to thank my other first reader, Janie, who saved me much embarrassment with her keen eye for typos, and a special thanks goes out to all the models who agreed to become "zombiefied" for the early covers: the zombie family of Zane, Zoe and Stacey; Devin; Zachary; Desiato; and Cherisse, Cherisse, Cherisse (I think you were on roughly half the covers, Cherisse). Thank you again, Desiato, for designing the many costumes. They were perfect. I also owe thanks to the many wonderful readers who have reached out to me online with feedback and encouragement, and to Kayleigh, who is perhaps the series' biggest fan.

A NOTE ON READING ORDER

The fairy tales in this volume have been rearranged to reflect the chronological events of the greater narrative. If you would prefer to read the stories in their original publication order, the series would be read as follows (using this book's chapter numbering): 5, 2, 1, 3, 4, 6-12.

CONTENTS

1   The Zombie Pinocchio   1

2   Hansel and Gretel Are Dead   38

3   Blood Red Riding Hood   78

4   Beauty Is a Beast   115

5   Zombie Cinderella   156

6   Zombie Cinderella II: The Ball   194

7   Revenge of the Little Match Girl   227

8   The Curse of Peter Pan   270

9   The Little Mermaid of Death   321

10   The Headless Horseman   374

11   Skull White   417

12   Sleeping Beauty Wakes in Hell   459

13   The Screams of Pocahontas   519

ZOMBIE
FAIRY TALES

Through me is the way to the city of woe;
Through me is the way to eternal pain;
Through me is the way among the citizens of Hell.

Abandon all hope, ye who enter in!

— *Dante*

THE ZOMBIE PINOCCHIO

He needed hands. Hands were all that remained. Then his boy would be complete.

Geppetto took a cautious step forward, keeping his eye on the sleeping gravedigger. His legs were cramped from spending the night huddled behind a bush, waiting for the gravedigger to end his drunken revelry. Now the early dawn lit the cemetery in a blue-gray light, and the air smelled heavy with moist soil. He tapped under his coat for perhaps the hundredth time in the last hour—the hacksaw was still hidden there—and he continued on.

The mausoleum door had no handle. An iron rod leaned against it in the brown grass, and he used it to pry open the heavy stone door. It opened with a gasp, and he slipped through. He gave a last look at the gravedigger, and then pulled the door shut as much as he dared.

It was dark inside, and the air thick with the now too familiar scent of death. He lit a match and gazed at the crypts lining the walls, covered with dust and cobwebs. He brought the flame to the wick of a candle in an ancient candleholder, melted over with the remains of hundreds of dead candles. Then he shook out the match as the flame took hold, not even flickering in the airless chamber.

1

He studied the caskets for signs of disturbance, bending down and trying to read the names. He blew at the dust on the engravings, and a cloud of grime flew back into his face, clouding his glasses and making him choke. He put his hand over his mouth and his eyes darted toward the door. He blinked, his eyes watering, and breathed in through his nose. But the dust had caught in his moustache, and before he could stop himself, he let out a bellowing sneeze.

He stood, silent, and waited for the gravedigger to barge in. It had been too easy, this collecting of bodies. Between the plague and the gravedigger's negligence, Geppetto had been able to gather almost all the parts he needed within the week. It would have been easier still if there were such a thing as a perfect whole. But at most he had been able to find a decent foot here, a passable jaw there. He quickly learned that if he wanted a perfect boy, he would have to make one himself.

But now so close to the end, like a cruel joke, he would be caught. And for nothing more than a sneeze.

He waited another moment, waiting but with no interruption, and then crept to the door to peer out.

The world was covered with a blanket of fog. He couldn't see a thing.

Then Geppetto realized that his glasses were covered with dust. He took off his small gold-framed spectacles, rubbed them clean on the hem of his coat, and looked again.

The gravedigger had sat up, and was looking around him with eyes that seemed to struggle to keep open. He faced the mausoleum, held his gaze for a moment, and then fell over on his side. Almost instantly, Geppetto heard the wheezing of his snores.

Geppetto sighed. He had been given another chance.

Sometimes, when his luck would seem too good to be true, he would think it was the supernatural intervention of his dead wife. He gave a mental thanks to his darling, and then turned back in toward the darkness.

And at once he saw what he hadn't before. There, on the bottom row of crypts, was a scuffmark in the dust. He bent down, and saw that the handle of the small casket had been cleaned by the hands of the priest and crypt keeper. He pulled the coffin onto the floor before him, and lifted the lid.

The candlelight flickered on the white pure hands of the dead boy, folded across his chest like angel's wings. The boy himself was less impressive.

His eyes and mouth had been sewn shut, his nose twisted, his features snobbish and cruel. Even his frame was misshapen, bent like a question mark in his coffin. But he had one saving grace: because he had been the only son of a wealthy family, he had never used his hands for anything. And they remained in mint condition until his dying day.

But Geppetto had to make sure they would work.

He pulled out a measuring tape from his pocket. He lifted up the boy's lifeless hand, tightening the tape from the tip of the fingernails to the joint of the wrist. He put his thumb on the mark and went over to the candle.

At the light, he took out a parchment from his back pocket that had an outline of a boy broken into parts, like the map of a terrain divided into countries. He stared down at the black marks and scribbles, then back at the measuring tape, then again at his notes.

A cold, cruel smile crinkled the skin around his eyes and lifted the edges of his lips past his gray moustache.

The hands were perfect.

He replaced the parchment and measuring tape in his pocket, and brought out the saw. He returned to the boy, drawing up his arm from the elbow, and placing the teeth of the saw just below the wrist. He bent around to see the angle of the cut from both sides, nodded, and drew the blade across the skin.

The skin cut quickly, almost as if it were nothing at all. It was the bone that took some effort. He dragged the jagged edge of the saw back and forth against it in even, methodical swipes, and let his imagination stray to thoughts of his perfect boy.

One that would love him, and keep him company in the lonely evenings after the toyshop had closed. One that would be the envy of the neighborhood, bright and tall and proud. And, what made him most perfect of all, one that would never die.

He was thinking this, done with the first hand and nearly halfway through the second, when the body's arm grew suddenly heavier. Geppetto looked down, confused, and stopped the motion of the saw.

The arm was pulling back to the body.

The boy was struggling to sit up, rocking his shoulders against the sides of his coffin. The skin of his face stretched as he tried to open his eyes and mouth, and a low growling came from his throat.

Geppetto shook his head. It would take more than that to stop him. Besides, he had already seen some of these plague victims return. They tried to attack, but could only succeed if you let them. And he wanted those hands too much to let go.

He pressed his elbow down on the boy's chest, pinning it in the coffin, and rushed to finish. He sawed in quick succession against the bone, getting the odd image in his mind of trying to start a fire by rubbing two sticks together. He was surprised he wasn't drawing sparks. As he worked, the boy's other arm raised, nothing more than a stump, and feebly knocked against Geppetto's side.

And outside, the light grew brighter and brighter.

Finally, the hand dropped to the ground with a dull thump. He pushed the boy back into the coffin, shut the lid, and shoved it back into the wall before the thing could object. He took the hands and placed them fingers down into the inner pockets of his coat, one on each side. He blew out the candle, and looked back out to the cemetery.

It was dawn. The gravedigger was still asleep, nestling in his tools with a bottle in his hand, but beyond the cemetery there were people on the streets, rushing past toward the marketplace, or down toward the different stores in town. If anyone saw him—just one—how would he ever explain himself? What would a toymaker be doing hiding in a mausoleum all night? And if they opened his coat... there would be no explaining that.

But he couldn't stay here. If he left the door open, someone would notice and look inside. Or close it absent-mindedly, and lock him inside with the dead. This door took effort to open from the outside. There wasn't even a handle on the inside, not even a groove. And he doubted anyone would hear him, no matter how hard he knocked. Better to be found out than to have it end that way.

He closed his eyes and took in a deep breath through his nostrils, and then let it out between his lips. He would have to risk it. There was no other way. The longer he waited, the worse it would be. He had to do it now.

He opened his eyes, narrowing them against the morning light. His eyes darted back and forth, watching the towns-folk crossing each way on the street outside the cemetery. Then, as casually as he could, he pushed open the stone door of the mausoleum, stepped outside, and walked slowly past the tombstones toward the main path that led to the gate. The sky was overcast, hiding shadows and giving the cemetery a cold gray color that blended with his drab coat. Nobody from the street turned toward him.

He had made it nearly to the gate when the gravedigger snorted, waking himself up. Geppetto kept his face blank, his eyes forward, and continued at a leisurely pace toward the main gate. Out of the corner of his eye, he saw the gravedigger watching him. Then, when he had placed one shoe on the cobblestone of the street, he saw the gravedigger shrug and fall back over into what must have been a very enjoyable sleep.

Geppetto entered the crowd on the street. No one was looking at him. He walked forward, letting the flow of traffic take him away from the cemetery. The boy's hands pressed against his stomach with each step, and he felt almost giddy. He had to work to keep the corners of his lips from smiling too openly. His eyes, though, he couldn't control those, and they twinkled behind his glasses as he walked.

He looked at all the bored, tired faces passing him, and thought: If only he could tell them. Because the best part was, of all the people in the town, he would be the absolute last person they'd expect to do something strange. They thought he just sat home alone each night, content with his empty little life—that is, if they thought of him at all, which they probably didn't. And here he was, with a dead boy's hands in his pockets, about to go home to sew together his perfect child, a child that will outlive all of theirs, a child that could *never* die—Oh! How he wished he could tell them.

But he knew better. He kept his face blank, his steps slow, and walked at the pace of the others down the street and around the corner, until the current had dropped him off at the stoop of his toyshop, which was also his home. He knocked the cemetery dirt from his shoes, replaced his keys in his pocket, and patted his coat for perhaps the hundred-and-first time that night, and—

And the saw was gone. He felt again, his door open ajar. There were the dead boy's hands, there was his measuring tape, his parchment, his matches. But the saw? His stomach dropped. It was back in the mausoleum. Right on the floor, covered with blackened blood right in front of the dead boy's coffin.

He stood, deciding between going inside, and turning right back around to the cemetery. And as he wavered, a voice called his name from the crowd. He looked up, and there was the priest, coming forward against the crowd in his black cassock, holding up a hand to wait.

It's over, Geppetto thought. They've found the saw. That's all it took.

The priest joined him on the stoop, his ruddy face sprinkled with beads of sweat. He was a stout man, with a bald patch on the top of his head, and a circle of dark hair ringing his temples. His eyes opened wide with enthusiasm, and at once Geppetto could see he knew nothing.

He stared at the priest, waiting for an explanation. He didn't have time for games. But the priest only looked at the door, waiting to be invited inside.

Geppetto clenched his teeth, fighting an audible groan, and said, "After you."

They walked inside, and Geppetto shut the door behind them. It was dark in the toyshop. The windows were shuttered, and the counters and shelves floated in the shadows. A thin band of light from the doorway sliced through the room, and landed as a vertical stripe on the body of the priest. One of his eyes glowed pale green, the black pupil constricting in the light.

"You had something to say?" Geppetto asked.

"Oh," he said, and his eye smiled, "you can open the store. I don't mind waiting. We priests may live in the church, but we understand a business is a business."

Geppetto had no intention of opening the store today. Not with the perfect hands pressing against his stomach. But he was too tired to think of a reason to tell the priest for being closed, so he walked to the end of the store, and began taking down the shutters. Light flowed into the toyshop, revealing wooden trinkets and mechanical toys cluttering the shelves. Most had a thick layer of dust. Geppetto didn't care; he might have cared once, but he didn't now.

He set down the final shutter and turned to the priest, waiting. The priest stared out the window, his thumbs looped through his rope belt, and watched a cart pass by, loaded with the latest victims of the plague. They were piled like logs, an arm from an unseen body hanging out the back, its blackened fingernails dragging on the street.

"These are hard times," the priest said. "None of us knows how long we have left."

Geppetto was silent. He had no interest in encouraging a theological debate.

The priest turned away from the window, throwing up his hands as if washing them of the scene. "But we must move on! Tell me, Geppetto, how have you been? What have you been doing?"

Geppetto glared at the priest, trying to deduce any hidden meanings. There seemed to be something else the priest was asking. "Why?" he asked finally.

"Oh, no reason." The priest looked down at his hands and smiled. "People have their own reasons to be away. I know a man in town, a Mr. Van Winkle, who enjoys taking sabbaticals in the woods. He says he finds the best worship in the beauty of nature." The priest frowned. "I haven't seen him in my church in over a year. Apparently, no one has, not even his family. But I suppose we can hardly compete with the perfection of nature."

Geppetto scoffed. "Perfection?"

The priest laughed. "I don't see it either. True, there is something beautiful about the trees and flowers, but to say *every* creature is perfect? Only man is created in God's image, after all. The rest can be quite hideous. For instance, have you ever looked at a toad, Geppetto? I mean really *looked* at it?" The priest shuddered. "The devil's work, I'm sure."

Geppetto stood in the center of the floor, distracted by the missing saw and the hands under his coat. "Well," he said, "it's always a pleasure to have you visit." He took a step to the door, and the priest held up a hand.

He shook his head with regret. "I wanted to give you a chance to come forward on your own, but…"

He let out a heavy sigh.

"Did you think I wouldn't guess? I know, Geppetto. I know your entire scheme."

They stared at each other in silence. Finally, Geppetto asked, "Excuse me?"

The priest counted on his fingers. "Bringing dead children gifts. Loitering around cemeteries. Your general *moody* behavior." He dropped his hands. "There's more, I'm sure, but I don't need to go on, do I?"

Geppetto couldn't move. His eyes flashed toward the door. If he ran—he might make it if he ran. But to leave it all behind, just now, the moment he had it complete?

"It's all very obvious," he continued. Geppetto cringed, and the priest rolled his eyes. "You're shopping for a wife!"

Geppetto straightened. *Wife?*

"Now, the Widow Abigail. You remember her? She's the short thing with the crooked walk? She took a fancy to you the day you brought that delightful marionette to her boy's grave—may he rest in peace—and hasn't stopped talking about you since."

There were no words. Geppetto stared, dumbfounded, feeling an anger growing inside him. To be caught was one thing, but to be distracted for something as senseless as gossip? "I think you'd better go."

"Come now!" The priest chuckled. "Let me play matchmaker. After all, you've been a widower for nearly a decade. And, let's face it, time has not been kind."

Geppetto crossed to the door and opened it, ushering the priest out. The priest didn't seem to mind his abrupt departure, and sauntered to the door, stopping on the stoop to put a hand on Geppetto's wrist.

"Just do me a favor," he said. "Meet her. Decide for yourself. Surely, anything is better than being alone?"

Geppetto tried to turn away, and the priest tightened his grip, brushing against the front of his coat, almost touching his fat red hands to the perfect white fingers beneath.

"Fine," Geppetto snapped, pushing the priest away. "Do whatever you like. Just *leave*."

The priest gave a little bow and took a step away. "God bless, God bless."

Then he stopped, just as Geppetto was closing the door. "Oh, one more thing."

"What?"

"Open some windows first. It smells a bit ripe in there." He gave a little smile, then turned on his heel and swam back into the crowd. Geppetto heaved the door shut, and breathed out in relief.

At last he was alone, and free to make himself alone no longer.

He stood back, and realized he was shaking. He pictured his wife's face, her golden skin and soft smile. She had easy eyes. They looked at the world and made everything she gazed on peaceful and right. And when she had looked into Geppetto's eyes—

"No," he told himself, tightening his hands into fists. This was not a time to give in to the loneliness. He was merely tired. How long had it been since he'd had a good night's rest?

Ten years.

"No!" he shouted, pounding his fists against the door. "This will work. This *must* work."

He looked down at the shutters, and then ran to them. He placed them on the windows in a mad rush, as if trying to defend against a storm on a sinking ship. Then he went to the door, bolted the lock, and threw down the security bar.

He took in another deep breath, and his face drained of all emotion. He felt better now, locked away against intruders. Against priests who like to talk too much, making suggestions that he find a new wife. Against the world that kept waiting for him to move on. To forget.

But why move on when he had a way to continue life

where he had left off? To create the child they never had? The life they never had?

He felt the hands under his coat and they touched him with a hot flash of hope. He gave one look back toward the closed shutters, and sneered at the world outside. He walked through the toyshop to a wooden staircase on the back wall, and climbed up, completely focused now. He took a key from his pocket and opened the door at the top, locking it behind.

This floor was a cramped space for storage, filled with shadowed boxes and tools. It smelled strongly here of death and rank bodies, but he kept the window boarded shut. In the corner was a cot that Geppetto used infrequently. Lately, he had taken to sleeping at his desk. But that was on the next level.

The top level, the attic, was accessible by a small spiral staircase. It creaked under his steps, and rattled as he made his way up to a latched doorway in the ceiling. He pushed open the latch, and a blast of rotten air met his nose. He curled his lips and climbed up to this secret room, and bolted the latch at once.

He struck a match and lit the lamp hanging from the center of the slanted ceiling. The walls were wooden boards, unable to keep out foul weather, but they protected against the light. He had sealed the small window here with bricks. This was a space untouched by daylight, protected from the prying eyes of the town outside.

In the center of the room was a long, low table. Spread out on this table were bundles wrapped in brown cloth and tied with twine. These were arranged in the shape of a small person. He took the hands from his coat pockets, and placed them at the ends of what would be the figure's arms.

There was a moment, staring at the parts before him on the table, when he felt frozen. What if this didn't work? He had seen some of these children rise from their coffins—it was rumors of this that first gave him the idea—but what if he sewed his child together and nothing happened? It was almost better not to try than to face the disappointment of failure. Of going back to the way things were before. The thought of all those lonely days and lonely nights terrified him. He wouldn't go back to that. He couldn't. He would rather die.

"Yes, I would rather die," he said aloud. And he made up his mind that, if this didn't work, he would kill himself. The mental image of his body swinging back and forth on a noose, outside his window for the entire town to see, gave him the strength to continue.

He pulled up a stool, and began unwrapping the parts. A length of arm. The knob of a knee. Aside from the smell and discoloration, they were still in remarkable condition. Whatever this plague was, it preserved the dead better than anything he had ever seen.

All but the head. The head he had chosen was from a boy who had drowned in the lake outside of town, not from the plague. Geppetto had wanted his boy to have a sweet face. A loving face. Not one with those monstrous black circles around the eyes.

When everything was unwrapped and laid out, the table looked like the cart of a fish vendor. Everything in shades of gray, looking flabby and raw, with clean cuts down through the flesh and bone. It smelled much worse than any fish vendor, though, and Geppetto found himself wishing that he hadn't sealed the window. But only for a moment. The stench wouldn't kill him, and it was worth it.

Next was the sewing. This required much concentration. The needle had to be pulled delicately through the flesh to avoid ripping the skin, and he had to work to keep the stitches even, so that they wouldn't embarrass his son.

Children could be quite sensitive about such things.

He worked the greater portion of the day threading, pulling, and assembling his child. It wasn't until he had made the last stitch and cut through the last thread with his teeth that the doubts returned.

Why hadn't he come alive yet? He was together now. There weren't any more parts.

He looked down at the child on the table, the gray body held together by black thread. Every limb was perfect, without blemish. He leaned under the table and pulled out some old clothes he had stolen from a corpse, and dressed the boy, trying not to think about how he wasn't moving.

But it was like dressing a doll. The body, misshapen and dense, flopped down as soon as he let go. He propped it up in the center of the table, and the eyes stared at him blankly, wide open and dead.

"You can come alive now," he said to it. "There's nobody watching."

He waited a moment, staring. Then he said again, "It's okay. You can live now. *Please*."

Nothing happened.

"Maybe you need a little help."

Geppetto slid the body back to the center of the table, and unbuttoned the boy's shirt. His toolbox was in the corner, and he went to it, calling, "Just a minute!"

He ran back with a small knife, no larger than a pen, and used its thin blade to cut a line down the child's chest, where the ribs met. He threw aside the knife, rolled up his sleeve, and shoved his hand inside the child's chest. He slithered past wet and cold organs, until his fingers wrapped around what he was sure was the heart.

"Okay?" he shouted. "I'm going to help you live."

He squeezed the heart, released, and squeezed again.

"Please," he begged, and tried again. But it wasn't working. Why did he think this would work? It was nothing but hope. Unfounded, unreasonable hope. "*Please*, there's nobody else."

The corpse didn't respond, and Geppetto took out his

hand. He wiped it on the side of his pants, and then picked up the thread. He didn't bother to make these stitches even. His hands and arms felt heavy, and he laced up the chest and turned away. Exhaustion spread through his body.

He dropped to his knees, and began to sob. The only way his child would ever walk and dance like normal children would be if he fixed it up with strings, and led it around like a human marionette.

He was half-tempted to try this, but the other half of him recognized the futility of such a gesture. He slumped to the floor, curling into a fetal position, and wrapped his arms around his head.

"Why?" he asked. "Why did you have to leave me?"

He sobbed, envisioning his wife. She was the one with the power of life, not him. He closed his eyes, and in his exhaustion entered a state not quite dreaming, not quite awake. He saw himself standing in the toyshop, the bright sunlight making the whole store sparkle. His wife was there, dressed in a gown of shimmering blue. She had her relaxed smile, and she gazed at him with her temperate eyes. She glowed, otherworldly, like a nymph or fairy, and placed a hand on Geppetto's shoulder.

"Why are you so sad, my husband?" she asked. Her voice was golden and warm.

"Because I'm alone," Geppetto said. "You left me."

"But I didn't leave you alone," she said. "What about little Pinocchio?"

"Who?"

She smiled. "Our son, of course." She stepped aside, and behind her stood the boy he had created, perfect, alive. He was free of lacerations and stitch marks, and looked up at Geppetto with adoration.

He bent down to the boy and threw his arms around him. "I knew you'd be okay," he said, "I knew it." He squeezed the boy, feeling the heart beating inside his chest, and said, "You'll be a good boy. You'll be perfect."

The child whispered, a coy smile on his lips, "But, Father, *I'm* not a boy. Not a real one."

"What do you mean, Pinocchio?"

"I'm dying."

He giggled, his skin changing from a golden tone to gray. His entire body began to wither like an old flower. Geppetto tightened his grip around him, but the child's limbs fell off, one by one, and hit the ground. Finally, his head rolled from off his shoulders, and dropped like a cannonball, exploding into pieces as it hit the floor with a thunderous blast.

Geppetto woke up on the hard floor, his hand covered in grime. His body was racked with aches, and his foot was dead asleep. He kicked it against the floor, feeling the pinpricks of the blood that flowed back into it. He had no idea what time it was. The room was dark, the candle extinguished. He pulled himself to a sitting position with a groan, and reached into his pocket for his matches. He lit one, blinking, and rose to his feet.

The table was bare. He turned to the hatch and saw it was open. And from the level below, he heard another thunderous blast, the same one from his dream. He looked back at the empty table, then held the match high in the room to check the empty corners. Then he turned to the hatch, seeing nothing below, and placed a foot at the top of the spiral staircase. The match blew out at once, but he didn't care.

He ran down the stairs, hearing movement but unable to see. He should have been afraid. There might be other explanations for the boy's absence. He might have been found out. Intruders might be ripping apart his store in search of other bodies. But he didn't think so. Anyone that might be accusing him would wake him up, not leave him sleeping. There's only one thing that this could be. He lit another match. There's only one explanation:

Pinocchio.

The boy—for that's what he was now, not just a corpse—

had his back to Geppetto and was busy overturning boxes across the room. The cot had already been knocked over, and the table next to it had been smashed into splinters. Geppetto picked up a lantern that had been thrown to the ground, and lit it with his match. At that expansion of light, the boy stopped. His shoulders were arched and his head hunched, and his hands curled into claws. Then, slowly, he turned at the waist and faced Geppetto.

He looked like a little leprechaun. He was short, maybe coming up to Geppetto's waist, with an impish face and eyes that gleamed. His skin was still gray, and dark circles formed around his eyes, but that did nothing to dim his appeal. He was the most beautiful creature Geppetto had ever seen.

He took a step forward in bare feet, the dark marks of the stitches stretching on his ankles and below his knees.

Geppetto bent down and opened his arms. "Pinocchio! Come to me, my Pinocchio."

The boy pressed his foot on the ground, his eyes on Geppetto, and dragged his other foot forward. But when he leaned his weight against it, he became unbalanced and fell to the floor, face first. He hadn't even put out his arms to break the fall, and he didn't make any attempt to get up.

"Oh!" Geppetto cried, and ran forward. He set the lantern on the floor, and lifted up Pinocchio, setting him back on his feet. The boy seemed dazed, but otherwise unharmed. And stepping back to look at him, Geppetto clasped his hands together and felt his eyes fill with tears of gratitude.

"You're really here," he whispered. "Oh, my dear Pinocchio, you're *really* here."

The boy wasn't paying attention. He raised an arm before his face and stared at the stitches that wrapped like a bracelet around his wrist. Except that beneath the bands of the bracelet, fibers of red flesh peeked through. He looked up at Geppetto.

"Oh, those." Geppetto smiled. "Those are from when I

sewed you together. I'm your father, Pinocchio. Can you say 'father'?"

The boy looked back down at the stitches. Then, with an effort, raised his other arm and pressed his fist against his palm. He bent back the hand until the gap on his wrist opened like a jaw.

"No!" Geppetto said, rushing forward. He spread apart Pinocchio's hands, and held them there. He looked deep into the boy's eyes, his eyebrows raised, and then looked down at the arm.

There didn't seem to be much damage, other than the stitches being stretched. Geppetto sighed and took the injured hand, and began tightening the thread like shoelaces. "You must be more careful. Your stitches still have to heal. Then we'll take them out, and you'll be just like everyone else. Well, almost." He smiled. "You'll be better." Finished, he sat back on his knees.

Pinocchio turned his dark eyes back to his wrist, but didn't try to touch it again. Instead he opened his mouth.

A blast of foul air emerged, and his dry tongue flopped. There was a rasping sound, but no words. Pinocchio closed his mouth, his eyebrows lowering, and then opened it again. His lips stretched back over his teeth as he tried with more effort to speak. But again only a dry rasp sounded from the back of his throat.

"What is it?" Geppetto asked. "What are you trying to say?" He put a hand on the boy's shoulder, but Pinocchio pulled away.

The boy was angry now, groaning in frustration and pressing his hands on either side of his head, shaking it back and forth. His mouth was open but silent.

"What's wrong?" Geppetto shouted, rising to his feet. But the boy was getting worse.

What if he can't breath? Geppetto wondered. What if I sewed him up wrong and he can't breathe?

He looked down, helpless, as Pinocchio gasped and moaned.

The boy dropped his hands from his head and his eyes widened, darting around the room as if he were seeing phantoms. He overturned more boxes, sending toy soldiers and marionettes spilling to the floor.

Geppetto chased after him, begging wildly. "Please, stay still, let me help, oh what's wrong?" But the child was in a rampage. He found a crate of chess pieces, looked inside, then threw it to the ground. The pieces spilled and rolled, and the boy walked over them, unfeeling, unseeing, as he cried out in his hoarse groans.

Then, as he was about to crash into a carton of delicate figurines, he stopped abruptly in the middle of the room. His foot was still raised in motion. It was as if he were a wind-up doll that had been alive one moment, and then dead again the next. And this silence scared Geppetto more than the rampage before.

But before he could say anything, he heard cries from outside. There were shouts coming from the street beneath the window. He looked back to Pinocchio, and saw that the boy had tilted his head toward the window, listening.

The boy's whole stance changed. He looked at the window as if he had seen a deer in the forest, and took careful steps toward it, as if he might scare it away by moving too quickly. All the while the cries from outside echoed in. It was the high-pitched trill of children, and Geppetto couldn't tell if the quivering voices were laughing or sobbing.

Pinocchio reached the boarded window, and pounded on it once with his fist. Then he drew back his arm slowly, and threw it against the wood from his elbow, as if his hand were a rock in a sling.

"Stop that," Geppetto said, and came forward pulling the boy away. He knelt and looked at the boy's hands. "Look what you've done," he said, holding it in the boy's face. "It's covered with splinters. Do you know what I went through to get you those hands?"

Pinocchio stared back at him, and even in his dull expression, there seemed to be a hard defiance in his eyes. Geppetto let him go, but as soon as he did, the boy went right back to the window, and start pounding on it again.

"We can't open it," Geppetto said, pulling Pinocchio away. "People might see in."

Pinocchio turned to him, a corner of his lip raised in a snarl. He opened his mouth and gave a fruitless gasp. Geppetto cringed at the stench. It was like the blast of air that emerged when breaking the seal of a coffin.

"Okay," he said. "I'll open it a little. Just enough for you to look out. But that's *all*. Do you understand?"

The boy closed his mouth, and turned expectantly to the window.

"You see?" Geppetto said, going to the window. He pried his fingers under a plank of wood, and tugged at it. "When you're nice, you get nice things." He pulled again, and gave a short grunt as he ripped off the plank. Pinocchio came forward and tried to push him out of the way.

"Hold on. Let me look first. To make sure it's safe."

He looked out at the street below. Everything was bathed in red light. He couldn't be sure if it was twilight or dawn, though, as he didn't know how long he had slept. Running in a circle on the cobblestones were a group of children. Boys. They were laughing and running in and out of each other in a game that seemed like some sort of frenetic waltz.

Geppetto turned back to Pinocchio, who was too short to reach the gap in the window. "Come here," Geppetto said, bending down and putting out his arms. "I'll lift you up."

The boy stared at him for a moment. Then looked up at the rectangle of glowing red. Then looked back at Geppetto.

"Don't be shy, now," Geppetto said, scooting forward and turning Pinocchio around and placing his hands beneath his arms. The boy was cold, the same temperature as the room, no different than the toy soldiers littering the ground. Geppetto shook the thought from his mind, and lifted the boy to the window, holding him around the middle from behind and leaning forward to the window as they looked down together.

"That, Pinocchio, is the town. And those, those are other children." They both watched as the children ran, throwing long black shadows across the red street. "But you mustn't ever be jealous of other children, Pinocchio. Because all those children will grow old and die. Some won't even grow old; they'll just die. But you, my son, will live forever."

They gazed at the children below, almost like watching an inferior species of fish flickering past in a stream, and Geppetto nuzzled against his son.

Finally, here was the child he had never known. Here was the life he had been living without. And all the years of bitterness, of loneliness, all the times he had watched the other townsfolk parade their families into his store and then out again, leaving him behind in the darkness as they played with their children in the sun—all the things he had never had and had always wanted—all of it was repaired, here, now, in this grateful moment pressing his warm face into Pinocchio's shoulder.

But then he felt a rumbling from inside Pinocchio, and leaned back to hear him moaning. The window reflected back their faces: Geppetto's worried eyes behind his glasses, and Pinocchio's elfish face scrunched in a grimace.

The boy lifted his hand again and knocked it against the window. He did this only once, then turned to lock his eyes with Geppetto. His beautiful face had the same agony as that of the rebel angels, just as God's lightning struck them to the earth below.

"What is it? What's wrong?" Geppetto asked. And then, as if in answer to his question, the tinkling chimes of laughter rose from the street below. His son's face twisted at the sound with a pain all too familiar to Geppetto.

"Friends," he said. "You want friends."

Pinocchio squinted his eyes. If he were able, Geppetto was sure the boy would be dripping tears.

"I'm sorry, Pinocchio." He looked deep into his son's eyes. "For now, until you're well enough to go out, it's just you and me. That will have to be enough."

The boy turned back to the window and raised an arm. Geppetto caught it before he could hammer with it.

"You won't be able to watch if you keep doing that."

But the boy slipped out of his grasp, and threw his arm against the glass with such force that it cracked. The break splintered out like a spider's web in the windowpane, and Geppetto knew that Pinocchio would not give up. He was determined to have a friend, and he would keep fighting until he got one.

"If we must, we must." He pulled Pinocchio back into the room, and bent down to him. "If I bring you a friend, will you promise to be quiet?"

Pinocchio stared up at him with eyes that screamed mutiny. But he nodded his head forward once.

"Good boy." Geppetto stood up and surveyed his son, seeing him now as a stranger might. The gray skin and stitches, the diminished mobility.

The smell.

"Maybe," he said, scanning the room, "maybe if we found something to…" His eyes paused on a hat. "Aha! Exactly what the doctor ordered!" He picked it off the ground where it lay trampled, and smoothed it out with his fingers. It was a green woodman's cap, narrow and pointed in the front. He placed it on Pinocchio's head. "There! It fits perfectly."

The boy stood with his arms slightly raised, and his eyes strained upward to look at it.

Geppetto raised a finger.

"Don't touch. Now, I'll be back in a moment. Remember your promise. Not. A. Sound."

The boy looked at him, his expression blank.

"Good boy."

He turned to the door, reaching inside his coat for the key. This door, at least, needed a key from both directions. He undid the latch, taking one last look at his son before closing the door, and turned the key. Then he ran down the stairs into the clean air of the toyshop. Breathing it in, he seemed to be waking up from a dream. And when he opened the door to his shop, it was like stepping out into another world.

Was he really the same Geppetto that had entered that door not so long ago?

No. He was no longer alone.

Outside the children had begun to disperse. He saw that it was not dawn. The sun was setting rapidly, and already the red light faded into a salmon haze. As he approached, only one little boy stayed behind, a sandy-haired child with dirt smeared on his face. He was looking down at something held in his hands, frowning. His face was vaguely familiar, a boy who had been brought into his shop at one point or another in his life. Almost all the children in the town had. Geppetto took another step forward and the child looked up.

There was a purple bruise underneath one eye. The boy took a step back.

Geppetto dropped to one knee and gave a friendly smile. "No need to be frightened," he said softly. "It's just me, Geppetto."

The boy relaxed a little, but kept his distance. And Geppetto thought how much more perfect his Pinocchio was than this child.

He asked, "Did you have a fight with your friends?"

The boy's eyes widened. "Those aren't my friends," he spat. "I hate them."

Geppetto kept the smile on his lips, but his eyes narrowed. Maybe this boy was right for Pinocchio after all. "Oh? What happened?"

The boy turned his body toward Geppetto. "They didn't believe me. You won't believe me either, even though it's the truth this time." He waited for Geppetto to disagree, but when he didn't, the boy was encouraged to continue. "It really happened this time. I saw her myself."

"Saw who?"

"The mermaid." The boy studied Geppetto a moment. "She lives in the bog in the woods outside of town. I saw her." He held a hand to the side of his mouth and whispered, "She eats children."

Geppetto stared at him in silence. The boy arched his eyebrows, and his chin shuddered. "I knew you wouldn't believe me!" he shouted, stepping back. "I knew it!"

Geppetto lifted a hand. "I believe you, boy." The boy stopped, but was unconvinced. "It's the truth. You know how I know?"

The boy's lips puckered. "How?"

Geppetto continued in a gentle voice. "Because I once heard a wise man say that if a boy tells a lie, especially a big one like that, his nose is sure to grow." He smiled. "And your nose isn't growing."

The boy smiled back, and took a step forward. Then he frowned. "But my nose didn't grow those other times, when I really did lie."

Geppetto shrugged. "Maybe it takes a few times to kick in."

The boy sniffed, and wiped his nose with the back of his dirty hand.

It was nearly dark now. The sky had turned royal blue and the first star had appeared. There wouldn't be much time left.

Geppetto bent forward and said, almost in a whisper, "Did the boys give you that bruise?"

He nodded. "But that's nothing compared to what my pa will do when I get home." His eyes watered. "But it's not my fault! The other kids broke it, not me." He put his hand forward and held a golden pocket watch in his palm. It was cracked down the center. "It was in my back pocket when they threw me to the ground."

"Oh that?" Geppetto said. "That's nothing. Why, I could have that fixed in no time."

The boy's eyes went wide. "Really?"

"Sure. A watch is no different than a wind-up doll." Geppetto stood up, towering over the boy, and held out his hand. "Come on. It'll only take a minute."

The boy looked up at him, and then turned away to look down the street, as if considering running away. Geppetto held his breath. He could feel the eyes of Pinocchio from above, ready to pounce out the window the second Geppetto failed.

Please, Geppetto thought, and his eyes glanced upward at a star that twinkled like a diamond in the sky. Please, he wished, let Pinocchio have this friend. Let me bring this to him tonight.

He felt the soft skin of the boy's hand touch his own, and he closed his rough fingers around it. He looked down at the child, and tightened his grip some more. "Quickly," he said, and they crossed the street and jogged to the toyshop door. Geppetto paused once on the stoop and looked back at the darkening street. It was empty; no one had seen. He opened the toyshop door, and yanked the boy inside.

"This is really nice of you," the boy said as Geppetto slid the lock into place, and peered out through the cracks of the shutters. "The other boys, they said it was like all those times I said I saw the wolf. But there was no wolf."

"There are wolves," Geppetto said, "even if you can't see them." He turned to the boy in the darkness, his black figure outlined by the fading light coming through the shutters. "Let's go upstairs."

The boy quieted. Then he asked, "Is that where your tools are?"

"That's where we're going."

If the boy was frightened, he didn't show it. He simply nodded, and then walked to the stairway. He waited at the bottom, and Geppetto motioned for him to go up first. Geppetto followed behind, and the boy stopped several times, perhaps figuring that something wasn't right, and turned back toward Geppetto.

"Go on," Geppetto urged. And the boy started again.

They reached the top, and Geppetto dug the key out of his pocket. He reached over the boy's shoulder and slid it into the lock. He thought of Pinocchio's outburst, of his demand that a friend be brought to him that instant. And Geppetto thought of how he had folded instantly, like all the parents he had seen in his shop, giving in to their child's tantrum, and buying the toy they had sworn they would not purchase. He always thought he would never be like that; but then, he had never been a parent until today. He chuckled to himself, and pushed open the door. The things you do for love.

He led the boy forward. "Inside," he muttered. Then he shut the door behind them.

The candle burned in the lantern he had left. He glanced around, not seeing Pinocchio through the overturned crates or past the spiral staircase. But he knew he was there.

"Ugh," the boy said, cringing. "What's that smell?"

"Don't be disrespectful." Geppetto walked past him, toys cracking and crunching under his shoes. "Pinocchio?" he called out. "I brought you a friend."

Then in the shadows there was movement. Pinocchio had been resting against a pile of crates across from them, so completely motionless that neither had seen him until he lifted his head to look at them. The boy behind Geppetto gave a yelp.

Pinocchio was sitting with his arms wrapped around his ankles and his hands dangling over his feet. He looked past Geppetto, his eyes wide and blank.

"There you are," Geppetto said. He took a step aside, so as not to be standing between Pinocchio and the boy. Then he turned to the boy and said, "This is my son, Pinocchio. You will play with him while I fix your watch." And while the boy stared at Pinocchio rising to his feet, Geppetto plucked the watch from his hand, and started rummaging through the boxes trying to find some tools.

Pinocchio took a step forward, and the boy ran to follow Geppetto. He tugged on Geppetto's coat and whispered, "Please, what's wrong with him?"

Geppetto didn't look up. "Nothing's wrong with him. He's—had an operation."

"No," the boy said, backing away to the door. "I want to go. You can keep the watch." He tried the handle, but it was locked. "If you don't let me go, I'll—"

"Nonsense," Geppetto interrupted. "You will play with my son. Then you will go home, and not tell a single person what you saw here today."

The boy shook his head. Geppetto took a step forward.

"And do you know why this will stay between us?"

The boy looked at him.

"Because," Geppetto said, "even if you do tell, no one will ever believe you."

Geppetto knew he was crossing a line here. He didn't like to be mean, especially to children. But this was for Pinocchio. And, besides, what harm would it really do this boy to play with his son?

Pinocchio took another step forward, his eyes locked on the boy.

Just then, from down below, there was a deep resounding knock. All three in the room looked up in surprise, and glanced at one another. Then there was another pounding on the front door, even louder this time, and the muffled sounds of a shout.

Geppetto took out his key and crossed to the door. "Stay here. I'll be right back."

The boy ran to him, and threw his arms around Geppetto's leg. "Please," he begged, "don't leave me with him."

Geppetto kicked him off, and slid through the opening of the door before the boy could follow, and locked it shut. There was another knock, and Geppetto raced down the stairs, only realizing when he was at the front door that he had the boy's watch still in his hand. He shoved it into his pocket with the key, ran his fingers through his hair to straighten it. Then he called out, "Who's there?"

"It's me," called the priest. "Open up, Geppetto."

His voice didn't sound threatening. It sounded jolly, even, and Geppetto unlocked the door and opened it a crack.

Outside stood the priest, his stout red face beaming, and next to him in the shadows a grizzled old woman squeezed into a tight-fitting bodice.

Geppetto eyed each one suspiciously. "What is it?"

"Come on, now," the priest said. "Let us in. I've come to make an introduction."

"It's not a good time." He started to push the door shut, and the priest stuck his foot into the gap.

"Ah ah ah," he said. "You wouldn't turn away a fair maiden on your doorstep, now would you, Geppetto?"

Geppetto eyed the old wench. She had painted her face nearly white, and dabbed rouge heavily over her cheeks.

"Just a hello," the priest said, "and then we'll be off. I promise."

"I don't have time."

The priest clucked his tongue, and pressed his weight into the door. "Tut tut, Geppetto. You know it's a sin to lie."

He was too strong for Geppetto, and the door opened.

He stood back, glaring at the priest, and the two entered the darkened toyshop, the wench eyeing the shelves with puckered lips.

"Are you going to offer the lady a chair?" the priest asked, nudging him in the ribs.

There was a scuffling sound from above, and all three looked up.

"What was that?" the priest asked.

Geppetto looked at him. "Rats."

"Awfully big rats." The priest shook his head. "You really shouldn't let things go like this, Geppetto. Look at you! You're still wearing the same clothes as yesterday, even."

"I fell asleep at my desk."

The priest smiled, and whispered to the wench. "See? A hard worker. He just needs a feminine touch to help around the house."

The wench held a hand to her nose. "The air certainly has a masculine flavor to it."

Another boom from upstairs.

"You know, Geppetto," the priest said, "I could introduce you to an excellent man at catching rats. A piper. You've never seen anything like it."

"He doesn't need a piper," the wench said, and took Geppetto's hand into her own. Her skin was like crumpled paper. "He needs a wife."

Geppetto slapped her hand away. "I already have a wife," he said, and looked upstairs.

The wench glared at the priest. "I thought you said he was a widow."

The priest whispered, "He is. He never quite got over it though, especially the way she died."

The wench's mood lightened, and she leaned in with curiosity. "Oh?"

"In childbirth," the priest continued. "He lost her and his newborn son in the same God-given hour." The priest raised his voice. "But it's been *ten* years. It's time for him to move on and find a bride among the living."

Geppetto turned to them. "I have no interest in the living. And I have no interest in continuing this conversation." He looked at the priest. "Would you like to know why I haven't been to your church? Because you're a gossipy windbag who could put Christ Himself to sleep in your pews. I have no use for any of you. Now get out."

He puffed out his chest and bumped up against the priest. But the priest just shook his head. "Your wife is dead, Geppetto. This won't bring her back."

"Get out!" he shouted, and lunged at them. The wench screamed and they both backed away to the door. He had them nearly out when there was a great crash upstairs, and the shattering of glass.

"What is going *on* up there?" the wench cried.

The priest pushed back inside. "I demand to know what is happening."

"It's none of your business!" Geppetto screamed.

The priest tried to move around him. "Either you let me up, or I will fetch the palace guards and *they* will let me up."

"He's hiding something," the wench agreed.

Geppetto held up his hands. "I will check on it." He backed away, leaving them at the doorstep, and then turned and ran up the stairs. He fumbled in his pocket, dropping the pocket watch, and took out the key. He slipped through the door and then quickly locked it again behind him.

He turned toward the room and gasped. Before him, hanging from the rails of the spiral staircase, was the sandy-haired boy. His arms had been twisted around the bars, and tied with string. His chest had been split open, his ribs spread out like butterfly wings. His eyes were wide open even in death, and his mouth had been jammed full of toy soldiers, stretching his jaw unnaturally.

And behind him, the window was open, the glass broken,

and the boards tossed onto the floor in shards. Geppetto crossed to it, his shoes slipping in the blood that coated the floor, and shined in the candlelight. He got to the window and leaned out.

Below, crawling down the side of the building like a spider, was Pinocchio.

"Wait!" Geppetto yelled after him, but the boy leapt to the street, and scuttled down the lane.

There was noise behind him. The priest was calling to him, pounding on the door to the room. Geppetto looked down at the street, thought about jumping, but it was too far. He turned back to the door with the key in his hand.

"Are you in there?" the priest was yelling.

Geppetto slid the key into the lock as quietly as he could. "Yes, I'm in here," he yelled, turning it and letting his voice mask the click.

"Then let us—"

He threw open the door before the priest could say another word. It had worked, he had taken them by surprise. The wench threw up her hands and let out a shrill scream. The priest took a step backward to avoid the door, and his heel landed on the broken watch. He slid, throwing out his hands to balance himself, but Geppetto lunged into him instead, knocking him down the stairs. Geppetto ran down after, stepping over the priest, and scrambling across the toyshop floor. It was only when he had taken a step out the door that he heard the wench give a lungful of a scream, and he knew she had seen the body.

He ran down the cobblestone street, heading left, the direction he had seen Pinocchio take. The air had cooled, and a light misting rain was falling. It made the street slick, and gave the cobblestones the appearance of glass bubbles under the moonlight.

"Pinocchio!" he called out when he reached the end of the lane.

He wasn't sure which direction to take; the road split here in three directions.

"Stop him!" the priest shouted from behind. He was leaning out the second story window, and waving his hands at the empty street. Geppetto chose the leftmost path, turning the corner and making his way deeper into the town.

He stayed in the shadows, keeping to the edge of the buildings like a rat racing along a wall. The streets were dark now, the shops closed, and he didn't see any sign of Pinocchio. Had he followed the wrong direction? He turned away from the marketplace toward the residential side of town.

Here there were windows lit, doors left open with bands of yellow light cutting across the blue-black street. He passed more cautiously, listening and watching for any sign of disturbance.

But still, he wondered: how could Pinocchio have killed that boy? Was it intentional? Did he do it out of spite for being left alone? Or was he merely curious? Taking apart the boy like Geppetto had taken apart clocks in his youth, spreading out the gears on the table and then being unable to put them back together again?

His poor boy! Alone on these streets, thinking Geppetto was mad at him. He had to find his Pinocchio. He raced through the night, past the windows of laughing families, turning corners and splashing his feet through puddles in the dark.

Then, turning down a lane and creeping past a home with his back pressed to the wall, he heard a scream from within. It echoed out into the night, resonating like the gong of a church bell. He stopped, and leaned toward the open window to listen.

It was a woman. A man ran into the room to join her.

"My baby," she cried, "her bed is empty!"

Before the man could respond, across the lane came another woman's cry. And then another from the next street over. Then three more, and more still, until the night air was filled with wailing.

A door was thrown open, and Geppetto was framed in its spotlight.

"There!" a man's deep voice called. "He's crouching by the window!"

A woman's voice joined in. "He's trying to steal more children!"

Geppetto didn't stop to correct them. He ran out of the light and around the corner, racing frantically as more doors were thrown open all along the lane, and parents spilled out into the night. Even those without children came out to see what the noise was about, and in a minute's time, the streets were as crowded as in the day.

A woman behind him called out, "What's happening?" and a voice returned, "A childnapper's loose!"

Geppetto backed away against the wall, and felt a puff of warm air on his neck. He turned and met the sleeping head of a donkey. It rested in a stable that faced the street with a low door. Geppetto glanced back, saw the crowd distracted, and lifted one leg over the door. No one noticed, and he pulled over the second, and dropped to the ground. He pressed against the side wall, out of the range of the donkey's hooves, and burrowed into the hay. He faced out toward the street, able to see out but still covered enough by the straw that no one would notice him.

Feet ran by. He saw the flames of torches being lit. Then more shouts, as word travelled through the group that the kidnapper was known. That, by the priest's own account, it was Geppetto behind the attacks, and that he must be captured and brought to justice.

Geppetto stayed very, very still.

After an hour, the crowds began to lose some force. The townspeople had been joined by the polished boots of the palace guards. At one point, one of the guards had even peered over the side of the stable with a torch and stared down, directly at where Geppetto was buried. Then he had moved on. Shortly after that, the streets began to clear. The windows remained lit, but most were closed, so that only shards of light escaped, looking like long fingers pointing to all the spots that Geppetto might be hiding.

He didn't feel it was safe to move, not even now. But he knew he couldn't stay here much longer. In the morning, whoever owned this stable would wake. And if he was caught, he might never find Pinocchio.

He pushed himself up from the hay, but before he had even sat up, he heard voices coming around the corner, and dropped down again.

It was the voice of the priest. He had a line of palace guards following him, and he was chatting to his captive audience without cease.

"You should have seen his eyes. And the things he said! Mad, I tell you. Simply mad."

They crossed the stable and stopped at the end of the lane to chat. Whatever hopes Geppetto had of escape were lost now. He rested his head back down, and turned away from the group in disgust.

And there, at the opposite end of the lane, was Pinocchio. He was crossing the lane from right to left. Geppetto turned back to the guards, but they were oblivious to him, their eyes on the priest. He looked to Pinocchio. The boy was getting away.

Should he shout out? But what would he say?

The donkey shifted above him, snorting and raising its hooves. And it gave Geppetto an idea.

He leaned forward and unlatched the gate of the stable. Then rising to a crouching stance, he untied the donkey's rope, and gave it a tug forward.

The donkey, even half-asleep as it was, obeyed the command and started trotting. Its hooves clapped against the cobblestone, and Geppetto hid behind it as it walked, shielded from the view of the guards.

He heard a lull in the conversation. The priest must have turned to see what the guards were looking at. But then a moment later, the priest resumed, and Geppetto walked hidden by the donkey down the street.

He was nearly at the end of the lane when the donkey stopped. He pulled on the rope, but it would not budge. Maybe it had woken up, or maybe it had one of the animal's characteristic moments of stubbornness. Geppetto pulled on the rope again, and the donkey shook its head.

The conversation stopped. One of the guards called out, "What's going on there?"

Geppetto dropped the rope and ran. He heard more shouts from the guards, but he was around the corner before they had reached the end of the lane. He saw Pinocchio ahead, and doubled his pace. The boy turned another corner, and then another, the dark streets a labyrinthine maze.

"Pinocchio!" Geppetto shouted, even though he knew he should be silent with the guards so near.

The boy stopped in the middle of the street at his call, and turned back to him. He was still wearing the cap, and his feet were bare. Geppetto cringed thinking of those feet having to be exposed to the wet and cold, and took a step forward.

Pinocchio dashed to the right, and disappeared into the darkness of another alleyway. This one was even narrower than the rest, and completely dark. Geppetto approached, looking up at the clotheslines strewn between the buildings. The flapping bits of fabric hanging from them almost looked like teeth, so that when he stepped forward it was like stepping into the mouth of a giant whale. But he continued nonetheless, and was soon swallowed by the darkness.

He felt his way forward. "Pinocchio," he whispered. "Pinocchio, stop. Why are you running? It's me, your father."

He could not see anything. Reaching inside his coat, he

took out the last of his matches and struck. It lit the alley before him, revealing Pinocchio pressed against a dead end.

"There you are, my son," Geppetto said, stepping forward and smiling. "Now, come and let's get out of here."

Pinocchio didn't move.

"It's okay. Those men can't hurt you. No one can." Geppetto shook his head. "Do you think I'd hurt you? How could you ever think that? I love you, Pinocchio. I'm not even mad at the trouble you've caused. I don't mind, really, because now we can run away together." Tears were forming in his eyes. "Please, Pinocchio. You can have anything. Just—just tell me what you want."

Pinocchio looked up at him. His mouth opened, and he brought his front teeth down over his bottom lip. A low utterance escaped, not more than a whisper, but clear enough:

"*Frrrr-ennns.*"

Geppetto dropped to his knees. "Friends?" he asked. "I can make you friends. I can make us an entire family. I might, I suppose, I could even make myself a wife." He smiled, and looked up at Pinocchio.

The boy took a step away from the wall. His head was slanted, and he shook his head no, slowly, as if underwater.

"I don't understand," Geppetto said.

And Pinocchio outstretched an arm and pointed, shifting his gaze up the alley. Geppetto turned, raising his nearly extinguished match in the air.

There, creeping down the wet walls like lizards and beetles, were the kidnapped children. Their faces were blank and gray, their eyes black. There were nearly a dozen of them, boys and girls, descending into the alley with their mouths hanging open.

"Are these," Geppetto asked, "are these your friends, Pinocchio?" He turned back to his son, and the boy had taken another step forward, his lips raised in a snarl.

The other dead children formed a line blocking the exit

to the alley, and they shuffled toward Geppetto, lifting their fingers twisted into claws, ready to strike. From this distance, he could see their mouths were caked with blood.

"No! Stop them!" he yelled, and the image of the sandy-haired boy, tied up and split down the middle, flashed in his mind. "Get away from me!"

The children had surrounded him, forming a circle like a pack of wolves, and were revolving closer and closer. Their faces flashed before him: dull eyes surrounded with black circles, translucent skin, and bloody gaping mouths.

They stopped circling. The children bent down, Pinocchio included, and prepared to pounce. The match burned to his finger, and Geppetto shouted at the sensation, dropping it to the ground in the pitch-blackness.

A shout returned his. "He's in here!" And at the other end of the alleyway, the yellow light of torches lit the ground. It was joined by the thudding of boots and knocking of wooden soles against the cobblestones.

The children, still crouched, looked toward the light. As it brightened the darkness, their circle expanded outward. Geppetto saw they meant to scatter, and he sprang out, catching Pinocchio by the wrist. There was another shout of the guards, and all the dead children fled, skittering up the walls like cockroaches. Pinocchio struggled against his grasp, and Geppetto strengthened his hold.

The footsteps had reached the alley. Pinocchio looked up with his face clenched in rage, like an animal caught in a trap.

"They think I've done it," Geppetto tried to explain. "But if they see you, they'll understand."

Pinocchio snarled. He whipped his head forward and sank his teeth into Geppetto's hand, piercing the skin and tearing at the flesh. Pain spread up Geppetto's arm like lightning. His fingers let go of Pinocchio's wrist, and the boy jumped away. He had already escaped up the wall by the time the thudding footsteps of the guards had reached his end of the alley.

The guards shackled Geppetto, chuckling and prodding him. Geppetto couldn't hear a word. He could barely even feel the wound on his hand, even though it was oozing blood and throbbed terribly. He kept seeing Pinocchio's eyes right before the boy had bitten him. That look of absolute loathing. Like he was upset he had even been created. Like he wanted nothing to do with Geppetto.

Pinocchio didn't love him at all.

He stared at the blackness of the alleyway, and he knew he would be blamed for his child's crimes. Geppetto had been too good at keeping his plans a secret. No one had ever seen Pinocchio; they would never believe him now.

He would be killed. There was no question about it, and his face crumpled in despair.

And then a thought came to him. He thought of Pinocchio slipping through the night, playing with his friends in the darkness. Pinocchio happy. Pinocchio, who in time would realize who had provided him with that happiness. That life.

A smile tickled Geppetto's lips as they dragged him away. Yes, they could hang him. Burn him, whip him, whatever they liked; it didn't matter now. He had already done it. Bless his twisted soul, he had *done* it.

He had created a love that would never die.

HANSEL AND GRETEL ARE DEAD

"I can't see," Gretel complained, edging forward in the crowd. She was a slight girl, dressed in rags, with a tired look in her eyes despite her youth. Hansel took her by the hand, and together they weaved through the throng until they were nearly at the edge of the gallows.

But he was short, too. Even though he was two years older than his sister, they were the same height, and people often mistook them for twins. He stood on his tiptoes, but he couldn't see anything.

Before them, blocking their view completely, were two women snickering to each other with their hands over their mouths. They were sisters. The first was exceptionally tall, and the other abnormally wide, but they were both equally ugly. Hansel tugged on the petticoat of the thin one, and both women turned to him as if he had insulted them.

"Please," he asked, "my sister and I can't see."

The fat one's eyes bulged and she bent down to Hansel with her hands on her hips. She took in Hansel's poor clothes and sneered. "Can't see? What's that got to do with us?"

Hansel cringed at her crassness. "If you'd let us in front," he said, trying to be polite, "we won't take up much room. Then we could all see."

Gretel stepped forward. Hansel could tell this took all her bravery; compared to Gretel, these two women were giants. "We just want to see the hanging," she said.

The thin sister rolled her eyes. "Then you should have gotten here sooner." The fat one nodded in agreement, and then the two sisters turned forward, pressing together to block as much of the view as possible.

"Please, miss," Hansel said, "we—"

But he was interrupted by the sound of trumpets.

"They're starting," Gretel whispered, squeezing his hand. "We're going to miss it."

"Hold on," he said, glancing behind. No one was looking. "I have an idea."

"Oh no, Hansel," Gretel whined. "Not one of your *ideas*."

"Shh."

He crouched down and edged his way forward, holding his hands up like lobster claws. And, before Gretel could stop him, he reached out and pinched the fat woman in the rear.

She jumped up, shrieking, and Hansel led Gretel through the gap that had opened in their confusion. He took her right to the steps of the gallows and pulled her down.

They huddled there, peeping over the wooden steps as the two sisters attacked a lone man standing behind them.

"That wasn't a nice thing to do," Gretel said, but her face was flushed with joy and excitement, and Hansel could tell she approved. He smiled back at her, and they both turned to watch the stage, waiting for the show to begin.

It was an overcast day. The open square was brighter than what Hansel was used to near his home in the dark woods, but the town seemed especially bleak for November. The trees were already bare, and a sharp wind passed through the streets, slicing at the townsfolk with icy knives.

But there was something more about the town that was different, a shift in mood separate from the time of year. The faces in the crowd seemed more exhausted, their eyes harder. And he noticed there was something different about the way they gathered at the gallows. Like there was something fearful in the air.

"Look!" Gretel whispered. Hansel turned to see the palace guards shepherding up a grey-haired man with a pale face and black circles under his round glasses. He was old and hunched, but he struggled against the ropes that bound him, snarling and snapping at the guards. Hansel shrunk back. The man seemed as wild as a wolf.

"It's the toymaker!" Gretel realized. Hansel opened his mouth to correct her, but then he looked at the man again, and realized she was right.

He hadn't even recognized Geppetto, yet they had visited his shop countless times.

"But he was always so friendly before," Hansel said.

Gretel shook her head and hid behind him. "He doesn't look so friendly now."

It took three guards to pull Geppetto up the stairs with ropes. The toymaker's bare feet stomped up the stairs, his toenails black, his skin ivory white and covered with dark black veins.

But worst of all was his expression as they slid the noose around his neck. His eyes were protruding as they rolled at the faces in the crowd, until they stopped at the steps of the gallows, right at Hansel and Gretel. The two ducked down, but not before seeing the beginnings of a smile on the old toymaker's face.

"He saw us!" Gretel whispered.

"Shh!"

The orator began reading the charges. "For the murder of our town's children, twelve known and countless unknown, we hereby execute the villain Geppetto."

"Children?" Gretel asked, turning to Hansel. He shrugged, and then they both were curious enough to look over the boards of the gallows.

Geppetto stood with the noose hanging over his shoulder like a scarf. His hands and legs were bound by rope, and he seemed to be paying no attention to the orator's statements. His gray hair stuck out in messy tufts and his clothes were ripped and wrinkled. Even his glasses were bent down the middle, and hung askew on his face.

"Does the prisoner have any last words?" the guard asked.

Geppetto perked up. "Indeed," he screeched. There were gasps at his voice. Instead of the humble and gentle tones he had used previously, Geppetto's voice was now high-pitched and devious. He smiled, looking at the crowd, and said in a matter-of-fact way, "No point in killing me. It's already begun." He paused here and turned to Hansel and Gretel. He spoke to them directly in his devil's voice. "The world's gone mad. It's no longer safe for *children*."

He broke into a grating cackle at this thought, his eyes wide and teeth flashing. Then he turned to the crowd.

"You're all as good as dead!" he cried. "There's no stopping it now; it's spreading as we speak. There's no hope—"

The floor dropped out from under his feet, and the rope snapped as it caught Geppetto's weight. Hansel and Gretel dropped below the floor of the stage to see his legs swinging back and forth, inches above the ground.

His feet twitched. Then, a moment later, went still.

Gretel let out a sigh of relief. The guard came forward on the stage and held a gloved finger to Geppetto's neck. He nodded to the orator.

"This villain," he announced, "is—"

Geppetto's eyes opened and a hellish cackle echoed through the square. The orator blinked, and looked to the guard.

The guard just stared down at Geppetto, a look on his face like he had woken up in the wrong bed. Geppetto laughed back at him.

"Again!" called out the guards. They pulled Geppetto

back to the platform, shut the trapdoor, and tightened the rope. The guard nodded, and the door was released again. Geppetto fell—and went right on laughing.

Gretel backed into Hansel. "Why doesn't he die?" But Hansel could give no answer. In the other two hangings he had witnessed, the condemned had died instantly.

The crowd, which had been astonished into silence, now broke out in shouts.

"Demon!"

"Witchcraft!"

"Satan's fiend!"

They pulled up Geppetto back to the stage of the gallows, and the officials huddled together, debating their options. The executioner held up his axe, and the orator shook his head, gesturing to the crowd.

"Hansel," Gretel said, pulling at his arm, "let's go. I don't want to be here anymore."

"Just a minute," he pressed. "I want to—"

Geppetto lurched up at the sound of their voices. His smile was gone, and his eyes had clouded over white. Beneath the turned backs of the guards, Geppetto snaked his way across the stage right toward them, snapping his teeth and snarling.

Gretel screamed, and the officials turned. Hansel pulled her to the ground, and they saw Geppetto's demonic face peer down at them over the edge of the stage, his eyes almost glowing with wild rage and hunger. He made a move to lunge at them, mouth first, and Gretel screamed again. Hansel opened his mouth to yell for help, unable to look away from Geppetto's crazed eyes.

And then, in the next moment, they saw the head explode in a shower of blood. It rained down, painting their faces with flesh and gore, and fell into their gaping mouths. It tasted awful, like rotten eggs mixed with brown sugar.

The children backed up, spitting and wiping their faces.

They looked up and saw the executioner still holding the axe he had lodged through Geppetto's skull.

"Away from here," he shouted at them. "Go!"

Hansel got to his feet and took Gretel by the hand, and they ran back through the crowd, pushing against stomachs and backs, until they had gotten free of the square. They ran, stopping finally in a dark alleyway, dazed and shaken.

"My eyes," Gretel said, "I got it in them." She looked up at him, the whites of her eyes streaked with red veins. His own eyes tingled at the sight of hers, but mostly he kept tasting the flesh on his tongue, and remembering the image of Geppetto's head sliced in half. It was making him nauseous.

He spat, glad he hadn't had any breakfast he could lose. "Let's go find Father. He's probably looking for us by now."

Gretel nodded, taking a step back toward the street. She stopped. "But Hansel, he'll see the blood."

Hansel grimaced, looking at the splatter of blood on the front of their clothes. They weren't supposed to be at the hanging. "We'll have to wipe it off the best we can. The rest we can smear with mud. We'll say we tripped."

It was agreed. They wiped off each other's faces, and then smeared a handful of mud over the blood on their shirts.

"There," Hansel said, eyeing his sister. "We look a mess, but at least it could have happened anywhere."

Gretel was equally satisfied, and together they went back to the street, avoiding the eyes of anyone they passed. As they walked, the wet filth on Hansel's clothes made him shiver. His eyes started to itch next. He rubbed them with his knuckles, but touching them hurt. They felt puffy. He saw Gretel scratching her face, too, and he stopped to look at her.

Dark circles had appeared around her eyes, shadowing her face like a skull. Her eyelids were red, almost bloody, and her skin had turned pale.

"Hansel!" she said, looking at him with shock, "you look awful!"

"Me?" he asked, and he found that his throat was sore, making it hurt to talk. "You should see yourself."

"But your eyes!" she insisted. "You look—" She cut herself off.

"What?" he asked, stopping in the street.

She shook her head, but he refused to move on until she continued. "Well," she said, "you look sick."

They were silent. He knew she meant more than sick. She meant dying.

His eyes itched again, and he gave in and scratched them before moving on.

They found their father by the cart, his hat in his hand and the cart still full of wood. There was a look of hunger in his sunken cheeks and desperation in his glassy eyes. He didn't even notice as they approached, and was mumbling something to himself and pinching the brim of his hat with his dry fingertips.

"No buyers today?" Hansel asked softly. His father jumped at his voice, and then looked down at them, his shoulders relaxing.

He shook his head. "No one at the stands. It's like the whole town knew we were coming." He gave an ashamed smile, and his children looked down, pretending not to notice.

No one asked what they were all thinking: What would their mother say when they came back with no money?

Gretel coughed, the choking sound rattling her entire frame. Their father looked at her. "Gretel?"

She looked up at him, her eyes bleary. She looked about to fall over.

"She's just hungry," Hansel said. "That's all."

Their father looked at her for another moment, and then said, "Get in the cart. Both of you. I'll be right back." He put on his hat and walked toward the marketplace. As soon as he was out of earshot, Gretel leaned into Hansel.

"He didn't sell again."

"I'm not surprised." Hansel looked over the nubs of damp wood piled in the cart. Their donkey, which was older than Hansel and Gretel combined, was sleeping with an angry expression at the front of the cart. They climbed onto the back, trying not to wake it, and waited.

"Mother's not going to be happy," Gretel continued, wanting reassurance.

Hansel had no reply to that. He didn't think she'd be happy that they were sick, either. But he didn't want his sister to worry about that.

They heard their father's voice behind them, apologizing to someone he had bumped into, and a moment later he rounded the side of the cart, a strained smile on his face.

"No kids of mine are going hungry," he said, and held up two round rolls of bread.

Gretel looked to Hansel in fear. Hansel kept his eyes strictly on his father.

"Dad," he said gently, "how much did those cost?"

Their father shrugged, putting the warm rolls in their hands with a grand gesture. "Don't worry about it."

"But you didn't sell any wood," Gretel insisted.

"We'll sell more next time." He looked at them, his eyes pleading, and then added, "Eat the bread. I don't want your mother to see it when we get home."

Hansel put the roll to his mouth and bit off a piece of the crust. He tried to smile as he chewed, and when he swallowed, his father laughed, satisfied.

"There!" he said. "Can't argue with warm bread, now can you?"

He looked to Gretel, and she bit off some of her roll as well. Their father nodded, and then looked back to the cart full of wood. His smile dropped. "Well," he said, letting out a sigh, "I guess we'd better get back."

The children were silent, chewing their bits of bread as their father walked to the front of the cart. It rocked as he

45

climbed up, and they heard the donkey startle awake. A moment later the ground underneath them began to rush by as the cart jostled along the street.

Gretel spit out her piece of crust into her hand. She looked at it a moment, and then threw it over the side of the cart.

"You should try to eat it," Hansel said, although he hadn't taken another bite from his roll, and the smell of the bread made him want to vomit. "It's not bad bread," he said.

"I just want to sleep." She handed over her roll.

They had reached the border of the town, and the trees of the woods were already casting shadows upon them. She leaned back against the wood and closed her eyes, squinting them shut and grimacing at every bump in the road.

As the cart left town, the temperature fell instantly, and instead of the dank and crowded smells of the town, there was the smell of mist and soil. Hansel and Gretel pressed up against each other for warmth, and Hansel closed his eyes, the ride starting to make him feel nauseous as well.

What would they do if no one bought wood from them again? He and Gretel had collected berries in the woods before, and their father caught the occasional squirrel, but that was in the summer months. It was November now. What would they do when winter came? How would they survive?

They bumped along the path in silence. Hansel had fallen into a light doze, not quite sleep, and not quite awake, when Gretel squeezed his fingers. He blinked his eyes and looked at her.

"What?"

She gestured with her eyes out to the shadows in the woods. The day was now almost black. Dark storm clouds blocked the little sunlight that had fallen before, and the air had the smell of rain in it.

He didn't see it at first. Then, focusing about twenty feet into the distance behind them, just beyond the edge of the path, there was movement. If it hadn't moved, he would have never guessed anything was there. But the movement, the change in shadows, revealed the shape of a man.

Hansel sat up with a start, forgetting his illness, his attention giving him energy.

They both watched diligently, but they saw nothing more.

"Maybe we scared it off," she whispered.

"Who would follow us all the way out here?" he wondered.

Before they had time to inquire further, the cart jerked to a halt. At first Hansel thought that his father must have seen something, too. But then he noticed the trees; they were familiar.

"We're home," their father called out, and the cart rattled as he climbed down. He came around the back to help them down, and Hansel quickly hid away the two rolls of bread under a log of wood.

Their father set them down on the ground as they heard the door of their home creak open. Their mother, a thin woman with a high forehead, came forward from their small hut holding up a lantern. She had a scarf wrapped around her hair, and a gray apron tied around her waist. She came up to the children—and stopped as soon as the light had reached them.

Her eyes widened, and her mouth opened, unable to speak. She took a step back, and then turned to her husband with a vile look of hatred. She ran to him, holding up a fist to beat him.

Their father merely flinched but put up no defense. "How could you!" she shrieked, her scarf falling into the mud. "You stupid, stupid—*how?* Don't you have eyes? How could you bring them back like this?"

"Like what?" their father asked, and Hansel felt worse than before. He wanted to disappear.

"Look at them!" their mother screeched, pointing a finger.

Hansel looked at Gretel, and they each saw in each other

what the light had revealed. Their eyes were worse than before, now black patches on their face, with intricate black veins running out from them like gnarled roots. Their skin was almost translucent in its paleness, and their lips pale and blue, even under the lantern's glow. And Gretel's expression—such fatigue, like she was ready to lay down and die. Was that how he looked, too?

Their father forgot his fear and took a step forward to investigate.

"Stay back!" their mother shrieked. "Or you'll catch it too."

He stopped, looking like he wanted to offer an apology but couldn't find the words.

Their mother motioned him closer to her, and they stepped away to talk in private. But their mother had a shrill voice that carried, and the children heard every word.

"We can't have them in the house," she said. Their father mumbled something, and she replied, "Because they're sick! There's no cure for that. It's already spread across the town. Honestly, don't you pay attention to anything?" Another mumble. "And how are we supposed to afford that?"

Then silence. Hansel and Gretel crept closer to listen, but their mother turned her head and snapped at them. "Go to the cart, children. This is adult business."

They obediently went back to the cart.

But it didn't matter, because now their father was openly shouting. "How can you expect me to do that? I can't kill my own children!"

"They're dead already. You saw their faces!"

"I can't," he said. He sounded like he was crying. "You can't ask that."

"We can't let them in our house. We'd be dead too. And I refuse to stand by and watch them die. They deserve better than that."

"But *kill* them?" There was a moment of silence. Then, softer, he asked, "How?"

"With the axe," she answered without hesitation. "Short and sweet."

"Oh no, not with an axe." Hansel could tell his father was shaking his head. "I could never do it with an axe."

"Then take them away," their mother suggested. "Take them far out into the woods, so far they'll never be able to find their way back. And then return without them."

Their father was silent. Gretel took hold of Hansel's hand.

"They're children," she continued. "They won't even know what's going on. They might even like it. And then we wouldn't have to worry. They'll be in the Lord's hands."

Something on their father's face must have betrayed him, because their mother suddenly said, "I'll come along."

She wasn't taking any chances.

He let out a deep sigh. "Okay," he said, defeated. "We can do it together."

"Deep into the woods," she said.

"Deep into the woods," he agreed.

And a moment later, they were at the rear of the cart. Hansel and Gretel looked on them with terror. Surely they couldn't go through with this?

Their mother smiled at them. "Guess what, children? We're going on a trip. All of us." She held her smile a moment too long, and the light of her lantern reflected against her eyes, revealing that they were watering in the corners.

Their father just stared at them, his expression pained but distant. It was like he was already picturing them in their coffins.

Hansel and Gretel said nothing. Their mother nodded, and then their parents went to the front of the cart and climbed on. There was a slap against the donkey, and they knew their mother had the reins. The cart went off with a start, and they jerked down the path back into the dark woods.

All four of them were silent. They had gone nearly a mile when Gretel's head suddenly snapped up.

She cupped her hands against Hansel's ear and whispered, "The bread."

He was confused, but reached under the wood and gave her the two rolls. Her eyes brightened with excitement. She tore into the rolls, ripping one apart with her fingers until she had a small pile of scraps in her lap. Hansel watched completely engrossed. Then, delicately, she lifted up a piece of bread and held it between her thumb and forefinger for him to look at, urging him to understand. He shook his head, still not getting it. Then she smiled impishly, and threw the breadcrumb over the side of the cart.

Then, when they had traveled a little farther, she threw another.

Hansel sat up straight. She was making a trail. She was making a trail with the breadcrumbs. He wanted to kiss her, he was so filled with gratitude. He took the other roll of bread and began stripping it into small scraps, and they took turns throwing off crumbs as they continued through the woods.

The scraps were visible only if you were looking for them. Their parents would never notice. And then they could follow the breadcrumbs back home. They could do it.

They were nearly at the end of their supply of bread when the cart slowed to a stop. Hansel took the rest of his breadcrumbs and stuffed them into his pocket, and Gretel hid hers in the front pocket of her dress.

"Children," their mother's voice called out. It seemed hollow in the emptiness of the woods. "We're stopping here to rest for a bit." The cart rocked as she climbed down with the lantern. She rounded to the back and waited for them to find their own way down.

She looked at Hansel with a strained smile. "I need you to look after your sister while your father and I go off looking for firewood."

Hansel's eyes went to the cart filled with logs before he could stop them.

"*Better* firewood," their mother explained. "We won't take long."

She led them around the cart to the center of a clearing. There was something lazy about her excuses. Hansel already knew his parents planned to abandon them, but he had expected better of them. Gretel had as well.

"There's nowhere to sit," she said, not wanting to step farther into the clearing.

"Take a log each from the cart," their mother said.

Their father, who had been looking off into the woods with concentration, spoke up now. "Don't be afraid. We'll be back soon."

Then he looked to his wife, and nodded for her to return to the cart. She jumped inside, and without another word, she slapped the reins and they were turning back down the path.

The children watched as the light of the lantern grew dimmer. Before rounding the corner, their mother looked back, her eyes glowing in the candlelight. But it wasn't for one last glimpse.

It was to make sure they didn't follow.

Then they were gone.

Both children stood staring into the darkness, unable to think of what to say or how to feel. They absentmindedly threw the last of the breadcrumbs onto the ground, one by one, until both of their pockets were emptied. Then Gretel started to cough, and Hansel realized how cold it was.

"Well," he said, "I think we've given them enough of a head start."

Gretel didn't respond, and he couldn't make anything of her blank expression. But when he started walking, he heard her footsteps crunching the dead leaves behind him.

The day was already dying. If their parents had abandoned them an hour later, it might already be too dark to see. But as it was, they had enough light to find their way along the path, their young eyes able to discern the specks of bread every few feet along the way.

"Do you think they'll be mad?" Gretel asked.

"About what?"

"That we came back?"

Hansel thought about it. "I think we're the ones that should be mad."

It was getting colder. Left to their thoughts, the children started feeling the aches in their limbs. It was so much easier to ride in the cart than it was to walk. And even though he hadn't wanted any of the bread, Hansel still felt hungry. He wanted to get back home and into bed and have the whole day over, like it had never happened.

Twilight took hold, quieting the birds and waking the crickets. There were the sounds of small feet scurrying past them, jumping from tree to tree, or running along the leaves. The smell of the soil intensified as the worms and beetles dug themselves up from the ground and swarmed across the earth.

Hansel had the distinct sense that he didn't belong here. The woods were a wild place, and the creatures weren't friendly toward children who wandered through their homes.

Then they heard it: a scream.

"That's Mother!" Gretel said, and Hansel took her hand and ran toward the sound.

They were closer to their parents than either had realized, not more than a bend in the path behind them. They saw the light ahead and ducked behind a tree.

Their mother was standing on top of the pile of wood, holding up the lantern. Their father was clutching the harness of their donkey, trying to keep it under control as it shook its head back and forth.

Then they saw it.

Encircling the cart, barely discernible from the shadows, were the outlines of a group of robbers.

"Stay back!" their mother called out, but her activity only

seemed to excite them, and they took another step closer. They stepped into her circle of light, and she screamed again. Hansel gasped. The people weren't robbers at all. Their faces were twisted in rage, and they had the same white eyes Geppetto had at the hanging. They shambled at crooked angles, reaching out toward the cart and snapping their jaws together with harsh clacks.

The donkey brayed and their father lost his grip. It shook itself free of the cart, and then retreated, running into the darkness of the trees.

Their father took a step to follow it, but then their mother shrieked again. The men were dragging their fingers along the base of the woodpile, reaching up toward her ankles. But their father kept back, standing still.

"He's not going to help her," Gretel whispered, clutching Hansel's hand.

A man started climbing the side of the cart like a spider. Their mother set the lantern down and picked up a log from the pile with both hands. She raised it above her head, but the hand of the man shot forward and grabbed her by the ankle. She tried to pull away, but he was too strong.

Gretel let go of Hansel's hand and ran to the center of the path. "Father! Help her!"

Their father looked up, confused and alarmed. Their mother turned toward her as well. But the man at her foot didn't turn. He pulled on her leg, and knocked her flat on the woodpile. There was a thud as her head hit the logs, and a crash as the lantern rolled off the cart and smashed onto the ground.

Then it was dark. Full dark.

"Gretel, run!" their father's voice came from the darkness.

Hansel heard Gretel take a step back, and he went out to her in the darkness. Their eyes had adjusted to the dark just enough to make out the shape of strange men climbing the sides of the cart. There was frantic movement among the shadows near their father, the sound of several sets of feet shuffling through dead leaves—some toward the cart, some toward their father, and some moving swiftly toward Hansel and Gretel.

"Run!" their father called. He sounded ready to shout again, when his voice was cut off, and his body was thrown to the ground. Gretel reached a hand forward to help, but Hansel took her hand and pulled her hard toward the trees. She would have tripped, but he held her up and kept her moving, dragging her feet along the dirt until she started moving them again.

They made it to the trees and began to dodge between the branches. Hansel put his parents out of his mind and focused completely on the task at hand: a branch that he must duck under; going left around a tree trunk; noticing a rock that stood out and stepping over it. Moving, always moving, as he heard the crunch of the leaves and branches behind him. There was only one thought that ran through his head, repeating unfinished but finished enough: *If they did that to adults. If they did that to adults.*

For a long time that felt like a single moment they ran hearing the men directly behind them. Then they ran hearing the men behind them only sometimes. Then they just ran.

Hansel might have kept running the entire night if he were alone. But Gretel couldn't keep up. And once the immediate danger was gone, her body seemed to lose all ability to stand, let alone run, and she was too heavy for him to carry. So they stopped in the darkness, panting, and listening to the sounds of the woods.

After a moment, Gretel whispered, "I think we're alone."

"Shh!" Hansel said, and listened again, turning his head in every direction. He tried to look, too, but even with the moon peeking through the branches above, he couldn't see beyond a few feet in any direction.

He didn't believe the men were really gone. They were

still out there, somewhere, and might be trudging around, separating and going in every direction. It wasn't safe to be out in the open.

What made the danger even worse was that Hansel had no idea where they were. They were already beyond the woods that he recognized before they started running. And now? He had no clue.

Gretel pulled at his grasp. He tightened his grip around her, not wanting to be disturbed in his thoughts. She gave a petulant huff and pointed with her free hand. It was a thick tree. Hansel didn't see it at first. Then he noticed Gretel was pointing down, and he saw the hollow opening at the base.

They could hide there.

He let go of her hand, and Gretel went toward the hollow on hands and knees. She was about to enter it when he grabbed her shoulder. She turned to him, upset but obedient. Hansel picked up a pebble and threw it into the dark opening of the tree. It hit the back and he listened for the scurrying of animals or snakes. He heard nothing.

"Okay," he whispered, and they bent down and climbed inside.

Gretel went in first and curled around the back of the hollow. Hansel came in next and pressed against her, but even with squeezing his feet stuck out of the opening. He covered his legs with a few dead leaves, and then lay back inside the tree.

The ground was hard and they were both pressed together in an uncomfortable position, but it felt safe and that was all that mattered. Gretel passed out in an instant, while Hansel was determined to stay awake. He listened to the sounds outside, the frogs croaking and the hoots of owls, and despite his best intentions, he was soon fast asleep next to his sister.

He was woken by the sound of sharp chirps and screeches. He opened his eyes to the dull morning light. His sister was waking behind him, mumbling to herself. She must have forgotten where they were.

Hansel hadn't.

He kept perfectly still and listened to the woods.

But the only sound came from a small bird just outside their tree, peeping desperately as it hopped over the dead leaves. It was a chick, practically new born. Its bare skin had ugly pink wrinkles, covered with fuzz instead of feathers. The grey skin of its eyelids was stuck shut, and its flightless wings lifted feebly as it opened its beak and cried out.

Gretel sat up behind him, watching the bird.

"It's fallen from its nest," she whispered. She made a move to climb out, and Hansel put up a hand to hold her back.

"Me first. It might not be safe."

He slid out from the hollow, and put his finger to his lips to tell Gretel to keep silent while he looked around.

He stood and peered up. It looked like any other part of the woods. The weak morning light made the leaves above glow. He saw a sparrow peek down from a nest in the tree they slept in. It stared at him for a moment, then went back to hopping from branch to branch, chirping in all directions with glee.

"You can come out," he said to Gretel, careful to keep his voice low. She climbed out, eyeing the chick and careful not to touch it. Brown leaves were caught in her hair.

"It fell from its nest," she said, looking down at the bird. "We have to help it."

Hansel nodded, even though he wasn't sure how they could. But it felt too cruel to just leave the chick there, when it was so helpless.

"Maybe we can find it some worms," he suggested.

Gretel lit up at the idea, her blackened eyes scanning the dirt.

But before they could search, there was another plop on

the ground. Another baby chick had dropped to the leaves. Hansel looked up to the nest, and saw the sparrow hop out, then hop back in. Its tail was still hanging over the edge as a third chick became visible, hovering over the edge.

"It's pushing them out!" Gretel said, her eyes opening wide.

And sure enough, a third chick went tumbling through the air and landed in the leaves on the ground. Hansel stared at the three chicks, all too young for feathers, working their wrinkled pink wings and opening their mouths with high-pitched chirps.

"They can't even see," Gretel said. "Their eyes are still closed."

The sparrow jumped from its nest to sit on a branch, and cooed merrily to itself.

The children stared at it, squinting against the sunlight. Gretel blinked. "It meant to push them out," she said quietly. "It meant to."

"Come on," Hansel said, taking her hand, "let's start walking."

She resisted, looking down at the chicks.

"After we find someone," Hansel said, "we can come back to help them."

Gretel looked at him skeptically, but she didn't argue, and together they walked deeper into the woods.

They were lost. There was no point in trying to pretend otherwise. But Hansel kept up his pace, figuring they were bound to run across something sooner or later. The woods couldn't go on *forever*, after all. Besides, it wasn't safe to stay in one place, not with those men in the woods.

Gretel slowed. "Hansel," she said, and he looked at her. "Our arms."

She held up her arm, her hand holding his. The white skin of both of their arms was crossed with black veins. Hansel felt his stomach lurch at the sight. He looked at

Gretel, about to comfort her, when he noticed how raw her eyes looked.

His own felt sore and puffy. It even hurt to blink.

"At least we can still walk," he said. "And maybe this is as bad as it gets."

Gretel nodded, and they started walking again, looking at the trees without seeing them. After a little distance, he saw her open her mouth to speak and then close it.

"What?" he asked.

"Nothing." They walked a little farther. "But—what if there's no one to help us?"

"What do you mean?"

"What if there's no one left but us? What do we do then?"

He had no answer to that. It seemed better not to answer.

They continued walking.

The morning mist had begun to thin, and in the clear light the woods seemed suddenly unfamiliar. Even the trees were species Hansel had never seen before, sprinkled with red blossoms. The air smelled different, too, rich with the scent of a different kind of tree sap than in his woods, something sweeter. The stench of it was making him dizzy.

He didn't say anything, but he was thinking about what Gretel had said, about no one being left. They had traveled so far. What if they really had walked past where any people were? What if they were in a woods no one had ever seen? The leaves were brown, and the sky was grey; that was normal enough. But there was an untamed energy in the air, a wildness to the way the wind blew. He took in a breath, and the air felt new here. Like it had never been breathed before.

But what choice did they have? They walked on. Gretel held his hand tightly, and he could tell by the way she glanced around at the empty woods that she had noticed the difference, too, and it scared her. They were more than lost. They had entered into a new world.

They walked slower now. They felt like intruders, creeping through the strange woods. And the longer they walked, the more silent the woods became. Back home the woods were noisy, but here there was no wind to rustle the leaves. There was no buzz of insects. Hansel realized he couldn't hear a single bird. What kind of woods doesn't have a few birds making noise in the middle of the day? The only sound—the *only* sound—was the sound of their feet crunching the leaves, and as everything else grew quieter, their steps seemed to grow louder and louder.

The only reason the woods were ever quiet back home was if the birds were hiding from danger. And it felt like that. It felt like some unseen predator was watching them.

Then, suddenly, Gretel stopped. "Hansel," she said. Her voice had an edge to it, cutting through the silence like a slap. He instinctively began to shush her, but she insisted.

"Hansel. *Look*."

She didn't point. He followed her eyes through the trees to their left. And there, illuminated by a slant of sunlight, was a gate.

He looked at Gretel, and she nodded. They made their way on tiptoes through the woods, stopping behind the trees nearest the gate, and peered out.

The gate did not belong here. It rose from out of nowhere and towered above the children. It was made of thin branches tied together with twine, but not neatly; the seams and top were crooked, and it looked ready to fall over. Whoever made this had no experience making gates. It was more like a gate made by an animal.

It connected to a low wall on each side, made of stone bricks piled on top of each other in random heaps. And between the spokes of the gate they could see a tended pathway that curved into the distance between the walls.

They stared at the gateway.

"Who would live out here?" Hansel asked. The woods

had been silent; they still were. And here was a gate and a path where even birds wouldn't nest.

"Maybe we're near a town," Gretel suggested. But neither one thought that likely.

Hansel took a step out from the trees. Gretel stayed behind as he made his way up to the gate. But when he began to look at it closely, her curiosity won out and she joined him.

"It doesn't seem real," he said, reaching out to the gate and sliding his hand along the rough branches. Gretel did the same. It seemed they both needed to touch it to believe it was real.

"Ow!" Gretel cried, snapping her hand back. Hansel jumped at her cry, falling away from the gate.

"What? What is it?"

She grimaced. "Splinter." She held up her finger. A drop of blood bloomed on its tip like a spot of dew.

Hansel let out a breath, and turned back to the gate.

It had opened a crack. Gretel must have nudged it forward before she pulled away. The children looked at each other. There was fear in their eyes, but they were both so intensely curious that there was no decision to be made. They pushed the gate open and went through. Gretel closed it behind them, her finger leaving a bloody fingerprint on the inner side of the gate.

They walked slowly down the path, looking at the strange piles of rocks on either side that made up the walls. The gaps had been filled in with mud, and the imprint of hands and fingers had been dried into them.

They turned the corner of the path, and the walls went outward to encircle a small clearing. At the center of this clearing was a small black house surrounded by a colorful garden. Everything had been decorated. Even the path had been paved with snail shells and bird feathers. The children stepped forward, marveling.

Low hedges lined the path to the house, trimmed into

unnatural shapes. Hansel stepped close to one, trying to figure out what it was.

"I think it's a person," Gretel said quietly, looking at it. She pointed to two gaping hollows at the top. "Eyes." And at another wide hole below. "A mouth."

Looking at it gave Hansel chills. "It looks like it's screaming," he said.

"It's just not very good." Gretel turned to a line of dead trees behind it. Hanging from bits of twine were ornaments and small bells cluttering the bare branches. Gretel stepped closer, squinting her eyes.

The ornaments were clusters of objects stuck together with mud. Seeds, nuts, and sticks were wedged into them, but also—and this is what attracted Gretel's attention—iridescent wings plucked from butterflies. She poked one, and it twirled on the branch, sending shimmering reflections onto her face.

"Birdfeeders?" Hansel guessed, stepping next to her.

Gretel frowned. "But there aren't any birds."

Hansel stared at the spinning seeds and nuts. He reached out and pulled off a shelled walnut, tugging it off the ornament. "People feeders?" he said with a smile, and popped the walnut into his mouth.

It tasted bitter. Worse than the bread. He chewed it slowly, and forced himself to swallow. As disgusting as it was, he was too hungry to be picky.

At his example, Gretel reached out, careful to avoid the bells, and pulled off a few seeds from an ornament. She gagged at the taste, but swallowed them down. As she chewed, her eyes traveled over the rest of the yard.

The house itself loomed over the garden, a black center to the circle of color, like the pupil of an eye watching over them. And next to the house was a tent of branches and leaves. Inside this tent was a picnic basket, its contents covered by a red napkin. Gretel spat the seeds from her mouth, and started toward the basket as if mesmerized.

"Gretel, wait," Hansel called. There was something off about this entire garden. Everything was too quiet. Too... planned.

But Gretel ignored him. The basket drew her through the tall grass like a magnet. Hansel stayed behind, afraid to follow her small form as she approached the tent of branches. She stopped, everything as silent as a dream. Then she reached out her hand, and took another step forward.

A roar of thunder broke the silence of the garden. Gretel screamed in panic, her whole body tensing and trembling. Hansel ran forward and gasped.

The metal jaws of a bear trap had snapped around Gretel's leg, just under the knee. It had been hidden by the tall grass, and placed directly before the basket. Its teeth had bitten almost completely through her leg.

Gretel pulled against the trap in a frenzy, ripping her skin as she tried to yank her leg out.

"Hold still!" Hansel cried. Gretel didn't seem to hear him. She didn't even seem to see him. The metal teeth of the trap had sliced through the flesh of her leg, down into the bone. Hansel tried not to look at it—it looked like the meat at the butcher shop—and gripped both sides of the trap with his fingers. It was covered with grime and rust. He pulled with all his strength, but it didn't budge at all.

"Okay, okay," he whispered to Gretel. "I'm going to try again."

But she didn't hear him. She seemed like she was dying. Her voice cracked from the screaming, and her yells sounded like the howls of an animal now, not a child. Hansel gripped the teeth again, and pulled, straining against them, kicking his feet into the dirt with the effort. He could feel the vibrations of the trap scraping against the bone of her leg.

Hansel fell back, flapping his fingers in the air. They had the indentations of the device pressed into his skin. But it hadn't budged. Not at all. Not even with all his strength.

After all they had been through, they were caught now? There must be a way out. What happened to animals when they were caught? What did they—

All the color drained from Hansel's face. He looked at Gretel.

Tears streamed down her face, her hair sticking to the drool that bubbled out as she screamed. He put a hand on her shoulder, and she looked at him, her mouth open and panting.

"Gretel," he said softly. "I can't get the trap open. I'm going to have to find something to… remove your leg."

Gretel's eyes went wide, and she let out a wild howl of anguish.

Just then, they heard the door of the house open and slam. Gretel was silent at once as heavy footsteps ran across the garden. Hansel looked at his sister, and she looked back. They were saying goodbye with their eyes.

Around the corner came a bent old woman. She wore a dark cloak that seemed to drape off nothing but a skeleton, and in her hand she held a long knife, almost a dagger. She had been ready to lunge at whatever was in the trap, but at the sight of the two children, she stopped and stared, her expression completely blank.

Then, like the dawn breaking across the dark horizon, her expression began to warm. She lowered the knife and placed it on a loop of her cloak. Then she came forward without speaking, and put her hands on either side of the trap, and pried it open.

Hansel's mouth dropped open. He couldn't budge the trap. And this old woman, who looked as feeble as a house of cards, pulled it open with one effortless motion. She scooped Gretel up in her hands, and turned back toward the house, Gretel's leg dangling down like a pendulum.

"Wait!" Hansel cried. He scrambled back to his feet, and chased after them. It wasn't until he was at the steps of the house that he recognized something he had seen before he ran out of the corner of his eyes: the red napkin had fallen off. The basket was full of rocks.

The old woman went into the house and didn't close the door behind her. Hansel followed her inside, the house almost black to his vision after the sunlight. He saw the old woman drop Gretel on a couch and then disappear into another room. Hansel went forward reaching out his hands like a blind man, his eyes still adjusting, and made his way to his sister's side. She wasn't moving.

"Gretel," he whispered. "Gretel, wake up. Listen: the basket was full of rocks. You don't use rocks to catch animals, they wouldn't smell it. The trap wasn't meant for animals."

He heard shuffling behind him, and then the heavy groan of the door being closed. The room was thrown into blackness, and he heard the clack of locks being bolted.

He turned toward the darkness, his hands spread across the couch, trying to block the old woman from his sister. There was the strike of a match, and an orange glow filled the room. The old woman came toward him, her face lit from below, wrinkling in on itself as she peered at them.

She was hideous. Her nose bent down like a shriveled carrot over her wrinkled turtle's mouth. She had long gray hair that hung like limp seaweed over her shoulders and down her back. But her eyes—her eyes were wild and wide, covered with milky white cataracts. Hansel had no doubt that she lived alone. No one that goes among people could let herself look like this.

"Stay back," he said, but she didn't lose a step. She came forward, shoved Hansel to the ground, and bent over his sister like a vulture. She reached inside the sleeve of her cloak, pulling out a length of cloth, and set the candle on the ground. Hansel was silent. The old woman dexterously spun the cloth around Gretel's leg, like a spider spinning silk around a fly. She was shaking her head and mumbling to herself. Hansel couldn't make out a word.

She finished wrapping the leg and stared at Gretel for a moment. Then she turned to Hansel, gazing at him. She slanted her head sideways, the way dogs do when trying to make out a sound.

Just then, Gretel moaned, turning on the couch. Her eyes were rolled up in their sockets. The old woman went to her at once, and reached out a hand to stroke the side of her face. She had exceptionally long fingernails, almost as long as the fingers themselves, and Hansel worried she might scratch Gretel.

But Gretel seemed comforted by the gesture. She focused on the old woman in the dark, and smiled.

"Mother?" she asked.

That his sister could confuse the old hermit with their mother disgusted Hansel.

The old woman cooed something unintelligible, and then bent down to Gretel's forehead, pressing her puckered lips against the girl's skin. She made an exaggerated smacking noise, and when she pulled away, a strand of saliva stretched like a cord between them.

Hansel didn't want to be this house anymore. Even the woods were better than this.

"Gretel," he said, "we have to go. I'll carry you."

The old woman looked at him sharply, her gentle expression turning hard. He made a move toward his sister, but the old woman put an arm over Gretel.

"Mine," she said. Her voice was rough, like an out-of-tune instrument. And with that one word, she pushed Hansel aside, and plucked Gretel off the couch. Hansel looked up from the floor to see the old woman rush through a dark doorway into the next room.

"Gretel!" Hansel yelled. He picked up the candle and followed after.

The next room seemed to be some sort of kitchen. He didn't see them, but what he did see made the hair on his head stand on end. A massive black oven was in the corner, and hung up on the wall next to it was a line of large knives coated with blood. In the middle of the room, hanging open, was a trap door leading down to a dark cellar.

It was the only place they could have gone; there was no other exit. He took a step toward it. He held the candle over the opening and saw the beginning of a narrow wooden stairway leading into the darkness.

He didn't want to go down there. He wanted to return to the sunshine. To be free among the trees, where there would be places to run, places to hide. He might have turned around, too, if he hadn't heard the low notes of a lullaby floating up from below.

The old hag was singing to Gretel. He couldn't leave her alone with that.

Hansel swallowed, and took a step down the stairs. He tried to hide the candle by keeping it close to his chest, but the light streamed out into the cellar, sending long bands into the pitch black. When he was halfway down the stairs, the light finally reached the floor, and he was able to make out the shape of the old woman huddled in the center of the space below. She was sitting with her back to him, rocking back and forth with Gretel in her lap, humming a nonsense song.

Hansel crept down, making his way to the dirt floor. The room smelled like the underside of rocks. When he got to the base of the stairs, he noticed marks lining the stones of the walls, and he brought up his candle to see.

The walls were covered with handprints. Children's handprints, made with blood—an uncountable number of them.

Hansel lowered his eyes and turned away. He felt nauseous all over again, like he might faint. He had to stop altogether and concentrate on breathing in and out, the light from the candle growing darker in his vision.

He just had to get Gretel. Then they could find someone else to help them.

If there was anyone else. They hadn't seen anyone else all day, and no one knew they were here.

But he couldn't lose his head. Not when Gretel was depending on him. He focused on the sound of the air going in and out of his lungs. It was quiet and soothing. And the light of the candle grew bright again in his vision.

It was too quiet. The humming had stopped.

Hansel turned to see Gretel slumped over alone in the middle of the floor. He scanned the room, and couldn't see the old woman at all.

"Gretel," he whispered, running to her. He slid to his knees and set down the candle, and then lifted her head into his lap. Her dark eyes looked up at him, and then a weak smile formed on her lips.

"Hansel," she said, "isn't it lovely?"

"We're going to be okay," he said. "We're going to get you out of here."

"Out of here?" she asked. "But we're home, Hansel. We're safe now."

"No, Gretel. She's coming back down." He tried to lift her shoulders, but she was heavy now, her body limp. He looked down at her leg. The bandage had been soaked with blood, and her foot rested at an unnatural angle.

"Does it hurt?" he asked her.

She smiled. "I don't feel anything. Mother made it better. She built this house out of gingerbread, you know. So we would never go hungry again."

Hansel clenched his jaw.

"But, Hansel," she whispered, "I can't eat a bite. I'm still hungry, but I can't eat a bite."

"I'm going to find someone to help us," Hansel whispered. "I'm going to hide you, and then I'm going to find someone to help us." He reached down under her arms, and looked around. There was a line of crates along the wall behind them, and he dragged her to them. She was so heavy. It was like she was dead already.

He brought her to the wall and leaned her against it. Then he went to the crates and stacked three in front of her. The third crate was open on top, and as he placed it, Hansel almost dropped it.

At first, it looked like the crate was entirely full of dead rats. But that seemed wrong. He knew it was wrong. And he went forward to look closer.

It wasn't rats. It was—shoes? He picked one up from the pile. It was no bigger than the size of his hand. It must have belonged to a toddler. The entire box was full of these little shoes. Why did the old woman keep these? What had happened to the children?

He dropped the shoe back into the crate and finished moving it to block Gretel. Then he went around behind it and bent down to her.

"I'll find help," he whispered. "I promise."

She looked at him, a serene grin on her lips, and then dropped her head.

Hansel tried not to think of the way she looked when he left her. He meant to go right up the stairs and out the door, but as he crossed the center of the cellar, he heard the creek of a footstep above him. The old hag was coming back.

Quickly, Hansel ran and hid underneath the stairway, climbing on top of a pile of dirt and rocks. It was a loose pile, and he had to be careful not to dislodge anything. If the hag hadn't seen him before, when he was standing right at the base of the stairs, maybe she would be too blind to see him hidden here. That is, *if* she hadn't seen him before.

Her steps sent down dust as her weight bent the stairs above him. The candle was still in the center of the room, and Hansel wished he had thought to put it out. The hag reached the bottom of the steps. She walked out into the center of the room, looked down at the candle, and stood facing the far wall.

Hansel backed up farther under the stairs.

If he could just get upstairs, Hansel thought, he could sneak out through the front door. He could run through the garden, out through the gate, and back out into the open woods. He had outrun those other men; he could outrun an old woman. Then he would run and run, never stopping until he had reached another town. And he'd find someone, *anyone*, to bring back to this house. He'd save Gretel. She'd be okay. And then they'd lock up the old woman so that she could never hurt another child again.

People like that shouldn't be allowed in the world, he thought. It didn't—

Didn't make it safe for children.

He remembered Geppetto at the gallows.

No. He shook his head. If the world wasn't safe, then he would have to make it safe. He crawled over the dirt, noticing that the ground was bumpier here. He kept his eyes on the old woman. It was only then that he noticed the knife in her hand, its blade glinting in the candlelight. She took in a deep breath of air through her nose and closed her eyes, smelling it.

Hansel knew this was his last chance. He crouched down and pushed off, ready to run up the stairs. But as he crouched, his eyes drifted down. The candlelight flickered. And Hansel saw that his hand was twisted in the hair of a rotted corpse, a little boy his own age. Its hollow eyes glared up at him, its lips rotted off and mouth open. It looked like it was screaming at him, asking for his help. Hansel looked away, facing back under the stairs. In the candlelight he saw that he was crouching on a heap of bodies, all of them children, in various stages of decomposition.

The light grew even brighter, and Hansel looked up to see the old hag standing over him, the knife raised in her hand.

"No!" Hansel cried. He raised his hands to shield himself, but the knife came down with a flash. He felt it pierce his chest, digging itself between his ribs. The edges of his vision went dark, and the old hag leaned over him, her face filling his view. Her white eyes met his, her grey hair falling down and tickling his face. She smiled at him, her teeth brown and rotted, as her sour breath filled his nostrils.

"Sweets," she cooed. "My little sweets."

He felt the knife poking inside him, and then the sensation of her hands ripping at his chest, trying to pull up his ribs.

He thought of the box of shoes.

And then everything went black.

* * *

The old woman wiped the sweat off her forehead, smearing blood on her face. She sighed in relief. The worst part was over.

Reaching inside her cloak, she pulled out a stained canvas sack. She looked down at the boy, his ribs spread open like wings, and used the knife to slice all the way around the heart in a circle. The blood was thick here, and spilling over the boy's chest. But she didn't care about the blood. She only wanted the heart.

She lifted it out, cutting the last of the hanging tendrils, and placed it into her sack. Then she bent down to the child, undoing its shoelaces. It peered up at her with its eyes still accusing.

Why did they have to look like that? It wouldn't do them any good now.

She shook her head, and tossed the boy under the stairs with the others.

Then she turned toward the crates with a hungry leer. There was still the other. And she knew the other would be the real sweet one.

She left the sack and candle on the ground, and picked up the shoes, letting them hang by the laces off the hook of her fingernail. Then she made her way across the floor to the back wall, where there were the crates, and the over-powering smell of the sweet girl.

She was the one that the woman really wanted. The boy had been sour. He would do, there was no sense in wasting him, but he was on the cusp of being too sour. Another year and he would have been ruined.

But the girl...

She dropped the shoes into the crate with the others, and pushed aside the entire stack with one quick movement.

"Oh!" she said, putting a hand to her chest. The child was so beautiful! It lay with its head resting on its chest, like a little doll thrown in the corner. "Oh, my little sweets!" she said, bending down and scooping up the girl in her arms. She took her to the center of the room, and sat down next to the candle and the knife.

She sniffed in the young scent of the girl's hair, closing her eyes to savor it. Then she set her down, careful to hold her head and not let it knock against the floor.

This was her baby.

She combed the blonde hair with her nails, and picked up the knife. She wiped the blade across the front of her cloak. A blade had to be clean for a creature as sweet as this.

She leaned down and kissed the child on the forehead, and it opened its eyes, looking up at her.

The little thing saw the knife and started to whimper.

"My sweets," said the old woman with reproach. It al-ways angered her a little, that these children were so ungrateful. Why did they have to hate her so? Was it because of the way she looked? Well, she couldn't help that! She'd lived a long life.

Besides, if they didn't like the way old people looked, they should be thanking her for saving them the pain of ever growing old. Not fighting and struggling like this little brat was doing.

She leaned an arm down on the girl's neck to keep it still while she brought the knife to its chest. As the tip of the blade scratched her skin, the girl screamed out.

"Shh," the old woman said, "shh, my sweets."

But she kept pushing in the blade. There was no reason to stop. You could spend all day petting the things, if you wanted to, and they'd still fight you. She knew. She'd tried that enough. Better to do it quick. To not be attached. And it's not like it made the hearts taste any different.

She gouged away.

Afterward, looking down at it with the cavity in its chest, she wondered if it knew how precious it was to her. She hoped so. Life was lonely without friends. Then she took off the shoes and threw the body into the pile with the rest.

She made her way back upstairs, closing the hatch to the cellar, and emptied the sack of hearts onto the kitchen table. She cut the girl's heart in half, and then placed the other half and the boy's heart into a clay jar to save for later. Normally, she'd try to ration better, but this was too sweet to resist.

She started a small fire in her oven and held the heart over the flames with tongs, turning it as the fire made the juices bubble. Then she took it out, half raw. There was no point in overcooking it. Hearts were better tender.

She took a bite and moaned, letting her head roll back with pleasure. Who could ever forsake this? she wondered. As far as she was concerned, anyone who denied that it felt good to eat the succulent hearts of children was lying to himself, and she had no patience for liars. She gobbled up the rest of the heart, and licked the tongs clean. Then it was time for bed.

Smacking her lips, she made her way across the house, through the entryway, and up a small ladder to a loft. She slept here, naked, throwing her cloak over herself as a blanket and curling up in a bed of straw.

And as she closed her eyes, she wondered if there were others like her. She was sure there had to be. One living in each town, maybe, or each street. And all of them lonely like her because they had to keep their lives a secret. She yawned and turned over, thinking of it, of all the others. And it wasn't long before she fell asleep, and dreamed of all the friends she'd never know.

* * *

It was the smell that woke her.

She sat up in bed, rubbing her eyes, noticing it was too bright. Smoke curled up from below, and she could hear the crackle of the oven in the next room.

She pulled her cloak over her body and sat listening. She could have sworn she had put out the fire in the oven. It was part of her routine. Nevertheless, she slid her legs over the edge of the loft—and froze.

At her movement, there was a squeak of a chair leg being moved in the kitchen. She gasped at the sound, and held her breath.

Her doors were locked. She was sure her doors were locked. There was no opening for anything larger than a rat to get inside the kitchen. And a rat couldn't move a chair.

Someone had found out her secret. One of the parents, maybe.

It was quiet now, and she climbed down, placing her feet carefully on the floor. Her stomach gurgled, and she felt nauseous. But she would have to tend to that later.

The doorway of the kitchen was lit up with the orange glow of the fire. She took careful steps across the floor, her eyes wide and searching the corners of the room as she walked. How she wished for a knife. A woman living alone should never be without a knife. She reached the kitchen door and stood, gaping.

There were children everywhere. Their corpses were propped up in the chairs around the kitchen table, their sunken faces flickering in the orange glow of the fire. Others, some not more than skeletons, sat leaning up against the walls, encircling the room. Dirt was smeared across the floor where they had been dragged, and still clung to their clothes and faces.

The fire blazed in the oven, and she saw the knives gleaming at her from the wall. She stumbled forward between the legs of the children, making her way across the room, and pulled the biggest knife from the wall, clutching it desperately.

There was a shuffling sound in the shadows of the room. She saw movement out of the corner of her eye, but when she turned, she couldn't see anything at all. She looked down at the children, barely able to make them out in the darkness. Looking at them again, she almost fell over.

Not only had someone dug them up, but someone had put *shoes* on each and every one of their feet.

A giggle came from the darkness, and she swung the knife in the air. But it was no use. What she needed was a candle.

Holding the knife up with one hand, she patted the pockets of her cloak with the other. She found the nub of a candle in her far pocket, and pulled it out. Then, brandishing the knife, she backed up toward the oven.

She stood in front of it, throwing a long shadow down the center of the room, and watched for movement. Seeing nothing, she bent her knees, and opened the door, feeling its heat radiating outward. Still holding up the knife with one hand, she leaned back into the oven, holding out the nub of the candle into the flames. She darted her eyes backward, and lit the wick.

Relieved at the light, she pulled out her hand and turned back to the room with the candle. But as soon as she had, she revealed two children standing in front of her that had been hidden by her shadow. It was the two from earlier that day.

The girl lunged at her, pushing her toward the oven. The hot metal hit her back, and she lost her balance, falling backward onto the floor. The girl pounced on her chest, and threw a handful of the old woman's gray hair into the oven. The long strands caught on fire at once, flames shooting up to her head.

She jumped up, tossing off the girl, and ran back and forth in the kitchen, batting her head with her hands. She screamed out, the fire leaping from her hair to her shoulders, and began to lose sense of her thoughts, only aware of the desperate need to put out the fire.

Her last thought, before the fire overwhelmed her mind, was of the corpses. Of how it's indecent for children to wear shoes if they have no place to go.

And then she thought nothing more.

* * *

Hansel watched the old woman stagger blindly through the kitchen, swatting at the fire on her head and knocking into the walls and table. She looked like a human matchstick, but she wasn't going down.

Gretel rushed the old woman, and Hansel went forward and joined her. Together they bit at her legs, tearing through the cloak with their teeth, and swallowing chunks of flesh. The old woman hollered, bucking with pain as she flailed and tripped over the corpses, finally hitting the ground.

Gretel took hold of the old woman's shoulder, reaching right into the flames. She looked up at Hansel, and he put his hands on the woman too, surprised that the flames didn't bother him either. He couldn't feel anything at all.

And together they dragged the old woman the short distance across the floor to the oven. Gretel opened the door, and pushed the old woman's head inside the flames.

They stood back. The skin of the hag's face melted off in

chunks like butter, and her mouth fell open in a never-ending scream. Gretel put her hand in Hansel's, and together they watched as the old woman's body shuddered its final spasm.

The kitchen was bright with flames now, the dead children's clothes igniting after the old woman had bumped into them. Gretel gave Hansel a tug, and they made their way past the corpses and into the living room. The fire was just spreading here, and they made their way leisurely to the front door. It took both of them, and several tries, to turn the bolt on the door. By then, the living room had begun to heat up, and by the time they stumbled out into the garden, even the roof of the house had begun to kindle.

It was night now. But they could see better at night than ever before, and made their way along the path and back toward the front gate. They got to the front, where Gretel's thumbprint of blood seemed to glow in the dark, and Hansel opened the gate. The two took a step out, and stopped.

Ahead of them, too far in the distance for their eyes to have seen in life, was the shape of a man moving toward them. Even without knowing how he knew it, Hansel knew this man was alive. Gretel seemed to know this, too, and motioned to look at the house behind them.

It lit up the night like a torch. It must be drawing whomever it was right to them.

Hansel looked back at the approaching figure, and found himself growing hungrier and hungrier as it grew closer. He had taken a few bites from the old woman, but he was still starving.

It wasn't until the man was close enough to see them too that the children recognized him as their father. He came forward, his clothes in shreds, and squinted into the darkness.

"Hansel? Gretel?" he asked, standing across the clearing.

The children were still, and he came forward a few steps.

"Your mother is dead," he told them. "Those—*things*— tore her up."

They stared at him without reaction as the fire blazed behind them in the night.

He laughed nervously. "I didn't think you'd still be alive." He shrugged, ashamed. Then, running out of things to say, he bent down before them and opened his arms.

Hansel looked at him, feeling within himself two forces fighting against each other, although he could already tell which was stronger. The weaker part recognized this as his father, and rejoiced at his return. But the stronger part was overwhelmed by the irresistible fragrance of flesh coming to him through the air. He sniffed, finding that he could still pull in air with some effort, but he didn't exhale.

And then all at once the last of his restraint crumbled, and he flew through the night toward his father. This was what he wanted all along. He heard Gretel join him at his side, and together they tackled the man, throwing him to the ground.

Their father's face lit up with joy at their embrace. He thought his children had forgiven him, that they would all live happily ever after.

And then his children chewed the smile off his face.

BLOOD RED RIDING HOOD

She was too good to be true.

He followed behind her on the path, like a moth driven to the flame of Satan's fire. The grandmother whispered something in his ear, and he nodded his head, not hearing a word. It was as if he wasn't even in the woods anymore. Not among the grey trees, not among the cold. He had escaped the pointless emptiness that had haunted him wherever he went. All the huntsman felt now was love, an overpowering, *burning* love for this little Red. This little Red Riding Hood.

"I *said*," the old woman emphasized, squeezing his arm until he had to look at her. She glared at him through her smeared glasses. "Shouldn't we be turning back?"

His eyes were still on the girl. She bent over to look at something in the dirt. "Sure, sure," he said to the old woman, and pulled away from her. He was a tall man, broad and powerful, with thick dark hair under his cap. As he crossed the path, a smile spread across his face, crinkling the skin around his eyes. "What have you got there, Red?"

The girl's back was to him, her red cloak hugging the lines of her back. She was a teenager, nearly a woman. At his voice she turned her head toward him, and looked up with a shy smile, dimples forming on her cheeks. She had a small

78

upturned nose, like a little pixie, and large hopeful eyes. Her eyebrows rose to a concerned arch as she looked at him.

He couldn't breathe. He wanted to hold her so much.

"Breadcrumbs," she said. He looked down at the pile of crumbs. Little black ants climbed over the stale pieces.

"I saw the birds pecking over here," she explained. "And then I turned up the leaves to see what they were getting at." She kicked the pile lightly with the toe of her shoe to demonstrate, and when she extended her foot, it revealed a flash of her white stocking. The fabric stretched over her delicate ankle as if it were painted on, and he shuddered at the sight of it.

"Do you want to feed the birds?" he asked.

She shook her head, a thin strand of hair falling across her forehead. She pushed it back beneath the hood of her cloak. "I think it's supposed to be a trail. It leads into the woods."

He leaned in closer to her, his shadow falling across her face. "Maybe we should follow?"

She inhaled to respond, but before she could, the girl's grandmother was behind them. She poked the tip of her cane into his back.

"Do you hear that?" she asked.

He turned to her and grimaced. But then he heard it, too.

Off in the distance rang the howl of a wolf. It was followed by a chorus of yelps from the rest of the pack. They were perhaps a mile away, perhaps less.

He stood up, and little Red did the same. She came up to his chest in height, even though she was nearly full-grown. And he towered over the grandmother. They both huddled near, looking into the trees.

"There's nothing to be afraid of," he told them. "Wolves know to stay off the path. Especially in the daytime."

"We'd better head back, anyhow," the grandmother said. "This cold is kissing my old bones with ice. It'll snow soon, I'm sure of it."

He looked up at the low-hanging clouds. "It might," he said. "But we've got some time."

"Red," the grandmother snapped, "go up ahead a bit. I want to talk to our gentleman friend in private for a moment."

The girl listened, her eyes glancing at the huntsman when he was referenced, and then she nodded at the grandmother. She turned and went ahead on the path.

"Stay where I can see you!" the grandmother called after her. Then she took the huntsman's arm in her own, and they began walking.

She leaned in and spoke quietly. "I need to know your intentions with the girl. Her mother might be willing to give in to any suitor that comes to call, but I know better than that. I know what men are like."

The huntsman shook his head. "My feelings for her are entirely pure."

The grandmother laughed, a hoarse sound like the cough of a goat.

"What's so funny?" the huntsman asked, feeling embarrassed. "My love *is* pure. It's completely innocent."

The grandmother wiped away a tear, and then turned to him. "Oh, my dear," she said gravely, "love is never innocent. And frankly, I'm not even sure if love is all that important. Why does the girl even need a husband?"

At her statement the hurt was turning to rage inside of him. He had a temper. He knew he had a temper, and should work to control it. Especially now, with this old woman who held the power to make the girl his own.

But he hated her. If he was honest with himself, he hated her.

What did she know of love? Her blood ran cold.

And then there was Red. Lovely little Red. He looked at her in front of them, seeing the sunlight like a halo around the edges of her hood. He really did wish she'd take that thing off. He wanted to see more of her. But at the same time, being hidden by the hood made her more attractive. Until he saw it, her body underneath was *exactly* as he imagined it. She was perfect.

"Now take me for example," the old woman said. He cringed at her voice, breaking his moment. He didn't want to listen to her. He wanted to watch his beloved. But she continued. "My husband has been dead for nearly ten years, and these have been the happiest days of my life. I live alone, and I love it. Everything stays where I left it; nothing is out of place. And it's all *mine*. No sharing with anyone. That's what happiness is all about: having a room to yourself, and no children or husbands to break the silence."

The idea of that sounded terrible to the huntsman. He wanted the girl to warm his bed at night. He wanted her in his arms. He wanted... *her.*

His heart beat faster thinking about it, and again he was completely distracted from the moment by his passion. What if he couldn't have her? What would he do then? He could kill himself. But then she'd just end up with another. And the thought of that made him want to scream. Imagine: her walking down the aisle in a white dress for someone else. Jealousy surged through him at the thought of this imaginary competitor, and a low rumble escaped his throat.

The girl stopped abruptly.

"What is it, Red?" the grandmother asked.

But Red was silent. Her eyes were on the trees next to her on the path. She took a careful step backward, the white of her heel winking from beneath the hem of her cloak.

"What are you doing?" the grandmother snapped.

"Shh," whispered the huntsman. His body grew tense, and his hair stood up on end. He could feel it. He could feel it before he saw it.

As Red took another step backward on the path, the heavy foot of a wolf emerged from the trees. Its head was bent low, its eyes narrowed and teeth bared in a snarl.

"Careful, Red," the huntsman said to her quietly. "Hold your ground. Let us come to you. If you back up anymore, it may pounce."

"I thought you said the wolves wouldn't come near the path?" the grandmother accused.

"They must know winter's coming." Then he added quietly, so that only the grandmother could hear, "It makes them hungry."

They reached Red and he moved to put his arms around her shoulders. The old woman sidestepped him and got between them, throwing herself over the girl. He felt like smacking the crone. Did she think he couldn't protect them? But he held his tongue, and met the eyes of the wolf.

He saw at once this was no ordinary wolf. To begin with, there was its size. It was huge, as tall as the women, and sturdy enough that, if it were feasible, they could have ridden it like a horse. Only alphas got this large, and the fact that an alpha was the first to emerge filled the huntsman with dread.

The second thing that he noticed was that it was wounded. It walked with a limp, dragging one paw sideways through the dust of the path. The creature's silver coat had bald patches, and where the fur remained it was matted and encrusted with gore. Some of this gore was from its victims, like the blood around its muzzle, but there were also open wounds up and down its flank. There was a gash on its side that revealed the white bones of its ribcage, and another on the haunch of the left leg through which a line of pink-grey muscle stretched and constricted as it took another step. And its eyes—huge black globes that stretched open until they bulged, giving the wolf an expression both crazed and empty.

"Stay together," the huntsman whispered to Red and the old woman. He moved between them and the wolf, shielding the women with outstretched arms. "He won't attack a group of our size, not if we show we'll put up a fight."

He reached down slowly, and pulled a hunting knife

from a holster on his boot. The blade gleamed, and he saw the wolf take notice.

He had killed wolves before, even a few this large. A pack of wolves would be a problem, but just one, he could handle that. And *if* he could kill it, if he could save Red in front of the grandmother, he would be the family hero. Her parents would be so grateful they'd give him Red that very night.

"Maybe we should split up," Red suggested.

"No," the huntsman said, not breaking his gaze with the wolf. "He'll just go after the weakest of us—your grandmother. No, stay together and we will all survive. If it comes to battle, I can handle one wolf."

The wolf took another step forward, almost as if testing his claim. Its lips curled back into a leer. Thick saliva pooled in its lower lip and dribbled down in long strands. Now that it was closer, the huntsman could smell it. The rank stench made his eyes water. It smelled sour, like the rotten corpse of a plague victim.

The wolf stopped its advance, and stared at them for a moment. Then it lifted its head to the sky, formed its mouth into a funnel shape, and let out a howl like no howl the huntsman had ever heard before. It was a broken gurgle of a howl that had within its notes both sadness and pain.

"What's wrong with it?" the grandmother asked.

"It's dying. Only a wolf this close to death would come onto the path. Especially alone."

But as soon as he had said that, a rustling came from the bushes on all sides of them. He felt the old woman and the girl press closer to his back. He turned to the shadows, and saw glowing eyes staring back at him from the trees.

"There's more of them!" shouted the grandmother. Air was wheezing in and out of her chest. She took a step backward, away from the group, and the huntsman shot out an arm to hold her in place.

"No," he bellowed. "They will *all* go after the one who is

alone. Our best bet is to fight them. The alpha is weak. If we can kill him, the rest won't touch us."

"I'm not killing a wolf!" the grandmother cried. She looked at the eyes in the darkness, and her pitch began to rise. "They're all around us! Look at them. It's an attack! It's an attack and they're going to—"

"*Quiet*," the huntsman said. "I've got it handled."

But the old woman kept going. He could hear her sobbing, heaving in wet sniffles. "I don't want to die," she moaned. "I need more! I'm not done with life. Don't you hear me? I'm not ready!"

"Grandma, *please*," the girl said. "I'm sure—"

The wolves came forward from the shadows, and Red hushed. These wolves were smaller than the first—the huntsman had been right, it *was* the alpha—but they were still solidly built, and designed by nature for killing. What was more, if the alpha had looked wounded, some of these looked like death. There were five total, and a few were even missing parts. One had no tail. Another had its stomach ripped open, and was trailing dripping guts along in the dirt. But the worst one emerged last, behind two others on the left side: it was missing the lower half of its jaw, tongue and all, so that the entrance to its throat stared at them like a quivering blowhole under the roof of its mouth.

"No, no, no," the grandmother began chanting. She was shaking her head, and tried to move back again. "No, no, no, no, *no*."

The wolves shifted their gaze to her.

"Stay with the group!" the huntsman ordered, but she took another step away. The wolves took a step toward her. The huntsman reached out to grab the old woman, and she screamed at his touch.

"I will not die!" she yelled, her eyes wide with panic behind her glasses. He could see the wild fear of death in her look. She would run if she could. He tried to hold her still, grabbing the shawl draped over her shoulders, and she struggled against him. Then, before he could protect himself, she lifted up her cane and whacked it down with all her might on his kneecap. The bone shattered with a crack, and he crumpled to the ground.

"Grandma!" the girl cried. "What have you done?"

But the old woman didn't lose a moment. She snatched the girl's wrist with her hand, looked her right in the eyes, and said, "Run."

The huntsman curled on the ground, holding his knee, and saw the wolves advancing on him. He turned back to the two women, and saw them running down the path. He reached out a hand toward them, his fingers grasping at the empty air.

"Stop!" he cried.

And then the wolves were upon him.

He comprehended the smell before the pain. Rotting guts. Rancid blood. The sweet musky odor of disease. All of that, compounded by the stench of dog.

The alpha bit into the muscle of his shoulder, sinking its fangs deep into the flesh. This hurt dearly, but it wasn't truly pain until the animal twisted its head, ripping the flesh into shreds.

He cried out in pain, and the wolf growled in response, growing excited by the kill. The huntsman forced himself to turn away from the blood, and faced the path to ask for help. But the woods were empty now, Red and the grandmother out of sight. A moment later large paws blocked his view as the other wolves advanced.

His knife. Where did his knife—

The alpha released his shoulder. The huntsman was dizzy with pain, the wound sputtering blood with each heartbeat. His good hand went to the wound instinctively, covering it, feeling it in disbelief. There was a cavity where his shoulder should have been, and he looked up to see the alpha chewing on a meaty filet of flesh, the blood trickling between its teeth with each chomp.

It made him lightheaded to watch. Or maybe it was the loss of blood. So much blood. He looked down at the growing puddle forming in the dust, and saw his life seeping away from him for the wolves to lick up.

He didn't want to die. Suddenly, passionately, he didn't want to die.

His vision darkening, he glanced around, looking for the knife. He shuffled his feet, dragging them forward and back across the path, and his boot knocked against something solid. He looked at his feet, and even though he wasn't standing, looking at his feet was like peering down over a cliff, the ground below falling farther and farther away. It was giving him vertigo.

The alpha paused in its chewing, noticing the huntsman again. He didn't have much time. With all of his remaining strength, he sat up and shot his good hand to the knife. His fingers grasped the handle, and he turned back to the wolf. It had dropped the meat of his shoulder to the dust, and now crouched to jump. The huntsman drew the knife up in an arch over his head, and just as the wolf lunged toward him, he brought it down and lodged it in the crown of its head.

The wolf's skull at first resisted the blade of the knife, the huntsman's blood-coated fingers sliding down the knife handle. But the inertia of his stab brought his fist to the hilt of the weapon. It caught at the rim, and drove the blade down into the wolf's head, right between its pointed ears.

The wolf gazed at him with its empty eyes, and then stumbled over its front paw. It fell sideways onto the path, its red tongue flopping onto the dirt, and its eyes wide open.

He stared at it, almost not willing to believe it was dead. And then seeing it, he laughed. He had killed the alpha. The others would see it too and leave him alone. He would be a hero, he would marry Red, and have her in his bed tonight.

He imagined her face warm with candlelight, dabbing a cloth to his wounds.

But as the thrill of the victory settled, his shoulder felt worse than before. He winced with the pain. The raw flesh felt like it was on fire, but it shot out daggers of ice through his veins in all directions. He looked down at his arm, and saw the blood in his veins blackening outward from the wound. He felt a ripple of nausea pass through his intestines. He looked up, preparing to vomit, and saw the other wolves were still there.

The pack surrounded him. They stared at him with their leering smiles, and closed in the circle further.

"But I killed your alpha!" he said, his voice escaping in a gasp. He felt cheated. These wolves were breaking the rules. Then he looked again at their disfigured forms, their missing limbs and crazed eyes. This entire pack had gone mad. There were no rules among it.

The huntsman shuffled back. He knew he shouldn't retreat; it was a sign of weakness; but what choice did he have? He couldn't fight five more. Not now. He could barely lift his arm. Bitterness spread through him. "But I killed your alpha," he moaned. And then the pack took another step toward him, and his bitterness heated to panic.

He turned back to the alpha and lunged toward it, groping for the knife. At his movement, the pack broke into a run, and within a moment he was besieged with sharp bites. One snapped at his boots, its teeth poking through the leather. Another went for his calf, the sensitive area under his knee. The other three were going for his arms and hands as he struggled to free the knife from the alpha's skull. He tugged at it, pulling with all his weight, and clenched his eyes shut with the effort.

The knife dislodged with a slurp, but he wasn't ready for it and lost his balance, falling over and landing on his back. A wolf was underneath him, and it wriggled out as he gained his orientation. The others lost no time in returning to him, and a silver wolf bit into the wound on his shoulder, locking its teeth onto his bone. It shook its head, trying to tear his entire arm off.

"Ahhh!" the huntsman cried. He looked at the snout of the wolf, the bristles of whiskers under its black nose, and saw its reddened teeth pierce into his flesh. It was so crisp in his vision, each hair on the wolf's head outlined distinctly, a line of white fur running vertically up its muzzle. He saw in its black eyes the reflection of the woods and of his own blood-splattered face.

And seeing himself in such stark detail, the attack felt less real. He became detached from the moment, as if watching a scene from below the surface of a lake. And a thought came into his mind, complete and with perfect clarity:

It should be the grandmother here instead of him. It should be her, and he should be with the girl. He was meant to be with the girl.

The wolf twisted its muzzle deeper into his shoulder, and the pain shocked him back to the moment. Spasms shook his body, and his fingers curled around the handle of the knife at his side. He knew he had to stab the wolf. He had to stab them all to survive. He fought to take control of his senses, squeezed the knife, and flung his arm at the wolf on top of him.

The knife landed in its side, going into its chest to the hilt. He knew wolves, and he knew it was a blow right to the heart. The jaw on his arm loosened. The wolf turned its head to look back at the knife in its side, then turned back with a blank expression. The huntsman's lips raised in a cruel smile.

But the wolf didn't die. It didn't even seem to feel the knife. It might have turned to it simply to be sure it had been stabbed at all, because a moment later it was on him again, digging into his flesh.

The other wolves came near now, and the man knew he was finished. He felt the jaws of the wolves clamp down on him, one onto each leg, another going for his other shoulder. He was pinned. Then the fifth wolf came up to him, the one with no lower jaw. He stared into its black eyes, hate filling him, and dared the wolf to try anything.

The wolf came to his neck, lowered its head, and stuck its snout beneath him. Then it brought up its head, lifting the huntsman a few inches off the ground. The other wolves followed, lifting their heads, and the jawless wolf began to push as the others dragged the huntsman into the trees.

He was already in the darkness before he could fully comprehend what was happening. Sharp twigs snapped against his skin as the wolves tugged and pulled him against the brush of the woods. He was in such dizzying pain at this point that he barely felt the occasional jab of a rock into his back, or when the wolves would falter and drop a bit of him, letting an arm or a leg drag on the dirt until it tore his skin away. He didn't feel it; or rather, he felt it all, and the pain was so absolute he could no longer distinguish its nuances.

Deeper and deeper into the woods he was taken. His body was relaxing. Wherever the wolves were taking him, he might be dead before he got there. And his mind drifted, his eyes rolling back in his head, only catching occasional glimpses of the black trees pointing to the grey sky above, their tips all pointing to the same center point.

He had heard stories of people surviving a wolf attack. But he'd never heard of being dragged into the woods like this. Perhaps that's because the only people who ever experienced this didn't live to tell about it.

The wolves took him downhill, and with the slant he was able to see their destination: up ahead was the black mouth of a cave. It was shaped like a tombstone. It was their den. The panic rose in him, waking him as if he had fallen through the ice of a pond.

"No," he said, seeing the cave growing larger and larger before him. "No, not there. Anywhere but there."

He struggled, unable to break the manacles of their jaws. He knew once he went inside he would never come out again. If he could distract the wolves, even for a moment, even just to stay alive for a few more minutes—

But he couldn't do anything but watch. The wolves dragged him forward to the mouth of the cave, like a sacrifice brought to the idol of their god. Only then did the wolves release their grip, and the huntsmen dropped. He fell into the cave, past the lips of the rock, and deep into the vaulted throat of its void.

And then the entire world went black.

* * *

Red. Everything came back in a flash of red.

Blood.

The cloak.

The... *girl*.

He sat up in the darkness and could see. He couldn't think but he could see. There were bodies all around him. He was in a pile of bodies. He was in the cave. The wolves had dropped him into a pile of bodies in the cave. But he was not dead. He didn't feel alive but he was not dead.

He was buried in the bodies, and pushed them off of him. There were other humans. Animals. Parts of things he couldn't even tell what they were. The bounty of a million kills.

He pushed himself out of the pile and looked around at the ribs of the cave walls. Then down at the pile of bodies. Bones mostly. He could see them even in the darkness. And then he looked up to the circle of light from the outside world. He crawled over the bodies, feeling their lumpy ruins under him as he climbed over them and up the incline of the cave floor.

A grunt escaped him. It took effort to control his hands. He meant to clutch the rocks but only knocked at them with the side of his palm. He was mashing his fingers again and again until the skin was torn.

But he didn't feel it.

He didn't feel anything at all.

He climbed to the edge of the cave, and pulled himself to the level ground outside. Then he pushed himself up from the dust to stand, his limbs twisted, his ankles at unusual angles. His shoulder couldn't lift his arm anymore, the muscle had been ripped so severely, and it swayed at his side when he intended to move it with force. It was strange, not to have control over your body. But he—

The red cloak. Red. It flashed in his mind again, and his head snapped up with a snarl.

There before him were the wolves, the dead wolves that had brought him here. They sat in a semi-circle around him, and when he looked at them, they lowered their heads. They were bowing to him.

He took a step forward, and they looked up at him, slightly, from the edges of their vision. He took another step to the left, toward the woods, and when they saw his direction they rose as one. But not to attack. They still had their heads lowered. He took a step into the trees, and they followed obediently at his heels.

He had killed their leader. They would listen to him now. Do as he commanded.

He was the new alpha.

And there was only one thing the huntsman wanted.

*   *   *

"If you ask me, she's better off without him," the grandmother said, tying a scarf over her head. "Men are nothing but trouble."

It was night, and they were back at the girl's house with her mother. A fire sputtered in the hearth, fighting to warm the room. Red, still in her cloak, leaned against the wall with her arms crossed, and watched as her mother wrapped the old woman in scarves like a mummy.

"Don't talk that way," she chastised.

"Grandma's right," the girl said. "He was weird. And even if he weren't, I never want to get married."

Her mother turned to her. She had limp dark hair tied behind her head in a bun. Her face was wrinkled but kind, and even her look of reproach was gentle. "Now, Red, you shouldn't say such things. It's a woman's duty to have a man."

"But I don't *want* him," Red protested. "I want to live alone, like Grandma."

Her mother shot the old woman a look. "Don't fill her head with lies, Mother. You had a man, just like everyone else. If you hadn't, I wouldn't be here. And if *I* hadn't, Red wouldn't be here. Even if you don't care for a man, it's worth it for that."

"I don't want a child," the girl said, turning toward the fire. "I want a garden instead. And I want it to be all *mine*."

"And where is this garden?" her mother asked. "Where is this house you'll live in?"

Red shrugged. "I'll build it."

"All by yourself?"

The girl frowned, then turned to look at them both by the door. "No," she said, and smiled. "Grandma will help me."

Her grandmother let out a laugh, and Red couldn't tell if she was amused by the statement, or mocking the implausibility of it.

"Oh, you say that now," her mother said, putting her arms around the girl, "but all that will change soon enough. You just haven't met the right man yet."

Red pushed her away. "Why can't you understand? There *is* no right man for me."

But her objections were cut short by a dull knock at the door. Red and her mother stared at each other for a moment before turning away.

"That's your father, dear," her grandmother said, going to the door. "And it's about time. I was beginning to grow worried."

She swung open the door, sending a long rectangle of light stretching into the darkness outside.

No one was there.

She peered out, tiny in the doorway, and raised her glasses to her eyes. Her lips puckered as she scanned in either direction. Red and her mother watched with tight nerves, seeing the old woman's hunched back as she leaned out exposed into the black night. Red was relieved when she turned back inside and shut the door.

The old woman looked at them and held up her hands with a smile.

"Must have been the wind," she said, trying to make a joke out of it. But no one laughed, and her own smiled dropped instantly.

"Are you sure?" Red asked. "You have trouble seeing in the daylight, let alone at night."

The old woman's hands started to fiddle with the knot of the scarf under her chin. "There's no one there."

Red's mother went back to dressing the old woman in silence. She pulled a pair of mittens over her frail hands, and the old woman looked up at Red.

Red was quiet. Both she and her grandmother had been on edge since the wolf attack. The woods no longer felt safe. And even though neither of them cared for the huntsman, her father had insisted on searching for him. He had been gone since the afternoon, and the day outside had since turned to black.

There was another knock at the door, and all three women jumped. They eyed each other for a moment, and then the grandmother nodded. She went to the door, and Red's mother stood back, shielding the girl.

"Who's there?" the old woman asked.

A moment of silence was followed by a gruff reply: "Open the door."

"Is that your husband?" the grandmother asked. Red's mother shrugged helplessly. All voices sounded the same through the thick door.

"Open the door, Greta."

The women breathed out in relief at the mother's name, and the grandmother opened the door. A lumberjack of a man sauntered in, towering over the women and looking down at them with a sunburnt face. He crossed to Red and kissed her on the forehead.

"How's my girl?" he asked.

"I'm fine, Father," she replied, looking down.

He smiled at her, and then turned to his wife with a frown. "I could use a glass of water. I've been out all day."

Greta nodded quickly, and went to the corner of the room to ladle out a cup of water. She brought it to him as he took off his cap and wiped his forehead with the side of his arm. He leaned back and gulped the water. Beads of sweat reflected on his Adam's apple as it hopped up and down. He burped, then handed the cup back to his wife without looking at her.

"I couldn't find any sign of him," he said, looking at his daughter. "I saw the blood on the trail and circled outward from there, double tracking over my steps just to be sure."

Red nodded, still looking down.

"I would have looked longer, but it's pointless in the dark. And by morning..." He shook his head. "I'm sorry, Red. He's gone."

The women were silent. Red tried to hide the excitement growing inside her chest. "Gone?" she asked carefully. "So—I don't have to marry him?"

"Oh, my little Red," he said, and pinched her cheek. "There will be another. And next time, you're not to wear your cloak. It makes you look fat."

She didn't say anything. She might have been able to argue with her mother, but with her father, all anyone could do was listen.

He smacked his lips and turned to the old woman. "You ready to go?"

"Are you sure it's safe?" she asked.

He glared at her, the corner of his lip rising. "Yes," he said, his voice cold, "I *am* sure. Otherwise I wouldn't have said it, now would I?"

The grandmother kept her face blank, but Red could tell she was furious. The girl put a hand on her father's arm.

"You didn't see these wolves, Father," she said. "There was something *wrong* with them."

He looked down at her hand, his eyes narrowing. The mother saw his look and came forward to take the girl away.

"Listen to your father, Red," she whispered, locking eyes with the girl until Red backed down.

"All right," her father said, putting back on his cap. "I'll be back soon." He took a step to the door and stopped. "And make her take off that cloak. She's not a child anymore."

Red's mother nodded, and her father went out the door. He left it open, not slowing down, so that the grandmother only had time to give Red a quick pitying glance before hobbling after. Red watched them disappear into the darkness, and she shut the door. Then she leaned back against it, clenching her eyes shut.

She was disappointed in her grandmother. Why did she have to submit to her father like that? Why did everyone have to obey him? Red would still have to get married, she knew that now, and she wouldn't have any choice about it. She also knew that, after tonight, her grandmother wouldn't take her side if she tried to fight it.

Red opened her eyes. Her mother was across the room at the sink, rinsing out the cup her father had used.

"How can you put up with him?" she asked, crossing to her. "It's like living with an animal."

"Don't speak about your father like that," her mother snapped. "He's a good man; he provides for us."

Red folded her arms, running her fingers over the fabric of her cloak. She looked up at her mother, raising her eyebrows like a small child. "Do I really have to give up my cloak?"

Her mother sighed. "I'm afraid so. If your father comes back and you've still got it on, we're *all* going to get it." She held out both hands before Red, palms up. "Best to do it quickly."

Red hugged her arms around herself, grabbing a fold of the fabric in each hand.

"*Now*, Red."

She wouldn't budge, and her mother grew impatient and tried to pull the cloak off of her.

"No!" Red cried. She pushed her mother away.

Her mother's eyes went wide. Then she came forward and slapped the girl hard across the face.

"How dare you disrespect me!" she cried. "Your father was right. The sooner we get you married and out of this house, the better."

There was a knock at the door.

"That's your father now," her mother said with a sneer. "And I intend to tell him *exactly* how you behaved while he was away."

She went across the room with her chin raised and opened the door. "Just wait until you hear what—"

But again, no one was there. The cold air blew into the room and stirred the flames of the fire, sending wild ripples of light across the room.

Red's mother turned to her with a shrug, her back to the

dark doorway. Her tired eyes were warm again, and she lifted a corner of her mouth in a shy smile.

And then in the next moment, a dark form flew through the door and knocked her to the ground. He was on top of her, holding her down. Red screamed out, and the man—it was a man, he was covered in blood—looked up at her.

It was the huntsman.

His face was smeared with gore, his hair sticking out in unkempt tufts. It was grey now, like the wolves', with streaks of silver against his dark hair. Blood covered his tattered clothes, and there were gashes all over his pale skin.

He tilted his head sideways, and his lips opened in an effortful smile. But his eyes were blank, and the smile was little more than a parting of his lips that revealed his front teeth.

He struggled to stand up, his ankles twisted. The flesh at the shoulder had been torn away to the bone, the arm dangling at his side as he worked to push himself up with the other one.

"Red!" her mother called out. "Run!"

She grabbed the back of the huntsman's shirt, and pulled him to the ground. He landed with a thud, his body not reacting. Then he sat back up, and started toward the girl again.

"Go to your room!" her mother shouted. "Lock the door, and *do not* come out."

She pulled on the back of the man's shirt again, but he was too strong for her, and when he took a step toward Red, he dragged her mother along the floor with him.

Red ran into her room and slammed the door. Her hands were shaking terribly, and she had trouble working the latch. She locked it, throwing down the bolt, and then stepped back into her room.

A moment later she heard her mother scream.

* * *

The huntsman didn't understand why the mother fought him. He hadn't done anything to her, and he only had the purest intentions for her daughter. But still the woman blocked the door to Red's room. She had even picked up the fire poker, and swung it in front of her like a sword. Did she really think that would stop him? Did she value the power of love as little as that?

He shook his head and tried to say, *Pardon me.* But it came out wrong. More of a growl than a pleasantry. But he would have to worry about speech later.

The mother rushed at him, a wild look in her eyes like a caveman hunter about to spear a boar, and lodged the fire poker into the middle of his chest. She looked up into his eyes with a triumphant smirk, and released her fingers to step away and watch him fall.

But he didn't fall. He didn't feel the poker at all. Didn't this woman know? She couldn't hurt his heart; it already belonged to Red.

Her eyes widened as he took another step forward, and swung at her with his good arm. He grabbed her by her hair bun, and pulled her to him. She was warm. She smelled good.

And the huntsman suddenly realized how extremely hungry he was.

He held her against his chest, and bent his mouth to her neck. He could hear the blood pulsing beneath. It was like listening to the sizzle of meat on the stove, and he couldn't resist for another moment. He bit into her neck, the blood spraying against his face like warm rain, and he chomped into her throat.

He chewed into the muscle of her neck like taffy, pulling his head back to tear away strips of it, and then clenching down on each bite to squeeze out the hot blood. It spilled over his lips and onto his chin, and he worked to slurp down what he could.

The nourishment of the flesh spread through him. It was

refreshing and relaxing at once, like taking a nap in the sun, and he felt his spirit reviving. His senses sharpened as well. The room seemed to grow brighter, the colors more pronounced. He could feel the pressure of the iron rod in his chest, even though he felt no pain from it. And, amplified over it all, he could hear the sound of the girl behind the door, each breath as it entered and left her parted lips.

Then he smelled something different. A warm smell, a body, a man. He could smell his sweat. The huntsman turned, the woman still in his arm. Her head hung low and spun on its single cord of flesh, like a bead revolving at the end of a length of thread.

The girl's father was in the doorway. His shoulders were arched, and he staggered back when he saw the woman in the huntsman's arms.

"What have you done to my wife?" he shouted, and the girl behind the door screamed at the sound of his voice. She cried hysterically, begging for help, and the man looked up toward the door. "Don't worry, Red," he called. "I'll get you out."

The huntsman let the woman drop to the ground. He took a step forward, the poker sticking out of him like a flagpole, and snarled. If this man wanted a fight, he would get one.

The man in the doorway didn't back down. He waited for the huntsman to take another step, and then revealed an axe he was carrying behind his back. He held the handle with both hands against his chest, preparing to raise it into the air. The huntsman's eyes went open, and he took a step back. His hand went to Red's door, pressing against it, but it was locked. And the girl's father took a step into the house, the axe held up over his head. Then he came at the huntsman, looking like the white-faced angel of death.

But the woman's flesh had helped his thinking. The huntsman lifted up one corner of his mouth in an attempted smile, and worked to separate his fingers. He held up an index finger as if to say, *One moment, please.*

It worked; it caught the father off-guard, and he had stopped long enough for the huntsman to open his mouth, suck in all the air he could into his dead lungs, and then work his lips together until they almost touched. He leaned his head back and let out the air, feeling it vibrate along his windpipe, and let out a jagged howl.

The man stumbled back, confused and frightened, as the huntsman lowered his face with a bloody grin.

"What was that?" the man asked, looking around. "Why did you do that? It won't save you." He chuckled, his confidence returning, and lifted up the axe. He had not taken more than one step when the first wolf ran through the door. It pounced on his back, and knocked him to the ground. He rolled onto his back, raised the axe without wasting a moment, and brought it down.

He missed. It lodged in the wooden floorboards, and before he could lean forward to try to pull it out, the rest of the wolves had arrived. He couldn't try anything more.

The man's cries lasted only a moment. Wolves know to go for the neck first, and his throat was torn out within seconds. They didn't stop there: they tore into his stomach, and pulled out his intestines like streamers, growling and snarling as they worked.

The flesh looked good, delicious actually, but the huntsman turned back to the girl's door.

He knocked on it with his good arm, and tried to tell her she could come out now; that there was no one left to stop them from being together. But his words came out in the same garbled chokes as his previous attempt, and the girl only screamed back at him. She wasn't going to open.

The huntsman wasn't a fan of modesty. He knew some liked it, but he never had much patience for girls playing hard to get. He turned back to the room and saw the axe stuck into the floorboards, its handle floating in the air. He patted the door with his fingertips, and then stumbled toward the axe.

The wolves were ripping into the father's ribcage, tearing apart the bones curled around the man's chest. Even the wolf without a lower jaw managed to join in, lowering its neck to the floor, and slurping up the blood through its throat like a straw. The huntsman walked past them and put his good hand around the axe handle.

It wouldn't budge. He tugged on it, leaning back his body, but its blade had been wedged into the floor almost to the handle. He tried to flop his other arm around to grab it with both hands, but he couldn't work the fingers. He tried wrapping his dead fingers around the handle with his good hand, but they wouldn't grip, and his bad arm fell back as soon as he let go. All he had managed to do was coat the handle with slippery blood.

He let out a groan and turned back to the locked door. Why wouldn't she open up? He had come here just for her. Didn't she know they were meant to be together? And at her memory he felt an emptiness in his chest that had nothing to do with the fire poker lodged there.

He felt like crying.

He turned back to the wolves, the sound of their chewing echoing in his ears, and was unable to think of a solution. Maybe some more food would help clear his mind. He bent down to all fours and crawled between the wolves. They were shoulder to shoulder in a circle around the father, their heads bent down and snouts inside his chest. The huntsman pressed his own mouth inside, his nose against the warm wet flesh, and let the sensations of eating sooth his worried mind.

She wouldn't open the door. He couldn't break down the door. And she probably wouldn't come out while he was still here. That much was evident.

But she had to come out at some point. And the

huntsman realized he already had a pretty good idea of where she'd go. There was only one place, really. And if he got there first, he could be sure to have everything prepared for a perfect honeymoon.

He lifted his head from the body, his teeth flashing under his face painted with red slime, and he sucked in a grateful blast of air into his lungs. He leaned back his head, and gave a joyful howl. The other wolves lifted their heads in solidarity, and their chorus of howls echoed into the night.

*   *   *

She wept with her back against the door until dawn. It was the longest night of her life. She wasn't sure if her parents were alive or dead. She assumed the worst; she had heard their screams. But then, she had thought the huntsman was dead, too.

What made it all worse though was how quiet it was. After the first screams, and after some strange gnawing sounds that her mind refused to comprehend, there had been nothing. Nothing for hours.

It wasn't until she had been listening to the birds outside for nearly an hour that she thought about opening the door. Birds wouldn't chirp like that with wolves nearby. She leaned her head against the wall and listened. No sounds. She raised her hand up, and knocked, three quick raps and then listened sharply for the sounds of someone on the other side being surprised or disturbed.

Again, no sounds.

Her breath went in and out, her chest heaving as she tried to prepare herself for what may be on the other side. She unfastened the lock, listening the entire time, worried that she may have been tricked. She waited another moment, and then pulled the door toward her.

She peeked her eye out of the crack and was blinded by

the daylight. She narrowed her eyes and scanned the room, her vision adjusting.

Red. Everything was red with blood. It was splattered on the walls and stood in sticky pools on the floor. Not seeing the huntsman or his wolves, she opened the door a little wider, until she could plainly see that the room was empty.

Her parents were gone. The floors were bare, and in the center of the room was her father's axe, slanting out of the ground like a trampled blade of grass. She ran to it at once and wrapped her fingers around the handle. It was sticky with blood, but she barely noticed. It was a weapon. It was a fantastic weapon.

She had to use both hands, pulling it up and down with all the weight of her shoulders until it started to wiggle like a loose tooth. Then she dug her feet into the ground and pulled back on it, letting out a grunt of effort that grew louder as she continued to tug at it. Then, finally, it slipped out of its groove, and she took a few steps backward to balance herself with the weight of it in her arms.

She stood for a moment holding the axe in the middle of the room, her shoulders rising up and down, her eyes on the open doorway. The sunlight lit up the room and the grass and trees in the distance. But she didn't trust it. She would probably never trust anything ever again.

She took a step forward, her shoes sticking to the blood on the ground. She felt something crunch under her step and looked down to see one of her parents' molars. Her heartbeat quickened at the sight, and she forced herself to look away and out the door. She didn't want to see anything in this room. She wanted to get out of this place, and to safety.

The plan was to run through the woods to her grandmother's house. It was only ten minutes away by walking. The town would have been her first choice, but she couldn't be sure to find it if she had to stray from the path. If she met any of the wolves or the huntsman on the way, she had to be able to run in any direction without getting lost. And she knew the trees between her home and her grandmother's house by heart. It was the obvious choice.

It was also a place with someone who could figure out this mess. Her grandmother would know what to do. Yes, she told herself, her grandmother would help and all she had to do was get there.

She approached the doorway on tiptoes, stopping after every step to listen. When she got to the door, she thought about shutting it and locking herself in against the world. It was tempting, but what good would that do? She didn't have enough food here to last more than a few days. Besides, she couldn't stand the idea of staying here, in this room, finding more *things*…

Her foot stepped off the firm stoop and onto the soft grass outside her home. She looked around, clutching the axe to her chest. She was still wearing her red riding hood, with the cap lowered to see better, and her hair blew in the breeze as she stepped through the clearing. When she reached the middle, she turned in a full circle, ready for something to dart at her from any direction. Then, when she didn't see anything, she ran into the woods, taking the path to her grandmother's house.

She walked down the exact center of the path, cowering as she held the axe close to her chest. It made her nervous to be so exposed, but it had the benefit of giving her some room to react if someone came at her. She scanned the shadows in the leaves, her eyes constantly darting from one side to the other, never settling.

She got to the part of the path that turned into the woods; she wouldn't be able to see her house from this point forward. She looked back with some regret, and then continued on.

The woods seemed to get darker here. She realized her hands were shaking, and stopped to look at them. When she looked back up, she couldn't move her legs. She was frozen with fear.

"Come on," she whispered to herself. "You can do this."

She wished she were bigger. It would be easier if she were bigger. She felt so small underneath the skeletal canopy of branches that arched above her on the path. And she knew she stood out from everything with her red cloak, that it made her even more vulnerable and likely to be seen, but she couldn't bear to take it off. It was her only comfort left.

"Okay," she whispered. She took a deep breath, and managed to take another step forward. It was easier to keep moving once she started, and a moment later she was walking briskly, almost running, as she reached what she recognized as the half-way point between the houses. Encouraged by this, she picked up her pace even more, until she really was running now, not able to slow herself down. She had to lift up the front of her cloak to keep from tripping, but it felt good to run, to have the details of the woods turn into a blur on either side of her. She sprinted around another bend in the path, and it was then that she realized she wasn't alone.

They were all around her, running next to her through the trees. Wolves. She saw their low shapes clinging to the ground. But not only wolves: people, too. There were people in the shadows, a horde of them. She screamed, unable to control herself, and leaned forward as she ran, moving her legs as quickly as she could, and turned another bend.

The path ahead was littered with obstacles. Someone had thrown branches over it. These people, she thought, these people in the woods must have done it. They're trying to stop me from reaching safety.

She wasn't going to let them.

She ran forward, hopping in between the branches and landing in the clear spaces of earth between. Some of the branches were covered with blood, and it wasn't until she had hopped through a great length of them that she realized they weren't branches at all: they were bones. The path was littered with yellowed bones. What had these people done? How many people had already died that she didn't know about?

She neared the end of the expanse of bones, and could now see her grandmother's house in the distance. But between her and the grandmother's house was another obstacle. Something was stretched across the path and tied to the trees on either side. She kept running, unable to make it out in the shadows, until she was right before the barrier.

And there, stretched out like a giant cobweb between the trees, were her parents. Their intestines had been ripped out and were strung into a taut net, into which pieces of their bodies had been wedged: arms, a length of hair, and in the center, side-by-side and gazing at her from eyeless faces, were their heads. Red screamed, the image of it forever burned into her memory.

Behind her, she heard the horde. She turned back to them as they came forward from the shadows. They were a disparate group, their heights and ages varied, their tattered clothes from different castes. She made out two small children that looked like siblings, a brother and sister wearing grey rags, and another boy next to them that looked like he had been pieced together out of parts. But there were more, so many more, and they were still coming out of the woods when she turned back to the web of intestines. She lifted her axe, and brought it down on her parents' faces. Their heads knocked to the ground and rolled past her feet, and she climbed through the gap. Hands grasped at the hem of her cloak, but she pulled herself through, her feet landing on the other side, and she ran the rest of the way down the path.

The ground was descending now, and she was able to run faster toward the house. She could see the red flowers her grandmother had planted outside on either side of the brown door, and wanted it to be like it was before, before any of this had started.

"Please," she begged, "please let me make it. Don't let this be the end."

That's when she heard the wolves. They had sidestepped the blockade and were racing on either side of her, closing in for the kill. She screamed out, her muscles on fire, and called out, "Grandma! Grandma, let me in!"

She reached the door and saw it had been left open. She pushed it forward and squeezed inside. A wolf lunged after her, snapping its teeth, and crashed against the door as she pushed it shut.

Red screamed out, unable to control herself now. She could hear the wolves scratching against the door, and knew the people in the woods wouldn't be far behind. The room was dark, and she had to set down the axe to secure the door by feel, sliding down a heavy wooden beam into place. Shaking, she turned toward the room.

It was almost pitch black. The only light came from a small window the size of a sparrow's nest near the peak of the roof. It sent a shaft of light down through the room to the grandmother's curtained bedframe.

"Grandma?" Red asked, her throat burning after the run. Her breath came out in heaves, and she started to realize that it was odd for it to be so dark. Her grandmother should have lit a candle, or started a fire in the hearth. It was cold in here, too, almost colder than outside. "Grandma, what's wrong? Are you sick?"

A hand emerged from a space in the bed curtains, issuing Red closer.

The girl rushed to the bedside. "Oh, Grandma. You have to get up. The huntsman, he killed Mother and Father. He tried to kill me. And outside, there were these people, they—they—the whole world's gone mad!"

She took her grandmother's hand in hers, and dropped it at once.

"Grandma, your hands are like ice!"

She took a step back, and her shoe stuck on a patch of blood.

"You're hurt," she said, looking down. "Did he do this to you? Let me see."

"No," her grandmother whispered. Her voice was weak and hoarse, and it sounded like her tongue was swollen.

Red stepped forward and threw open the curtains of the bed. Her grandmother was there, barely able to lift her head off the pillow. She had changed into her long-sleeved night-gown, and wore a matching sleeping cap over her hair. The covers of the bed were bundled up almost to her chin, and she looked at Red from behind her thick glasses with a blank expression.

"Grandma, your face," Red said, leaning closer. "You look awful." Her skin was a dull grey color, and it sagged at her cheeks and had strange bulges under her cheekbones. Someone had beaten her, and badly.

"Did *he* do this to you?" Red asked. "Let me light a candle, I might be able to clean some of your wounds."

Her grandmother lifted a hand and waved, a gesture that said *Don't Bother*, but Red went to the other side of her bed anyway, and found the candle and matches. Her grandmother turned to look at her. Red lit the candle, holding her hand around the flame as it caught on the wick, and then looked up at her grandmother.

Her grandmother was sitting up on the edge of the bed. Only she was bigger than she should have been. A sinking sensation began in Red's stomach as the shadow of the form stared at her. It was her grandmother, only it *couldn't* be her grandmother. Red took her hand from the candle and gasped.

"Your eyes," she whispered. "What's wrong with your eyes?"

Those weren't her grandmother's eyes. The sinking sensation turned into a free-fall of panic inside her, and her hand shook uncontrollably as it held the candle. She took a step backward, and the heel of her shoe landed on something. She turned to look down, and saw she had stepped on a foot. It still had a shoe on it, and next to it was another foot, also with a shoe, and both had legs that led under a pile of clothes heaped up against the wall.

Red turned back to the form on the bed that looked back at her. She squinted to see it better.

Then the form reached up to its face with one hand. The skin on the back of the hand was scraped away, and there were thick black hairs covering the knuckles. It reached up and spread the fingers wide, poking into her grandmother's face as the old woman stared back without any expression at all. Her eyes were dark and dead as the fingers curled, the nails digging into her skin under her cheekbones, and clawing away strips that dangled like worms from the edge of her jawline.

"Grandma, stop," Red begged, unable to take her eyes away.

And then the old woman reached farther up, to the peak of her hairline, and began to peel the skin off her forehead like an orange. Underneath the skin was grey, and she dragged her hands past her eyes, knocking off her glasses, past her nose and chin, until she held her face in her hands. It wasn't the grandmother; it had never been the grandmother. The huntsman looked up at Red, his mouth in a grin, and his face covered with pink gore like a newborn.

He threw the old woman's face to the ground, and Red screamed, looking down at it.

"Her face," she said, unable to comprehend. "You were wearing her face." She looked up, her body shaking all over, and saw the huntsman take off the grandmother's nightcap and rip through the thin nightgown.

"No," Red whispered, stepping back. The huntsman reached his arm out toward her. "No!" she screamed, and stepped to the edge of the wall, her eyes looking back toward the door. If she could reach the axe—

But she hadn't gotten halfway around the bed when the huntsman lunged at her. He wrapped an arm around her throat and pulled her to the bed.

"No!" she screamed, kicking her feet into the air. But he was too strong for her. He threw her down against the pillows and pinned her down with his weight, lying on top of her.

She closed her eyes and shook her head, struggling underneath him. She felt his cold fingers press against her face, touching her cheeks, and her eyes opened involuntarily and looked up at him. His skin was torn and rotten, and patches of his scalp peeked through the temples of his forehead. She coughed, his rancid smell singeing the inside of her nostrils.

His face lowered ever so slightly toward hers, and her eyes opened wide in revolt. She tried to move away, and he held her head with his hand, and pressed his lips into hers. She screamed out with her mouth closed, thrashing her hands and feet and unable to get him off of her. She couldn't breathe, crushed by his weight and the pressure building in her lungs like she was being held underwater.

He pulled back, and left the taste of her parents coating her lips. She gagged, about to vomit, and started to hyperventilate.

She just wanted to die.

He leaned down to her again, and she didn't think she could take any more of this. What if it went on for days? What if he never stopped? His lips tickled her neck, and she was almost grateful when she could feel his teeth sinking into it.

*　*　*

Little kisses, he thought, that's all they were.

He didn't understand why she struggled against them.

Didn't she know he'd never hurt her? And he nibbled at the skin under her ear, tasting her sweet blood first on the tip of his tongue, and then savoring it as the rich flavor spread across the middle of his mouth and all the way to the back of his throat. She was ambrosia and nectar. Her parents were swill compared to this purity made flesh.

Yet still she struggled. He leaned back down and ran his tongue along her neck until he felt the hot surging of her pulse underneath. He had found a major artery, and cut into it delicately with the tips of his teeth.

Blood sprayed out like a fountain, and he opened his mouth and swallowed mouthful after mouthful. It still amazed him how much blood a person had beneath their skin. Truly, what you could see with the eyes was the least interesting part of a person; it is what was inside that counts. He gulped her down, until what had been inside of her was now inside of him. It saturated every cell of his being, expanding and constricting his muscles, heating him like being dipped in warm water. It made the room brighter, and sent vague objects hidden in the shadows into stark clarity.

The warmth escalated to a feverish intensity until he felt ready to burst. Then the blood seemed to bloom, expanding and dancing inside of him, and sent shivering waves of pleasure all the way down to the tips of his toes. He smiled, recognizing the sensation for what it was: the divine feeling of pure love.

He sank back to the bed as the last spurts of blood left the girl's neck. He was completely relaxed, and reached his arm around the girl to cuddle with her. She twitched, fighting him still, but without the energy from before. He held her, his head on her chest as he listened to her heart squeeze with effort, and then expand outward in a spluttering gasp, silent forever more.

And he knew she was his now. His little Red Riding Hood.

* * *

They spent the day lounging in bed together, blissful newlyweds. He ran his fingers through her hair and watched as the dot of sunlight rose up on the wall and then faded away again. Then he watched it start anew the next day. He could spend all eternity like this. He might have, too, except that when the dot of light reached the middle of the wall on the second day, the girl's body jerked.

She was waking up.

Her arms stretched out like a butterfly's wings stiff from the chrysalis. Her red cloak was starched with blood, the folds caked onto her in patches as she sat up. She turned first one way, and then the other, as she took everything in.

She turned to him, and he gestured to the room and smiled. "Our new home," he tried to say, but the whisper caught in his throat. It was so much work to talk, and words weren't worth the effort.

Red stared at him. The gash on her throat had turned black, but there were still red splatters of blood on her chin and dabs of it on her earlobes. She was the most beautiful thing he had ever seen. He put his hand in hers. She looked down, and pulled it away. He reached toward it again, and she hissed at him like a swan.

Then before he could stop her, she had climbed out of bed and was shambling toward the exit. She pushed off the beam, letting it clank to the floor, and shoved open the door. She had taken a step outside before he was even on his feet.

He scrambled after her. She was heading to the trees, he could see that. She was trying to leave him.

"No," he gurgled, and sucked air into his lungs until his chest was double its normal size. He couldn't lose her, not now, not after all this. He leaned back his head, and let out a howl that shook the trees and rattled the frame of the house.

She didn't even turn around.

A moment later the wolves arrived. He was still their alpha, a fact she would learn soon enough. They emerged from the trees, their fur more matted than when he saw them last, and they formed a line blocking the girl's path into the woods. She hissed at them, and they snarled back.

He came to her, and took her hand again. She struggled to pull away, but he kept his grasp firm. She was his wife now; she would have to learn to respect him. He was sure in time she'd realize that he only had her best interest at heart, and perhaps as the years went by, she would learn to be grateful.

Either way, she was his, and she wasn't going anywhere. He spun her around toward the house, and they both froze.

There in the doorway was the grandmother, staring back at them. Her face looked like a slab of beef wearing a wig and dentures. Blood coated the front of her dress like a bib, and she had found her glasses and stuck them into the meat of her face, although they hung crookedly without having a nose to rest them on.

She curled an index finger to motion them toward the house.

The huntsman recovered from the shock first. He was glad the old woman was willing to forgive and forget; he could do that, too. After all, they were family now. And maybe *she* could talk some sense into Red.

He pulled the girl closer to the doorway. The grandmother looked at them. He couldn't be sure, but he thought she was smiling. It was hard to tell without a face. They met her on the stoop, and she reached out a hand to touch the side of Red's face tenderly. The huntsman felt a pang of jealousy; Red wasn't letting him touch her like that. He turned to the old woman.

Up close he could see the tendons of her face stretch. Her bulging eyeballs rolled from the girl up to him, and she took a half step back. Her hand went behind the doorframe, and a moment later it emerged holding the axe.

The huntsman's mouth went open, air gasping into his lungs. He leaned his head back to howl, and she swung the axe.

The blade landed on his lips, splitting them down the middle, and then continued through his teeth and tongue and mouth. It divided his head in half, went through his neck, and stopped finally between his shoulders.

The old woman let go of the axe, and the huntsman fell to the ground. He did not get back up. Still, the old faceless woman leaned down to him, dug the axe out, and then held it up against the wolves.

Red watched in amazement as the wolves stared at the old woman for a moment, their minds catching up to what had just happened. They turned from the old woman to the dead huntsman on the ground, and then back to the old woman again. Then, one by one, they lowered their heads and bowed to their new alpha.

The grandmother took a step toward the trees. She walked three paces, stopped, and then turned back to Red. She held out her hand, inviting the girl to join her.

The girl looked down to the body at her feet. She remembered her parents, and the life she had lost but never wanted. She was free now. She was totally free, and no one would ever tell her what to do again. She pulled the bloody hood of her cloak over her head, and caught up to her grandmother.

Before they continued, Red stopped to put a hand on her stomach. The old woman nodded. She was hungry, too.

Together they turned toward the woods, the faceless grandmother heaving the axe over her shoulder, the girl wearing her favorite red cloak, and the dead wolves following obediently at their heels.

And then together they disappeared into the darkness.

BEAUTY IS A BEAST

Belle stared at her father in disbelief. "What do you mean, 'job'?" she asked cautiously.

"A job! That's what I mean!" her father said, and he laughed. Maurice was a short trollish man with a ring of white hair around his bald scalp. "I thought you'd be happy about this, Belle. We can finally leave this town."

She looked at him, wanting it too much to believe him yet. They were standing on the side of the street in the marketplace, people passing in either direction around them. She saw a trio of gossipers on the next curb gawking at them, trying desperately to overhear their conversation. She took her father's arm and walked him into the shadow of an alley.

"What kind of job?" she asked quietly.

He wobbled where he stood. It was barely noon and he was already drunk. "Oh, nothing much." His eyes flicked to the left, and then looked back at her. "A—a *gardener*. Yes, as a gardener." He held his eyes on Belle's for a moment, and then turned away. "At an estate deep within the woods, where help is hard to find. Especially with winter approaching."

Belle nodded. Then she said, "A caretaker position? We would live there, then?"

"Yes!" her father agreed quickly. "That's why you must

come, too. It's a permanent move." He smiled. "Yes, *permanent.*"

Belle looked off into the town in a daze. She had straight brown hair tied in a ponytail, and a clear, youthful face with wide eyes and a regal bone structure. It didn't matter that she wore a plain blue-grey peasant's dress; she looked like a queen. Or would have, if not for the meek hunch to her posture, and the way her eyes darted from side to side with insecurity.

She had never felt that this town was their home, not in all the years since they had moved here. It didn't help that her father drank whatever money they could scrape together, and held debts at every storefront. And it didn't help that Belle had no desire to escape her shameful poverty through marriage, not if marriage meant being tied to a life here, forever trapped in a town that didn't understand her.

"We'd get to leave?" she asked, a hope growing inside her like a seed planted on a cliff. "We'd never have to see these people again?"

"Never!" her father said, smiling now, but still watching her face closely. "But we must leave at once."

Belle felt herself smile. It was the first time she had smiled in weeks. "Okay," she said. "What do we have to do?"

Maurice's pale face stared up at hers, his eyes greedy. "I need you to rent us a carriage. Just a simple horse and carriage to take us through the woods. Then we'll be on our way."

Belle agreed. She took his arm, and they walked out of the alley into the dim sunlight. The day was overcast, and a sharp December wind ruffled their hair. As they walked, Belle could see the townspeople glaring at them. She cringed. Why did everyone in town feel that she was their business? What had she ever done to them?

They were blocked momentarily by a cart rolling past, overflowing with plague victims. Belle followed it with her eyes for a moment, and saw it stop by the cemetery. There, she knew, the bodies would be dumped into a ditch. There were no headstones for the poor. That would be her fate, too, if she stayed here.

"Come along," she said, and pulled her father through the street.

They walked to the blacksmith, and Belle used their last three gold pieces to rent a horse and carriage. She knew it was wrong to rent something that she knew would never be returned, but she didn't have a choice. Still, when the blacksmith pulled the ancient nag out of its barn, and handed her the reins, she could not meet his eyes.

After the blacksmith had left, Maurice patted the horse's muzzle. "Cheapest beast I ever bought," he said, and they continued home.

They rented a small room in a shambling tenant house near the center of town. Belle waited outside with the cart while her father went in to pack. They would be skipping the bill on the room too.

Belle was giddy with nerves. No one suspected a thing.

But just as she thought that, a voice called out to her from the street. "Belle!" She looked up and saw the ruddy face of the priest looking back at her. He gamboled up, his black cassock swishing as he walked. "Have you heard?"

Belle cringed. The priest was the biggest gossip in town. He was the absolute worst person to greet them as they were trying to make a discreet exit.

"What is it, Father?" she asked.

"The Princess is dead!" He realized his own enthusiasm, and composed his face to be more somber. "Yes, dead. The Prince really does have poor luck when it comes to brides, it seems. Goes through them like cheap dinnerware."

Belle glanced back to the house. If she could just get rid of the priest before her father came out, they might have a chance. "Well, thank you for telling me," she said, and started to look away.

"But Belle," he said, and reached forward to clutch her forearm. "Don't you know what this means? For you, I mean?"

She looked down at her arm. She hated to be touched. "What?" she said, clenching her teeth. This was no time to make a scene, but if he didn't take his hand off of her—

"Public decree states that, until an heir is produced, a prince must not be without a princess." His stale breath fell upon her neck. "That only leaves one option: he's going to throw a ball! Isn't that exciting?"

She pulled her hand away from him with a grunt. "A ball? Whatever for?"

"Well," the priest said, leaning closer, "he hasn't announced it yet, but I've heard that he's run out of women in court that will have him. They're all convinced there's some curse on the Bluebeard Estate, which is ridiculous, but it means that he'll have to look to the greater population for a bride. And *who*," he asked, "is more beautiful than you?"

She leaned away from him. "I have no interest in being somebody's trophy."

"Oh, pish posh! I've heard the prince is quite charming."

"He's not my type."

"*Royalty* isn't your type?" The priest studied her for a moment. "Then who exactly *is* your type?"

Belle looked off into the distance. "Someone who isn't from around here. Someone," she sighed, "someone like me."

The priest scoffed. "There's no one like *you*, Belle."

She looked down at her hands. She was starting to believe that this was true. Maybe she would be alone forever. But then her eyes narrowed. If she *did* have to be alone forever, she'd at least do it on her own terms, and away from this provincial little town.

Just then her father emerged holding a bulging suitcase. "I think that's everything," he said, and stopped when he saw the priest.

The priest seemed to notice the cart for the first time. He gazed on it suspiciously, and watched as Maurice loaded the suitcase onto the back of the cart.

"Going somewhere?" he asked.

Maurice and Belle looked at each other. Her face turned bright red, and she fumbled for a response. "I—I—" She felt like she was going to cry. She had wanted to escape so much. She should have known nothing ever worked out for her, nothing—

"Father!" a shrill voice called out. All three looked up to see a small homeless girl running toward them from across the street. She held up a bundle of matches as she ran.

The priest ducked down, as if trying to shrink into nothingness. "I have to go!" he gasped, and immediately started away from the cart. He disappeared down the street, and the little match girl followed.

Belle let out her breathe. "What was that all about?" she asked.

"Probably doesn't want to buy any matches," Maurice answered. He climbed into the cart, and took up the reins.

Within minutes, they had left the cobblestone streets of the town and turned onto the dirt path of the woods. Belle shut her eyes tight and wished that this would work out. That her father wasn't going on another wild goose hunt; that her life would improve; that she would be happy in her new home. The fear that it might not work out coupled with the intense desire for change filled her with such hysterical energy that she didn't know whether to laugh or cry. All she knew was that she wanted a different kind of life, and if this road took her there, then it was the road she was supposed to be on.

She leaned back against the headboard of the cart, and let her mind wander as she watched the dark branches fly past her. And soon, exhausted by emotion, and lulled by the hypnotic beating of the horse hooves, she fell into a deep sleep, and let the cart take her wherever it might into the deep, dark woods.

*   *   *

She smelled the sweet perfume of roses before she had even opened her eyes. The cloudy fragrance stained the air, and she blinked open her eyes to see it was already dusk. She sat up, the cart drawing to a stop, and looked around surprised.

"Why did you let me sleep so long?" she asked her father.

But he didn't answer. He stared forward, his small eyes watching the horse and his expression grim.

They had just pulled up to an iron gate draped with twisting vines, which blocked the view beyond it. There were no roses. She sniffed again, and couldn't find their trace in the air. Was it possible to dream a smell? she wondered. A smell and nothing else?

Her father jumped off the carriage and went up to the gate. It let out a long creak as he pushed it open, and Belle gasped.

Before her, at the end of a dark path, was an immense black castle. It was the largest building she had ever seen, bigger even than the palace. There were no candles lit within its towers, and its outline stood black against the fading light. Wisps of fog shrouded its turrets and spires, making them seem immaterial and ghostly.

Her father climbed back into the cart. He prodded the horse forward through the gates, and Belle gazed at the dead wasteland of brambles and grey soil around them. Even the path was decayed, with black weeds reaching out like shriveled hands from the wide cracks.

"This," she asked in disbelief, "*this* is the garden? How are you ever going to tend this?"

Maurice coughed and set his gaze on the castle ahead.

They continued down the path until they had gotten to

the front steps of the castle. These led up to massive double doors, two stories tall and bolted shut.

"Stay here," Maurice said, climbing down from the carriage.

The air was calm and still as he approached the doors. And while he climbed up the great stone steps, Belle was distracted by the sight of a single red rose.

It grew out of the side of the castle wall, and seemed to be swaying in the wind, only... there was no wind. What was more, she was sure that it had not been there a moment before.

Belle looked up at her father. His back was turned to her. She quietly climbed down from the cart. Then she tiptoed along the castle wall, toward the mysterious rose. She bent down to it, the fragrance filling her nostrils, and put her hand on it.

Its stem was sticking out of a crack as wide as a finger on the base of the castle wall, and when she tried to pluck it, something shook it from inside. She looked through the crack, and could just make out movement on the other side. There was someone there, watching her.

"Belle!" her father screamed, and she jumped. She looked over to him, and he was motioning for her to join him at the door. She then looked back toward the wall.

The rose had fallen to the ground. Whoever had been holding it before was now gone. She picked up the rose, clutching it to her breast as she stood, and made her way up the stairs.

The doors of the castle were now open. She followed her father inside a great entryway lit by an enormous chandelier of flickering candles. Belle stared up at the vaulted ceiling, and then let her eyes follow a stone column down to the ground. The floor had been polished by countless boots and heels, so that it shined like melted wax, and Belle could see her amazed expression reflected in it.

There was a cough, and Belle looked up. A grand staircase, as wide as a courtyard, made up the back of the room, and lining either banister were the many servants of the castle. They had been so still that Belle hadn't even noticed them until now; their drab grey uniforms blended seamlessly into the shadows. Walking down the exact center of the staircase was an imposing woman dressed in black. She was an older woman with a hooked nose and dull grey hair tied back in a bun.

"Is this her?" she asked, looking directly at Belle but apparently talking to someone else.

"Yes," her father answered. "Just as I promised."

"What's going on here?" Belle asked, but everyone ignored her.

The woman in black stepped forward. She reached out and grasped Belle's chin with long, thin fingers. Then she turned the girl's face from side to side, as if inspecting her.

Belle pulled back and looked at the woman as if she were crazy. "What's wrong with you?" she asked.

The woman in black stared back at her, her expression bored and detached. "How old are you?" she asked in an emotionless tone.

Belle looked to her father, and he nodded for her to answer. "Nineteen," she said.

The woman sneered. "A little older than we'd like." She kept her cold grey eyes locked on Belle. "And are you a virgin?"

"*What?*"

"She is," her father answered. Belle looked at him in astonishment, and he continued, looking past her to the woman in black. "She hates to be touched, and has refused every man that has shown any interest."

Belle felt the warmth of her blush. She was too confused to know what to say. This felt like a dream. Like she had fallen asleep back at home, and woken up in a crazy nightmare.

"So do we have a deal?" Maurice asked.

"Does anyone know that you are here?" the woman in black responded.

"No one," he answered proudly. "And not only do they not know where we are, they don't even know that we've left."

A corner of the woman's thin lip turned up. "Excellent," she whispered. Then she looked down, and noticed the rose in Belle's hand. Her eyes widened, and she took a step back. "What is that?" she gasped, and pointed at the rose. "Where did you get that?"

Belle looked down at it. "I found it," she said. "Outside."

The woman's face blanched, and she stepped back farther. She gestured for one of the servants to come forward. "Take that away from her," she whispered. A plump man with a pencil-thin moustache approached and held out his hand for the rose. Belle gave it to him reluctantly, and then he retreated back to the line of servants by the stairwell.

The woman in black lifted her gaze and nodded. A moment later, servants were pushing shut the giant doors of the castle. Belle turned to watch, and when she did, she felt shackles clamp down on her wrists.

The woman in black laughed as Belle looked down in surprise at the restraints. "You're not going *anywhere*."

She looked up at her father. "Help me!" she cried.

But he stood still. "I'm sorry, Belle. This was the only way."

"Only way for what?" she yelled. She tugged against the shackles, but they were firm. Hands were on her shoulders, and the grey-clothed servants started to pull her along.

"To pay off my debts. I've sold everything I had, and it wasn't enough." He didn't even have the decency to look ashamed. "And now I've sold you."

"Sold me? To whom?"

But before he could answer, the woman in black stepped up to him. "I suppose you want your payment?" she asked.

He nodded eagerly, and she reached inside a pocket of her dress. "This should settle our account." She pulled out a dagger, and Maurice took a step backward, holding up his hands. She slipped behind him, towering over him, and easily slashed the blade across his neck.

Belle screamed. Her father's eyes opened in shock, and his hands went to his throat. The blood spewed out of him in hot bursts, a thick stream like a fountain spraying into the air and splattering across the waxy floor. His fingers were coated with blood as he tried to feel the wound on his throat, as if he didn't quite understand what was happening, and then his eyes lost focus. He dropped to his knees, and fell onto his side in a puddle of his own blood.

The woman in black stepped around him, lifting her foot so as not to mess it in the blood, and wiped the dagger on her dress as she made her way toward Belle.

Belle shrank back, and the woman's eyes seemed to inhale her fear.

"Not so brave now, are we?" she asked.

Belle swallowed. Behind the woman, servants dragged away her father's corpse. She looked up into the emotionless eyes of the woman in black. "Are you going to kill me?"

The woman laughed. "No," she said. "That is not my place. You are to be *prepared*."

"Prepared?" Belle asked. "For what?"

The woman in black leaned in closer, her face in shadows. "For the Master." She stepped away, and met eyes with one of the servants. "Take her upstairs. I want her ready as soon as possible."

"Yes, Madam," answered a round woman with a lilting accent. She gave a short bow, and then nodded toward whomever it was that was holding Belle in place.

She was pushed up the grand staircase, taking the stairs two at a time to keep up with the pace of her captors. They seemed to be in a rush to get away from the woman in black, because once they were upstairs and out of her sight, they slowed at once. They were silent as they led her down a great dark hallway lined with suits of armor and immense dusty paintings. Everything seemed to be on such a grand scale in this place that Belle felt like she had been shrunk down to the size of a mouse, and was crawling through the home of a giant.

She was brought up another staircase, this one narrower and steeper than the first, and soon emerged in a long hallway. Both sides of the hall were lined with an uncountable number of doors, and all of these were closed. Belle stared at them as they walked, feeling a pit of nausea grow in her stomach.

This floor didn't look like a palace. It looked like a makeshift prison.

Or mental asylum.

After they had passed nearly thirty doors, the servant woman stopped and pulled out a ring of keys. She thumbed past several, and then used a long spindly one to open up the door. It creaked open, and she walked inside into the darkness.

Belle was pushed forward. The room was ice cold, and the servant woman went around lighting candles.

"That's better," she said cheerfully, waving out the match. "Bring her in."

The room was lushly decorated. A four-poster bed stood in the center, with lace curtains drawn down over the sides, and around the room were arranged gold-finished chairs and tables. Black marble statues stood on pedestals. A tissue paper room divider languished near the far wall, and in the opposite corner rested a heavy armoire with one door slightly ajar.

Belle glanced around. The room had no windows and no other doors.

The door shut behind her, leaving her alone with two servants: the older one who had led her in, and a younger one, a slight girl with black hair who looked no older than Belle herself.

"What is going on here?" Belle asked. "This is madness."

The younger servant gave a weak smile. "No need to be scared."

"Just routine, dear," agreed the older servant. She smiled kindly as her relaxed blue eyes twinkled.

Belle might have found their attempts at consideration more reassuring if she hadn't just witnessed her father's throat being slashed apart. The fact that these servants regarded her father's death as typical business only unnerved her even more.

"Now what we need you to do," the older servant continued, "is to take off all of your clothes."

Belle took a defensive step away from them.

"It's just to give you a bath," the younger servant said. "And if you behave, we can take off your shackles." She took a step toward Belle. This time, Belle didn't step away. "That's a good girl. Easy, now."

Belle allowed them to lead her behind the room divider to a tub that had been filled halfway with murky water. They pulled off her clothes, ripping apart the sleeves to remove her dress without taking off the shackles.

"You'll get new clothes, dear," said the older servant. "But first you must wash."

They held her elbows as she stepped into the tub. Her toes dipped into the water, and she pulled back her foot with a cry. The water was ice cold.

"The faster you get in, the faster you get out," the older servant said. They pushed her into the tub, and her feet slipped against the ceramic sides. She fell on her tailbone, the cold water rising up her back halfway and sending goosebumps all across her flesh. She held her hands over her naked breasts as the two servants scrubbed her clean. Her whole body was shivering, and her teeth chattered. By the time they pulled her out of the water and wrapped a towel around her shoulders, she was sniffling and sneezing from the cold.

They patted her dry and rubbed oils into her skin, as if marinating a chicken. Then, finally, they brought her to the armoire and let her put on some clothes.

"We have to undo your restraints for this step," the older servant warned. "But I wouldn't try anything. Guards are waiting outside the door, and Madame can be called as well. You don't want us to call Madame."

Belle was silent. She held up her hands and waited as they unlatched them. As the manacles fell away, her wrists felt light without their weight, almost floating. But as soon as she was free of one form of bondage, she was ensnared into another. The two servants fitted a corset over her stomach, pulling the laces so tight that she could barely breathe. Then they pulled on layer after layer of clothing, until at the end she must have had nearly thirty pounds of fabric falling off of her.

By now Belle had begun to guess what awaited her. There was only one explanation that made sense: her father had sold her to the estate as an in-house courtesan. She was being manicured and groomed for the Master's bedchamber. What else could it be?

"But why," she said aloud, "why so many layers of clothes? Won't they just be taken off?"

The two servants looked at each other. The older one gave an awkward smile. "The Master likes to… *unwrap* his guests first."

Belle cringed.

Once she was dressed, they raised the pair of shackles again.

"Are those really necessary?" Belle asked.

"They're for your own protection, dear." And they clamped them down on her wrists.

The pair of servants continued in silence. They gave Belle a stool to place underneath her gown so that she could sit as they finished her preparations. The younger servant stepped behind her to start combing out her hair, while the older one came forward with a palette of makeup and facial creams. She stared at Belle's face, trying to decide where to begin.

"You have marvelous skin, dear," she said, talking more to herself than to Belle. "It makes my job much easier."

Something about her casual tone made Belle seethe with rage. How could these two fools be so nonchalant about kidnapping and murdering innocent strangers? Did they really expect her to just sit there and agree that, yes, she had beautiful skin and it made their jobs much easier? Even when it was their jobs to prepare her to be raped by some madman while her father's corpse was thrown into the woods?

Belle let out a cry and shot her bound hands up to the older servant's throat. She pulled the woman toward her, and bit her nose as hard as she could. Both servants screamed, and Belle dug her teeth in farther until she could taste the coppery flavor of her blood. She let go, the blood trickling down her chin, and dug her hands into the servant's pocket. She pulled out the ring of keys, and stood up.

The younger servant had taken several steps back. She had both hands up, the comb still in one, and she was shaking her head with her mouth and eyes wide open. Belle ignored her and continued to the door, fumbling with the keys, trying to find the one that would fit inside her shackles.

The door opened and she stepped behind it, hiding herself from the incoming guards. They stepped into the room and stared at the older servant as she tried to speak, her words muffled by the flow of blood. Belle ran out the door and into the hallway. She found the right key—a small black one, the size of a fingernail—and let her shackles fall to the ground. She ran over them, pulling up the front of her immense gown, and raced down the small staircase, the winding hallway, and made her way back to the front entranceway. She stared at the two main double doors, and had put one foot down on the top step when she was startled by a calm voice behind her.

"And where do you think you are going?"

Belle couldn't help it—she looked back. There was the woman in black, her austere face without expression. She had the knife in her hand, and all Belle could do was flinch as she saw the woman swing it at her, handle first. Its blunt end connected with the crown of her head.

A hot flash of white overlaid Belle's vision, and then she fell into a heap on the stairs.

* * *

She had been bound and gagged by the time she regained consciousness. She was back in the small bedroom again, and the back of her head throbbed.

"Nice of you to join us," the woman in black said. She was standing in the doorway with her arms crossed. "And just in time, too."

Belle tried to reply, but her words were garbled by her gag. The two servants were still in the room, the younger one next to Belle, and the older one a few steps behind her. She had a white bandage on her nose, the cloth wrapped around her entire head.

The woman in black turned to the younger servant. "Why don't you show our guest the result of your efforts?"

"Yes, Madame." She gave a quick bow, and then turned to a low table next to the armoire. She lifted a small hand mirror and held it before Belle.

Belle looked at herself. Her hair had been curled and styled, and her face had been painted with makeup so thick that she now had the complexion of a porcelain vase. Only her dark eyebrows and eyelashes stood out from her white face, her brown eyes almost floating in the white cloud of her skin.

They had decorated her with jewelry as well. Sparkling earrings dangled on either side of her face, and a diamond necklace rested against her exposed collarbones. Her dress was low-cut, a golden ball gown that was even more glamorous than the one she had been in before. The younger servant smiled, noticing her looking at her dress.

"We had to change it, miss. After you spilled blood on the other one." She thought about it a moment. "It would have been fine if it had been your own blood, but since it was ours, the dress had to be switched for the Beast."

"The *Master*," the woman in black snapped. "Don't let me catch you calling him anything else in my presence, is that understood?"

The servant girl nodded, and the woman in black calmed.

"Well then," she said, "I think we're ready for the Master."

They lifted Belle up by the ropes around her arms. She had been tied together much more tightly than before, her palms facing each other and the rope wound around her wrists and forearms. The end of the rope extended from between her palms, and the servants used it as a leash. They walked her out of the bedroom and back into the long hallway. The woman in black led the way, and anytime Belle began to struggle, she would pause and turn to look at her. Her eyes, empty of all expression, made her seem capable of anything, and Belle remembered how easily she had killed her father, almost on a whim. This was a woman without feeling, and Belle was sure that if she hadn't been reserved for their master, she would be dead already.

They led her down to the ground floor and past the entryway. Her father's blood had been completely removed, as if he were never there, and the efficiency of the staff sent chills through Belle. They approached a small doorway, and the older servant brought out her ring of keys.

This door led down into a narrow spiral staircase. The air was dank and cold, and the black stone steps narrow. Belle looked back at the woman in black, and she prodded Belle forward.

They descended into the depths of the castle. The spiral staircase let out into an underground tunnel, the walls and ceiling covered with sheets of grime. The air smelled worse here, almost like a tomb, and the chatter and scurries of rats echoed off the walls. Torches were lit at odd intervals, but the majority of the tunnel lay in shadow.

This had to be some mistake. A master of the estate would never live down here. Belle tried to speak, moaning against her gag.

"Not now," the woman in black answered. They continued down another stairway, these steps crumbled and broken. Belle tried to place her feet carefully, but it was hard while being simultaneously pulled forward and pushed from behind. Another locked door met them, and the older servant struggled with her key in the rusty lock until the heavy door swung open.

This next level was little more than a tunnel dug right into the dirt, the ceiling covered with cobwebs and dead roots. The soil muffled the sound here, and as they went forward, dirt caught on the hem of Belle's gown. No one seemed to mind, and she was brought before a heavy prison door with a lone torch burning next to it. This wall had been reinforced with stones, but not the smoothed and fitted stones of the castle above. These were little more than boulders, sticking out at odd angles and held together with moss-covered clay.

Belle was shaking, with tears in her eyes as she looked around at the surroundings. This was not right. This was most certainly not right.

The woman in black leaned toward a barred opening in the prison door, peering into the darkness within.

"I don't see him," she whispered. "Quickly. Before he returns."

The older servant peered through herself. She lifted the beam that blocked the door, and then thumbed through her keys. Meanwhile, the younger servant had begun to untie Belle's mouth gag. Before she let it fall, she looked into Belle's eyes and whispered earnestly, "Please don't scream. It will only bring him faster if you scream."

Belle opened and closed her mouth, the edges of her lips raw from the gag. "I thought you were bringing me to your master," she said quietly.

"And so we are," the woman in black said. "Put her in."

The two servants opened the door, and then the woman in black shoved Belle inside. They slammed the door shut, locked it, and threw down the beam. Belle turned toward the cell, the ruffles of her gown rustling. The only source of light was from the torch outside the door, and it fell upon a muddy floor littered with old clothes and patches of straw. Her feet sunk into the dirt, and she took a step forward.

"I don't understand," she said weakly. "Why have you—"

Her foot bumped against something, and she stepped back to look.

It was a severed hand.

"Oh!" she cried, and turned in a circle all around her. Her eyes had begun to adjust to the darkness, and now she saw that more than clothes were left in the mud. All around her, strewn about the cell, were the gored remains of human beings.

And then she noticed what *kind* of clothes these remains wore:

Ruffles. Satin gloves. A foot with a high-heeled shoe.

Women that had been murdered here. Women that had been *prepared*. Belle gasped and turned back to the small barred opening of the door. Her arms were still bound together, and she lifted them to the bars.

"Please," she begged, "let me out. I'll behave. Just take me out of here."

The woman in black smiled at her. She reached into her pocket, and lifted up a metal triangle. She tapped it with a silver wand, and the chime reverberated throughout the underground chamber.

"No," Belle said, backing up. "You can't do this." And the woman in black chimed the triangle once more.

It was a dinner bell.

There was a sound from above them like the feet of a large dog banging against the floor. It continued across the ceiling of the cell, and then moved to the back by the darkness.

"The Master," whispered the woman in black. She took the torch from the wall and held it up to the opening in the door. The two servants huddled up next to her, all three faces pressed against the bars. "The Master is coming."

With the light raised, Belle could make out a small square opening at the back of the cell. It was slightly higher than her knees, about the size of a small fireplace. She could hear whatever it was crawling forward from behind the darkness, and in a moment two grey hands pressed into the mud outside the opening.

It was not a man. It could *not* have been a man. It was a beast.

He came forward out of the opening on all fours like a dog, a bulky figure wearing clothes so smeared with mud that they seemed almost a second skin. His hair was long and tangled, and his shoulders twisted at an unnatural angle. He shambled forward, pressing his face to the mud and seeming to sniff it. Then he lifted his head and stared at Belle.

Belle nearly collapsed at his gaze. There was something wrong with this man, something more than dirt and grime. His face was grey, with black circles around his eyes, and thick black veins crisscrossing his cheeks. His lips were blue-black, and they hung slack from his open jaw. He grunted, putting a hand forward in the mud, and Belle screamed. She backed away to the door, unable to get away any farther, and yelled at the creature.

"Stay back!" she cried. She raised a foot to kick it, but the motion was lost under the many folds of her dress.

What the servant had said earlier flashed in her mind: *He likes to unwrap his guests first.*

He was going to kill her. This was the end. Belle clenched her eyes together, the tears running down her cheeks. What had she done to deserve this? All she had wanted was to get out of the town. But not to *this*. Even her father must not have known what was really going on here.

The Beast moved forward, and she could smell him now, a fecund mixture of rotten odors, rancid and sharp. She coughed, choking on his stench.

"Please," she begged. "Please don't touch me. I can't take it. I—"

She felt him pulling at the hem of her dress, and she looked down. He was climbing up her front, pulling himself up into a hunched standing position before her, like a bear on its hind legs. The skin of his face was bloated, and his eyes were pitch black. Overall, he looked like someone who had the plague.

To be completely truthful, he looked like someone who had *died* from the plague.

A low, inarticulate groan emerged from him. His breath was like a hot blast from a sewer, and she turned her head away. She pressed her entire body against the door, every muscle in her clenched.

His hands lifted slowly, his fingers wriggling like fat grey worms. He placed them on her temple, sliding them into her curled hair. They were cold and stiff, the touch of a corpse. Belle shut her eyes and squirmed against the sensation of his touch, her face turning red.

Then he lifted his other hand and placed it on her cheek,

his sticky palm kneading into her cheekbone. Belle couldn't take it anymore.

"I don't like to be touched!" she snapped, and pushed him away with her bound hands. She huffed out in relief, and wiped her face on her shoulder. In her discomfort, her fear had entirely vanished, and she looked at the Beast, meeting his black eyes.

"Move back!" she said in a firm voice, as if housetraining a dog. "I need some air."

He stared at her for a moment, and he then took a step back.

The three outside the door were amazed, and instantly started to whisper.

"Did you see that?"

"He won't touch her."

"Do you think—do you think he's cured?"

They were silent, watching the Beast just as Belle was. He stepped back into the shadows, and rested against the wall.

"He's cured!" the younger servant said. "He's not attacking her at all. This has never happened before, has it?" She turned to face the woman in black.

She glared at Belle inside the cell. Then, without looking away, she said, "Open the door."

The older servant looked at her nervously. "Madame, are you sure?" The bandage made her voice especially nasal.

Belle almost cried with relief. They were letting her out. Any other day she might have been thrown into this cell and torn apart by that animal. But instead she had the good fortune of arriving on the day he was cured. She took a step toward the door, and the woman in black yelled at her.

"Stay back! Away from the door!"

"But I thought—"

"Back!"

Belle took a step back, and the woman in black waited a moment before she slid the door open partway. She kept her eyes on the Beast. "We have to be certain," she said quietly. "What we need is a test."

Then, suddenly, she gripped the young servant girl by the arm and pushed her through the opening of the door. They slammed it shut behind her, and the lock bolted.

"What are you *doing?*" she screamed. She turned and saw the Beast lift his head toward her. "Madame! Quickly!"

But the woman in black watched her with her cold eyes. She made no movement to open the door. The Beast took a step toward the servant girl, crossing the small cell with his slow, irregular gait. Belle took a step back, not wanting to get in his way. The servant girl wrung the bars of the door.

"Please! I don't want to die. I don't want to *die.*" She sobbed as she said this last word, extending it into multiple syllables.

But the only person who was moved by her outburst was the Beast, who took the last few steps toward her and reached out his mud-smeared hand to grab her by the back of the neck. She screamed, her eyes bulging, and he pulled her away from the door easily. Her arms flapped at the air, trying to find something to clutch onto, but there was nothing. The Beast dragged her to the wall, and tossed her to the ground. Then he bent down to all fours, and pinned her with his arms.

Belle didn't want to watch but she couldn't turn away. The Beast ripped off the layers of the servant girl's dress, tossing them behind him like wrapping paper. He tore away the fabric that covered her stomach, so that the girl's pale quivering flesh was exposed to the cold dungeon air, and then buried his face into her.

When he lifted his head, he pulled up a bloody tube of intestines with his teeth. The servant girl screamed, her body convulsing, and dark blood oozed over her pale belly. The Beast swallowed down the end of her intestine whole, and kept swallowing as he pulled more out of her. The long streamer of guts was taut between her belly and his mouth, connecting them like an umbilical cord. Finally, the Beast bit down and chewed on his end. The other half of the intestine curled back inside of the girl like a frightened snake.

She was still alive, and she reached her hand back toward the doorway. She moaned, sending splatters of blood from her stomach like the eruption of a volcano. It sprayed across the Beast's face, dripping down his lips and hair as he greedily licked up her blood.

He grew wilder, sliding his hands up her body, from her gaping stomach, to her neck, to the sides of her head. He twisted his fingers into her hair, and then slammed her head against the cell wall. She was instantly silent, and he slammed it again, until he had broken her skull in half like a coconut.

As he reached down into the wet cauliflower of her brains, the woman in black clucked her tongue. "I suppose we overestimated his recovery."

The older servant just stared at her, unable to respond, and the woman in black turned away to leave the dungeon.

"Wait!" Belle cried, and went to the cell door. "I'm still alive. He won't touch me. You can let me go."

The woman in black smiled. "Oh, my dear," she said, "let you go? We can never let you go. You know too much."

"You can't just leave me in here!" She lowered her voice. "Not with him."

The woman in black gave a polite shrug. "I'm sure whatever it is that's keeping him from eating you will clear itself up, soon enough. And then neither of us will have to worry about it again."

"No!" Belle cried, but it was too late. The woman in black had already turned down the tunnel, and the older servant was following behind her. "Please," Belle said, feeling weak now. "Can't you please show some pity on me? At least untie my arms."

The older servant stopped a moment. Then she gave a bitter smile. "Now you want to play nice," she said, her voice distorted by the bandage. "You should have thought twice before you did this." And she pointed to her nose.

Belle's mouth opened in shock. The servant laughed, and then disappeared down the dark corridor.

It was now eerily silent in the dark chamber. The only sounds that remained were the gentle smacks of the Beast's chewing, and Belle's heaving breaths as she turned back toward the small muddy cell. She eyed the Beast, and after a moment he noticed her stare. He brought up his face from the floor, his mouth and chin covered with blood, and stared at her a moment. Then he lifted a section of the servant girl's skull, her brains jiggling on it like gelatin on a dish, as if to share.

"No thanks," she whispered, and wasn't sure how to feel at his offer. It was horrifying to see him dismember the girl in front of her, but at the same time, she didn't think he was going to attack her. Not this moment, anyway. For now, as his offer seemed to imply, she was to be his guest.

She sat down in the mud of the cell, using her many layers of fabric as a cushion. She stared off into the darkness as the Beast consumed the servant girl, who no longer looked like a girl, or like much of anything, really. And Belle thought about what to do now.

The situation looked absolutely hopeless. She was trapped in the bowels of a castle, locked up with a cannibalistic beast, with no one to help her and no one in the world that even knew where she was. Her father was dead, the servants hated her, and the woman in black was beyond reason. The only person who might even go looking for her from town was the blacksmith, and even he wouldn't really be looking for her, but rather his missing horse. And even if he did set out searching for it, which Belle thought extremely unlikely, and even if he did find the castle, which was unlikelier still, he would only go so far as the front stoop before he found it, and would never go searching in a dungeon three levels down. Furthermore, he wouldn't even notice the horse and carriage was actually missing for another week, and by then she would most likely be dead.

She dropped her head onto her bound wrists and started to cry. She couldn't help it; she was so exhausted from the long ordeal, and the feeling that even after all of this, she was just as alone as when she started.

When she had finished crying, she felt somewhat better, even if the dull dread of the situation was still upon her. She looked up, wiping her eyes on her upper arm, and was shocked to see that the Beast was gone. Her head turned to the corners of the cell, but they were all bare. Then her eyes rested on the small square opening in the wall. It was where the Beast had entered; it must be how he had left. She bent down, trying to peer into the pitch black hole, but unable to make anything out. She couldn't tell if it was a proper tunnel, or merely a cove in the wall. For all she knew, the Beast was only a few feet back, sucking off the meat from a fresh rib, and staring back at her. But somehow, she didn't think so.

And then she remembered when she had first approached the castle with her father. She remembered the rose held out   •
from the narrow crack. That must have been the Beast; it couldn't have been anyone else, and it would explain why the woman in black had been so upset when she had seen Belle with the rose. The Beast must have tunnels all throughout the castle. Why else would they still feed him, unless there was a chance he might try to escape if he were hungry? And a rose—a rose wouldn't grow underground. It could only grow on the outside.

Her chest heaved with her excitement, and she felt light-headed. She couldn't breathe.

"The corset," she muttered, and reached awkwardly over her shoulder, trying to undo its laces with her bound wrists, but with no success. She looked down at her impressive gown, and felt its weight and girth like an anchor. She looked back at the opening.

She had heard the shuffling of the Beast from within the tunnel. She stopped, her breath catching in her chest, and stepped back to where she had been sitting by the door, and lowered her arms to her waist.

The Beast crawled out as before, only this time he carried a single rose, the stem held between his teeth. He entered the cell and stood up, still hunched, and shuffled over to Belle. Then he took it from his mouth and held it out to her, his fingers still dripping blood.

She tried to reach for it, but she couldn't with her bound wrists. "I'm sorry," she said. "I can't."

He crawled across the cell to her, until his face was level with her hands, and set down the rose. Then he reached out to touch her.

She flinched away. He grumbled, and then reached out again. This time she forced herself to keep her hands still. Her heart was racing as she saw his slimy grey hands place themselves on either side of the rope. At the pressure of his touch, for a moment she was convinced that his friendliness had all been a trick. He had intended to eat her all along, and was simply looking for a way to do it without having to chase her around.

No, she told herself. That was foolish. He ate that other girl so easily. He could have done the same with her if he wished.

But then he bent his mouth down to her wrists, and started chewing.

She screamed out and tried to tug her arms away, but he held them tight. He was gnawing on her. She could feel his teeth scratching against the ropes, digging into them and nipping at the twine. She pulled away again, and this time she was able to get one hand free. She hit him with her fist on the side of the head, and he looked up at her, a strand of drool like an icicle dripping from the corner of his lip.

She fell away from him, landing in the straw, and slapped away the feeling of his hands from her wrists. It was only then that she looked down, and realized her hands were free. She looked closer, noticing the indentation of the rope against her skin, but beyond that there wasn't a cut or a scratch. He hadn't been trying to eat her; he was trying to help her. Just as she had needed.

Belle felt incredibly stupid. "Oh." She pushed herself up and flexed her wrists. "Thank you."

The Beast nodded, and then bent down to pick up the rose. When he handed it to her, she noticed a fresh gash on the side of his cheek. The skin had been torn so that the bone of his upper jaw showed through the gap, and Belle put her hand over her mouth. She had done that to him.

"Beast," she whispered. "Your face."

He stared at her for a moment, then slowly brought up his hand to feel the skin of his face. But he was tapping on the wrong side.

"No, it's over there." Belle pointed. "On that side. Can't you feel it? It's so deep."

The Beast kept patting his face until he finally got to the wound. He poked it lightly, and then dropped his hand.

"Doesn't it hurt?" Belle asked, and the Beast shrugged. She leaned forward to check again. "It looks pretty bad, but there isn't any blood. I guess it's can't be that serious."

He nodded, and then gestured toward the rose.

Belle gave a forced smile. "Thank you." He kept his eyes on her as she put it to her nose and sniffed in its fragrance.

"Oh, that's nice," she said, luxuriating in the sweetness after the sour stench of the dungeon. She pressed it to her nostrils, using it as a filter for the air, and turned to the Beast. She looked at him, and now that she wasn't so fearful for her life, she took more notice of his clothes.

His clothes were filthy, covered with countless days' worth of muck and gore, but they were regal garments nonetheless. She was pretty sure that his coat was once a royal blue, and the golden tassels still glinted even in the low light of the torch. The elbows had been worn away, and one sleeve was ripped halfway from the jacket shoulder. But even so, this was not the outfit of a slave or a beast. It was as fine as what a prince might wear.

"You really are their master, aren't you?" Belle asked. "Even though they keep you locked up."

He looked away, and Belle thought it was out of shame. This encouraged her, as only gentlemen felt shame. She took a step forward.

"Why are you down here? How did this happen?"

He looked up, his blackened eyes meeting hers, and opened his mouth. He groaned, trying to speak, but unable to articulate the words. Belle lifted the rose to her nostrils to mask the stench of his breath, and studied him for a moment.

"Can you take me to where you found this rose?" she asked.

His posture straightened, and a corner of his mouth lifted in what was either a sign of affection or a misshapen snarl. He turned toward his little door, and bent down to all fours. He was nearly through when Belle called out to him.

"Wait."

She wanted to follow, but her dress would never fit through. Without a moment's hesitation, she reached down and ripped a handful of the lace, grasping it with both palms and pulling it down the length of her gown. It was like stripping wallpaper. When she was done, the gown was still voluminous, but she could maneuver it better now. She reached around to her back, and ripped the stitching of her corset. She let out a deep sigh of relief.

Then she descended to her knees, and crawled after the Beast, leaving the rose behind in the cell.

It was indeed a tunnel. Her hands slapped against stone covered with a layer of dirt, and she hadn't gone more than a few feet when the light became so weak that she couldn't see anything at all.

"Beast?" she asked, and then wondered if he might be offended by the title. "I can't see."

A moment later she heard him rap his knuckles against the stone, and she continued on in that direction. They made their way through the tunnel in that way, with the Beast tapping for her to follow, and Belle calling out whenever she felt lost.

After what felt like ages, Belle could see thin shafts of light up ahead. They crawled forward, and Belle pressed her face against the slim openings, sucking in the clean, fresh air from the outside world. Then she looked through the gap, and saw the front gates of the castle. This must have been the underground tunnel that the Beast had watched her from before, when he had given her the rose.

There was a rap of knuckles against stone, and Belle started moving again. It was easier now that she had some light to see by, but the climb of the tunnel had begun to wear her out. Her dress had picked up several pounds of mud on the way, soaking it up like a sponge, so that she felt not only dirty but like she was lugging a cart behind her.

But it wasn't much farther. The tunnel kept getting brighter and brighter, until at last Belle could see a white circle of light ahead: the day. It had been evening when she arrived at the castle; the light now must be from the early rays of the next dawn.

They emerged in a circular courtyard enclosed within the castle walls. Unlike the outer yards, which were dead and grey, this small expanse of land was completely green. Grass covered the ground like a carpet, and well-trimmed trees and bushes grew here. This is where the roses were, and Belle stepped forward in awe as she approached a rosebush with flowers as large as saucers. It smelled wonderful here, the air misted with the perfume of nature.

The Beast led her to a small pear tree by the far wall, and Belle eagerly plucked a piece of fruit and bit into it, the sticky juice quenching her parched throat. She hadn't even realized how hungry she was until she bit into something edible, and quickly devoured half the tree's fruit within minutes. She was about to reach out to a neighboring tree when the Beast blocked her with his arm, and gently kept her in the shadows. He looked up, motioning with his eyes, and Belle saw the woman in black appear on a rounded balcony about three floors above them. She came forward and leaned against the railing, looking dissatisfied with the garden, and then turned back inside.

Belle waited a moment and then stepped back into the light.

"If we can get up to that balcony," she said, "we could have a chance at escape."

She looked at the Beast.

"Or, if you truly are the Master of the estate, we could have a chance of returning ownership to you. So that you would no longer be a prisoner within your own walls."

The Beast stared back at her, and for a moment she wasn't even sure he understood a word she was saying. And the way he stared at her now—he was as still as a statue. That's when she noticed for the first time that he wasn't breathing. Had it always been that way? She really wasn't sure what his condition did to him. She had never seen a plague quite like this. It seemed to kill you even before you were dead.

"We should head back," she said after a moment. The Beast seemed to wake up from whatever hibernation he had been under, and he led the way back to the tunnel.

As they crawled back to the dungeon cell, Belle couldn't help but wonder exactly what she was doing with this man.

She had seen him rip apart and devour a helpless woman right in front of her not more than an hour ago. And yet— he seemed so harmless now. How could that be? Everything had seemed so strange ever since she and her father had left town.

Her father.

Was he really dead? It had all happened so quickly. She half expected to wake up from this other world into her own bed again. And she didn't know if she wanted that to happen, if she wanted this adventure to end or not.

They were crawling back through the outer tunnels when Belle heard voices talking through the walls. She listened, and heard the nasal voice of the older servant woman that had dressed and bathed her earlier.

"—would not touch her. Swear on my life. Madame kept a cool face about it, but I know the mistress. She was shaken."

"But how long has it been?" a second voice asked. This one was male. "He can't possibly be getting better now?"

"Ages," the servant woman agreed. "And to think he used to be so sweet." She sighed. "And then one day out in the woods, a single scratch on the arm that killed him. Or so it seemed. And then not more than a few hours later, the Master was on his feet once again. Only… he wasn't our Master anymore."

The man replied, but his words were lost in the walls.

"Left at once," the servant woman said. "Just left his son behind to be looked after by Madame. Can't say as I blame him, but it's a cold move, nonetheless." There was a moment of silence, and then she added, "But this girl, he seems to like her. And not killing for once is a step in the right direction. But we'll see how long it lasts."

There were taps from up ahead in the tunnel, and Belle moved on, following the Beast back to their underground chamber.

It smelled worse than she remembered. The stink was

like a slap in the face, and she groped in the darkness for her rose. She clutched it to her nose, and stared at the Beast, thinking. She pictured his life here in the dank cell, having women thrown in for food, and his only source of pleasure in the brief trips up to the garden. It seemed like such a sad life, even for a beast.

Belle decided that however she escaped, she would set the Beast free in the process. He may be dangerous, perhaps inhuman, but he had helped her. He was *still* helping her. And no creature with kindness deserved to be kept in a cage.

She sat down in her corner, and the Beast settled into the mud across from her. "We need a way to get to that balcony," she said. "It's too tall for us to climb. Maybe we can make some stilts out of what we have here, or from the tree branches." She looked around, and the Beast did the same. Again, she wasn't sure if he was helping her search, or merely imitating her gestures. It was hard to tell how much he was thinking on his own.

She searched the floor, pushing aside the torn pieces of fabric, and nudged against a long dry bone. She lifted it, feeling its weight in her hands. It must have been a femur at some point in its existence, but now it would make a perfect club. She could smash Madame in the face with this, and incapacitate her for good.

But not from down on the ground. She threw the bone back to the floor and pushed aside the hay. There was a tatter of an apron caught on a rib bone. She tried to pull it up, and the rib kept it down, locking it into place. Belle's eyes opened wide, and she let out a laugh, pulling on the cloth and feeling it hold.

"I've got it!" she cried, and bent down to her knees, clutching up all the loose strands of cloth. She began tying them together into one long sash. "We'll make a rope out of all the leftover clothes," she explained to the Beast. "And then we'll tie one end of it to a few bones, and use it as a grappling hook." She pulled the fabric taut in the air to demonstrate. "We'll *climb* up to the balcony!"

They spent the next few hours tying together ropes and bones. The Beast lacked the dexterity to help with the construction of the devices, but he helped by rummaging through the mud and straw, and dumping what he found into organized piles. They only had one interruption during the entire process: a manservant entered to replace the torch. At his approach, Belle sat on top of her creations, ruffling out her gown to cover the evidence like a swan sitting atop eggs in its nest. And as soon as the servant had left, she went right back to work.

When she finished, Belle had to sit and close her eyes to focus for a moment. She was exhausted. She hadn't slept since she arrived, and she knew it was no way to begin a battle. Her stomach growled, too. The fruit from the tree had barely been a snack, and she was starving.

Her stomach growled again, and the Beast looked up. His pale skin glistened in the torchlight, and his black eyes squinted with concern.

"I'm fine," Belle said. She needed sleep, but there was no use trying to rest when her mind was so active. She pushed herself to her feet, and gathered up the rope. Then she turned to the Beast, her eyes narrowed in determination.

"Let's go."

* * *

The sky was dark with low-hanging clouds when they returned to the courtyard. The temperature had dropped considerably, and there was frozen dew on the leaves and buds of all the plants. The entire garden shimmered as if sprinkled with diamonds, and Belle thought it looked almost magical as she dumped her pile of bones and victim-spun rope onto the grass.

A flash of lightning bolted across the sky, and Belle felt a raindrop land on her cheek. It was half-frozen slush, not quite snow, not quite rain. And Belle knew that they only had so much time before the balcony would be coated with the slick substance, and they would have no chance of securing an anchor for the rope.

"I'll climb up first," she said, "then you follow."

She picked up a hook, composed of several bones tied together into a talon shape, and began swinging it in a circle at her side to gain momentum. Once she felt the pull of the hook, she released it, throwing it toward the balcony with all her might.

The bones flew directly at the side of the castle, nowhere near the balcony. They hit the stone wall and shattered on impact before tumbling back to the garden below.

"I guess it was smart to make a back-up," she muttered, and moved to pick up the next hook. The Beast stepped forward, and grasped at the air, gesturing for her to give it to him. Belle handed it over.

The Beast took it and stepped back more toward the center of the courtyard. He stared up at the balcony for what felt like an entire minute, and then started to rock the hook back and forth like a pendulum, about an inch from the ground. The arc of his swing grew, and he released the hook. It flew through the air and landed with a crack on the balcony above. He stared at it for a moment, and then handed the length of rope to Belle.

She was impressed. She tugged on the rope until the hook caught on something above, and began to hoist herself up to the balcony. She had tied bones at intervals along the rope, to make it easier to climb, but even with these it took great effort to scale the rope.

When she was about halfway, the slush began to fall more heavily. It numbed her fingers, and made the knots and bones of the rope slick. Her shoes kept slipping with each step, and she began to think this was altogether a stupid idea, and one she wished she wouldn't have started in the first place. It wasn't until she had placed one arm around the railing of the balcony that she let herself look down. The rope was so thin that it looked like her feet were hanging in the empty air. She felt dizzy from the sight of it, and almost lost her grip completely.

She hugged the banister and rolled onto the balcony. Then she motioned for the Beast to follow her up.

He tried to grip the rope and his hand slid off. He tried again, using both hands this time, and slid again. He stared at the rope a moment. Then he lifted a foot, and fell over. Apparently, he could not climb ropes.

Belle waved her hands for him to stop. She tried to mouth "Wait there," but she wasn't sure if he understood. But given that he couldn't go anywhere else at the moment, she felt it was safe for her to move on.

She tiptoed across the balcony, and opened a tall door. She barely stepped inside when a voice came from the darkness.

"Don't move!"

Belle turned, completely ignoring the command, and saw the old servant woman with a feather duster in her hand. Her nose was still bandaged, and she was backing up toward the door.

Belle would never be able to outrun her, and even if she could chase her down, by then she'd have woken the entire castle. So Belle did the only thing she could think of: she put a hand to her forehead, swooned, and collapsed to the floor.

She waited with her eyes closed, listening. For a moment she didn't hear anything. The soft slush of the rain fell on the back of her neck, and she refused to feel cold, to shiver or move at all.

And then she heard the rumble of a footstep.

And then another, louder this time, as the servant woman came closer to investigate.

That's it, Belle thought. Just a little closer.

She waited until the servant woman had bent down over her, and then Belle kicked the old woman down to the ground. Belle hopped to her feet, and dragged the woman out onto the balcony.

She dropped her at the railing. There was a flash of lightning, and Belle put her arms around the woman, groaning as she worked to lift her. Her legs buckled, but she managed to half carry, half roll the woman over the railing, and toss her down into the courtyard below.

She fell like a brick and landed in the middle of a rosebush. Belle looked down to see the Beast jump on her, biting into her at once, and the woman's cries were instantly silenced.

Belle snuck back into the room, more carefully now, and crept her way to the door. She opened it a crack, and saw a guard practically sleeping on his feet at the end of the hall.

She stepped out the door, and glanced around for a weapon. She looked to her right and left, not seeing anything at first beyond the suits of armor lining the halls. And then her eyes landed on a mace in the hands of the armor directly across from her, and recognized the decorations for what they were.

She took down the mace, surprised at its immense weight, and took a few steps toward the guard. She had made it nearly halfway to him when he looked up, the sleep shaken from his eyes.

There was no time.

Belle ran at him. She lifted the mace to her side, and rammed it into the guard's stomach. He doubled over in pain, but he was not incapacitated. Belle reached down and grabbed his hair, and slammed his head against the wall. It was the same attack she had seen the Beast use on the young servant girl back in their cell. He let out an *oof* sound, and she tried again, using her entire body in the swing, and smacked his forehead into the stone.

He went limp in her arms, and she let him fall. She looked up, blood splattering her face, and smiled.

She lifted her dirty gown above her knees and ran down the hall. She raced down a narrow stairway, turned onto the lower floor, and found a reinforced door that, by its position, must have faced out to the courtyard. She heaved the brace from the door, and unlatched the lock. She wiped the sweat from her forehead, and then pulled open the door.

It was the courtyard, the plants sparkling like glass crystals in the icy slush. The Beast crouched with the servant woman in his arms, tearing open her chest and letting the steaming blood spill onto the grass.

"Beast," she whispered, and he looked up from the bloody frame. He dropped the servant, and shambled inside after Belle.

She turned to him. "Listen," she said, "we need to get to the front entrance. Do you know where it is from here?"

The Beast let out a low moan that Belle interpreted as agreement.

He started to shamble through a low archway at the end of the corridor. Belle followed him through the twists and turns of the castle, at times wondering if he even knew where he was going. But at last they arrived on the top steps of the grand staircase. The massive double doors to the castle loomed below them.

"Come help me," she whispered, and galloped down the stairs, taking them two at a time.

She pulled at the huge doors, leaning her body backward and using her entire weight. The Beast came up behind her, and with a single hand pulled back one of the tall doors.

Outside the slush fell onto the steps. The wasteland outside had been stained black by the rain, and in the far distance were the trees of the woods.

"We're free," she whispered. She turned back to the Beast with a smile. "Oh, Beast, we're absolutely free."

He raised a lip to smile back at her, and she turned to step into the fresh air.

As her foot stepped onto the stone of the front steps, a hand shot out. A dagger flashed. And Belle felt her chest pierced with an explosive burning.

She dropped to her knees, clutching the dagger that had been stabbed through her heart, and looked up to see the woman in black smiling over her.

"Did you think you could escape?" she asked. "No one runs off on my watch." She eyed Belle with her emotionless grey eyes, and pulled the bloody dagger from her chest. She lifted it above her head to strike again, and the air was torn with an animal howl of rage.

She looked up just as the Beast lunged at her. She dropped the dagger as he knocked her to the steps, and then picked her up and shook her like a rag doll. She tried to fight him off, but he threw her to the ground and held her down.

"You don't have the nerve," the woman in black gasped. She smiled up at him, blood running in a line down her chin. "You wouldn't kill your own mother."

The Beast cringed and the woman in black laughed.

"That's right," she said. "Forget the girl. I'll get you plenty more where she came from."

Belle clutched at the wound on her chest, and the Beast turned back to her. His black eyes softened for a moment, and then narrowed. He turned back to the woman in black, his mother, and lowered his teeth to her. He bit her, tearing away the skin between her collarbone and her breast. Then he stood up, lifting her over his head, and threw her down the front steps of the castle. She rolled into a heap at the start of the path, and did not move again.

"Beast," Belle gasped. She could feel the life leaving her body.

He turned back to her, and bent down to her side. She

looked into his eyes, and reached up to touch the side of his face.

"Goodbye, Beast."

Her hand fell limp to her side.

The Beast screamed out, putting his hands all over her trying to revive her. He pressed against her chest, and blood smeared his fingers. He stood up, looking around for something to help. But there was nothing.

Then he saw the dagger. He bent down to it, and held it in his hands, staring at the blood on its blade. Belle was gasping on the ground, about to take her last breath. He tried to think, grimacing at the effort.

Belle had been stabbed in the heart. She needed—

And then he knew. He knew what he had to do.

He clutched the dagger, and pointed the blade at himself. Then he lunged it into his chest, right between his ribs. It didn't hurt; nothing hurt anymore. He cut an opening between his ribs, and then reached inside himself, his dull hand searching, pressing past his blackened innards, until he wrapped his fingers around his heart.

He let out a groan as he ripped it out of himself, and looked down on his black organ as the white slush fell onto it. Then he bent down to the girl. She wasn't dead, not yet, but he didn't have much time. He took the dagger, and cut her open. Blood spewed out onto her dress, and the girl looked up at him, an expression of hurt and betrayal in her eyes. He opened his mouth, but he couldn't explain, and he hoped that this would work. That she wouldn't die thinking he had tried to kill her.

He ripped the opening in her chest further until he could fit in his entire hand. Then, as the girl's body erupted in spasms, he shoved his heart inside of her.

Her eyes went wide, and her teeth clenched. Then the fight left her body, and she collapsed once and for all.

The Beast carried her limp body back inside the castle.

He trudged up the grand staircase, and back through the twists and turns of the estate, until he came back to the courtyard. He pushed open the door, and walked to the center of the garden. He laid the girl next to the rose bushes, and stared down at her.

She was dead.

He folded her arms across her chest, and smoothed out the ruffles of her gown. Then he stood up, and gathered all the roses of the garden. He buried her with them.

Once she had been covered, the Beast looked back up to the castle. A flash of lightning lit the high turrets, and he knew what he had to do.

While Belle slept in death, the Beast made a slow journey through the castle. He went down every hall, entered every door. He tore out the throats of every servant and house-keeper, dragging his bloody feet from one room to the next, biting them all. They were the reason Belle was now dead, and he had no sympathy for them. It was his castle now.

He returned to the courtyard. The rain had stopped, but the sky was still dark. He bent to his knees next to her corpse, and waited.

* * *

Roses.

She was dreaming of roses.

Their petals fell from the sky like red snow, and coated the earth with their velvety texture. There were no more people, no more places.

Just roses.

* * *

He wasn't sure how long he waited by her side. It might have been days, it might have been hours. If she were to remain dead forever, he wouldn't have moved from that spot for all of eternity.

But eventually, she did move.

The roses shuddered. They fell away as Belle sat up, her face pale and dark shadows around her eyes. Black veins stood out on her skin, and her mouth hung open slack as she sat there, gazing around the garden. A dark circle of dried blood coated the front of her dress.

She turned toward the Beast.

He had saved her, but would she know that? Would she be mad that he had let her die? Would she still want him?

He reached out his hand and placed his palm on the side of her cheek. She didn't flinch. She didn't turn away. She stared at his arm, and then her own hand raised and she curled her fingers around his wrist.

But instead of pushing him away, she pressed him closer. She moaned, relishing his touch.

Because for once, she couldn't feel a thing.

And she had never been happier.

ZOMBIE CINDERELLA

A cold December breeze shook the last dead leaf off the gnarled branches of a great oak. Cinderella watched it flutter to the ground like a snowflake and land on the fresh dirt of her father's grave. She shivered, pulling the grey shawl tighter around her thin shoulders.

"Cinderella!" came a whiney voice from behind.

Cinderella turned to see her stepsisters and stepmother squeezed into the black chariot that had carried her father's small coffin to this bleak patch of dirt. He didn't even have a headstone, she realized. They couldn't even spare him that.

"Hurry up," her stepsister whined. "It's cold." She was a fat thing, wider than she was tall, and took up so much of the carriage that they couldn't latch the door properly. It hung open with a gap, and had to be held during the ride to keep from flying open.

"Mother," began her other sister, who was as tall and thin as her sister was short and fat, "make her move."

Her stepmother peered out at Cinderella, her cold sharp eyes glowing from the dark of the carriage like a rat from a dark corner. Her gray hair was pulled back tight against her scalp, and gave no temperance to her hard eyes.

Cinderella looked back at her, crossing her arms. She

hadn't meant it to be a look of challenge, but she wasn't used to following orders, and her stance displayed as much.

Her stepmother arched her shoulders, glaring at Cinderella. Then she called to the driver, "Let's go! We'll catch our death waiting!"

The driver, a gray-whiskered man with a crushed top hat, stared out at Cinderella with drunken eyes. "What about the girl?"

"She can walk," her stepmother called, the smug satisfaction of her tone impossible to miss.

The driver rustled the reins and the pale horse moved forward, almost sleepwalking, through the cemetery gates. Cinderella saw her fat sister smile and wave at her as they rounded onto the street. Then they turned a corner, and Cinderella could only hear the echo of horse hooves clopping on the cobblestones, growing fainter and fainter until it was as quiet as a memory.

The cemetery was empty now, and silent. The overcast sky sent a looming shadow over the space, and the dark figures of the headstones and crosses took on an unfriendly color that gave Cinderella goosebumps. It felt like the monuments were watching her. She had an urge to flee, to run after the carriage and return to the safety of company, but her pride kept her in place. She didn't need *their* help.

Stubborn, she sat down on the edge of the dead grass next to her father's grave. She missed him already. The idea of living with her stepmother and stepsisters filled her with dread. It might have been better if she had gotten sick, too. Better to be dead than live with them.

She hated everything about them. Her sister's fat face and the other's bored eyes, like she's always about to fall asleep looking at you. But most of all she hated her stepmother. And what was going to happen without her father there to be on her side? There was no one to help her now.

Cinderella lowered her face to her hands and began to

cry. It was better to cry alone. To not show any weakness in front of her new family. But her tears were interrupted by the sound of a snap behind her. She turned.

A few rows behind her, stepping closer, a woman dressed in black held out her arms toward Cinderella, her long white fingers twitching like albino crab legs. She wore a thick black veil over her face.

Cinderella wiped the tears from her eyes with the back of her arm. "I'm sorry if I disturbed you," she said quietly. It seemed indecent to be loud in such a desolate location. "I thought I was alone."

The woman in black didn't answer. After a moment, she took a step forward, and immediately stumbled into a headstone, cracking her knee against the rock.

"Oh!" cried Cinderella and rushed forward to help. "Are you hurt? Miss?"

The woman's head lurched up at the sound of her voice, and Cinderella noticed the woman's dress was tattered and smeared with dirt.

Cinderella lifted a foot awkwardly to scratch the back of her ankle, and the woman stared at her from underneath her veil.

"I'm visiting my father," Cinderella explained, gesturing toward the grave.

The woman didn't reply, but Cinderella could feel her gaze intensifying. It made her nervous.

"He died. I mean," she stuttered, "are you here to see someone, too?"

The woman tried to speak, but only a hoarse rasp came out. She tried again, enunciating her syllables, but unable to do more than give a low moan. Then she lifted her white hand and pointed at Cinderella.

"You're here to see me?" Cinderella asked. She felt a surge of hope. Hadn't she always heard stories like this? About a benevolent old guardian appearing at a time of tragedy?

The woman in black made a motion for Cinderella to come forward.

Cinderella took a step closer. She imagined this woman whisking her away from her evil family, like a genie or a fairy godmother. A magical woman, standing here between the tombstones, ready to grant her any wish.

The woman in black seemed taller up close. Even though she was hunched, she was still as high as Cinderella. She was much broader, too, and easily weighed several times what the slight Cinderella did.

"Did my father send you?" Cinderella whispered. "Before he died?" There was no answer, and Cinderella began to wonder if she knew this woman. And without asking, Cinderella reached out and lifted the woman's veil.

Underneath the woman's face was gray, her eyes clouded white, and her mouth open and slack.

"Oh!" Cinderella cried, stepping backward. She covered her mouth with her hands. She might be sick now. This old woman had some kind of plague.

The woman in black came forward, drool bubbling out from the corner of her mouth. Cinderella took another step back and stubbed her heel on a gravestone. She winced, but before the pain had a chance to dull the old woman lurched forward and took hold of her wrist.

"Let go!" Cinderella shrieked. She tugged at her arm but the woman's grasp was firm. Her yellowed fingernails dug into Cinderella's skin. Then the woman's mouth opened, and a gust of rotten breath steamed out, sour like spoiled milk. She leaned forward, her broken pointed teeth bared, and Cinderella understood that this woman meant to *bite* her.

Cinderella took the offensive. She heaved her shoulders into the woman in black, knocking them both to the ground. While the old woman failed to figure out her new position, turning her head from side to side, Cinderella pulled back with all her might. Her wrist dragged against the woman's nails as she yanked it free, leaving four long gashes that stung at once.

Her wrist in her hand, Cinderella got to her feet and stumbled to the cemetery gates. The woman in black moved to stand, and Cinderella ran out to the street, her tiny wooden shoes slapping against the cobblestones.

She meant to find help, but realized at once that the town was different. To begin with, the streets were empty. Normally they would be filled with worker women, bartering over the price of bread in the town square. Now there were boarded up windows and neglected alleys. Garbage was piled in heaps on corners, the filth falling past the gutters and into the streets. Even the windows of the village toyshop were dark.

What had happened here? she wondered. Had she really been that oblivious the last few months waiting by her father's side? Something flashed in her mind, a quote by the grave-digger: "Not enough room for bodies. You're lucky to get a spot by yourself these days." What did that mean? And that woman in the cemetery—what about her? She seemed positively raving.

Cinderella looked behind her to make sure she wasn't being followed, and saw that she was leaving a trail of blood as she ran. She looked down at her wrist, and saw the bright red blood, almost glowing in the gloom of the streets. She would be spotted for sure. She tore off her shawl and wrapped the fabric around her wrist. It flowered in crimson patches against her cut, but it stopped the dripping, and that was good enough. She continued along the streets, breathing a sigh of relief once she got past the limits of the town, and onto the open road that led back to her estate.

She felt safer here. There were less places to hide, especially in winter, when there were no flowers and all the grass was dead. And, if it weren't for the memory of her father's absence, and the dread of facing her new family again, she might have skipped along under the clouded sky.

But as it was, she was wounded and desperate to get indoors before it snowed. She wanted to wash her wound, maybe make a pot of hot cider with fresh cinnamon and nutmeg, and curl up in a blanket in her room. From there, she could stare out the window at the falling snow, and think of how white and bleak the world was now without her father, and how he would have approved of her grief.

It was two miles back along the road; her teeth chattered as she neared the estate staring at the dead trees, their branches forming a dark canopy over the lane. When her father had gotten sick, it was like the entire estate had gotten sick with him. All work ceased on the property, and what was once a bright corner of the world, fragrant with fresh blooms and the friendly sound of sparrows, was now overrun with weeds and blackness. She thought of the dark streets of the town. Maybe the whole world had died along with her father.

A cold blast of air hit her from behind. It went right through the fine fabric of her mourning gown, and chilled to the bone. She clutched her arms to her chest, shivering as she neared the family gate lined with large black crows.

The gate was open. That was odd, she thought. Normally her stepmother made it a point to keep it locked at all times. She entered, and saw a brilliant white horse standing by her front stoop. It was clad in a royal blue harness, and its rein was leashed to the railing.

Cinderella approached, her feet crunching on the dry brush that was once a garden. The horse turned its head.

"Shh," Cinderella whispered, making a calming motion with her hands. The horse's nostrils flared, as if it smelled something it didn't like, and it cowered backward.

"Easy," Cinderella whispered, and she edged closer. "I'm just going into the house."

But the horse wouldn't have it. It backed away until its rear hit a line of dry bushes. The branches snapped, and the horse's eyes flashed with panic. It shook its rein from the railing, and reared up on its hind legs, kicking out its front hoofs toward Cinderella. The girl backed up, and tripped over the front stoop of the house. The horse let out a loud whinny, and then came forward to trample her with its hooves.

Cinderella could do nothing more than hold an arm over her face. Her only thought was that she would soon join her father, and that was probably for the best.

"Whoa!" came a man's cry from behind. He ran forward and placed himself between Cinderella and the horse, waving his arms and shouting, "Whoa, Nellie! Whoa!" He wore a blue coat with brass buttons, and shining black boots. A thin braid of white hair stuck out from the rim of his tricorner hat.

The horse lowered and scooted back and forth. The man reached his hand behind his back and waved it at Cinderella, ordering her to move away. Cinderella scrambled backward and up the porch. But as soon as the fear of being trampled was lifted, her arm throbbed worse than ever, her skin stretched by the fall. She felt lightheaded, and remembered she had been too grief-stricken to have a bite to eat in the morning. Now all she wanted was a warm meal and to cuddle up in the soft blankets of her bed.

"Cinderella!" shrieked her stepmother from behind. "Get up at once!"

Cinderella blinked. Her stepmother had changed clothes already. Now she wore a tight-fitting black leather bodice, and a short black leather jacket with pointed shoulders. In her hand she wielded a black cane, one that she used for appearances only.

Cinderella tried to sit up, and swooned to the side.

"Oh, my Dear!" her stepmother cried, coming forward. Her sharp heels clacked against the doorstep. "Are you all right?"

"I do feel a little peaked," Cinderella said.

"Not you, stupid," her stepmother sneered, pushing past her. She went to the man's side and placed a hand on his arm. He was looking down at Cinderella. He had a pink bloated face, and a nose like a doorknob, but his kind eyes held genuine concern as they looked down upon her. "Is she all right?" he asked the stepmother. His voice lowered. "She looks a bit pale."

That was a kind way of asking if she had the plague.

"Oh," the stepmother said, waving her fingers at Cinderella, "that's how she always looks. Don't pay her any attention, your grace. We don't." She smiled at him, a lecherous grin that crinkled the skin around her eyes. He gave a weak smile back.

"Well," he said, taking the horse's reins in his hand, "I'd better go on." He paused a moment, looking at Cinderella. "Remember, the invitation is for *all* eligible maidens."

Then he was off, walking his horse to the gate, and riding it down the dark lane.

Cinderella climbed to her feet, her vision darkening as the blood flowed to her limbs. "Invitation?" she asked.

Her stepmother pursed her lips. "It doesn't concern you," she said, grabbing Cinderella by the arm and dragging her through the door. "Now come inside. You've already wasted enough time skipping about."

They went inside the darkened house. The curtains were drawn, and no lamps had been lit. Her stepmother pushed her to the windows, and Cinderella open the curtains, sending a streak of light into the dusty chamber beyond the entryway.

Her sisters were sitting on the edge of a dilapidated couch. The thin one ran her fingers through her hair, and the fat one puckered her lips like a pufferfish.

"Oh, *Mother*," the thin one cried, "I'm so excited for tonight. I think I'll wear the blue gown, the one with the ruffles." She picked up the hem of her mourning dress. "Anything to get out of this *black*."

"I'm more worried about our makeup supplies," her sister said, her eyes desperate. "I think I'm all out of that shadow that thins my face. You know, the blue one?"

Her sister nodded, and they held hands as if their lives were in danger.

"Girls, girls," the stepmother cooed, "don't worry. You'll both be *beautiful*. We've got plenty of time to prepare before tonight."

"Tonight?" asked Cinderella.

"But I've never been to a royal ball!" moaned the fat sister. "What if I don't recognize the prince? How will he propose to me?"

"We can practice our dance steps together," her sister said, patting her on the shoulder. "I can teach you. I'm an *excellent* dancer."

"You're going to a ball tonight?" Cinderella asked. When no one answered, she stepped into the center of the room. "You're going to *dance* on the night of Father's funeral?

"He's looking for a bride," the thin sister explained. "The prince."

"And the king has ordered every eligible maiden in the county to attend," added the fat one.

"And there will be less competition than usual," the thin one realized, smiling.

The fat one's eyes opened wide, and her mouth twisted in glee. "Because of the plague! Half the town is dead! Isn't that wonderful, Mother?"

"*Girls*," the stepmother said, "don't speak that way. You know there'd be no competition for either of *you*, no matter how many maidens were present."

The sisters beamed.

"I think we should stay home," Cinderella said. "I'm feeling ill as it is."

"That's just as well," the stepmother said. "You're not going."

Cinderella felt a bit insulted at not being allowed to go, but she didn't have the energy for a fight. So she shrugged, and moved to step out of the room. "I think I'm going to lay down for a little."

Her stepsisters giggled on the couch, and gave a conspiratorial look to their mother. She stifled a smirk, and took a step to follow Cinderella out of the room. The sisters immediately followed.

Cinderella didn't care. Even though she was hungry, she could barely keep her eyes open. She wanted to get to the dark quiet of her room, and shut the doors, blocking out the inane chatter of her sisters as they prepared to disgrace her father's memory. She slumped up the wooden stairs, clutching the rail, and came to the first door on the left. Her room.

She went to walk through the door and knocked her head right into it. It was locked. She tried the handle again, but it didn't move.

She turned to the others.

"Why is this door locked?" she demanded. "Open up my room immediately."

The stepmother smiled. "I'm afraid that's impossible."

"Fine. I'll get the key from the kitchen."

Her fat sister smiled. She pulled a chain from around her neck, lifting a key from her bosom. "You mean this key?"

"This room will go to my daughter," the stepmother said, leaning into Cinderella, pushing her against the wall. "It's a disgrace that two such wonderful girls should have to share such a small room when you have a great big room all to yourself."

Cinderella clenched her teeth. She had grown up in that room. It was more than a space: it housed her memories. But her scratch was itching, and this entire situation was giving her a headache. She'd get back the room later, when she was at full strength. "Fine," she said. "Then show me to my room. I need to lay down before I faint."

Her sisters giggled. Her stepmother's lips formed into a thin smile.

"I will show you your new quarters," she said, "but there will be no time for a nap. This place needs a good cleaning, and your sisters need help preparing for the ball. You can't expect them to go as they are."

"In black?" Cinderella asked.

"Exactly. It's ridiculous. Now follow me."

The stepmother turned and went down the stairs. Cinderella narrowed her eyes at her pointed shoulders and moved to follow, but her fat sister pushed her against the wall.

"Me first!" she squealed, and she stomped down the stairs giggling.

"Me too!" cried her other sister, and pushed Cinderella against the wall a second time, even though she wasn't in the way at all now.

Cinderella followed after, rubbing her shoulder. There would be a bruise there later.

They walked downstairs, and Cinderella was surprised to see her stepmother lead the way into the kitchen. It was a cramped, dark space with a black stove and a soot-stained fireplace. Her stepmother slapped her arm against the round stove. "This," she exclaimed, "will be your new home."

Cinderella looked around. "The stove?"

"No, you stupid, obstinate, ugly girl. The *kitchen*. We can no longer afford maid services, not without your father's income. You will be responsible for preparing the meals and keeping the household in order."

"But where am I to sleep?" Cinderella asked.

"The floor has been good enough for thousands of generations of mankind, it will be good enough for you."

Cinderella looked down. The floor was caked with black muck. "But it's dirty."

"Then clean it." Her stepmother walked around the room. "Now, before you do that, we desire a little lunch.

But you'll need to do the dishes first. Nothing's clean. And then you will modify some dresses for your sisters to wear to the ball. And then you will bathe them, dress them, apply their makeup, and arrange their hair."

Her sisters nodded, finding the idea sensible.

Cinderella looked at her sisters, wanting to smack them. "Let them do their own hair. I want my room back."

Her stepmother went forward in a flash, pinching Cinderella's ear between her fingers and twisting it hard. Cinderella let out a shriek and dropped to her knees.

"Listen you ungrateful little creature," her stepmother growled. "This is my house now, and there is no one left who cares for you in it. You will make yourself useful or you will wind up in a grave like your father. Is that *understood?*"

"My father?" Cinderella asked, and her stepmother pinched her ear harder. It felt like it would be ripped off, and Cinderella let out a howl of pain.

"Is that understood?" her stepmother growled.

"Yes," gasped Cinderella.

"You will do as you are told?"

"Yes!" Her stepmother let go of her ear, and Cinderella fell to the hard stone floor.

"Now," her stepmother said, "I believe it's time for lunch. We will be upstairs."

She turned to go, ushering her daughters with her, and then paused in the doorway. She looked back at Cinderella, narrowing her eyes and curling the corner of her lips.

"One more thing. I won't have good clothes ruined. Get out of your dress."

"What shall I wear?" Cinderella asked, her confidence shaken.

"In there," her stepmother said, whipping her finger to the broom closet. "The old maid's garments."

Cinderella wanted to object, but she knew her stepmother was eager for a chance to ring her other ear, so she went to the small closet and opened the door. Inside was a mop and bucket, covered with cobwebs. Behind that, mashed into a corner of the space, was a crumpled pile of gray rags.

"Change into them now," her stepmother said. "I want to air out that dress you're wearing immediately."

Cinderella bent to her knees, and pulled up the rags. They were crusted to the floor, and when she pulled them up, they held a hard shape. She brought them to her nose and coughed. The clothes smelled like a musty sewer drain. She looked up to her stepmother, pleading with her eyes. But her stepmother glared back, her ringed fingers laced over her cane.

Cinderella pulled apart the clothes, cracking them together to loosen the shape. It was just one garment: a simple gray dress with an indecently low collar.

"Can I have," she whispered, "a moment to change?"

Her stepmother shook her head. "No time for that. Do it here."

Cinderella looked at her sisters, leaning forward over their mother's shoulders, eager to see what Cinderella looked like naked.

Cinderella clenched her teeth. She set the gray dress on the cold stove, took in a heavy sigh, and then went about removing her mourning gown. She unlaced the back carefully, savoring the feel of the black satin ruffles, and then pulled it over her head. She handed it to her stepmother, who handed it back to the fat sister. "And the rest."

Cinderella removed her stockings, her corset, and finally, her lace bloomers, handing each over in turn, until she stood shivering in front of her family, trying to cover herself with her thin arms, naked except for the shawl tied as a bandage around her wrist.

"Look at how *small* she is," exclaimed the fat sister, her eyes widening.

"How short, too," said her other sister. "You can really

tell how insignificant she is, when she doesn't have her fancy clothes to hide behind."

"She won't be fooling anyone, anymore," the stepmother agreed.

Cinderella tugged the coarse servant's dress over her shoulders. It was ill-fitting, and the sandpaper fabric chaffed against her fair skin. It was cold, too. She grew eager for the sisters to leave so that she could start a fire to warm the air.

"Aren't you forgetting something, Cinderella?" her stepmother asked.

Cinderella looked around the room, then back at her stepmother. "I don't... think so."

"You forgot," her stepmother said, "to say *thank you*." Then all at once she pushed Cinderella to the ground and into the ashes of the fireplace. The sisters laughed behind her. "This is where you belong, Cinderella—among the dirt and trash and cinders." She turned to her daughters. "Kick up the soot onto her, girls, so that she will remember her place is in the kitchen."

The sisters came forward gleefully, and kicked up a black cloud of soot onto Cinderella, sullying her servant's uniform, and caking her arms and face with dark powder. Her eyes were burning, and the soot made her sneeze, but the sisters kept kicking more and more soot into the air, until finally the stepmother said, "That will be enough, girls." She leaned down to Cinderella in the fireplace. "Now, what do you have to say?"

Cinderella glared back at her, tears washing white lines down her blackened face. She pursed her lips in defiance.

Rage flashed across the stepmother's face, and she lifted her cane as if to strike.

"Ahh!" Cinderella cried out. "Thank you!"

"Say it again," her stepmother growled, holding up the cane.

"Thank you!" Cinderella screamed at her, tears flowing.

"Again!"

"Thank you!" she cried, her voice echoing throughout the house. She broke down into sobs and repeated, barely articulating the words, "Tha-*ank* you."

The stepmother was satisfied. "Now," she said, lowering her cane, "I don't know about you, girls, but I'm famished. Who wants an early lunch?" The sisters cheered, and the stepmother led them out of the room, stopping only once at the door to make sure Cinderella didn't object.

Cinderella was too stunned to move. She sat in the cinders, her mind blank, her body aching. If she had been given the option, she would have passed out and gone to sleep. Her limbs felt heavy, and they shook with uncontrollable spasms. But she couldn't sleep. If she slept, they'd come back and beat her. She pulled herself out of the cinders, and raised to her feet, leaning against the stove to keep from falling over.

She thought of the day ahead of her. Of having to clean the filthy house. Of having to bathe and dress and pamper her ugly stepsisters, so that they could go to a frivolous ball on the day of her father's funeral. She thought of the empty sitting chair by the front window that her father would never fill again, and thought of all the evenings that were to come with no one to talk to, with no one to love her, no one to show her even the smallest kindness. How would she ever get through this? She didn't even think she could last through the day. How would she ever be able to face the *years* of loneliness before her?

But when she asked herself these questions, the only answer she heard was a small voice inside her head. It said: "Better make them lunch, or they'll beat you." And she knew this was true, and set to work digging out the pots and pans necessary to make a soup.

By the time she brought up the lunch trays, her sisters were already laying out gowns to wear to the ball.

"Cinderella," her fat sister said, taking her soup from the

tray without even glancing in Cinderella's direction, "I need you to let out the sides of this gown. The cheap fabric has shrunk again."

Cinderella nodded. She walked to the thin stepsister with the tray in a daze.

"This one needs to be lowered," the thin sister said, taking her dish. "I don't know who they design these things for."

They slung the gowns over Cinderella's shoulders. She carried them out of the room, and hung them outside the door before gathering the tray to take into her stepmother's room.

When she entered, she found her stepmother sitting at a small table scribbling down figures on a parchment. Cinderella came closer and saw that they were numbers—finances—that the stepmother quickly covered at her approach. Cinderella gave her the tray of food wordlessly, and turned to leave.

"Oh, Cinderella," her stepmother chimed, "I need you to do one little chore for me."

Cinderella kept her expression blank. The cane was still leaning against the desk.

Her stepmother continued. "Tear the sheets off the bed and wash them. I'd like to use the bed for myself tonight."

For the last few months, her stepmother had been sleeping on the chaise lounge. The bed was reserved for her father in his illness. He died in those very sheets. The pillow still had the indentation of his face pressed into it.

Cinderella swallowed, closed her eyes, and ripped off the sheets. She tried not to think about what she was doing, but when the sheets fluffed out, the smell of her father filled the room. She bunched the sheets into a ball and turned to run out of the room before she began bawling.

"*Cinderella*," her stepmother chastised, stopping her at the door. "Aren't you forgetting something?"

Cinderella turned back, utterly confused. Then, bitterly, she remembered.

"Thank you, Stepmother," she whispered, feeling as sullied as the sheets in her hands. Her stepmother nodded, and Cinderella went back to the hall, shutting the door behind her. She passed by her sisters' gowns, her arms too full with the sheets, and went down the stairs blindly, unable to see over the large pile of laundry. She was nearly at the bottom when a bowl struck the back of her head, splattering hot soup onto her neck and shoulders. Cinderella lost her step, and fell forward onto the floor. The mound of laundry broke her fall, but it might have been better to hit the floor rather than have her nose shoved into the sheets full of her father's scent.

She turned, hearing giggles up above, and saw her two sisters laughing at her from the banister.

"*Disgusting* soup," the thin one shrieked. She must have been the one to throw her bowl, as her hands were empty, while her sister still held hers.

"And not nearly enough," her fat sister added, and tossed her empty bowl at Cinderella. Her aim was off, though, and it shattered on the floor. They laughed, but their laughter stopped instantly when the stepmother's door flew open. She came out hunched over with annoyance, cane in hand.

"Cinderella!" she cried, looking down. "Stop pestering your sisters and clean up this mess!"

Cinderella held her tongue, the soup running down the ends of her hair, and merely looked up at her stepmother. The stepmother went back into her room, slamming the door, and a moment later there were two more slams as the stepsisters followed.

Cinderella stood up. Her head throbbed, her eyes burned, and the scratch on her arm itched worse than ever. She set the pile of laundry down in the kitchen, and then started peeling back the bandage from her hand.

It was worse. The veins all around the scratch had darkened, looking like black spider webs on her skin. The scratch had puffed up, and yellow mucus oozed out. It throbbed terribly, and Cinderella worried that it might be the plague. The idea of death frightened her, and she tied the shawl back around her wrist, trying to forget about it. Maybe if she ate something, maybe then she would feel better.

She found a small helping of soup left in the pot, and she dished it out into a wooden bowl and ate with her fingertips. The soup was cold, and after two mouthfuls, her stomach gurgled. She barely had time to run outside before she vomited into the bushes.

Feeling weaker than before, she went back inside. She struggled with the mound of sheets, carrying them out to the yard to the water pump, and dumped them into a tin basin. She pressed and fought with the pump until the sheets were covered with cold water. Done, she leaned against the pump, her eyes closed, and let the winter breeze tickle the skin of her hot forehead.

Leaving the sheets, she hobbled back across the dead weeds and went back to the kitchen.

A large black rat had found her bowl of soup. It looked up at her with its red eyes and twitched its nose. Cinderella stared back, and the rat dunked its head back into the bowl.

Well, she thought, someone may as well enjoy it. Besides, she'd rather leave food for a rat than for her sisters any day.

And, maybe, once the rat grew large enough, she could hide it in one of their beds. She could keep it in a crate for a day beforehand, so that it was hungry enough to bite anything that came near.

She smiled at the rat as she left the kitchen. It may be her new best friend.

Upstairs she found her stepsisters sitting together on her old bed, full of whispers and giggles. They frowned as she entered, and she smiled back at them. She was remembering the rat.

"Mother was right," the thin one hissed. "Nothing more to her beauty than her clothes. She looks like death now.

Look how black her nails have become in such a short time. She's weak, is what she is."

The fat one nodded. "Disagreeable face, too." She squinted her eyes at Cinderella, and then lost interest and announced, "You will prepare a bath for us. Hot water. And while we bathe, we will supervise the mending of our gowns, and you will favor us with compliments of how beautiful we will be tonight."

"That's a sensible plan," agreed her sister. "Except that I would like compliments about my personality, as well as my beauty. For I was blessed with both."

"Just beauty for me," the fat one said. "Besides, men don't care much for personalities. I've been told so by my admirers on several occasions."

Cinderella took up the gowns and followed the sisters downstairs. They chatted among themselves while Cinderella put a pot of water on the stove to boil, and then went back and forth to the water pump to fill up the rest of the tub. She was glad for the chance to rest on her knees when the fat sister needed someone to wash between the rolls of fat on her back. Cinderella scrubbed, fighting back a wave of nausea that was only partly related to her task. She day-dreamed about that night, after the sisters and mother would be off, when she would be free to rest.

Next, the thin sister scrubbed herself as the fat one stood with her arms out, the fabric of her dress stretched over the bulge of her stomach. Cinderella felt like she was trying to prepare a pumpkin for the ball, and soon after, when it was the thin one's turn, a broomstick.

She had a fever now, she was sure of it, and the room felt alternately hot and then cold. Her arm was feeling worse, too, and the veins had blackened all the way to her shoulder. She finished her chore, lengthening and tightening and let-ting out the gowns, her fingers shaking the entire time.

The sisters ran up the stairs while Cinderella lugged

buckets of water out to the yard, splashing them into the dirt. It created a bog, shining black and slick like oil, and she stared down into it. She thought, That's what my father's grave will look like when it rains.

"Cinderella!" The scream came from the second floor window. The fat sister filled the frame, a wig sitting sideways on her head. "Quit daydreaming and get up here!"

Cinderella dropped the bucket into the mud and walked back to the house.

The next few hours were a blur. Cinderella felt disconnected, as if she were watching from underwater as her sisters flitted around her. Their movements and sounds were distorted, and she only had enough awareness left to experience random flashes of moments—her fat sister puckering her lips in the mirror; the crinoline texture of a dress as it caught in the air and seemed to descend with a sigh; her thin sister's fingers gripped around a brush like a dagger.

She would have remained in her daze longer, but a sharp whack to the back of her head startled her to attention. She fell off the stool and slumped to the floor. Confused, she turned and saw her stepmother standing above her, a broom in her hand.

"You ungrateful brat! What will happen when your sisters meet the prince tonight, and he wants to marry them? He'll want to pay a visit to the house—this messy shack—to ask me for their hands in marriage."

"Both of them?" Cinderella asked, no trace of mockery in her tone.

"It very well might be," the stepmother said. "Princes are known to be fickle, and this one goes through brides like pairs of socks. If he should ask for both, who am I to stand in the way of my daughters' happiness?"

It was then that Cinderella noticed there was blood on the broom handle. She reached her hand to the back of her head. "I'm bleeding," she observed in astonishment.

Her stepmother waved a hand. "A little pain never hurt anyone. Now," she said, collecting herself, "this house needs a proper cleaning, and there isn't much time." She looked at her daughters. "When is the soonest you could expect the prince to return?"

The fat one rolled her eyes. "Well," she said, smacking her lips, "it depends. We might dance until morning, even if he wants us the moment he sees us. You know how I like the royal dances."

"Pfft," her sister exclaimed. "You mean you like the food. I haven't once seen you dance. Not that I blame you. I don't care much for dancing myself." She gave a meaningful look to her mother, her eyebrows raised. "If I had it my way, physical contact between strangers would be forbidden. Between newlyweds, as well, for good measure."

Her fat sister nodded. "You're right. Forget the dance. If the prince wants us, he'll have to leave when we're ready." She paused, thinking. "What time do they traditionally break down the buffet?"

"Midnight."

"Then we may be back as early as midnight," the fat sister answered.

The stepmother nodded. "Midnight," she grumbled. "That isn't much time. I had counted on having the night to work through, at the least. But if it's midnight, Cinderella will just have to work twice as hard." She turned to Cinderella, who was still on the floor. "Get up, you lazy toad."

"Could somebody," Cinderella whispered, her vision blurring, "help me?" She crawled on the ground toward her stepmother and tried to pull herself up on her gown. Her stepmother whacked her on the crown of her head with the broom. Then she threw the broom down at her.

"Help yourself up, then follow me. I will show you what needs to be done."

Cinderella crawled to the side of the room and made it to

her feet using the wall as a brace. She shuffled to the door, feeling woozy, and clutched the banister as her stepmother raced down the stairs.

"This floor is filthy. Look, there's even muddy footprints from when we came in from the cemetery. These tiles used to be white, you know. And do you see how the grime has built up in the cracks? You'll have to scrub that away. It doesn't look nice. What would the prince think?"

Cinderella reached the bottom step, and she stared down at the floor. It had a thick layer of muck on it, caked on for generations. She doubted if the tiles were ever white.

"And the walls and windows need to be scrubbed. And the weeds outside, remove those. Have you finished those sheets yet? And the cellar—let's clean that out. Make it nice."

Cinderella could barely follow. Her head was light, and she felt herself slip to the floor. "I can't..." she whispered, "I can't..."

"Of course you can," the stepmother snapped. She whacked Cinderella in the shoulder with her cane. "And I'll see to it that you don't slack off again, as lazy girls are apt to do."

Cinderella took a step forward and fell to the ground. She tried to push herself up, but her wrist stung with the effort, and she gave up. She would take a beating if she must, but she couldn't clean the entire estate, not by herself, not in her condition. She slumped to the ground in passive defiance.

"Up! Up!" the stepmother screamed. She came forward and smacked Cinderella in the back with her cane. Cinderella refused to move. She hit her again, and Cinderella still refused. Then, panting, the stepmother stood back. "All right. You can start with the floors." And she whisked herself away to the kitchen.

She returned a moment later, holding a water bucket with a brush in one hand, and something she concealed behind her back with the other.

"I've got a surprise for you, Cinderella…"

Cinderella looked up, her expression firm, but her eyes were panicked. She wanted to know desperately what was hidden but she refused to ask.

The stepmother stepped forward. Silently, with her eyes wide and her lips parted, she set down the water bucket and took another step toward Cinderella. Her smile widened. Then she brought out a fire poker from behind her back, the tip glowing orange.

Cinderella's eyes went wide at the sight of the poker. "Okay," she gasped, holding out one hand to shield herself as she scrambled to her feet with the other. Her stepmother had hit her before, but she had never severely injured her. But now that her father was gone, what was to stop her? "Okay," she repeated, huddling into a corner. "I'll clean. I'll clean."

The stepmother sighed. "I knew you'd see reason. But who knows what you'll remember the *next* time." And she lunged forward with the poker, and pressed its tip into Cinderella's thigh.

Cinderella screamed out. It felt like an animal biting her. The sizzle of her flesh rose to her nostrils and the smell of it, of her own flesh—*burning*—her mouth opened and she vomited out a frothing sour spray. The stepmother pulled the poker back, and Cinderella sank to her knees, tears streaming down her face. Her entire body shook, and the burn felt like a fire she couldn't put out.

Her stepmother clucked her tongue. "What a mess you've made, Cinderella. You're just creating more work for yourself." She pushed forward the bucket.

Cinderella took up the brush. She sniffled, dropping it into the water. "Why must you be so cruel? What have I done to deserve this?"

"Done?" her stepmother asked incredulously. She laughed. "It's not what you've *done*, Cinderella, it's what you *are*. You're ungrateful. Spoiled."

"But why are you so cruel?"

The stepmother shook her head. "You have no idea how the world works." Then, remembering, she pointed at the floor. "Keep scrubbing, Cinderella. This isn't a vacation."

Cinderella mucked black water over the grime of the tiles. She choked on the smell of the water. But she kept scrubbing.

"If my father were here, he'd—"

"Well he's not!" the stepmother cawed. "He's dead. And now I'm stuck with you. Such an ugly thing, not even a person, really. You've got no personality. No talents. You're like a cinder pretending to be a girl."

"I could," Cinderella cried, "I could do more than scrub floors."

"Yes, is that right? And do what?"

Cinderella spoke before she had time to edit herself. "I could go to the ball."

Her stepmother cringed, and she made a move toward Cinderella with the poker, but then reconsidered. She lifted her head and belted out, "Girls! Girls, come downstairs."

Cinderella scrubbed as her sisters came down the stairs. Her stepmother started right away.

"Your sister is lazy, girls. She says she's entitled to everything you have. She says that she shouldn't have to work, and that *she* should go to the ball."

The slack, bored expressions of the sisters transmogrified into the snarling faces of wolves. "*Her!* At the ball?" They advanced on Cinderella.

"She wants to push us back to the gutter!" the stepmother cried. "She wants to throw us from our own house!"

Cinderella dropped the brush and huddled back against the wall.

"Here," the stepmother said, handing the poker to the thin sister. "If she won't clean, she's of no use to us. Make her clean."

The thin sister's eyes lit up. She looked to her mother for permission.

"Let's just kill her," the thin sister said, pleading. "Why can't we just kill her?"

The stepmother smiled. "Patience, dear. There's no reason to kill her. Not while the house is so dirty." She took a step forward. "Besides, it's more fun when you draw it out."

The sisters nodded. They had understood something beyond the words, some reference Cinderella wasn't privy to.

"I want this house clean," the stepmother said, her sharp heels clacking across the floor and up the stairs. She called back over her shoulders, "I want it spotless."

The sisters chuckled. "You heard Mother," the thin one said. "Get to it."

Cinderella tried to push herself up to stand, but her hand was numb and she slipped.

This was not good. She was losing feeling in her arm. It probably needed to be amputated. And instead of going to a doctor, she would have to clean floors.

"Look at her arm!" the fat one cackled.

"Disgusting!" the thin one agreed.

They snickered to themselves as Cinderella struggled over to the bucket. She felt around for the brush with her good arm, and went back to scrubbing without a word.

After a minute, the fat sister let out a bored sigh. "That's enough with the floors for now. Let's move to the kitchen."

Cinderella moved to stand up.

"No," said the thin sister, blocking her. "You will walk on all fours. To remind you of your place."

"Yeah!" agreed the fat sister, picking up on the idea. "Like a ragged old mutt!" She laughed, and pushed Cinderella down.

Cinderella didn't have the energy to argue. She had trouble standing anyway. Balancing her weight on her knees and her good hand, she crawled on all fours to the kitchen, the sisters hooting for her to go faster.

"Come on, Doggy!" the fat one squealed. "That's a good little thing. You're a good doggy, aren't you? Aren't you?" She was smiling now, but her mood seemed ready to turn black, and when Cinderella delayed, she saw her stepsister glance toward the poker.

So Cinderella nodded. This made them laugh.

"She agrees!"

"Say it!" cried the thin sister. "Say it!"

Cinderella cringed. But even in this momentary lapse, the thin sister raised the poker, and Cinderella blurted out breathlessly, in her soft voice, "Good doggy. I'm a good doggy."

The sisters cheered, and slapped Cinderella's rear playfully as they herded her into the kitchen.

Cinderella felt like she might drop at any moment, her arms were so weak. What would they do if she fell? Would they burn her? Would she ever wake up?

"Oh, look at this mess!" the thin sister cried in mock-surprise upon entering the kitchen. "All these dishes! And look at the counters—disgusting!"

But her fat sister didn't share her amusement. She looked at the counters with wide eyes. "This?" she asked, "This is where my food is prepared?" She opened a pot and a rat jumped out, scrambling across the counter and out the door. She turned to her sister. "She's trying to poison us. She's trying to poison us like Mother poisoned her fath—"

"Shh!" her sister said, holding a finger up to her mouth and giving her sister a loaded look.

They turned to look at Cinderella, seeing if she followed.

She had. Cinderella gasped. She pulled herself to her feet and looked around the kitchen, realizing, shaking her head. "His food. She poisoned his food. That's why he never got better." Her father was dead because of them. They were murderers.

"Why did you tell her?" the thin sister seethed.

The fat one shrugged. "Oh, what does it matter now?"

"She could still turn us in. If Mother finds out we told, she'll—"

"She'll be furious!" the fat sister realized, her eyes wide with fear. "What will we do?"

The thin sister's eyes darted around the room, thinking quickly. Then she looked down at the poker. "Hold her still," the thin sister ordered.

Cinderella struggled against the fat sister, but she was too weak to put up much of a fight. The thin sister walked over to the oven and shoved the poker deep inside. She turned to Cinderella, smiling. Then she pulled out the poker, the tip of it glowing bright orange. "Open her mouth."

"No!" Cinderella screamed, trying to free herself. But the fat sister worked to open her jaw as the thin one came forward. They pressed the hot poker against her lips and Cinderella couldn't help it—she screamed out—and they shoved its tip inside her mouth, pressing it down on her tongue. She could hear it sizzling. She could even smell it.

"You won't tell any of our secrets now."

The sister dug the poker in deeper, and Cinderella saw the room go black. She slumped into the fat sister's arms, and they finished without any struggle.

After, they let her drop to the floor.

"The house is still dirty," the fat sister whispered, wiping off the front of her dress. "Mother won't like that."

"Let's not tell her. Not until after the ball. If we come home with a prince, she'll forget all about the house."

The fat one nodded. They looked down at Cinderella. "Is she…?"

The thin one leaned down. "She's not breathing. And look at her. Her skin. It's pale as a corpse." She reached out a hand and placed it on Cinderella's chest. The fat sister turned to look upstairs, her feet restless. The thin sister shook her head. "Heart's not beating."

"We have to hide her."

They glanced around the kitchen, and both stopped at the fireplace.

"We could burn her," the thin sister suggested.

"No," the fat one said, shaking her head. "The smell would wake Mother."

Then they both paused, looking upstairs, and listening.

"We'll have to cover her with the cinders for now," the thin sister said. She bent down and the fat sister followed, dragging Cinderella to a dark corner of the kitchen. "Quickly. Cover her with ash."

They worked, tossing ash over the body, burying it in a thin layer of grime.

"You can still see her shape," the fat one whispered.

"Only if you look for it. Who would look for a girl in the cinders?"

They stared at the corner. Then the fat sister shook her head. "Mother isn't going to like this at all."

The thin sister dunked her hands into the sink. "We'll have to tell her we had no other choice."

"Tonight?" She dunked her hands in the water, too. "What about the ball?"

"No, no," said the thin one in a soothing tone, shaking the water from her fingers. "Not tonight. Tomorrow. By then it will be old news."

The fat one nodded, wiping her hands on her dress, and the thin one pulled her along. She took one last long look at the fireplace, and then together they went upstairs to finish preparing for the ball.

* * *

Shortly after dusk a bedazzled coach arrived in front of the family estate. It had multi-colored bells that tinkled as it approached, and the two sisters, who had been dressed and waiting by the front door for nearly an hour, heard it at once.

"It's here! It's here!" they squealed. Their mother, also hearing the bells, had come down the stairs. She approached her daughters, straightening their lace and bows, and held their faces in her hands.

"My daughters," she said, full of pride, "my beautiful daughters." She sighed. "The prince won't be able to contain himself. I'll be a grandmother by morning."

The sisters giggled, basking in the attention.

Then the stepmother straightened up. "Where's Cinderella? She should be here to carry the tail of your gowns."

She made a move to storm off to the kitchen, but her daughters held her back.

"Don't, Mother, don't," they cooed. "We can carry our gowns. It will be practice for when we arrive at the palace."

The stepmother nodded, appeased. But then she made another move toward the kitchen. "But where *is* that girl? These floors are still filthy, and I don't have a single sheet on my bed."

The daughters held her back. "She was just hanging out the clothes last time we saw her," the fat one said. The thin one agreed. "And then she was to start on the floors."

The stepmother sneered. "Well, all right. Just as long as she's not lying down on the job."

The sisters exchanged a look.

"Just go upstairs," the thin one said, pushing her mother toward the stairwell.

"Yes, go to your window and wave us goodbye."

"And then sit there until we return."

The stepmother liked this plan, and she went upstairs as the two sisters collected the length of their dresses, and made their way out across the yard.

She went to the window and waved a silk handkerchief down at her two daughters. They waved up at her, and she waved back. Then the colorful coach groaned and creaked as the sisters climbed inside. The driver rustled his reins and they were off, jaunting down the dark lane toward town and the palace.

The stepmother leaned back inside, lingering over the image for a moment, and then walked to her desk, instantly bitter at the sight of the financial papers. Her husband wasn't nearly as rich as he had pretended to be. All that work seducing and procuring him, putting up and pretending—and for what? Not more than a butcher's salary. Her daughters had better lure that prince tonight. After all, the stepmother was a fine woman, the kind that needed a palace to feel comfortable. Now that her own looks were gone, her daughters were her only hope. And, if for some reason the prince turns out to be a pain, she could start poisoning his meals like she did with the others. And within a year, she'll have the kingdom to herself.

Smiling at her daydreams, she pushed aside the papers on the desk, and rested her head on the wood. She muttered to herself about how that lazy Cinderella didn't even have her sheets ready yet, but only softly, and without any venom. Thinking of a palace, of a throne and kingdom, she was quite content.

It was some time later—she wasn't quite sure when, she had been dozing—that the stepmother was woken by the sound of a large crash downstairs.

"Cinderella," she growled, jumping up at once. She would have to beat that girl into the ground just to get a good nap in around here. She straightened her hair with her hands, and then threw open the door and whisked down the stairs. When she got to the bottom, she found the house dark.

"Cinderella?" she snapped. "Why have you dampened the candles? I can't see a thing."

There was no answer.

The stepmother stood there, holding onto the banister, and called out again. "Cinderella!" she cried.

But she couldn't think of anything more to say. There was

something eerie about the darkness, something unnatural, that held her back.

But she was being silly! This was her house now, and she would not be pushed around by a little guttersnipe like Cinderella. She marched across the front hall with her chin held regally, and found the lantern by the entryway table. She struck a match, lifted the glass of the lantern, and soon a warm yellow glow lit the room. She was relieved to find the room empty. Then she narrowed her eyes, and took the candle with her into the kitchen.

"There you are!" she said upon entering. She saw Cinderella at once, sitting—*sitting!*—in a corner, staring at the black ashes at her feet.

The stepmother squinted at her. There was something off about her. The way she perched. As if her bones had been reassembled incorrectly.

But the stepmother dismissed this. The girl had been cleaning all day, and she was lazy to begin with. Her posture *would* be off after her day.

"Why aren't you cleaning? Did I say you could take a break?"

But Cinderella didn't respond. And from this close, the stepmother could see how dirty the girl was. She was covered from head to toe in soot.

The stepmother came closer, her heels clacking. "You will answer when you're spoken to," she warned.

Cinderella seemed to realize her presence. She turned, ever so slowly, to face the stepmother.

Cinderella looked awful. Even with all the soot on her face, it was evident she was sick. Her eyes were clouded and gray, while the skin around them had turned black. Her cheeks were sunken and slack, and all over her body her veins stood out, as black against her pale skin as dead roots in milk.

Cinderella had seen the stepmother's surprised reaction,

and her mouth curled into a smile, her teeth flashing before her mouth fell open, hanging slack. Gaping like a black void.

She had no tongue.

The stepmother gasped and took a step back, and this triggered an instinctual reaction in Cinderella. At once she sprang up and flung herself at the stepmother, knocking her to the ground. Suddenly the stepmother wished for her cane to beat off the girl, but she had left it upstairs, and before she could chastise herself further, her thoughts were silenced. Cinderella pressed her face into the stepmother's side—and bit her.

It wasn't a small bite, either. Cinderella bit into her like the fat sister chomped into a hot cake. She wasn't just biting the stepmother—she was tearing out chunks.

"Ohh!" the stepmother cried. She tried to bat away the girl, but her swipes were feeble. She was still in too much shock. She looked up to see Cinderella leaning over her, her mouth bloody, her teeth chewing on flesh. It was too much for her, and the stepmother fainted.

She woke to the sensation of being dragged across the floor, her head knocking against the tiles. She screamed out. "Help! Help me!" But there was no one to hear her cries.

Cinderella dragged the stepmother back into the main entryway, and threw her against the hard stones. The stepmother looked down at herself, seeing a large gash on her side, and then noticed the long streak of blood marking her trail from the kitchen.

She looked up to see Cinderella pacing the room, shuffling, using one good leg to move, and then dragging the other misshapen one behind her.

"You're going to be in so much trouble," the stepmother whispered. "Do you really think you'll get away with this?"

Cinderella didn't listen. She bent down and picked up what she had been searching for: the bucket and scrub brush. She hobbled back to the stepmother, and dropped them in front of her. Then she pointed down at them, struggling to articulate her fingers.

"You want me to… *clean?*" the stepmother asked, looking up at her.

Cinderella pointed again.

The stepmother thought it best to go along. She reached out with a shaking hand and picked up the brush.

"But there isn't any water."

A hissing sound came from Cinderella's throat, and in the next moment she had crouched, throwing her arm around the stepmother's neck, holding her head over the bucket. The stepmother struggled against the grip, but it was too strong, and she flailed, panicking, as Cinderella dragged a sharp fingernail across the stepmother's throat.

Blood spluttered out. The cut had missed the major veins—it would not kill her—but she felt her limbs growing weary and her head growing light. She was thrown back to the floor. Cinderella picked up the brush, dunked it in the bucket, and crammed the tool into the stepmother's hand. Then Cinderella pointed at the floor.

The stepmother let the brush drop to her side. "I'm not a maid," she said softly, holding her chin high.

Cinderella growled and pushed her to the ground. She pointed again, and this time the stepmother lifted the brush, and began scrubbing the floor with her own blood.

As she scrubbed, Cinderella circled. This was more terrifying than the pain of her cuts, as Cinderella seemed to be building up to something more. The bite that Cinderella had given her in the kitchen burned intensely, and the stepmother realized Cinderella must have some horrible disease. The plague.

The stepmother began to cry—hard, quivering sobs that came out of her stubbornly, sounding like the cawing of a crow. She couldn't remember the last time she had cried, if she had ever cried. But she cried now.

Cinderella made her dunk the brush again, and again, until the blood was gone.

"It's not fair," she murmured through her sobs. "I gave you a home. I took care of you."

At this, Cinderella lashed out and dragged the stepmother by the hair and threw her against the stairway banister. The stepmother closed her eyes, her hands rubbing her scalp, when suddenly she felt a sharp pain in her side, worse than any pain she had ever known. She looked down and saw Cinderella's fingernails digging into her flesh. She screamed, trying to push the girl away, but she was too weak.

And then the stepmother felt Cinderella's hands *inside* her. This was the worst of all the horrors yet. It was like a giant spider crawling inside her skin, biting her insides, and it made her squirm and nearly lose her senses completely. She was screaming, tears running down her face, and she felt like at any moment she might have a heart attack.

"Stop, please, stop," she cried, her voice weak.

Then, confused and horrified, the stepmother had the odd sensation of being emptied out. She looked down to see a line of intestines streaming out of her stomach. Cinderella was pulling them out, hand over hand, like a seaman piling rope on the deck of a ship.

The stepmother's vision grew dark at the sight, and she forced herself to look away. But then a moment later Cinderella stood up, the roll of intestines in her hand, and began circling the stepmother, wrapping her in her own intestines.

The stepmother screamed, her voice wavering, and tried to pull against her restraints. But when she moved forward, it tugged painfully at something inside of her. She was trapped, and she could do nothing but wonder what terrors might come next.

Then she realized Cinderella was looking at something. A rat had emerged from the kitchen. It was licking up bits from the trail of gore. Cinderella moved toward it, and it ignored her until she made one brisk motion and caught it, lifting it off the ground. It bit at her hand, and Cinderella smiled. She didn't even seem to feel it.

The stepmother shrank back what little she could as Cinderella approached and leaned into her, her gray eyes wide with delight.

"Please," the stepmother begged, "we can get a maid. We'll get you help. You're not well, Cinderella. Just please, let me go."

At this plea, a husky laughter emanated from deep within Cinderella. It echoed inside her frame and came out her open mouth amplified as if emerging from some deep pit of hell. The laughter continued as Cinderella lifted up the rat. It fought against her hard fingers, snapping its jaws and running its feet in the air. Cinderella smiled. Then she shoved the rat, head first, into the stepmother's mouth.

The stepmother's eyes bulged. She could feel the rat panicking inside her, scratching and biting at the inside of her mouth, its tail whipping across her face. She tried to spit it out, but the rat was confused, and kept trying to go deeper and deeper into her. The stepmother shook her head back and forth, whipping the rat out, until it hung down her chin and scratched its hind legs to free itself, dropping down the front of her dress and running along her legs.

The stepmother looked up. Cinderella was gone. Was it over? She thought of her daughters at the ball. It might only be a few hours before they returned. She could stay alive until then. She might even be able to free herself first. Hope began to flutter in her chest, rising like a phoenix from the coils of her pain.

Then she noticed a light like a candle glowing from the kitchen. Only it wasn't a candle, and it was moving. Cinderella appeared in the doorway, her face illuminated by the poker's hellish light. It wasn't over. The night might not even have begun.

"Please," the stepmother asked, the words coming out in a bloody slur. "You can have the money. I'll give you everything, I'll give it all back. Your father—"

Cinderella paused in her approach at the mention of her father, and the stepmother hurried on, dribbling out blood that she coughed up as she continued.

"Your father would want it that way. We'll move out. You'll never see us again."

Cinderella stepped before her, her eyes encircled by black shadows, and her mouth gaping black. She lifted the tip of the poker, and held it between the stepmother's eyes.

"Wait!" the stepmother cried, feeling as if she were hanging over the ledge of a cavern and about to fall. "I'm sorry, please."

But Cinderella ignored her, and in the next moment a searing pain blinded the stepmother. She tried to move away but felt a hand on the back of her head, holding her in place. The hot tip of the poker pressed deeper and deeper, until she felt it scratch against the bone. She could feel her skin melting. Then, suddenly, there was a white hot flash of light. And then nothing.

Cinderella stared down at the stepmother. The poker stuck out of her forehead like a flagpole, and Cinderella clutched it between her fingers. She yanked it out, and then brought it down against the crown of the skull. She heard a crack and could smell the brains within. She brought down the poker one more time, and the skull broke apart like a gourd.

She tossed aside the poker, and dug her fingers into the soft flesh of the brain. She scooped out mouthful after mouthful. It was the most delicious thing she had ever tasted, and she was desperately, insatiably hungry. She thought cheerfully to herself how much it was similar to scooping out the innards of a pumpkin, and that thought lent the occasion a festive feeling.

As she scratched against the inner skull, trying to get the last particles of flesh available, a grandfather clock began to chime by the front door. It belted out the hours—three, four—and Cinderella saw the large hand pointing straight up, and the little hand nearly touching. The chimes continued—eight, nine—and stopped finally at eleven.

It was eleven o'clock. There was something about midnight that Cinderella was supposed to remember. Her sisters? Something about her sisters. It was harder to think now.

Her sisters. Midnight.

The Ball.

Cinderella stood up and left her stepmother's corpse still tied to the banister. She dragged her stiff legs up the stairs, still chewing fragments of skull and brains as she climbed. She made her way to the master bedroom and saw the financial papers spread out over the table. She went past them, toward a large armoire that rested against the back wall.

This had been her mother's. Her father had refused to touch it after her death, and all her mother's beautiful gowns were still hanging right where she had left them. Cinderella ruffled through them with her soot-covered hands and pulled out her favorite: a shimmering blue dress. She ripped it off the hanger and dragged it behind her as she descended the stairs.

When she got to the bottom, she stripped herself of her rags and pulled on the blue dress. She threw the old clothes at the stepmother, as if ordering her to wash them, and let out a wheezing laugh from her tongueless mouth. She looked down and admired the scene—her stepmother's head hollowed out, her intestines wrapped around her body, and rats scurrying in and out of the crevices of her body, feasting on her organs. But best of all was the look of absolute horror frozen onto the stepmother's face, her wide eyes and her screaming mouth. Cinderella gave another laugh, and then turned to the door.

Eleven o'clock. There was still plenty of time.

Feeling glamorous in her sparkling blue gown, Cinderella hobbled out across the dead weeds of the dark yard and out onto the lane. She was getting hungry again, thinking of what awaited her: the palace decked with a million candles, the prince bowing to eligible maidens, and her sisters.

Her sisters. Cinderella growled at the thought, and made her way forward through the night.

She made her way to town and through the twisted streets, hurrying as best she could. She only stopped once, at the cemetery, where an old woman dressed in black hunched between the tombstones. Cinderella wanted to thank her for this opportunity to make her dreams come true, but there was no time. The palace glittered on the hill. And nothing could hold her back now. She waved at the woman and continued on.

Cinderella was going to the ball.

ZOMBIE CINDERELLA II: THE BALL

Her neck called to him.

The servant girl was bent over a table of lilies. The great ballroom was empty except for them.

The Prince approached, his hands rising. She didn't even hear him. He took another slow step, lifting his boots carefully from the marble floor.

He'd bet, oh yes, he'd bet she wouldn't even have time to scream.

Just then, the large double doors of the ballroom burst open. His father's booming voice filled the cavernous space.

"Son! There you are." His father was a short stout man, dressed in royal robes. He scuttled his way toward them. "We need to talk before I leave."

The servant girl bowed her head and started to back away. The Prince watched her retreat out a side door, wanting to stop her, but he couldn't very well go on with his urges while his father watched.

There were some things that were indecent to do in front of your parents.

The Prince turned to his father. He had dark brown hair, with each strand in place, sharp eyebrows, a straight nose, and thin pouting lips. His piercing eyes narrowed. "What?"

"It looks like I arrived not a moment too soon," he whispered. He gestured toward the room.

The great space was as large as a cathedral. The room had been decorated with flowers and ferns, and a table of refreshments placed along the sidewall. A platform for the orchestra had been erected, hidden by a row of potted shrubs.

His father shook his head. "How am I supposed to leave you alone at a time like this?"

"What are you worried about, Father?" the Prince asked. "This is supposed to be a celebration."

"I know what this is supposed to be," his father growled, pinching his son's arm. "And aside from you, I am the *only* person who knows what this is *supposed to be*." His rage was growing.

A temper. That was one thing the Prince had inherited from his father.

"You worry too much." He pulled away and began pacing forward, admiring the great chandeliers above them. "I think this is my second favorite room in the palace," he said. He stared up at the porcelain cupids and the ceramic ruffles that adorned the walls. "It's like being inside a gigantic wedding cake."

"For you," his father whispered, "a wedding cake is an ominous portent."

The Prince smiled. He had brilliant white teeth. "Maybe that's why I like it."

The King shook his head. He pulled the Prince away to the refreshment table. Plates of cheeses and red grapes had been piled. The Prince smiled at these, and began plucking grapes off the stem as his father talked.

"Do you know how expensive this has become for me? A ball is not a cheap affair, especially when it is followed by a wedding." He leaned in. "And then a funeral."

The Prince rolled his eyes, and bit a grape in half.

"And then, if that weren't enough, it's to be followed by

another ball! And another wedding! And another funeral!" He was throwing his arms up with each exclamation, and his voice was rising. The Prince smiled and gestured with his eyes toward a pair of servants entering with more flowers, and his father remembered himself. "All I'm saying is that this has gone on far enough. One, two wives—that was an inconvenience. But you are now beyond a number of wives that I can even count."

"This will be the thirteenth," said the Prince, lifting his chin with pride.

"This will be the last," his father said. He looked into his son's eyes significantly. "You must promise me that this will be the last. And when I return from my sister's, you must put this part of your life behind you. Enough is enough."

"But, Father," the Prince insisted. "You know I have my... *urges.*"

The King quieted as a different servant girl passed by, holding a basket of croissants, and bowed at them. The Prince's eyes followed her, and the King noticed.

"*Yes,*" he said. "Urges. That's what servants are for, *not wives.* Wives are for children. It would be one thing if all these women were dying in childbirth. But lately your brides have barely lasted beyond the wedding night. And how do I explain that to the staff?" He looked around, and then leaned in to whisper, "And how am I supposed to explain that, yet again, *somehow,* it seems we have misplaced your new bride's *head?* If I weren't the king, I would be at the gallows by now."

"But you *are* the king," his son said reassuringly. "And I don't know what you're concerned about. No one suspects a thing." He smiled, and turned to the servants. "Look at them, busy as bees. They're *happy* to have more to do, Father. The entire town is happy that they have another ball to look forward to." He motioned for his father to follow him. "You have nothing to worry about while you are away."

He led his father to the entranceway, where white marble steps led up to two monumental doors that were currently shut. He approached a table where rolls of parchment had been piled haphazardly.

"Do you see these, Father?" He picked up a scroll. "They are RSVPs to the ball."

"So?"

"Father," the Prince said patiently, "most of the kingdom only received their invitations this morning. And look at these." He picked up the papers and read at random. "'Delighted to attend.' 'Enchanted to make your acquaintance.' 'I have *two* daughters, each more beautiful than the last.'" He set down the papers. "See, Father? They couldn't be happier."

"And the expense?"

The Prince shrugged. "Add a new tax."

"Our population is already on the brink of death as it is. This plague—which I suppose you care nothing about—has reduced our numbers greatly over this past month. Crime has been on the rise. Shops and marketplaces are deserted."

"All the more reason for a ball," the Prince said. "It will boost morale."

"It will cause a rebellion." The King stood back, looking at the preparations. "And if they knew the truth… if they *found out*…" His face grew paler. "No," he said, "I will not have my kingdom destroyed like that." He turned to his son. "This will be the last ball. No more after this."

"But, Father—"

"I am the king, and my word is *final*."

He turned on his heel, and stomped away down the length of the great ballroom. The Prince watched him go, and then slammed his fist down on a bunch of grapes. Their juice splattered on the front of his royal garments, and dribbled down the table to form red patches on the white marble.

A servant rushed up to help him clean himself. It was an older butler, a white-haired man who looked like he was the progeny of a hundred generations of butlers. The Prince stared at him, thinking of how servants had a particular look to them, beyond their clothes and rank; that they were almost a different breed than those they served.

The last ball! The Prince snarled again, thinking of it. The butler cowered, wiping off the grape stains from the Prince's boots.

Then the Prince had an idea. He pushed past the butler and looked back at the table of RSVPs. The butler followed.

"How many people have been invited?" the Prince asked.

The butler coughed, composing himself. "Every lady in town of a suitable age and rank."

A look of devilry entered the Prince's eyes. "No," he said. "That isn't enough." He turned to the butler. "You must have every maiden here. Every woman that you can find. Forget about rank."

"Even the servants, Your Majesty?"

"No, of course not," the Prince said, wrinkling his nose. "They don't count. But all the other women in the kingdom, even the ones of lower standing. I want every eligible maiden to attend. And make it clear to them that this is not a request; they are ordered to attend, by royal decree."

"Yes, Your Majesty."

The Prince laughed, a loud bellow that echoed through the great ballroom. The butler bowed and went off to make arrangements, and the Prince skipped away, delighted with himself.

That will serve his father, he thought.

He was about to head out the rear door when he noticed the carpenters. He turned toward them.

"I have a small request," he said, approaching.

The carpenters all cowered, bowing their heads and saying, "Yes, Your Majesty."

"I want the doors locked. Reinforced." He gestured around the ballroom. "All these doors in and out of the ballroom, they are all to be closed off by tonight. Is that understood?"

"Yes, Your Majesty."

He could place guards outside the main entranceway, with orders to bolt the doors once the ball had begun. He laughed again, the brash sound echoing and sending chills down the servants' spines. And then the Prince left the ballroom, still laughing to himself.

His father would be none the wiser. By the time he returned, the Prince would have plenty of time to clean up. And what has been done cannot be undone.

He climbed a staircase lined with a royal blue carpet laced with intricate designs and flourishes, and then another staircase after that. Finally, he approached a wooden door, and took a key from around his neck. He unlocked the door and bolted it behind him.

He was in a round stonewalled room. There was a stained glass window on the far wall depicting a fawn hunted down by a pack of dogs. It showed the moment of the first bites to the beast's haunches, the look of terror in its eyes, and the excitement of the dogs as blood splattered in their faces.

This window sent a red light into the room, and the Prince turned to see twelve faces staring back at him. Each was placed at an equal interval around the round chamber, like the score marks of a clock face.

They were all women, their expressions twisted in the agonies of a horrific death. Only their heads remained, speared by a post jutting from the wall like hunting trophies.

The Prince turned and gazed on them with pride.

Then he began to chuckle. He imagined his father returning to his chambers, relieved that this would be the last ball. Then the Prince imagined the ball itself, the maidens marching into the ballroom like cattle, oblivious as the doors locked behind them.

He walked over to the window, and swung it open.

Cold air rushed against his skin. He was in a high tower of the palace, facing out toward the town. From this distance, it looked like a child's miniature village. Dark storm clouds crept over the horizon, promising storms.

He leaned out the window, and breathed in the air as if breathing in the life of the town.

He would have the people that walked like ants through the streets of the town below. He would have every eligible maiden.

He would have them all.

*   *   *

"It's here! It's here!" the sisters squealed.

Outside of their estate a bedazzled coach arrived, pulling into the pathway with its multi-colored bells twinkling into the night.

The two sisters had been lounging by the window, waiting for it to arrive for what felt like hours. Now they started hopping up and down in excitement. This caused the ground to quake, as one of the sisters was enormously fat and completely unaware of the effects of her size. Dust fell from the ceiling with each jump, and the glass of a lantern set by the door chattered.

Their mother descended the stairs, drawn by the noise. The thin sister stopped jumping. She was tall and unattractively narrow, with jowls that hung from her face like those of a Basset Hound. Her face was covered with a layer of white makeup, with a mole painted to the side of her sneering lip, and purple shadowing around her eyes.

Her mother approached, beaming with pride. "My daughters," she said, putting her hands on either side of the thin sister's face. The thin sister immediately pushed her away, and the mother moved onto the fat sister. "My beautiful daughters."

The fat sister smacked her lips. Her own makeup did little to help her appearance. She looked like a toad with ruby red lipstick.

Their mother led them outside, stopping only once to ask about their stepsister, Cinderella. They managed to appease her, to get her to agree to go back upstairs. Both sisters sighed with relief when their mother walked away, passing right by the kitchen door.

For the sisters had murdered Cinderella, and her corpse was buried in the cinders of the kitchen. If their mother found it now, they might not get to go to the ball.

And that would be cruel, the thin sister decided. She collected the length of her dress, and went into the coach with her sister. They waved at their mother, and then climbed inside as the colorful carriage creaked under their weight. Their mother was still watching from the window, and both sisters made sure to smile as the driver rustled the reins, and sent them rumbling along the dark lane toward town.

"Move over!" the thin sister said, pushing against the flab of her sister's side.

"I'm over as far as I can go," the fat one replied. "I'm practically falling out onto the road."

The thin sister pushed one more time before she was satisfied. Then she turned her gaze out the window. "It really is a disgusting night."

They were passing dead fields that loomed black under the moonless night. The air was cold and smelled like a swamp, and in the distant sky there were bolts of lightning high in the clouds.

"It had better not rain," the fat sister said, looking at the storm clouds. "After all I went through to prepare."

The thin sister nodded. "And we haven't even started with the night yet. We'll have to go the ball, introduce ourselves, talk to *people*." She shook her head in distaste. "It certainly is a heavy burden to become a princess."

The fat sister wasn't paying attention. She was rummaging in the folds of her gown. The thin sister grew curious, and turned to see her sister pull a handful of plums from a hidden pocket.

"You brought food?" the thin sister asked. "You know they'll have a feast when we arrive."

The fat sister bit into a plum, the juice spilling down her chin. "Just a snack," she said, her mouth full. "To keep my strength up." She sucked the juice from the plum, and threw the pit out the window. As she bit into the next one, her expression became pained with thought. "Do you think Mother will be upset?"

The thin sister frowned, the corners of her lips dropping like melting candlewax. "Cinderella had it coming," she said after a moment. "And I think she was sick. Perhaps Mother will believe she died on her own."

The fat sister nodded, sucking out the juice from another plum. "It was her time."

"I'll tell you this," the thin sister said, sitting up and holding out a finger. "I'm getting tired of Mother controlling our lives. I don't like anyone telling me what to do, like I'm some sort of puppet. If the Prince chooses me tonight, I might just leave Mother behind."

"Me too!" the fat one cried, and the two sisters giggled. "Let her starve!"

The fat sister spat the next pit out the window, and wiped what remained of the plums onto the floor of the carriage. A worried look creased her forehead, and she turned to her sister. "What about me? You wouldn't leave me behind, would you?"

The thin sister narrowed her eyes and smiled. "We'll see…"

The fat sister smacked her. "We'll see, indeed!" The thin sister smacked her back, and the fat sister raised her hand to retaliate, but then lost interest. Instead, she rummaged through her ruffles again, and this time pulled out a pile of chocolate-dipped macaroons.

"How much food did you bring?" her sister exclaimed.

The fat sister lifted her chin. One of them, at least.

"It's a long ride," she said primly. "And I always come pah-paarrrd." Her last words were mumbled by the cookies.

Just then, the carriage rocked severely. The sisters were thrown forward, and the cookies sprayed out of the fat sister's mouth.

"Hey!" she yelled to the driver. "Slow down!"

"Sorry, miss," came the driver's voice from outside. "But there's no avoiding it." The carriage rocked again. "The road is covered with bodies."

The sisters stuck their heads out either window and looked down at the road. Indeed, the entire path had been littered with corpses.

The fat sister sat back inside. "Damn plague," she cursed. "It's going to give me indigestion."

The thin sister sat back down as well, and they were rocked back and forth, bumping into each other.

But after a few minutes, the carriage slowed. The sisters looked outside at the marketplace streets in confusion. It was nothing but darkness. They were still miles from Bluebeard Palace.

"Driver," called the thin sister. "Why have you stopped?"

There was a moment of silence. Then he answered, "There are more people in the road, miss."

"Then go over them, like before," she returned, annoyed.

There was another pause. Then he said, almost delicately, "These people are alive, miss."

The sisters stuck their heads out the windows again. The night was getting colder now, and a harsh wind whipped past their ears.

Ahead was a huddled group of children, standing in the dead center of the road. Their bodies were thin and starved, their eyes black and hollow. They stood unmoving, staring at the coach.

"They're only peasant children!" the fat sister called. "Don't stop for that."

The thin sister concurred. She slapped the roof of the coach, and said, "Rush them. They'll move if they know what's good for them."

"Yes, miss." The driver slapped the reins on the horses, but they stammered. He slapped them again, but they refused to move any closer to the children. The sisters stared ahead out the window.

A child in the center took a step forward. His movements were stilted, as if he had to concentrate to move his foot and then concentrate again to rebalance his body. He was small and sickly, with scars covered with stitches running up and down his limbs. And when he moved forward, the children behind him took a collective step forward as well, walking over the bodies.

"What are they doing?" the thin sister whispered.

"I don't know," the fat one replied. "But fear makes me hungry, and I'm all out of cookies. Tell the driver to get us out of here."

They screamed at the driver. "The horses won't budge!" he yelled back.

"Then turn around!" the thin sister yelled, exasperated.

The driver worked to turn the horses around, and they were more willing to do this. The sisters sat back in the coach, and as the coach turned, the thin sister's window faced out toward the children. She pressed against the bulk of her sister's side, trying to edge back into the coach, but there was no room to retreat.

"Move back!" she snapped.

"I'm back as far as I can go!"

The children outside grew closer, and in the glow of the lantern the thin sister could begin to make out some of their faces. In particular, there were two—a brother and sister— that seemed familiar from someplace she had been. Then she placed them: they were the children from Geppetto's hanging. And she gasped at how their appearance had changed. They were still dressed in rags, but now there were dark patches of blood down the front of their chests. There was blood around their mouths, too, only this blood must have been fresh, because it glimmered in the moonlight.

"They're mad with the plague," she whispered to her sister.

The coach had turned halfway when it suddenly stopped. The sisters heard the slap of the reins, and felt the horses tug against the coach, but something was holding them back.

"Move!" the fat sister wailed.

"The wheel's lodged!" the driver yelled back.

"Then dislodge it!" the thin sister shrieked. "We're under attack!"

The driver jumped off his box seat. His boots landed with a soft thud on the flesh of the corpses. He scrambled past the fat sister's window, ducking down to look at the wheels.

"An arm's caught," he said, popping back up. "On your side, miss." He was looking at the thin sister.

She blanched. "Then remove it!"

"Just open your door and lean down. You can get it faster."

"No!" she cried. "I won't open the door. Not with *them* out there!"

She looked back, and saw the children were only five feet away now. She screamed out, and the stitched boy's mouth opened into a leer. Next to him was another boy, this one with bright red hair and a Pagan look to him, perhaps be- cause he was wearing all green, including what looked to be a shirt of leaves. Close behind him were smaller children, still wearing pale nightgowns, as if they had been snatched right from their beds.

The driver ran around the back of the coach, and bent down to the wheel on the thin sister's side. But just as he bent, the stitched child pounced on his back. He screamed out, standing up and trying to reach for the child.

"Get the arm," the fat sister said, prodding the thin one. "Get it *now*."

The thin sister, before she had time to doubt herself, opened her door slightly and reached down toward the wheel. Stuck between the spokes was a grey human arm. It looked to be male, judging by its thick size and hairy knuckles. She tugged on it, her fingers squishing into the decayed flesh of its wrist, and felt that it was still attached to a shoulder. With all her might, she leaned back and ripped it clean off, knocking backward into the fat of her sister's side.

The wheel was dislodged.

The sisters looked up just in time to see the stitched boy wrap his arms around the driver's neck. The boy bit down and blood sprayed out, causing both sisters to scream.

The thin sister, barely thinking, swung the severed arm at the little boy's head, right on the skull. He let go of the neck, stunned, and was lifting his head up when the thin sister hit him again, using the arm as a club. She knocked the boy completely off the driver.

"Drive!" the thin sister screamed, and the wide-eyed driver woke into action. He crawled along the side of the coach and up to his box. He slapped the horses fiercely, so that they cried out and broke into a run. A child in bed-clothes, not more than four years of age, leapt at the coach as they turned away. But the coach was moving too quickly, and the sisters felt a bump as the child was run over by the vehicle's wheels.

The coach raced and jostled and bounced back over the street of bodies, until it had escaped the children entirely. Its lanterns turned upon a clear road and started to travel uphill, in the direction of the palace. The driver kept the horses at a quick trot the rest of the journey, and the sisters fanned themselves until their breathing had returned to normal. It wasn't until they had caught sight of a line of coaches that were heading to the palace as well that the thin sister felt it was safe to throw the severed arm out the window, no longer feeling the need for a weapon.

But once in the safety of others, the sisters' attention returned to higher concerns, and they began to adjust their tempest-tossed appearances. Their high hairstyles were askew, and they worked to comb down each other's hair, reworking the piles of curls. As they got closer, and entered the torchlights near the palace, they noticed splatters of blood on their gowns, and repositioned their laces and flowers to hide them.

There were whimpers coming from the driver, and the thin sister whispered to him, "Shut up!"

"I'm sorry, miss," he answered, his voice shaking. "But one of those children bit me."

"That's none of my concern!" she snapped back.

He was silent afterward.

It felt like ages, but finally their coach was at the front of the line. The sisters sat, waiting for their driver to open the doors. When he did not arrive, they stayed in their seats, holding up the entire procession. Eventually, a palace attendant stepped up and bowed. He opened a door, and held out his hand to the thin sister.

She climbed out, readjusting her gown, while on the other side of the carriage, the fat sister nearly pulled down a second attendant, trying to pull herself out of the coach. She got to her feet, crumbs and bits of food falling to the floor. Then she and her sister turned with sneers toward the driver.

"Lazy oaf!" the thin sister said, and smacked at the driver with her fan.

He slumped over, leaning against the far railing of the driver's seat. Blood coated his neck, and his mouth and eyes were open and unmoving.

He was dead.

"This is so embarrassing," the thin sister mumbled.

"Is something wrong?" the attendant asked, taking a step forward. He hadn't yet seen the driver.

"No!" shouted the fat sister. "Nothing's wrong!" Quickly, she slapped the rear of one of the horses with her palm. It whinnied, and the pair broke into a run, speeding the coach down the lane and out of sight. The sisters both exhaled in relief, and turned toward the palace.

"Damn driver," the fat sister mumbled as they climbed the stairs, holding their gowns with both hands.

"Don't worry yourself about it, sister," the thin one said. "We've made it. After all this, we've made it. And *nothing* is going to spoil our evening."

The fat sister nodded her head in agreement, and together they went up the steps toward the lights of the palace. A storm rumbled in the distance sky. The air put goosebumps on their skin, and as they stepped inside, the great chimes of the clock tower began to ring out.

It was eleven o'clock.

The sound of the chimes rang out over the town, spreading over the dark streets in concentric circles like ripples on the surface of a lake. They sounded upon the gallows. They sounded upon the cemetery. And far out into the night, past the town and past the length of a dead field, all the way to the dark estate the sisters had left earlier that evening, they sounded.

But here the chimes were overpowered by the deep intones of a single grandfather clock.

And here, Cinderella looked up from the corpse of her stepmother, to the clock, and remembered:

It was time to go to the ball.

*   *   *

The Prince smiled from his perch high over the ballroom. He locked the door behind him and placed the key into the pocket of his dress coat. Then he turned to the room, his back straight and chin held high. He tried to hide his smug smile, but the devilish glee escaped through his eyes.

And why not? he thought. It's a ball, after all. He was supposed to have fun.

And he would have fun soon enough.

He descended the spiral stairway from the balcony, feeling the eyes of the proles below admiring his regal attire. He had a white dress coat with red cuffs and a red collar. Gold fringe hung from the shoulders, and golden ropes decorated the front of the jacket and accented the golden buttons and cufflinks. A golden belt sat high on his waist, and he wore crimson pants with gold trim on the sides that led to his shining black boots. He had an additional crimson sash over the front of his jacket, and held one white-gloved hand over it as he slowly descended the steps.

His other hand was at his waist, where a long silver sword lay at the ready. He almost laughed, feeling its hilt against his fingertips.

He stopped three steps from the polished floor of the ballroom for the women to admire him, turning from side to side like a peacock displaying its feathers. He flashed his intense eyes at the groups in the crowd, his hair impeccably combed, and tilted his head slightly to show off his fantastic jawline. Then, still with his hand on his sword, he descended the final steps, and walked into the cloud of admiration that had formed among the guests below him. '

The orchestra was playing, and he looked past the women that bowed on either side of him as he crossed the center of the ballroom. He looked to the drapes hung over the doorways that he knew to be locked. Already the air in the room had grown stuffy from lack of ventilation, but he didn't mind. Let them sweat.

He crossed with slow, careful steps, not glancing at the crowds on either side of him. He walked the length of the entire ballroom, to the main entranceway. The guards bowed as he neared, and he gestured with the slightest movement of his fingers for the captain to come near.

"What may please Your Most Royal Highness?" the guard asked, still bowing.

The Prince spoke in a low voice. "You have fulfilled your orders?"

"Yes, Your Royal Highness. The guards have all been briefed on the procedure."

"At the stroke of midnight," the Prince said, almost as a threat.

"At the stroke of midnight," the Captain repeated. He lowered his bow until his nose almost touched the floor.

The Prince looked at the massive double doors, which were now the only exit to the ballroom. They were solid enough to hold out an army. Or hold one within.

Satisfied, the Prince turned back toward the ballroom, molding his face into a pleasant smile.

"It is time for a quadrille," he stated. "I feel like dancing."

An attendant within earshot ran off to inform the orchestra. As the Prince stepped back into the crowd, the ladies all bowed to him, smiling with shy looks from behind their fans.

The Prince smiled back, and they found him charming.

*   *   *

"It's too hot," the fat sister complained. "I'm sweating like a pig."

The sisters were on the sidelines of the room. The fat sister had plopped down on an ottoman before the refreshment table, eating from the buffet by the handful with her back to the crowd. Her sister stood next to her with her arms crossed, grimacing at the dancers.

A lady stood not five feet from them, clapping her hands lightly to the time of the music. She called out the dance moves. *"A droite! A gauche! A la fin!"*

The thin sister rolled her eyes. *"A droite!"* she imitated in a high-pitched squeal. *"A gauche! A la fin!"*

The lady turned and raised her eyebrows at the thin sister, shocked at her impropriety.

"That's right," the thin sister said, standing at her full height to look down on the lady. "I'm talking about you. Why don't you give it up? The Prince is obviously not interested in your catcalls."

The lady's eyes went wide. *"Excusé moi?"*

"It's true," the fat sister agreed, turning with a mouthful of food. "You sound like a banshee."

The lady gave a *humph!* and walked away with her nose in the air.

The sisters let a moment of silence pass. Then the fat sister said, "Mother won't like it if she heard about how rude you were."

The thin sister rolled her eyes.

"If Mother cared so much, she should have been here herself. And you're one to talk—chowing down like a hog at the trough. *Custom* says that ladies are to wait until the interval to partake of refreshments."

"Yeah, well, this ball lacks custom."

The thin sister couldn't disagree. This *was* a strange ball. For one, the refreshments were placed right out on the sides of the dance floor, instead of in the adjoining rooms. And when the sisters had looked for a place to sit in private, they found all the side doors locked. The doors had even been covered with curtains so that no one would notice.

And the mood of the ball itself was strange. Perhaps the

evening had been colored by what they had seen on their journey to the palace, but the air in the room felt uncomfortable and tense. There were fewer men than usual, and the attendees were almost all women. The Prince was even dancing with them indiscriminately, smiling and laughing broadly at times when looking at their faces with bacchanalian hunger.

"If I didn't know any better," the thin sister said, "I'd say we were at the early stages of an *orgy*, not a ball."

"An awfully grim orgy, at that." The fat sister brushed her hands clean and turned toward the room. "Look," she said, pointing, "the Prince is sitting back down. Let's pay our compliments and get out of here."

There was already a line to greet the Prince by the time they had crossed the dance floor. They waited, fanning themselves and eyeing the dresses of the ladies around them cynically.

"Blondes should really be in delicate hues," the thin sister whispered, looking at a lady ahead of them in line. But her whisper carried, and the lady turned her head halfway to look back at her.

"And calico," the fat sister said, wrinkling her nose while staring at someone behind them. "It takes a fine woman to pull that off. Too bad."

They arrived at the front of the line. The Prince sat on the throne, one leg crossed over the other, and held his chin in his hand as if deep in contemplation. He didn't even look up when the sisters took their dresses in both hands and bowed.

"If it may please Your Royal Highness," the fat sister said, annoyed.

The Prince startled. He had a watch in his hand that he had been staring at, and he placed it back in his breast pocket. He started to look up, a smile already on his face, and froze. His eyes widened, and then his face fell into a frown.

The thin sister stifled a giggle. She had expected the Prince to fall in love with her on first sight, but she hadn't expected it to be this easy.

The Prince stood up, as if mesmerized, and took a step forward.

"Why, Your Majesty," the thin sister said, holding a hand over her mouth to hide her glee.

He ignored her, and took another step, parting the sisters with his hands and walking between them. Slighted, the sisters turned with bitterness, but their own expressions froze as soon as they did.

There, standing in front of the main entranceway, was Cinderella.

Everyone was staring at her in stunned silence. Around her was a vacant clearing, as no one wanted to get too close, even if they couldn't look away. She stood at the center, lopsided, one shoulder rising above the other as she turned her head to look around the room.

"I thought she was dead," the fat sister whispered.

The thin sister shrank down a little behind the crowd, peeping over. "It looks like she still is," she whispered back.

Cinderella's skin was grey as a corpse, and still covered with the black soot of the fireplace. Blood stained the sides of her mouth, dribbling down her chin and onto the hem of her dress.

"My Lord!" the thin sister exclaimed, now noticing the dress itself.

It was stunning: a light shade of blue that seemed to glimmer and sparkle even in the candlelight of the chandeliers. It looked like silk, and had poofs of white gauze on the shoulders, and long trails of diaphanous netting over the skirt of the dress. It was perhaps the finest gown at the entire ball, and worn by the most miserable creature in attendance. There were even muddy footprints in a trail behind her, revealing that she had come in bare feet.

Then, suddenly, as if announcing her arrival, the chimes of the clock tower began to ring. The hours vibrated through the air, sending chills through the ladies, and they started to gossip at once.

"What's wrong with her?"

"She's obviously a peasant. She doesn't belong here."

"Is that blood?"

They were so distracted by the mysterious stranger that the assembly failed to notice as the great doors of the entranceway shifted behind her. By the final stroke of midnight, their only exit to the outside world had been sealed shut.

And then Cinderella turned toward the sisters.

The fat sister saw this and tried to hide behind the thin one. It was like the moon trying to hide behind a needle. The sight made Cinderella laugh—a deep gusty cackle—before lifting her arm to point at the sisters.

The thin sister blinked in fear. Then her face grew cruel. "Don't hide, sister. We have no reason to hide from *her*." She crossed her arms. "Go ahead," she said to Cinderella. "Point all you like. You're only making a spectacle of yourself."

The fat sister took a step forward, looking from the thin sister to Cinderella. Then her eyes went wide. "Hey!" she cried. "She has no tongue." She smiled, narrowing her eyes at Cinderella. "Not so tough now, are you?"

Cinderella held her place, and continued to point, still as a statue. She could stand here all day. But then she saw a flash of red in the crowd. The Prince. And then a moment later the ballroom attendants were closing in on her. These men wore black, to set them apart from the guests, and to fade them into the background.

"You'd better come with us, miss," one said to Cinderella. He stood a few paces away, seemingly not willing to place a hand on her. She turned to him, feeling a bond between herself and the fellow servant.

"Can't you see you're not wanted here?" the thin sister

said, taking a step forward. "You're not even wearing gloves."

The fat one laughed. "There are people that go to balls, and there are people who belong on the streets."

Cinderella turned to her. The assembly around them watched the scene, shifting awkwardly. The music was still playing, as the orchestra was oblivious behind a screen of bushes brought in to hide them from view. A minuet had begun, but no one was dancing.

Cinderella didn't recognize any of these people. Her clouded eyes scanned the crowd for a familiar face, and the pampered women stared back at her as if she were supremely out of place, like a goat in the kitchen.

And a feeling that had been brewing in Cinderella for some time began to take solid form. It was a feeling of the unfairness of life. It was unfair that she, a person who had never done any harm to anyone, should lose her father and shortly thereafter be murdered herself. It was unfair that her murderers should go on to live and dance and insult her, without recompense. And it was unfair that these snobbish society women should look at her that way, with their cruel eyes, for interrupting their dance—their celebration as the town below them suffered with sickness.

And then a great relief washed over Cinderella, and her smile returned.

Life *was* unfair, she realized. But death wasn't. Death was equal to all.

It was time she dealt out some death.

She lowered her arm and gave a wide grin to the sisters, opening her mouth so that they and the other guests of the assembly could see the hollow cavern within. There were a few gasps, and Cinderella was pleased. Her blackened lips stretched as her smile grew even wider.

She moved toward the sisters, dragging one foot behind her on the floor.

"We can't let you—" one of the servants began. He reached out a hand to restrain Cinderella, and she whipped around at him, clutching his hand with her sharp fingers, and bringing her open mouth down upon it. She bit into the flesh of his wrist, tearing into the veins and feeling the hot blood spray against her face. The servant struggled against her, but his struggle only gave her strength. More of his blood flooded her mouth, until it was dribbling out, down her chin and back into his arm.

There were screams from the ladies, and Cinderella looked up, losing her grasp on the man. The sisters were already running away, pushing down the women around them in their retreat. They reached the main entranceway and pulled on the brass rings.

But the doors didn't budge.

The thin sister pounded on the doors. "Let us out!" she cried. "Let us out!"

The music had stopped. At Cinderella's feet, the servant's body started to spasm. White foam erupted from his mouth, and blackness spread through his veins. He screamed out in agony, his shoulders twitching. He gave one last shriek and then fell over, curling himself into a ball.

"They won't open the doors!" the thin sister called out to the room.

The fat sister nodded to the crowd. "We're locked in!" she confirmed. "There's no way out!"

Just then, the bitten servant lifted his head. His eyes were now completely black, and his mouth twisted into a snarl. His gaze fixed on a stately woman, plump with grey hair, who stood a few paces behind him. At his look, she pulled up the length of her purple gown and tried to retreat, but he was too quick. He leapt through the air like a flea, and knocked her to the ground. Then, as if it were part of the same movement, his teeth latched onto her neck, and he ripped out her throat with one clean tear.

Blood splattered the fine dresses of the nearby women in a delicate red mist. On all sides of the ballroom, the women tried to press through whatever doorways they could find. Every last one was locked, bolted, secured. Understanding went through the women like an electric shock. This had been done on purpose; they were not meant to escape.

The servant dropped the woman. He raised his head, blood streaming from his mouth, and set his blackened eyes on a fresh victim. He leapt, and the room filled with the same panicked screams as might be heard on a sinking ship, lost at sea.

They screamed the mindless howls of the damned.

*   *   *

This was music to the Prince's ears!

He laughed, watching the women rush by him in either direction. He hadn't smiled this broadly in what felt like years.

Finally, he thought, the party had begun. A real jubilee!

But wait. The actual music had ceased; his orchestra had been silenced. He shook his head and made his way over to their corner of the great ballroom. An occasion like this *must* be accompanied by music.

He rounded the hedges that hid the orchestra, and was dismayed to find its members cowering on the ground with their hands held over their heads.

"It's not an earthquake," the Prince mocked. "You can get up."

The conductor looked up at him. "Your Majesty?"

"Back to places." The Prince clapped his hands. "I'm thinking… a waltz. A happy, carefree waltz."

"With all due respect, Your Highness," the conductor said, raising his eyebrows so that little rolls formed on his forehead, "you can't expect my men to perform at a time like this."

"A time like this?" the Prince asked, as if the question were absurd. In the background, a trio of women's screams ignited—and then were prematurely silenced.

"Yes, Your Highness. When our lives are in jeopardy."

The Prince's lighthearted airiness vanished. He leaned down to put his face within an inch of the conductor's. "Let me make myself clear," he said, his tone chillingly expressionless. "If you do *not* play, your lives *will* be in jeopardy. I am the Prince, and it is my royal decree that we have *music—at—the—ball*." He growled his last few words for emphasis.

The conductor nodded.

"Well!" said the Prince, slipping back into his charming routine as he stood up, "I say it's time for music." He smiled. "Deny me that, and you will be executed."

He waited until the conductor and his orchestra started to lift themselves to their chairs, and then trotted back to the dance floor. A fountain of blood sprayed across the room at the same moment he heard the conductor tap the beat. The waltz had commenced.

The soft opening notes reverberated off the high walls, and the Prince reached for his sword. He took its hilt in both hands and admired the reflection of the candles on its silver finish.

"Ah, my old friend," he murmured, "we meet again. May I have the pleasure?" He bowed, and then started shifting his feet to the right, to the left, holding the sword before him. He twirled in a circle, drawing the blade through the air as if it were a dance partner.

Seeing him armed, a fine lady in pink with tumbling blond curls ran up to him at once.

"Your Majesty!" she screamed. She couldn't have been more than sixteen, perhaps making her début. She slowed before him, her cheeks stained with tears. "Thank the Lord you're—"

The Prince swung the sword like an axe and chopped

right through her neck. He had such force to his blow that he managed to decapitate her completely, her head falling with a thump to the dance floor. It rolled three times, and then landed facing him. To his surprise, the eyes blinked once. Then they remained wide forever.

The body tumbled like a great oak and spewed its blood into the air like a geyser. The Prince could hear the music, and it had a relaxing effect on him. As the body hit the floor, he exhaled, and then stepped away to continue with his dance.

He was radiant. He hummed along with the waltz, spinning as he approached another group of women. These, too, had the misfortune of turning toward him for aid, and he sliced off their heads—*one* two three, *one* two three—killing at the beat of each step.

He danced over the corpses, kicking the heads playfully through the remaining crowds, and felt the showers of blood rain down upon him like fairy dust. He smiled, blood dripping down his face.

This was the best night of his life.

* * *

Cinderella was enchanted as well. She had trapped her two stepsisters into a corner of the ballroom. She was flanked on either side by the dead, servants who had joined her cause and licked their blackened lips with hunger.

The two sisters huddled into each other, sniveling.

Cinderella laughed, a blast of sour air emerging from her open throat. The sisters choked, their eyes watering.

"Please," the fat sister begged. "You can have your room back. It smells, anyway."

The thin sister elbowed her.

"What?" the fat one whispered. "Maybe she likes that it smells."

The thin sister pursed her lips, allowing that this might be possible.

"And you don't have to worry about Mother," the fat sister continued. "We will take care of her."

At this, Cinderella shook her head.

"You... *don't* want us to take care of her?" the thin sister asked.

Cinderella worked her mouth, as if preparing to speak, and a muffled gurgling came from her throat. The two sisters leaned forward, working to understand. But instead of words, a bubbly broth sizzled from Cinderella's mouth. It spluttered a foul concoction that sprayed in all directions.

"Oh, disgusting!" the fat sister said, leaning back and holding her nose.

Bits and pieces of things regurgitated from Cinderella's throat: slime-coated chunks of brains, hunks of hair, and then last, a long finger wearing a dark round stone.

"That's Mother's ring!" the fat sister gasped.

The sisters looked up at Cinderella with alarm. Cinderella tapped her belly through her gown, confirming their suspicions, and then gave a throaty chuckle.

Tears fell from the thin sister's eyes. "I don't deserve this. *She's* the one that was always against you." She poked the fat sister in the side. The fat sister slapped her hand away.

"Not true," the fat one said, shaking her head. "Not true. I tried to stop her. But she overpowered me." The fat sister smiled, the rolls of her face doubling over each other. "Punish *her*. I'll help you do it."

The thin sister's eyes went wide, and Cinderella turned to her. "She's lying," she stammered.

Cinderella growled. She motioned for her servants to come forward.

"No!" the thin sister screamed out.

She squirmed and fought, but the servants grabbed her, holding her still by her hands and legs. Cinderella leaned over her, her dead eyes taking in the sight, and she literally drooled over what she saw.

"Sister!" the thin one yelled. "Help me!"

The fat sister shook her head. "I've got to think of myself."

Cinderella bent her head to the thin sister's stomach, and used her teeth to tear through the gown. The thin sister tried to fight, but could not escape the servants. Cinderella clawed at her quivering skin, digging through with her face, and pulled back two long flaps of flesh. Blood gushed out of the thin sister, and she shook violently. Cinderella watched as the parts inside of her vibrated as well.

Then Cinderella turned to face the fat sister. She held up a hand, and motioned with a curl of her finger for the fat sister to join her.

"I can't," she said, backing farther into the corner.

Cinderella looked to her servants. Together, they brought the thin sister to rest on the fat sister's lap like a human serving tray. The fat sister tried to sit up, but Cinderella pushed her back down.

Then Cinderella reached inside the opening of the thin sister's stomach, squishing past her intestines until she was elbow deep within her body. She clutched on something, and tugged her hand out. Wrapped between her fingers was the thin sister's kidney.

The thin sister cried out, her head swooning.

And then Cinderella shoved the organ into the fat sister's mouth.

The fat sister's eyes opened wide. Before she could object, Cinderella leaned forward and placed both hands over her mouth. She had no choice. Slowly, with many mumbled objections, the fat sister began to chew, her cheeks puffed out with flesh. And as soon as she had finished, Cinderella reached down into the thin sister and pulled out her spleen.

She fed the thin sister this way, piece by piece, to the fat sister. First, a few organs. Then, as the thin sister started to phase in and out of consciousness, Cinderella shoved the thin sister's hand inside the fat sister's mouth, and had her chew on the fingers to revive her sibling.

"I can't," the fat sister cried after swallowing down both of her sister's hands, "I can't do anymore. I feel like I'm going to explode."

She was bulging at the sides. The seams of her dress had split, and her flesh pressed through the openings like dough.

Cinderella had intended to keep feeding her fat stepsister until she exploded, but the thin sister was barely responsive. There was only so much time left if the final course was to be served *en vie*. She would have to improvise.

She stood up, and the servants mimicked her. She reached both hands to grip the fat sister's lower jaw, and had the servants lodge their fingers inside the flab of her lips. The fat sister's eyes rolled in every direction, trying desperately to see what was happening. She tried to speak, her tongue flopping inside her mouth like a fat garden slug.

Then Cinderella nodded her head, and everyone began to pull, each in their own direction. There was a snapping sound as Cinderella pressed down, breaking the jaw at the joint. She wiggled it back and forth to loosen it, and then ripped it out completely. She tossed it over her shoulder, and then picked up the thin sister, who was even thinner now without half of her insides. The servants stretched the skin of the fat sister's cheeks on either side, pulling it like taffy, and Cinderella shoved the thin sister's head inside the fat one's mouth.

The thin sister struggled, flapping her arms as she choked in the darkness, and the fat sister's face turned purple as she was also suffocated. Soon, the thin sister's feeble movements slowed, and the fat sister's eyes glazed over. They were dead.

Cinderella stood up, admiring her handiwork. It was a beautiful sight.

She left their corpses to the servants, and turned away. It was time to see the Prince.

*   *   *

The Prince stood in the middle of the ballroom, breathing hard, his entire outfit heavy with blood. His face was splattered with it, and coagulated rivulets dripped from his perfect hair.

The orchestra had stopped.

He looked around, and to his surprise some of the women he had slaughtered just moments ago were rising from the floor. He hadn't managed to decapitate everyone, and there were a good many women he had killed after they were weakened by strange bite wounds. It was these who struggled forward now, slipping in their own blood.

And the Prince decided it was a good time to end the night.

He half ran, half skidded across the ballroom floor, back to his staircase at the far end. He passed groups of servants along the way who were huddled around the bodies on the floor, feasting on their organs. The room smelled of blood and raw human meat, the stench intensified by the heat and lack of circulation.

When he reached the spiral staircase, the path was blocked by a thong of women.

"Out of the way," he shouted, holding up the sword. "By order of the Prince!"

They started shuffling forward.

The Prince lost no time and met their advance. He swung his sword and decapitated a brunette with braids. The others weren't frightened at all by his efforts, and reached out to him as he weaved between them, running up the stairs. He reached inside his coat pocket and pulled out his key.

But as he stepped onto the ledge, there was the mysterious

stranger standing before the door, the woman in the blue shimmering gown. Only now, her dress was covered with a heavy coating of gore.

"It's you," he said, and she pounced on him. They both hit the railing of the stairs, their bodies twisting in the scuffle. He swiped his sword, and managed to land the blade on her ankle, snapping the bone and slicing the foot clean off.

The woman didn't even seem to feel it. Instead, she used his momentary distraction to make an attack on his shoulder, ripping through the fabric of his jacket, and sinking her teeth into his flesh.

"Off!" he yelled, and kicked her in the stomach with his boot. She was knocked back by this, but immediately came at him again. He rose to his knees and jammed the key into the lock, falling forward as the door opened. She tumbled out with him, still clawing.

The Prince crawled forward on the ground, and quickly got to his feet. He felt a rush of blood run to his head, and was overcome with a wave of dizziness. He shook the sensation away, and looked down to see the woman roll onto her back.

As soon as she had, he raised the sword with both hands, and brought it down on her. He got her right in the heart, twisting the blade to make her suffer. She lifted her arms, and then let them fall, her eyes growing blank.

He stood back, feeling suddenly weak, and was relieved to see the woman didn't move again.

The Prince leaned forward and locked the door to the ballroom. He left his sword in the dead woman, and made his way upstairs with his hand on his throbbing shoulder. He climbed the long staircases to his secret chamber, and pulled a key from around his neck. He twisted it in the lock, but in his grogginess he dropped it. It bounced down the stairs, around the curve, and out of sight.

The Prince was too tired to care.

He sat down at his small writing desk in the center of the room, and put his head in his hands.

He was not feeling well at all.

* * *

Cinderella waited until she was certain she was alone before sitting up and pulling the sword out of her.

She stood up carefully, feeling off-centered on her stump leg, and then made her way up the blue-carpeted staircase, dragging the sword behind her.

She had only meant to kiss the Prince good night. And instead of behaving like a gentleman, he had lopped her foot off. She wasn't in pain from it, at least, but it was inconvenient to have her bone dragging on the floor, and throwing off her balance with each step.

It took her ages to climb the long stairways to the tower.

When she arrived at the top, she found the door ajar. She pushed it open, and inside was the Prince sitting at a small writing desk.

She stepped in and looked around. There were women's heads on spears encircling the room. Their expressions had been frozen in the frightful grimaces they wore at their moment of death. There was an empty spear as well, one that had been sharpened but never used that rested by the dark window.

"I'm sorry," the Prince mumbled, and she looked up at him. "You weren't supposed to see this. *No one* was supposed to see this."

His skin had turned pale, and he shivered with chills.

"My father will be so angry."

Cinderella looked at him. He had killed all these women— and for what? He didn't even eat them.

He was a scoundrel, and not fit to rule.

Luckily, Cinderella still had the sword.

She chopped off his head with one heavy blow. It fell to the ground of the small room, and rolled in a small circle like a spinning top. The stump of his neck spurted a few shots of blood high into the air, and then settled into a bubbling fountain.

Cinderella bent down and picked up the head. The eyes had already begun to blacken, and the skin was pale with the plague.

He might come back.

And Cinderella decided she didn't want him to come back. He was unjust. She looked around the room, and her eyes settled on the sharpened spike by the window. She shuffled over to it, the bone of her severed foot clinking against the stone.

She raised the head just as the eyes started to open and blink.

"Wait," it whispered.

But Cinderella was done taking orders. She slammed the head down onto the thirteenth stake, and pushed the spear to the top of the skull.

It didn't say anything more.

Cinderella tucked the sword under her arm, and turned toward the door. Outside the window, the first rays of dawn were warming the sky. It was a new day, a new beginning, and she was free now.

She didn't need the Prince.

In the kingdom of death, she was already a queen.

REVENGE OF THE LITTLE MATCH GIRL

"And just what do you think you're doing?" the priest asked. He looked down at the girl in rags, who had apparently spent the night sleeping on the steps of the church.

She sprung up awake, like a soldier expecting attack. Her wide eyes looked up at the priest, and she relaxed—but only for a moment. Then she immediately began to collect her things.

"Didn't I tell you yesterday," the priest asked, "that I didn't want to see you here anymore? Are you listening, girl?"

She paused, a bundle of matches in her hand, and looked up at him. Her eyes had the exhausted look of an old woman ready to die, even though the child couldn't have been more than eleven. Her face was crusted with dirt, and her limp blonde hair hung in tangles over her shoulders.

Her name was Ada, although lately she had been known simply as the little match girl. She had even began to think of herself by that title, it had been so long since anyone used her real name.

"I'm leaving," she croaked, her voice husky with sleep. Ada noticed that her breath was visible in the morning air, and she suddenly felt in her bones how much colder it was today than yesterday.

The priest tapped his foot. "I don't know why you don't sleep out in the alleyways like the other urchins," he said, more to himself than to her. "That's where children like you belong. Not muddying up the fine steps of the church of God."

She tucked her matches into the pockets of her grey rags. "I can't go in the alleys," she said. "It's not safe. There are… *people* there. Sinister folk." Ada felt a shiver go through her body, unrelated to the cold. She turned to the priest, taking hold of his baggy cassock in her hand. "I think," she whispered, "I think they've been trying to get me."

The priest blanched at her stark statement. Then he brushed her hand away, and scoffed. "Fiddlesticks! If people are after you, you probably stole something from them."

Ada sneered. "I didn't *steal*."

The priest rolled his eyes. "God protects the innocent. If you are in danger, then you must deserve it." He smiled, his fat cheeks folding in on themselves. "That's *logic*." He said this as if the girl had never heard of a thing called logic before.

She turned away. The wind scraped against her face like sharp bristles, and howled in the streets. The world was cold, and getting colder.

"Why?" she asked, her voice muffled by the wind. "Why would you never give charity to me or my mother, not once, not even when we needed it the most?" She turned to him. "Isn't that your job? Isn't that your purpose, to help the unfortunate?"

"My *purpose*," the priest said, his tone expressing offense, "is to do *God's* work. Not to provide for those bowing at *Satan's* church."

Ada looked up at him, her brows raised in confusion. "But we didn't…" she said, trailing off.

The priest explained. "Your mother was a harlot, girl. A common street whore. Her kind is never welcome among decent company."

Ada's face smoothed, losing all expression. Her eyes focused on something in the distance. "My mother is dead. She has been dead for a week."

The priest paused. He had been brushing off the steps with his foot, as if dusting away the invisible presence of the girl. He turned to her. "Dead, you say? Was she murdered?" He took a step forward, his eyes alight with curiosity. "Was it someone I know?"

She shook her head, tears forming in her eyes. "A horse cart ran her down in the marketplace." The memory of the scene filled Ada's eyes. She had been buying matches with the coins her mother had given her, and was turning back from the stand when the cart connected with her mother. They had been looking at one another, a smile on her mother's face. Then the next instant she was gone. "They didn't even stop."

"A cart?" The priest lost interest. "For the best, I say. The less of you there are, the less to reproduce." He turned toward the church doors.

Ada sniffled. "But where should I go?"

The priest shrugged without turning around. "How should I know? Now leave me be. I must have quiet while I prepare my sermon."

And with that he entered the church, and slammed the door behind him.

Ada stood for a moment staring at the bulky wooden door. Then the wind blew against her, and the cold brought her back to herself. She made her way down the church steps, and with the movement, she instantly felt pangs of hunger. These were stronger than the pain of the cold, and she knew she had to eat today.

If she sold her entire bundle of matches, she would be able to afford another bundle as well as a warm roll at the bakery. Maybe, she thought, even some hot ale at the tavern. They let you sit inside by the fire if you have the money for a glass. She would have to sell two bundles to afford that though. If each bundle held sixteen matches—she counted on her fingers as she walked—that meant she'd have to sell thirty-two matches to sit down by the fire. She might be able to do that. It was cold enough out. People should want matches.

She made her way through the twisting streets to the marketplace. Lately it had seemed like no one dared show themselves in the early morning except other beggars like herself; but today, not even the beggars were around.

Ada sighed. The plague had taken the vulnerable first.

To make matters worse, winter had settled on the suffering town with a vengeance. She hadn't seen the sun in a week. Storm clouds had darkened the sky, bringing sleet and slush, and a winter wind that tickled her skin like a ghost.

She looked at the empty marketplace.

"Where is everyone?" she asked aloud, turning in a circle.

The stands were all bare, their wooden planks dark and their cloth tarps wilted like old flowers. In the gutters encircling the square were piles of corpses, their grey limbs intertwined so that each body was indistinguishable from the next. They were heaped like sacks in the belly of a ship. Before there had been swarms of flies buzzing around them, filling the air with their noise; but it must have been too cold even for them. The air was silent.

She took a step forward, hearing the click of her shoes against the cobblestone, and listened as the sound echoed through the empty square. She kept going, thinking there might have been something left behind on one of the stalls—an apple, or maybe something she could sell.

Some of the other children used to pick the pockets of the dead. But she had never been able to do that. Not with the chance of finding her mother among the bodies.

She was leaning down over the counter of what used to be the fisherman's stand, her fingers trailing through the darkness that she could reach but not see, when she heard a sound behind her. It was a short scrape of a foot being dragged against the ground.

Ada turned back to the square with her back against the stand, her eyes darting around the marketplace.

It was still empty.

But she knew she had heard something. Even if she didn't see anyone, she knew she had heard something and that meant that someone was there. There were storefronts behind the stands, their windows dark, and between some of the buildings were alleyways black with shadow.

She felt watched. Like there were eyes staring back at her from the darkness. She took a step toward the center of the circular marketplace, where the stands had been cleared so that the carts and wagons could pass through. And she looked at the piles of the dead circled around her.

What she didn't tell the priest, what she couldn't bring herself to believe, was that some of the bodies didn't stay dead. Ada had seen them move before.

Her eyes darted from the corpses to the shadows of the alleyway. There was another scrape, the sound of a foot being dragged, but due to the echo of the open space she couldn't tell from which direction it originated.

"Please," she whispered. "Please don't let them get me."

She thought about running, but her hands and feet were tingling with cold; she didn't trust herself enough not to trip. And if she fell, that would be the end of her.

She stood in the center of the square, slowly rotating. Then she saw it.

Out from the shadows directly across from her came a small boy. It was too dark to recognize him, but his posture and the way he moved so disjointedly told her that he was one of *them*.

She took a step backward, and then thought better of it. Her gaze shifted behind her just in time to see two more figures step out from the fisherman's stand. Then all at once, like a pack of wolves emerging from the trees, there were the dead children at all points around the marketplace.

Ada was startled by how many of them there were. These weren't just the homeless children anymore, the other orphans like herself. These must be nearly all the children in the town. And they were coming for her.

They had stepped into the light now, weaving between the stands to the open cobblestones. There were boys and girls of every age, forming an unbroken lasso of bodies growing tighter around her. She recognized some of the faces: a brother and sister she had known that lived with the woodcutter out in the woods—or at least, they used to; and other children she had seen being dragged through the market by their parents. Then there were the scores of the homeless, whose numbers had grown with the plague, and then suddenly vanished. And last she saw a redheaded boy dressed in green. It was Peter, the ringleader of the boys, who had been fearsome enough when he was healthy, and now looked like a starved creature of Hell. He leered at her with dark eyes, and she faced him. He was still the leader of the pack.

"Don't come any closer," she warned, but her voice sounded weak, even to her own ears. A chill ran through her, and the children around her noticed. It seemed to excite them, and the air became charged with their increased appetites.

Peter took a step toward her—and froze. Then he turned his head left, and all the other children shifted to look in the same direction. Ada glanced at their distracted faces, and then she too looked.

At the end of the marketplace came a warm flickering glow, spilling out from around the corner of a side street. Just over the howl of the wind, there were the sounds of men's voices, the stomping of heavy footsteps.

The horde of children scattered, retreating like roaches back to the shadows.

Ada stood where she was, too surprised to move. From around the corner spilled out a new grouping of men. They brandished lit torches, and stampeded forward through the marketplace like a herd of cattle. They were alive, but perhaps just as dangerous as the children.

They didn't seem to see Ada at all. Their eyes were focused on the opposite end of the marketplace. And when they neared, they parted around her, swallowing her into the middle of the mob.

Ada started walking along with them, glad for the protection, and not wanting to be left alone in the marketplace after they passed. She had to trot, almost run, to keep up with their pace. Inside the group of men, the air had been warmed by their bodies and the torches they carried. She felt her fingers tingle as the heat sent the blood back into them.

She had no idea where the wave of men was taking her. She glanced at their faces, set with a kind of grim determination; they didn't even seem to notice that she had joined them. If they did, they didn't care. She couldn't see over their heads, being the shortest one in the center of a group of grown men. But something about the fierceness of their eyes made her afraid to ask what this was all about.

And then she realized she was the only woman in the crowd. A girl, perhaps, but still—the rest were all men. Grown men at that. Normally a mob had at least a few women in it, feeding the flames of gossip, or, alternately, trying to bargain with their men to be civil.

The crowd marched past the marketplace. The road became narrower, and the little match girl could make out the peaks of buildings on either side. They were passing the shopkeepers' district, and then turning out to a street with a marked incline. Ahead, looming over the heads of even the tallest men, were the high-perched walls of Bluebeard Palace.

It took some time for the mob to work its way up the streets. With the heat and the activity, Ada began to sweat. It was so hot in this inner circle that she even took off her gloves, slipping the small pair into a pocket of her dress. Now that she was warm, all of her attention was focused on her increasing hunger. Whenever the mob stopped, she knew she would have to sell them some matches.

Finally, the crowd reached the top of the hill, and pressed themselves against the outer gates of the palace. Ada looked up at the grand structure, the largest building she had ever seen. The cold stone walls were especially grey in the overcast morning light, and the few lights that glowed within the windows seemed weak, ready to die out at any moment.

All except one.

From a high tower, there was black smoke billowing out from an open stained-glass window. A fire burned inside, apparently contained, and the match girl had the impression that this was not part of the mob's doing. It was something purposeful on the part of the royalty.

But why would they burn one of their own rooms? Maybe someone had died there, and they were trying to flush out the disease. Or maybe they had seen the mob arrive, and wanted to destroy something before they found it.

The palace guards were already at the gate. A representative of the mob stepped forward, a burly man with a heavy stomach. Ada thought she recognized him as the town tailor, who had a reputation for his bravery, but she couldn't be sure. He held up a torch and shouted:

"We demand an audience with the King! We demand to know what happened to our daughters, sisters, and neighbors who attended the Prince's royal ball and never returned to see the sun again. We demand answers!"

The guards said something back, too low for Ada to hear. It was evidently a refusal.

"If you don't hear our request," the tailor shouted, "we will break down the gates and see him ourselves!"

The mob responded with a deep-set hurrah, and the

guards shifted nervously. They sent one of their numbers running toward the palace, and the men of the mob were momentarily calmed.

Ada knew this was her opportunity.

She reached into her satchel and retrieved the bundle of matches. She held them over her head and cried, "Matches! Matches for sale!"

The men took a step away from her without even glancing in her direction. She was undeterred. Ada was no stranger to being a pest.

"Matches," she said, working her way to stand in front of a man—the baker. "Ah," she said, "and how's business today, sir?"

His eyes darted down to her for a moment. That was all she required.

"I may be in your shop later today," she said, "for one of your warm rolls." At even the thought of food her stomach pinched and gurgled. She forced herself to smile, which was a pitiful sight on someone as dirty and small as she was.

"Shop's closed," he said gruffly, turning his back to her.

She circled to his front. "Always good to take a day for yourself," she said, her voice growing desperate. "Perhaps sit by the fire, have a nice smoke." She waved the matches in front of him. "Nothing like a good smoke by the fire."

He turned away, but another man who happened to overhear reached into his pocket, pulled out a cigar, and bit off the tip. Ada was ready with an outstretched match by the time he put it to his lips.

"Don't need that," he muttered. "No sense paying when you can get a light for free. Am I right?" And he leaned over to his neighbor, who held one of the lit torches, and puffed until his cigar caught. He inhaled, and then let out a cloud of smoke.

Ada coughed. She always choked on the smell of smoke, but she had the smell so closely associated with being able to purchase food that it made her even hungrier. It was a nauseous sort of hunger, though, and it left her lightheaded.

She continued through the crowd, finding the men distracted and irritable, and unable to find a single buyer for a match. At least it was warm, she told herself.

But the truth was, the crowd wasn't packed as tightly now as it had been when traveling through the street. Without the heat of exertion, the sweat on Ada's forehead, neck, and back had turned icy. The worst though was the sweat around her toes, which had turned cold first and now sent needles of pain into her feet. She reached into her pocket and pulled back on her gloves.

The men hushed, and Ada looked up to see the guard returning from the palace. He had a line of soldiers behind him with long barreled guns over their shoulders. Ada stepped behind one of the men for protection, and stashed her matches away in her satchel.

"Where's the King?" demanded the tailor.

The guard's proud face didn't even flinch at his cry. He walked up to the edge of the gate, and then pulled a scroll from under his arm. He coughed into his white-gloved hand, and then started reading.

"His Royal Highness, the King, wishes to express his concern over the recent disappearance of a great many women of the township." There were murmurs in the mob, and he raised his voice to speak over them. "*However*, due to a great many royal duties and tasks, he is unable to address you himself, and orders the immediate dispersal of all parties currently trespassing upon these gates."

"Where are our women?" a man from the crowd shouted, interrupting the guard. The rest of the mob raised their torches and let out a roar.

"*If* any parties should refuse to depart," the guard shouted over them, "their actions shall be regarded as treason, and punishable by death." He lowered the scroll and gazed at the crowd, a lingering trace of pleasure in his calm eyes. "That is all."

The men started to knock one against each other, goading each other on and refusing to let anyone retreat. Ada felt like a rowboat lost at sea, right as a typhoon had begun. If the men barely noticed her before, they had completely forgotten about her presence now. A man bumped her shoulder, and sent her into the legs of another man. She pushed herself off, and barely had time to balance when the tailor let out another cry.

"If they will not give us our women, we will take them ourselves!" he shouted. The men lifted their arms in solidarity. They were all standing in place now, and Ada was able to readjust her shawl. But this proved to be only the calm before the storm.

A shot rang out from one of the guard's guns. At the same moment, the tailor's head cracked, blood splattering out on the crowd as he fell to the ground. All panic broke loose, and the men lost their nerve, dropping their torches to the ground, and pushing their way back from the gates and toward the street.

The little match girl was shoved down in the melee. She hit the cold ground and managed to land on her palms, the dampness soaking through her thin gloves. Not more than a moment later, a hard boot kicked her in the side with such force that she flipped onto her back, landing hard on the ground. Another man stepped on her ankle as he ran, and through the pain, she had one disturbingly sober thought.

This, she thought, is how it feels to be trampled. *This* is how my mother felt when the horse cart ran her down.

The pain of that realization made all her limbs grow weak, and she slumped over on her side facing the palace, not able to get up as a third man whacked her in the stomach with the toe of his boot.

Her head to the ground, she heard their footsteps clomp

away down the lane. The guards at the gate retreated into the palace, and the little match girl was left on the ground among the searing stubs of wood that had been the torches. The ground was damp and icy cold, and the little match girl didn't think she'd be able to get back up on her own. Not for a while, at least.

She lay there in a daze, looking up at the curls of black smoke rising from the high tower of the palace. And she wondered, from whom did the King buy *his* matches?

It was only with dim awareness that she heard a set of footsteps approaching from behind. Maybe it was one of the men coming for the body of the tailor, which was still slumped near the palace gates. The steps came closer until a hazy shadow fell over her.

She hadn't considered the person might be coming for her. No one ever came for her. No one except—

Fear bolted through her, and she turned to look up at the stranger.

It was a woman, an adult. Ada's eyes squinted against the light, and before she had time to react, the stranger had bent down and scooped her up. The stranger carried her away from the gates, off the road, and into a throng of bushes that lined the edge of the palace. She dropped Ada in a muddy clearing, and then lowered to her knees, hovering over the girl. It was only then that the stranger's face was close enough for Ada to make out, even in the low light of the clearing.

"Grandma!" she gasped. Relief filled her, but only for a moment. Then she shook with double the worry of before. Her grandma, her father's mother, had refused to help Ada and her mother when they had lost their home. She had turned the other way as her own granddaughter and daughter-in-law were forced to become beggars. This sudden shift toward charity rang false to Ada, but there was a much greater cause for alarm.

Three weeks ago, her grandma had caught the plague—and died.

Ada struggled back. "Please," she said, "it's me, Ada!" Her grandma looked down at her, the skin around her eyes blackened like the sockets of a skull, and her white hair frazzled, with leaves and burrs stuck in the tangles. She looked very different than the dignified older woman that Ada had known, and seemed more comfortable now hunched over in the bushes like an animal.

"Don't you remember me?" Ada asked, still trying to back away. Her grandma saw this, and grasped her shoulder with a cold grip. "I'm your granddaughter!"

The old woman looked down at Ada, as if recognizing her for the first time. Ada forced herself not to look away, even though it meant seeing the blotches and tears of the old woman's sagging grey skin. Ada noticed that she still had her jeweled earrings in, and a bitter part of Ada couldn't help but think that some people never change.

"*Aaaa-duhhh?*" her grandma growled, struggling to enunciate the words.

Ada felt tears of joy form in her eyes. "Yes," she cried, nodding. "Yes, that's right!"

At this confirmation, a shift took place. A fire seemed to ignite inside the old woman's faded eyes, and Ada could almost feel the rage radiating off of her. The old woman opened her mouth to expose all of her teeth, and snarled with an unmistakable indignation.

Ada cringed. She had obviously taken the wrong tactic. Her grandma barely liked her in life; in death she wouldn't be bound by the rules of propriety.

Her grandma ripped away Ada's shawl, and started tearing at her side with her sharp fingernails. Ada screamed, but the old woman didn't stop. She pulled apart the fabric of Ada's dress until the girl could feel the cold air on her bare stomach.

"No," Ada cried. "It wasn't our fault. We didn't make him leave. He left us. *He left us!*"

The old woman paused at the mention of her son.

Her son, Ada's father, had disappeared in the spring, leaving his family and friends behind without a trace of his whereabouts. The old woman had blamed Ada and her mother for driving him away; this was the source of her hatred for the pair.

"I'm sorry he's gone," Ada said, trembling in the cold. "I didn't want him to go either. I—"

Ada's words were interrupted by a guttural moan from the old woman. She shook her head back and forth, like a dog shaking off water, and then refocused on Ada, the nails of her fingers digging into Ada's shoulder.

She opened her mouth, and clamped down on Ada's stomach like a snake.

Ada screamed out, kicking and beating against the old woman. She was cold and weak and beaten, but she wasn't about to sit back and die. She grabbed the old woman by her white hair, and pulled her head off of her with all her might. The old woman's head was forced back, but she wouldn't unlock her jaw. Ada saw the skin of her stomach stretching more and more as she tore the woman away from her.

"Grandma, no!" she cried. "Let *go*."

Ada dropped the head, and tried to gouge the old woman in the eyes with her thumbs. But her fingers were too stiff from the cold, and she only ended up poking her.

The little girl might have gone on scuffling with the old woman, except at that moment, another woman came out from the trees. She wore a shimmering blue ball gown smeared with gore. Even before she opened her mouth with a roar, Ada could plainly see that this new woman was one of *them*.

She hobbled forward, dragging along one foot that was nothing more than a stump, and seized the old woman's head with both hands. The old woman opened her mouth in surprise, and Ada was freed. She was about to turn to thank this mysterious stranger, when the woman in the ball gown turned toward her with a growl.

She wasn't saving Ada. She wanted Ada all for herself.

Just as she was about to lunge, Ada's grandma snatched the back of the woman's gown, and knocked her to the ground. Ada stood up on shaky legs, backing away. She had managed to grab her shawl, which was now wet and covered with mud, and pushed through the bushes back to the road. She looked back once, and saw her grandma wrestling with the stranger, both of their jaws snapping at each other like reptiles.

The little match girl stumbled as quickly as she could down the slope of the road that led away from the palace. The bite on her stomach ached, and she could feel the opening in her flesh tearing as she forced herself to move at top speed. She wanted to put as much distance between herself and those creatures as she could before stopping to check herself.

The day had gotten colder. Or, in her wet and torn garments, it certainly felt that way to Ada. She could still see her breath as her chest heaved in and out, and the vapor seemed denser than before. She could even see steam rising from puddles on the ground, and that never happened unless it was bitterly cold. She took off her gloves, which were so soaked that they were chilling her more than warming her, and stuffed them into her pocket.

When she finally reached the first outcrop of buildings in the town, her body was a patchwork of frozen and sweaty territories. She slipped behind the side of a building's front stoop, and started to inspect herself.

There were clear outlines of her grandma's teeth in an uneven red ring on her stomach. Some of the skin had been torn away, hanging down in a useless flap and revealing flesh that looked like raw meat underneath. There was blood, but not as much as Ada had expected, and the cuts were not deep.

It stung like nothing she ever had ever known though. Perhaps that was because of the cold. Ada looked closer, and saw little ice crystals forming on the coagulated blood. She needed to cover the wound, to protect it from the freezing air.

She looked at her garments. She was wearing a grey dress, a shawl, and carrying a satchel. Not much to work with. She knelt down and tore the hem off her dress. The thin fabric gave easily, and she was able to tear a long strip all the way around. She stood up, and pressed the fabric over her wound, wincing at the pain. Then she wrapped the remainder of it around her waist. She was so thin that it went around twice easily, and she tied the ends in a knot.

It hurt, worse than before, but she felt better knowing the wound wasn't exposed to the cold. She was also glad to see that the blood on her stomach matched the dismal coloring of her dress, and it would look like any other stain rather than a current wound.

It was dangerous to display a wound in a town beset by plague. And it was utterly stupid to do so while trying to sell matches.

Maybe, she thought, hobbling into the street, maybe since I look so pitiful, some kind souls will take pity on me, and buy my lot of matches in one go. Maybe this whole nightmare will be worth it, if it ends with me sipping a mug of warm ale by the fire before the sun goes down. It's only a bite, after all. Only a bite.

A smile formed on her dirty, exhausted face. But on her next step, her makeshift bandage pressed against her wound, and she winced. She forgot about pleasurable things, and concentrated on walking carefully back to the marketplace.

There were people here now. Perhaps not as many as

usual, but the small little huddles of shoppers were preferable to the emptiness of the early morning.

"Thirty-two matches," she whispered to herself. "Only thirty-two matches."

She walked past the piles of bodies, which were not nearly as threatening when there were people around, and made her way into the marketplace.

If only it were as easy to sell matches as it was to sell fresh bread and milk. The trouble was that anyone who really wanted to buy matches could go into the apothecary around the bend and buy an entire bundle, the way Ada had, for the same price she bought hers for. *Her* customers were merely impulse buyers, men who smoked but were too clumsy to remember their matches, or women who never planned more than a day ahead, buying only enough matches to light their fire until tomorrow.

Normally, there were plenty of people who didn't plan ahead roaming about town. But it seemed that those who hadn't planned ahead were the first to die, and everyone that remained had enough matches to last an entire winter.

But still, she had to try.

Using the arm on her unwounded side, Ada held up her bundle of matches into the air. "Matches for sale," she bellowed. Her voice quavered in an odd way, and she realized she was shivering. The wetness of the mud had soaked into her clothes, and even the patch of fabric around her waist was wet with her own blood. She sniffled, feeling the cold now in her fingers as she held them up in the air. "Matches!" she cried. "Matches for sale!"

Naturally, no one noticed her. Ada had learned that, when you appear in the same place selling the same wares, day after day, you had a tendency to fade into the background. She would have to be more assertive.

She started blocking passersby, standing in their way and waving the bundle of matches in the air. "Matches! Cheap, easy-burn matches!" Most people walked around her, avoiding eye contact. Every now and again she'd get a dirty look.

But this was her job. She knew she had a right to be here. Anyone could sell in the marketplace.

"Yes," said an older woman, locking eyes with Ada. "Matches." She reached into her purse.

"How many, madam?" Ada asked. "Three? Five?"

"Just the one," the old woman said. "That will get me through the night."

"Are you sure, madam? It's s-s-supposed to be especially c-c-cold tonight." The woman looked at Ada, noticing her dirty appearance. Ada sniffled, and the woman held her coin back.

"You're not… infected, are you, girl?" she asked, sneering as she surveyed Ada.

"Just c-c-cold," Ada said, her shoulders shivering violently.

But then, without warning, Ada was seized with a terrible coughing fit. She heaved and bent over with the pain of it, clutching her chest. The bite on her stomach burned with the movement. She struggled to breathe, at last clearing her throat by spraying out the blood that had been choking her. It landed on the cobblestones, a red speckling, and a few drops had flown onto the matchsticks in her hand.

The old woman shook her head, backing up. "Never mind!"

"But," Ada said, still coughing, "I'm fine!" She tried to chase after the woman, desperate for the sale, but the pain on her stomach throbbed, making her lose her balance. She stumbled forward, letting her feet find their way on the wet cobblestones without looking where she was going.

"Watch it!" cried a boy.

Ada looked up to see a boy about her age standing before her. He was plump, with fine clothes and ruffles around his collar. He had narrowly avoided her, and was staring at her through squinted, piggish eyes.

Then she noticed a butler behind him, carrying an armful of packages.

Ada looked back at the boy, her eyes bleary. "Do you," she said, sniffling, "want some matches?" She held up the blood-splattered handful.

"Don't *touch* me," the boy sneered. He knocked into Ada as he passed, making her lose her balance and sending her to the ground.

She barely even felt the fall. Her hands had grown numb, and her head was swimming. She sniffled, looking up from the ground as the boy and his servant entered the tavern. A blast of warm air traveled out from the open door, hitting her in the face with the smell of fresh-baked pies. Her muscles seemed to melt as she savored the scent, holding it in as long as she could, and then reluctantly letting it go in an exhale.

She struggled to her feet, and wiped her nose across the back of her hand. Her nose barely felt the touch of her hand. She wrapped her shawl around her head tighter, trying to keep her ears warm. She could still feel her ears, although she wouldn't mind if *they* went numb; they ached and burned with the cold.

She shivered, and turned back to the market.

Her eyes went wide with what she saw.

"No," she whispered. "No, no, no."

All along the marketplace the air was full of snowflakes. They fell on the stands and the cobblestones, fluttering down like ashes after a cremation.

Ada shook her head, her eyes filling with tears. She had hoped the weather might hold out another week. Christmas was coming, and usually around then even the sorry folk of the town felt charitable. Certainly they'd be more giving than now. But snowfall this early would only hurt sales, and make life on the streets even more miserable for her.

She looked out, her fears confirmed. The women in the marketplace were hustling away, holding their hats to their heads as they fled the first signs of snow as if it were raining molten lava. The shopkeepers and those attending the stands remained—for now—but they never bought matches, not even once. And Ada still had thirty-two matches to sell before she could sit down by the warmth of a fire.

She began to cry. She couldn't help it, the tears rolling down her face, and her nose running worse than ever. What was she supposed to do now? The snow fell, swirling in the air and then sticking to the ground, turning the cobblestones white. She looked up at the clouds, and could see the dense fog of more snow to come. There was no sign that this would pass. In fact, it looked like the start of a blizzard.

Ada sank to the ground, huddling her knees to her body, and holding her face in her hands. She had counted on selling the matches. Maybe not thirty-two—even in her mind, that had always been a bit of a stretch—but at least a few, enough to buy a roll of bread, or a few pieces of fruit.

But she hadn't even sold one. Not one! She couldn't remember another day that she had been so unfortunate, not when she was really trying. And what if tomorrow was no better? What if she never sold a match again? What happened to the people nobody cared about?

She lifted her eyes to the marketplace, to the piles of the dead, and had her answer.

She sat in silence until the last of the merchants were packing up. The snow was coming down more heavily now, forming little drifts and gullies, and erasing the familiar landmarks with white dust. Ada watched with detachment as a lamplighter used a pole to light the streetlamps. It should have filled her with fear that their light was necessary this early in the day, but it didn't. Her only thought was that, with all the lamps that he lit, night after night and day after day, he had never once bought one of her matches.

She heard the bell of the shop door opening behind her. She didn't bother to turn.

"Come along, Master Jack," said the humble voice of a servant. "Your mother is waiting for you."

"Look, it's *snowing*," the boy whined. "I hate snow!"

"It's only for a few minutes," the servant said, trying to placate the boy. "Then you'll be inside with a hot meal by the fire."

Ada looked up. The boy and his servant didn't notice that she was sitting there. Then she realized, since the snow was falling on top of her, she probably blended into the background even more than she usually did.

The pair set off into the blustering wind. The snow flurries masked them almost immediately, their outlines growing fainter in the fog as their feet crunched in the snow. Ada looked around her then, at the empty marketplace, the dim lighting. She was right out in the open if she stayed here. She wouldn't even be able to see anyone coming. Or anything.

Quickly, she got to her feet.

"Oh," she cried, putting a hand to her stomach. The bite pulsed with a sharp pain when she moved. She grimaced, and forced herself to trudge forward in the snow, listening for the sounds of the boy's complaints ahead of her.

The icy wind slashed her face, making her cheeks burn with the cold. She tried to wrap her shawl around her tighter, but was startled to find that her hands were stiff claws. She looked down at her immobile fingers, and saw how white her skin had become. There were blisters on her waxy skin, swollen and surprisingly firm. She fumbled in her pockets as she shuffled forward through the snow, trying to find her gloves. When she did manage to pull them out, holding them up with the palms of her numb hands, she found that the gloves were frozen solid. She let them drop to the ground, and thrashed forward in the snow, keeping her hands inside her shawl.

She followed the boy and his servant through the streets, working to keep up with their pace, and not at all concerned if they saw her following.

They didn't. They probably wouldn't have noticed her following even on a clear day, bright and sunny. People like that didn't notice girls like Ada.

Her hands and feet ached with cold. Ignoring the pain, she trudged carefully through the snow, suddenly worried she'd trip out here, in the middle of the street, and be run over by a passing carriage. She looked ahead, at the figures several houses before her, and then gasped as they suddenly disappeared. She opened her eyes wider, and dug her feet through the snow that now came up nearly to her knees, until she came closer. Then she saw that they hadn't disappeared; they had gone inside, and shut the door behind them.

Ada hadn't really planned this far ahead. She instinctually knew it was safer around people than alone, but she hadn't for a moment expected this pair to come to her aid. Still, she made her way the rest of the distance to the building, the cold whistling in her ears.

It was a townhouse, three stories tall and pressed up against its neighbor, with a small alleyway on the far side. Ada huddled down in the snow outside the large front window, cleared the frost on the glass with her clawed hand, and settled down to watch the scene inside as if watching a pantomime on stage.

The first thing she noticed was the fire, blazing in the fireplace directly across from the window. There were at least four logs feeding the flames, and a stack of fresh logs to the side of the hearth in a polished stand. To the right of the fireplace was the doorway, both to the outside, and presumably the next room. Two soft sitting chairs faced each other on either side of the doorway, with emerald green pillows with golden tassels. On the left side of the room was a Christmas tree, glowing with white candles, and hiding several large, intricately wrapped packages underneath.

But the main focal point of the room was in the center: a long table placed in front of the fire, laid with a bountiful feast. There was a golden turkey, its juices glistening in the firelight; bowls piled with stuffed figs, green apples, cherries, and grapes; steaming pies with lattice crusts; mountains of cookies, sprinkled with powdered sugar, chocolate chunks, and drizzled with sticky caramel; and, in the center of the table, with a serving ladle resting on the side, was a crystal bowl of hot ale, with fresh fruit floating on its shining surface.

Ada had her face pressed against the glass, trying desperately but unable to smell the great feast only a few steps away from her. Her stomach turned with hunger, and the wild notion occurred to her to break through the window, grab what she could, and run off into the street. She might have, too, if she had been able to manipulate her hands, and if she weren't trembling violently with her body's futile attempt to generate its own heat.

Besides, just then the servant opened the doorway to the room. He didn't notice Ada at the window, and busied himself with setting up a pair of tall candles on the table. Ada watched with some resentment as he pulled out a long match, which she was positive did not come from her, and used it to light the candles. Once this was done, he turned back to the doorway and gestured with a stirring of his fingers for the boy to enter.

The little master waddled in, his nose held in the air, and although Ada couldn't hear the words, she was sure that he was complaining about something. He pushed past the servant and sat down in the chair at the center of the table, facing Ada and the window. He didn't see her, too busy looking nowhere in particular as he talked out of the side of his mouth. The servant pushed in the boy's chair with some effort, and then struggled to tie a napkin around his neck.

Then Ada had the unfortunate pleasure of watching as the servant offered the boy first a prime slice of the turkey, then a plump grape, then a spoonful of mashed potatoes, and then an assortment of other rare delicacies which Ada had never even seen before—only to have the boy, each time he was offered one of these, turn up his nose at the selection, and push it away with his fat hand.

Ada gaped, watching as this pampered child turned down foods finer than any she had ever tasted, and she was in tears, watching as the servant returned the forkfuls and spoonfuls back to their dishes, untouched, to be thrown later to the dogs. All while Ada watched, freezing, starving, crying outside his window.

Finally, the servant's shoulders deflated as he must have let out a frustrated sigh. His lips moved, and whatever he said made the boy perk up and clap his hands. He slammed his fists down, and the servant rushed around the entire length of the table, searching for something, and stopping when he found one of the steaming pies.

He brought it before the master and laid it down before him. The boy took one look at it, and then stuck his thumb right into the center of it.

Ada was shocked. Even she knew better manners than that.

The boy pulled out his thumb, and brought it to his mouth, gobbling off the purple plum filling. The servant merely watched, standing by to occasionally dab some of the mess from the boy's chin with a handkerchief mono-grammed *JH*.

The door of the room opened again, and in walked the boy's mother, a beautiful woman with radiant blonde curls. She was dressed in a fashionable deep green dress with elab-orate bows, and she held herself with grace as she crossed to the center of the room. She planted a kiss on the crown of her little boy's head. He grimaced, and she ignored it, cover-ing his face with kisses as he tried to slap her away.

Then the boy froze, looking directly at Ada for the first time. His eyes went wide, and he shouted something, point-ing at her. Ada's reflexes were too slow to duck down, and a moment later both the boy's mother and servant were staring at her, too.

The boy was still yelling, and the mother put a gentle hand on his shoulder to quiet him. Without taking her eyes off of Ada, she walked regally around the length of the table, and then stepped up to the window.

Ada looked up at her, feeling her shoulders shivering, and knowing her eyes were marked with frozen tears. She looked up at this woman, and was reminded of her own mother. Maybe Ada reminded the woman of a daughter she never had, too. They looked into one another's eyes, and Ada felt that, at last, someone was looking at her. Someone was *noticing* her. And a hope that she didn't even know she was still capable of fluttered inside her chest. At last this nightmare existence was over, this lonely life, and she could be part of a family again.

Ada smiled shyly. The woman spread out her arms, as if to embrace her, even through the glass. And then she pulled the curtains shut, and left Ada in the dark.

It took her a moment to realize what had happened. The wind howled in her ears, and all the pain and misery she had been distracted from returned to her at once, more intense than before. It was colder now, not just outside but inside Ada as well. She couldn't feel her fingers, and her face was raw and numb. She hadn't noticed while watching, but the entire time it had been snowing, and the snowdrift reached all the way up to her waist. She pushed her way out of it, the snow sticking to her clothes, and stumbled, barely able to walk, around to the alley beside the house.

The wind howled again, this time louder. And then Ada realized the howls weren't the wind. The howls were wolves.

She saw them in the distance, indistinct grey specks at the end of the lane. Ada plunged into the snow, burrowing in it as best she could, and peeped out from the front of her snow pile.

She waited. It was a few minutes before she saw anything, but when she did, she had the sense not to move.

Walking down the middle of the snowy street was a pack of large grey wolves. In the center of the pack, riding the largest wolf, was a young woman wearing a long red cloak, with the hood pulled over her face. She was turning her head in either direction as the wolves made their slow way down the street.

Ada did not move. Ada did not move even when the girl in red looked directly at her, and she saw that the girl's mouth was coated with blood. She did not move after they passed, not even when she was sure they had enough time to get to the end of the lane. She did not move for what felt like twenty or thirty minutes.

Then, realizing all at once how long it had been since she had moved, panic rushed through her. This was serious, she realized. It was getting colder, and it didn't look like she'd be able to leave the alley safely until after the blizzard. The cold was piercing her ears so sharply that she started to worry they'd break off altogether. They hurt even more than the bite on her stomach, which was now tender and sore, but didn't throb unless she moved that area of her body directly.

Then she remembered the matches.

They were still in the satchel she wore over her shoulder, and with great effort she leaned forward and raised an arm to grab it. But when she tried to feel for it, she found that she couldn't feel her hand at all, just a dull tugging at her wrist. Confused, she pulled her hand back in front of her.

It was worse than before, much worse. The hand had turned a waxy shade of blue, all except her fingertips, which were black. The skin was blistered and swollen, but she couldn't feel anything. She lifted her other hand from the snow, and found it looked the same. She touched them together, and her heart raced with anxiety at the strange sensation of neither hand being able to feel the other. It was like holding two inanimate pieces of wood and touching them together.

The matches. She needed the matches now.

She leaned forward again, this time shifting her body back and forth until the satchel fell over her neck and head. The wooden matches spilled out in the snow, but the heads of the matches were still safe inside the satchel.

Ada pressed her hands through the sleeves of her dress and under her armpits to warm them. They felt like ice, and she wasn't sure if she was warming them or freezing her body even more. After what must have been five whole minutes, she finally had some feeling in her hands. Not in her fingertips—those were still numb—but in her palms, and the little crook between her thumb and index finger. And what she felt there was an incredible burning pain.

"Ow, ow, ow," she gasped, but refused to move her hands away until she could pinch her thumb and forefinger together to hold a match.

Then she took her hands out and used one to pick up a long match. She used her shoulder to wipe off the frost next to her on the brick wall, and scratched the head of the match across the clean space.

It sent off sparks at once, and Ada held the flame close to her, hunching down to protect it from the wind. She stared at it, and could feel its weak warmth on the skin around her eyes. She didn't know that even your eyes could be cold, and she didn't realize how cold hers were until she had the little flame next to them to warm them up again.

She looked deep into the flame, and as she looked, she imagined what it would be like to sit in front of a fireplace. What would her day have been like if she had been able to sell those thirty-two matches? She might be sitting in the tavern right now, warming her feet as she threw another log onto the fire. It would spark and—

The fire disappeared.

She held the burnt out match in her hand, the trail of smoke curling up. She sniffled, and felt dizzy. Already the warmth on her face began to chill, and without the match's warm glow the world seemed even more bleak and lifeless than before. She looked down at the satchel.

She had plenty of matches.

She reached down cautiously to fetch another. A sensible part of her had the nervous thought that if she used up all her matches, she might live through the night, but she'd be without anything to sell tomorrow.

Ada shook her head. So what? she thought. No one bought her matches anyway. And how else was she supposed to keep warm?

She scratched the next match on the wall, and held it close, using her hand to guard it from the wind. The flame danced before her. The smell, oddly enough, reminded Ada of her hunger.

She thought of the table set with splendors, the golden goose and plates piled high with fresh fruits and sweet cookies. Even thinking about it now, she could smell the food: the savory spices of the broth that basted the goose, the tart but clean smell of sliced apples, the deep cinnamon and brown sugar of a warm, crumbly cookie. If only that little boy hadn't been so selfish. If only that mother had invited Ada inside. Instead all that food is just sitting there, going to waste. And Ada thought of how even a little bite would have satisfied her for the rest of the night. She could practically see her hand reaching out, could feel the greasy tenderness of the flesh of the goose, the resistance as she pulled off a chunk, and how it would taste when she brought it to her mouth and—

The match went out.

Ada threw it down with spite. She reached down and took a handful of fresh matches, dragged them against the wall, and watched with greed as their heads caught with white sparks that soon turned into a warm orange glow. She held the bundle in front of her in the snow, her own personal bonfire.

She didn't know why anyone would refuse her matches. The heat coming off the large flames was extraordinary. If this could keep going, she might just be able to stay out here forever. She wouldn't even mind.

The flames lit up her face, reflecting in her eyes, and as she stared into the rippling waves of heat, she saw the skin of her hands blister and boil. She started shivering again, and it caused the flames to dance in front of her, making streaks that burned into her vision. She was lightheaded, and nauseous, but she smiled as she looked into the fire.

And in the fire she could see faces. First eyes looking back at her, then a mouth, and then the mouth smiled. She had the thought that she was growing delirious, but somehow she couldn't bring herself to care.

It was her mother's face in the fire. The vision's eyebrows raised, astonished at Ada's state. "What are you doing out here?" she asked.

Ada shivered. "Nobody wants me." She wasn't sure if she said this out loud, or asked it in her mind. But her mother seemed to hear her nonetheless. "Nobody will buy my matches."

"That's nonsense," her mother said. "I'll take the whole lot of them."

Ada didn't know how to react. "But... you're dead. You can't buy matches. Can you?"

"I can buy whatever I wish," she said primly. "And I'll take a few for your father as well."

Ada opened her mouth to speak, but her mother interrupted.

"And before you say, 'He's dead, too,' you'd better turn around and see for yourself."

Ada turned, and saw her father in the doorway, holding a

candle in his hand. He was just as Ada had remembered him, better even. He had color in his cheeks, and a kind smile.

He crossed the room—they were in a room now, her old house—and sat down across from her at the table. Her mother was sitting next to him, and he set the candle on the table.

"I'm here, too," said a familiar voice, and Ada turned to her left, and there was her Grandma, rosy-cheeked and laughing. "We're *all* together again."

"Oh," Ada said, "I thought—I thought you were dead."

The old woman smiled. "But I am dead, dear. But I *am*."

"We're all dead," her mother said. "Do you know how you can tell?"

"No," Ada whispered.

Then a peculiar thing happened. The candle in the center of the table started to float in the air. But not the candle, only the spark of the flame. Ada turned to her mother, to ask what was happening, but her mother put her finger to her lips to hush Ada.

The light rose into the air, and Ada saw the wooden planks of the ceiling fade away, revealing the night sky. The flame rose among the stars, and then streaked across them in a wild blaze.

Her mother whispered to her, "When you see a falling star, it means someone has died." And Ada turned to her, to ask who had died.

But instead of her mother's glowing face, Ada saw nothing but a brick wall.

It was dark, and she was in the alley again.

She tried to speak, but found her face was stiff. It was unbearably, unimaginably cold. The muscles of her neck were sore, but she forced her head down to see the cluster of burnt matches gripped in her hands. Her fingers were covered with snow. And below them, snow had covered her completely. It looked like she had sat down in a bath of sparkling white crystals. She couldn't see her legs at all; only the tops of her arms and hands were above the snow level.

Then she looked up, and snow fell from her shawl into her face. She didn't even feel it.

She saw stars in the sky, and was surprised it was already night. How long had she been sitting here? How long—

But she found her emotions were oddly neutral about her situation. She knew she should be worried; she could tell she was dying. But she just didn't care.

She was still looking up, and across the sky flickered a barrage of falling stars. It looked like the heavens were collapsing, raining down in a torrential downpour of fire and brimstone. And Ada wondered: How many people had to die for that to happen?

This was her last coherent thought. She had some dim awareness for a space of time after, mostly of the wind whipping past her ears. But soon enough even that was gone, and the little match girl became as insensible and lifeless as the snow around her.

*   *   *

She had died with her eyes open, smiling up at the stars that only she could see. But she woke up angry.

Even before the morning sun had lit the snow around her face from pitch black to a blank white, Ada was fuming.

But since she was essentially frozen in a block of snow, without the use of her limbs, she had some time to think.

She thought about how she had died. Not just in the snow, but how she had died in the middle of a crowded town, with many people who knew she was suffering, and who could have easily helped her. It would have cost these people nothing to simply let her sleep on the floor, or eat some of their leftovers. Instead they ignored her.

She also thought about what she had lost. She had some

consciousness now, but she knew she wasn't alive. She had seen the other children in the alleyways. She knew she would never grow up. She would always be the *little* match girl.

That was their fault, too.

The snow melted in front of her face, and she looked out at the mound of white that she had been buried in overnight. She was no longer cold. Or rather, she no longer *felt* cold. She had some ability to recognize that it was indeed still cold, the way she could recognize the changes in color with her vision, but it was not a sensation in her body anymore.

She also felt no pain. The only feelings that still circulated under her skin were a deep and unmitigated hunger roaring in her belly, and an equally hot rage bubbling up inside of her.

She twisted, cracking the ice that held her in place, and rolled out away from the houses. She was still stiff from her night in the cold, and her movements were jerky and un-natural as she pushed herself to her feet. She walked back to the street, gazing about her at the white wonderland of pure, unmarked snow.

Then she lifted her head up with a crack, and saw the house of the boy she had followed the night before. Her lips curled as she remembered the curtains being closed. She took a step forward, and saw that the curtains were *still* closed. Closed against her.

Well, not anymore.

Ada shuffled up to the window, raised her arm, and brought down the bone of her elbow against the frosted glass. It shattered, and Ada reached her arm inside to unlock the larger window. She crept inside, not bothering to close it behind her, and was happy to find that she could see very well even in the darkness of the room. It was almost easier to see here than it had been outside.

She dragged her feet across the wooden floor, leaving a trail of wet snow and mud. She went around the table to the fireplace. A few cinders were still glowing, but the fire was nearly out. Ada turned her head to the pre-cut logs in their tray by the fireplace, and hobbled over to pick up a few, throwing them into the fire.

She found a handful of matches on the table. One had been burnt already to light the candles, and she left that one behind. She lit the logs in the fireplace, and placed the remaining matches in her pocket. Then she sat down, and let her stiff limbs thaw in front of the fire. The feeling in them didn't return, of course, but she was able to move her fingers once again, each individually, and the stiff muscles of her neck and shoulders stopped creaking when she moved them, as if the warmth had oiled her sockets.

It was around this time that the mother stepped into the room. She entered yawning, an arm over her face, but stopped instantly as she took in the scene.

"My floor!" she cried, looking down at the wet pools of melted snow. Then she looked at Ada, and charged for her. "You little *urchin!* I will have you thrown in the darkest, coldest cell of the—"

Ada turned to her with a smile. On her pale and blistered face, it was a frightening sight. The tip of her nose had purpled from frostbite, and her skin had peeled away in grey patches.

The woman took a step back, and Ada pounced to her feet. She was glad for the fire; she wouldn't have had it so easy otherwise. The woman reached behind her for the door, but before she could lay a hand on the knob, Ada jumped and bit down on her wrist.

The woman tried to fight back, but she was no match for Ada and her hunger. With a quick slash to the throat, the woman was down. She didn't even fight back as Ada dug her teeth into her skin, and swallowed down the flesh.

When she was through, Ada flung the woman's corpse into the fireplace, and the ruffles of her fashionable dress caught fire with a billow of flames. The heat filled the room, and the black smoke that rose and collected at the ceiling didn't bother Ada one bit. She didn't need to breathe.

Then she heard steps in the hallway, and quickly hid behind one of the sitting chairs by the door. A moment later the boy was in the doorway, screaming for his mother. He ran through the room, and tried to pull her out of the fire. Her flaming body lit the carpet, and before the boy could stamp it out, Ada jumped on his back, and knocked him down against the table.

The boy, instead of fighting back, kept trying to turn around to see who else was in the room. Ada pushed him back down, and pressed his face into the plum pie from the night before. It, like all the other food, had been left on the table. It had been left there all night while Ada starved.

The boy choked on the pie, flailing his hands. He pushed himself up, and then suddenly started calling out toward the door. Ada turned.

There in the doorway was the servant, already dressed and groomed. He looked at the scene before him with an unreadable expression.

"Help me!" the boy cried. His face was covered with purple jelly, and he reached out a hand toward the servant. "She's trying to kill me!"

The servant's eyes went from Ada and the boy to the charred corpse of the mother on the floor. Then, without a change of expression, he turned on his heel and went out the front door. He closed it behind him.

"No!" the boy cried, and Ada smiled. She dunked him back into the pie, and heard him gurgle, bubbles coming up as he struggled to breathe. Ada listened as his breathing slowed and his heart gave its final uneven beat.

She threw him down on the table, and looked at his chubby limbs smeared with the sauces and gravies of the elaborate dinner. Ada was never one to believe in waste. She bent down, and filled her stomach to the bursting point with the flesh of the boy, nibbling back the skin and chomping into the pink muscle of his forearms, and then splitting open his chest to feast on his collection of young organs.

Satisfied, and warm, she looked back at the room. The flames of the fire had climbed the walls, and were curling the expensive wallpaper. The ceiling was already black, and soon the fire would eat through to the second story. It was time to go.

But before Ada left, she made it a point to throw open the curtains. Then she jumped back out the window, and hobbled away on the street. Townsfolk, seeing the smoke, rushed past Ada in the street to investigate, still not noticing her. She was turning the corner toward the market as the first screams split the morning air.

She scuttled across the center of the marketplace. She wore her muddy rags around her, the shawl blackened from the smoke of the house, and no one even turned in her direction.

When she passed the church, she paused. She saw the priest standing at the entrance, greeting the first parishioners as they arrived. Ada growled. She forced herself to keep moving. She wanted to wait until the church was full.

She continued on, working her way up the winding road that led to the palace. The snow of the road had already been split and trampled by carriages and horses, and she walked in the dead center of the road, not at all worried of being seen. She went eagerly up the hill, sniffing at the air, and was able to make out the scent of the group of men protesting yet again.

But when she got to the top of the hill, she smelled something completely different. It was the smell of death and decay—and reanimation. It was potent all around the palace, like cologne applied too liberally. And she realized that the women the men desired must be inside the palace somewhere, most likely eager for a reunion themselves.

She slipped between the legs of the men in the crowd.

No one looked down. They hadn't looked down when they trampled her, and she hadn't expected them to care now. She made her way to the front of the gates, and peered out at the guards on the other side. Then her eyes followed the palace wall to the wooded area where she had been bitten the day before. No guards waited there.

She hustled back through the crowd, and crawled through the snowy bushes. She could smell others like her here as well. She stepped out into a covered clearing, devoid of snow, and sitting in the middle with her back toward Ada was none other than her Grandma.

Ada took a step forward. She saw the old woman's head perk up. She sniffed, and then her head lowered again. The dead didn't hunger after the other dead.

Ada reached inside her pocket, and took out one of the matches she had stolen from the boy's house. When she was two steps away, she lit the match on the bark of a tree. Her Grandma turned at the smell, her gnarled mouth opening as she saw Ada lunge at her. But Ada was faster, and she gouged the lit match into the old woman's side. It caught on her dress at once, and she let out a roar of panic.

Ada watched as her Grandma stood up, trying to bat out the flames but only spreading them to the rest of her clothes. She groaned. Then she lowered her arms, and stumbled out of the clearing toward the street, where she could roll in the snow.

This was the diversion that Ada needed. She crawled up the wall, and then let herself fall to the ground on the other side. She didn't feel the effects of the fall, and started crawling on her belly toward the palace. Not even the guards on the front steps noticed her, and she slipped inside a small servant's door on the side of the palace.

Inside was a kitchen with boiling pots on a massive stove. A woman was salting the contents of the dishes with her back to the room, and Ada walked casually through the kitchen to the far door. She hobbled through, and found herself in a polished hallway of the castle, lined with monumental paintings of men on horseback and elegant mountain vistas. She fingered the matches in her pocket, but decided to wait, following the scent of death down the hall.

She paused outside the King's chambers. His door was open, and she heard him talking to someone she couldn't see.

"And then this mess! As if it weren't bad enough at my sister's. You won't believe what she told me. She has taken to bathing in tubs of blood. Fresh blood! I know, I can't understand it either, but *she* claims it keeps her young. Only it hasn't been working as well as it used to, apparently, and now she thinks—"

Ada crossed the open doorway and heard the voices continue, undisturbed, as she scurried down the hall. She went up one more marble staircase, and then came to a pair of gigantic wooden doors. The handles had been tied shut with thick rope, and there was a proclamation written above in red lettering. Ada couldn't read, but she had seen letters like this before: it meant to keep out.

She leaned up against the door, and sniffed through the crack. The rancid smell of death met her nostrils, and she knew she had found the right room. She reached inside her pocket, lit a match on the grain of the door, and held it under the rope until it caught fire. The flames ate away at the coils until they were thinner than shoelaces.

Then, suddenly, there was a pounding on the other side. Ada stepped back, and saw the doors bulging as some great mass pushed against them from the other side. She crept forward and turned the handle, and the doors burst open. A flood of the walking dead spilled out in a rainbow of ball gowns and fine dresses.

They were the women, and they were starving.

Ada watched as more and more of them streamed out of the massive room, clawing against each other, eager for the live bodies they could smell so nearby. She followed the horde as they worked their way down the grand staircase, using her matches to light the royal tapestries and furniture of the palace as she went. The women left the palace through a rear entrance, a distance away from the front gate where the crowd was standing, but the men saw them at once.

Ada crept down the stairs, walking behind the bushes and along the edge of the palace.

The men were shouting, furious and excited, as the women slowly worked their way across the snowy front lawn. The men began to slam against the gates, and the guards couldn't stop the throng. They broke through with a crash, and started racing through the snow toward the women they had lost.

They met about halfway. The men were already surrounded by the time they realized they should have turned back. The guards shouted, running up to the wild mass of bodies, but they wisely kept their distance as the women ripped into the men, their red blood splattering the white snow.

The match girl walked behind the guards, who were too dazed to pay her any attention, and down the middle of the path that led out the front gates. She looked at the broken spokes of the gate as she passed, and then at the crumpled body of a woman charred to black that laid on the ground outside them. She stepped on her Grandma's head as she walked, crushing through it like a dry husk, and went casually down the lane back to the town. Behind her, the castle's windows crashed as the heat from the fire spread and expanded, and great cyclones of black smoke twisted up toward the sky.

By the time she got back to town, church was in session. The high voices of the choir filled the air as she passed people in the streets, looking up and away from her toward the billows of smoke coming from the palace. She smiled to herself. They would have to start noticing her now.

She crossed through the marketplace, and was about to go up the steps of the church when she saw them: the dead children. They were still lurking in the shadows, but she wasn't afraid of them now. She put a foot on the stone step of the church, and as she did so, the gang of children rushed forward to stop her. Ada quickened her pace, and was through the small door of the church before they had even crossed the street. She looked back at them, triumphant, and closed the door. There was a beam on the wall, and she looked at it for a moment before shifting it down into place, blockading the entrance.

The church was dark. It was an old wooden building, and the pews were filled with well-dressed men and women with bent heads. Dozens of candles lit the space and filled the long room with the scent of incense and smoke. The priest was at the pulpit, his fingers laced and his head dropped. He was saying a prayer.

Ada smiled. She knew prayers wouldn't do him any good now.

Before the prayer ended, she slipped behind the last pew. In the back of the church was a small table with little candles, and a big jar filled with matches. Ada took the lot of them, and stuffed them into her pockets.

The priest resumed his sermon. The topic, Ada was surprised to learn, was charity.

"And how you treat the least among you," the priest proclaimed, "that is how *you* shall be measured."

Ada thought this an appropriate moment to step forward. She started to walk down the center of the aisle, the shawl over her head hiding all but the smile on her face. She could see through the holes of the lace, and saw the priest's stunned expression. Then he caught himself, and attempted to continue with his sermon.

When she was halfway through the church, all eyes were upon her. Still the priest blustered on.

Finally, when Ada was standing directly before his pulpit, bowing her head before him, the priest lost his composure. He jumped down, and came around to grab Ada by the arm.

"I told you," he whispered into her ear, "to stay out of my church."

She growled, and pulled back her shawl to reveal her full appearance.

Her tangled hair was filthy with mud, ice, and smoke. The skin of her face had been frozen, burnt, and bruised. It peeled off from her cheeks in glistening layers. Her ears had deflated with the cold, and her nose was blackened from frostbite, looking like a dog's. She was monstrous, doubly so because if it weren't for the sickness and abuse, she would have been a beautiful little girl.

There were gasps in the crowd, and Ada looked up to meet all of their eyes. She wanted them all to see what they had done to her.

The priest was unmoved. He came up behind her and shoved her toward the exit.

Ada spun on him and hissed. His eyes widened, and he took a step back. Ada jumped at him, grabbing a handful of his brown cassock in one hand, and lighting a match along the floor in the other. Before the priest knew what was happening, he was on fire.

He screamed, trying to stomp out the flame, but Ada circled around him, drawing the match along his legs, and lit him in a ring of fire. It climbed from the level of his knees to his chest. The priest raised his arms, his sleeves catching ablaze, and let out a chilling shriek.

The parishioners were stunned. The priest pushed by the match girl, and lunged at a young woman in the front pew. She screamed, seeing the fire jump from his arms to the ruffles of her dress.

And that's when the crowd reacted. Not by saving the woman, but by turning in the other direction, fighting each other to escape. The first ones at the door were too panicked to figure out how to work the latch, and in a moment the crowd had pressed against them so tightly that they couldn't have moved if they tried.

Ada watched and smiled. The flames from the priest lit up the room like the sun, and Ada walked along the side of the church, lighting the tapestries of the commandments on fire, one by one.

The priest, now a human torch, was still trying desperately to put himself out. His hair had caught fire now, and the skin of his face was bubbling as it was cooked to his skull. He stumbled to the entrance of the church, and joined the mass of people trying to press their way free. He was obviously too far gone to realize what he was doing, but nonetheless he reached out, pushing down the old women and children in an effort to get to the door himself. Some of those he pushed caught fire immediately, and writhed on the ground, screaming in agony, while others were trampled by the panic.

Smoke was collecting in the beams of the ceiling, and it was working its way down until the entire crowd was either burning or choking to death. Ada just watched, standing behind the pulpit, as the stack of people caught fire and burned like logs in a fireplace.

She shook her head, and then turned to exit through a small unlocked door at the back of the stage. It led past a small cubby of a room with a writing desk, and out into a side alley thick with snow.

She trudged out through the snow and into the marketplace. There was an explosion in the distance, and people running and screaming in either direction around her. Some were dead, some alive, but Ada didn't even bother to look up. She watched her feet dig through the snow as they took her to her normal place in the center of the marketplace, and she stopped, feeling like she might as well be in the middle of an ocean.

Despite her revenge, which she *had* enjoyed, the little match girl was feeling unfulfilled. She still had no mother and no father, nowhere to go, and no one to care about her. She was perhaps even more alone now than she had been the day before, and had neither her hunger nor her cold to distract her from the loneliness. She hugged herself, wanting to cry but no longer being able to.

Snow crunched around her, and Ada looked up. The dead children were back, their mouths sneering and eyes distrustful. They had encircled her, but the little match girl was too exhausted to feel afraid anymore. She held out her hands, as if to say, Come and get me. The children tightened their noose around her.

Then one boy broke ranks from the rest. Ada looked at him, meeting his eyes.

He was a small boy, but with perfect features. Or at least they might have been. Long gashes and stitches covered his entire body, as if he weren't a real boy, but a facsimile sewn together from parts.

She didn't move as he came closer. He raised his arm, his fist poised to strike, and slapped it down on her hand. Then, keeping his eyes on her, he nodded.

Ada was confused. She lowered her arms, and noticed a golden coin had been placed in her palm. Her black-tipped fingers closed around it. Then she looked back up at the boy, and he pointed toward her.

It took her a moment to realize he was pointing at the matches.

Ada selected a match from her pocket, and handed it to him. The boy smiled, and stepped back into the ring.

Then another child came forward, and another, and another, until everyone in the circle had given Ada a gold coin in exchange for one of her matches.

They stood before her, and Ada realized here were all the lost and forgotten children of the world, gathered together into one group. Some, like the sewn boy, might have been as bad off as she was in life. Others looked worse.

Ada had found her new family.

They were all holding their matches, waiting for her to start. Ada crossed through the snow, and led the way to the nearest stand. Very obviously, so all the children could see, she dragged the head of the match across the wood. The flame sparked, and she held up the match, ignited.

The other children came forward and lit theirs in the same way, until their entire circle looked like a candlelight procession. Ada's face glowed with approval.

And then together, matches blazing, they set upon the town.

THE CURSE OF PETER PAN

Wendy heard the footsteps on the roof, but she didn't tell anyone. She smiled, and went on combing the hair of her doll.

You see, Wendy was a girl who wanted to die.

"I'm sure you'll have an excellent time," she said to her parents, who were preparing to leave for some sort of impromptu town meeting. They were all in the nursery, which was located on the third floor of their townhouse, and her brothers were already under the covers in bed, even though they were wide awake. A fire roared in the corner of the room by the door, and lit the scene with a warm glow.

Mr. Darling paused in buttoning up his shirt and turned to Wendy. She looked back at him with an innocent expression. She was wearing her brown hair in curls, and had on a pale blue nightgown. She rocked the doll against her chest, making her look like a child much younger than her fourteen years of age.

Mr. Darling's eyes narrowed. "When are you going to get rid of those dolls?" he asked. Wendy turned away. She hated these grown-up conversations. They always resulted in her having to lose something.

"Oh, honey," Mrs. Darling said, putting a hand on her husband's arm. "Let her have her fun."

"Fun?" he asked. "With the world the way it is?" He looked into his wife's eyes with serious intent. "You do realize that every time we leave the house, we may never return? And what will happen to John and Michael then? Who will look after them?" He gestured toward Wendy. *"Her?"*

Wendy's mother looked at the girl, and there was an expression of disappointment and regret on her soft features. "She is a bit underdeveloped for her age," she admitted.

"Then it's settled," Mr. Darling boomed. "Tomorrow Wendy will leave the nursery, and learn to take care of the household."

Wendy shook her head. "No!" she cried.

Her father took her by the shoulders, and leaned down into her face. He whispered in a stern tone. "You need to be able to take your mother's place should anything happen. Think of your brothers."

Wendy turned to look at her brothers, John and Michael, sitting against their pillows in bed. They were straining to listen.

"Oh, they'll be fine," she said, swiping at the air to dismiss the idea. "If anything, *they* should be taking care of *me*."

"You are the oldest," her father said in a louder voice, standing up. "And tomorrow you will learn how to take care of the household with your mother." He raised a finger. "No more days playing in the nursery. And no more *dolls*."

He moved to snatch the doll from Wendy's arms, but she ran back to her bed in the corner of the room. She jumped into a pile of teddy bears and dolls, and buried her head in it. "But—but—" she stammered from underneath, "I can't tomorrow." She sat up, and picked up a worn brown bear. "Tomorrow Teddy and I are going to the market—that's what we call the bricks by the fireplace—to inquire about his wife. You see, she's been kidnapped by pirates, and—"

"Enough!" her father screamed. He lunged forward and snatched the bear out of her hand. Wendy screamed.

"I've had enough of bears and dolls," he said, and lifted the bear as Wendy tried to reach for it. "You are fourteen years old, Wendy. It's time to start acting like an adult. Not some silly little girl sitting around and telling stories and playing with toys all day. It's nonsense!"

Mrs. Darling came forward and put a hand on his arm. "Dear," she began, but he shook her off.

"Don't you dare encourage her," he snapped to his wife. "It was one thing when she was little, and she'd make us sit through her little games as if they were real. But, *honestly!* She's still doing it! Like a baby that won't give up the bottle." He looked around the room, and fixed his eyes on the fireplace. "Well, we'll put a stop to her games once and for all."

He crossed the room to the fireplace, and Wendy jumped out of bed to follow him.

"Please, Father," she cried, and was horrified to hear her voice crack. The tears would start soon, and there was no helping it. "Don't hurt Teddy!"

But he was determined. He held out the bear before the flames. "It's time to grow up!" he shouted. Then he threw the bear into the fire.

It hit the back of the fireplace, and then slid down behind the logs.

"No!" Wendy shrieked, and started to go after the bear. Her mother had to hold her back, or she might have gone right into the flames before she realized the danger.

The bear erupted in sparks, and its fur started to shrivel and turn black.

Wendy buried her face into her mother's arms, her chest heaving with sobs. But her father ignored her and crossed the room again. She looked up to see him scooping up the rest of her dolls and bears.

"No!" Wendy screamed. Her face was red and strained, and she fought against her mother, scratching at her arms.

Her father stomped back to the fire, and threw the armful of toys into the fire.

The hair of the dolls caught fire first, and then the dolls' clothes and the animals. Black smoke curled up the chimney, and Wendy dropped to her knees before the fire, watching her only friends disintegrate in front of her.

"Tomorrow," her father boomed, standing over her, "you will learn how to be a woman. You have been a child long enough."

John and Michael stood up on the bed and started whining. "But Father! We like having her with us."

He turned to them. "Get back in bed." Then he turned to his wife. "Quickly now, Mary."

They were collecting their things when there was another creek on the ceiling. Wendy's eyes went up, and her parents heard it, too.

"Lock them in," her father whispered, and her mother nodded.

Wendy looked at them, her face streaked with tears. "Why?"

"You'll be safer, dear," her mother said. She went to the window and checked the latch, jiggling it to make sure it would hold. Then she turned to John and Michael in bed, and pointed toward the window. "This is to remain closed. Do you understand?"

The boys nodded. Mrs. Darling joined her husband at the door, and took the key from her pocket.

"You treat us like prisoners," Wendy said bitterly.

"It's for the best," her mother replied. "You'll be safer."

"What if there's a fire?" Wendy asked, placing her hands on her hips.

She was pleased at the pause this gave her mother. The town had been overrun with fires the past few weeks, and the concern was a realistic one. But then Mrs. Darling shook her head, and continued to the door.

"You'll still be safer inside," she said. "There's no telling what you'd run into on the streets. And Nana will be in the house, blocking the door."

Nana was their guard dog, a St. Bernard who stank like a coffin. They had gotten her for free after her owner had disappeared, but the dog wasn't really much protection. She just liked to sleep all day.

Her father left the room without glancing back, but their mother took one last look at them from the doorway. "Good night," she said. Then to Wendy specifically, she added: "Behave."

She stepped out of the nursery, and shut the door. A moment later Wendy could hear the lock bolt from the outside. Nana barked as her parents passed in the hall. Then the front door slammed, and the children were alone.

Wendy did not move from her spot in front of the hearth. She sat watching her toys burn until the faces of the dolls started to melt, making them look like naked old ladies in the fire.

John and Michael slid down from their bed. John was older at eight years old, and Michael was barely more than a toddler. They both had brown hair and were dressed in well-worn pajamas.

Michael put his arm around Wendy and looked into the fire. "Are they dead?" he asked.

Wendy stared into the fire, the light reflecting off her eyes. Her face had drained of all expression, and the tears had dried on her face. "It doesn't matter," she said in a level voice. "None of it will matter when Peter gets here."

Before Michael could ask what she meant by that, Wendy stood up and walked to the window.

Michael waddled over to Wendy, and tugged on her nightgown. "Who's Peter?" he asked. John was also curious, and sat down on the edge of his bed, his eyes eager for an answer—or better yet, a story.

"Peter Pan, of course. He's the boy who visits our window at night," Wendy explained, as if she were commenting on the weather.

"Our window?" John asked. "But we're on the third floor."

Wendy gave a smug smile. "He can fly. How else would he get up here?"

Michael couldn't answer, so he sat down to listen as well. Wendy was still feeling on edge, and couldn't yet look toward the fire without feeling a mix of anger and loss, but having an audience made her feel a little better. It always made her feel better to tell a few lies.

"He lives out in the woods with the fairies," she said. "And he learned to fly from the birds. He doesn't grow old, because he has no mother or father to force him to grow up. He is the happiest boy in the world."

There was a creak on the roof, and all three children looked up. A smile grew on Wendy's face.

"That's him now," she whispered. "He must have waited until Mother and Father left."

"Has he really come before?" John asked. "*Really* really?" John was old enough to know that not all of Wendy's stories were true.

Wendy's smile dropped, and her face grew blank. "He has been here every night for the past two weeks, ever since the fires. I wake up sometimes and see him watching me through the window. I've been too afraid to let him in before, but now... now I may have no choice."

"I've seen him, too," Michael said in a whisper.

"Don't lie, Michael," snapped John.

"It's not a lie." He stopped his foot. "But I was too scared to get out of bed. And in the morning I forgot about it like a dream." He held up a finger. "And don't you call me a liar, because I know you've seen him, too!"

Wendy turned to John with her mouth open. She felt as betrayed as if he had read her diary. "Is this true?" she asked.

John pouted and looked down. "I don't know what I saw. It was dark." He looked up, and gave Michael a dirty look. "And how do you know what I saw?"

"I saw you looking when I was pretending to sleep."

"That settles it," Wendy said. "He wants us to join his gang. He wants to make us children forever."

There was the distant sound of thunder. All three children turned toward the window, and the light of the nursery fire flickered against one side of each face.

"He only comes in the dark," Wendy said. She turned toward the fire. "We should put it out."

She searched around the side of the fireplace until she found what she was looking for. She held up a dingy pail full of sand.

"Peter Pan," she called out in a loud voice, "we summon thee." She turned to her brothers. "You must say it, too."

Obediently, the two boys repeated: "Peter Pan, we summon thee."

"We summon thee, Pan," Wendy chanted, "to take us away from this life. We call on you to save our childhood from the perils of adulthood. Save us, and we will be yours."

"Save us," her brothers repeated, "and we will be yours."

Wendy took in a deep breath, and then tossed the sand onto the fire.

The flames went out, sending a cloud of smoke into the nursery and crawling along the ceiling. The room's colors changed instantly from the warm orange glow of the fireplace, to the midnight blues of the moonlight.

"Look," whispered John, and he pointed to the floor.

Stretched across the middle of the nursery was the black shadow of a boy. His head was at their feet, and the Darling children followed the length of it to its source by the window.

And there, outside the frosted glass, was a young boy

staring back at them. He had wild red hair and wore a tattered green outfit made from leaves. He smiled at them, and then tapped on the glass.

It was Peter Pan.

*   *   *

Mrs. Darling was looking back over her shoulder as she and her husband walked down the empty street.

"Mary," Mr. Darling chastised. "I'm sure they'll be fine. We're the ones facing a hard time tonight."

And at once, her mind was brought back to the business at hand. They continued down the lane, taking the long way around the marketplace, and started to see other couples joining them as they neared the old tavern and inn, their meeting place.

Mrs. Darling felt instantly more comfortable when they started to see other people. The *things*—Mrs. Darling didn't know what else to call them—tended to stay away if you were in a group. Especially a group of adults.

When they arrived at the tavern, there was already a crowd inside. Besides the parents coming from the different corners of town, there was also a large portion of the remaining populace that had been forced to move into the inn after the fires had ravaged the town. The Darlings squeezed in through the doorway, and found a spot toward the back. And just in time, because the meeting started almost at once.

"I'm sorry to call you so late," the innkeeper announced. "But with the King's guard on alert, it's not safe to meet during the day."

The room was silent, eager for any voice of authority.

"As you know, our town is at a moment of crisis. Commerce has come to a stop, and even the foundations of our community have been shattered. The church has been burned to the ground, the Palace has been under attack, and the King gravely wounded by the fires. We have no protection, and we have no solace." He looked around the room, letting his words sink in. "But that is not why we are meeting tonight. We are meeting tonight because the streets are no longer safe, and neither are our children."

There were murmurs of consent.

"I have called this meeting tonight because I have recently been introduced to a man who claims he can help us. He is a stranger to us, but he comes with the high recommendation of the priest." He paused here, embarrassed. The priest's recommendation was never worth much, and now that he was dead, it was worth even less. "In any account, I turn the floor over to this gentleman, and can only pray that he will save us from our living hell."

And just as he said this, the door to the tavern flew open. A burst of cold winter air flickered the candles, and drew gasps from the women. The crowd turned, and was stunned.

There in the doorway was a man no one in town had ever seen before. What was more, he was a man unlike *any* the town had seen before.

He was the Pied Piper.

He was tall, having to bend as he entered the doorway. He wore a long red jacket, which he wore almost like a cape, and underneath that a frilled garment with intricate white lace. He wore a wide-brimmed hat, which he wore at a slant, and it had a number of feathers tucked into the band. He had curls of black hair, and a moustache that curled in points at the ends.

And the man himself had a grand expression to match his outrageous style. He stood with his chin raised, his eyes slightly closed, not even looking at the crowd that had him as their complete focus.

The townsfolk didn't know how to react.

"I suppose you were wanting to request my services?"

the man asked, and opened his coat. He took out a long scroll from his inside pocket. With great to-do, he unrolled it, and began reading.

"'It is with greatest humility that we request your services, as soon as possible, in the matter of the eradication of a very particular pest that has gained control over our streets. Please come at once. We will pay *any price*.'" The man looked up, and smiled. He held out the scroll to face the crowd. "It is signed," he said nonchalantly, "by your priest."

It took some time for the crowd to soak this in.

Then, timidly, Mrs. Darling broke the silence.

"I'm afraid, sir, that our priest is dead."

The stranger contemplated this for a moment. Then he shrugged. "Tell me," he asked, "*does* this town have an infestation problem?"

The timid stares that met him back answered his question. They also told him there was something more going on.

"Tell me: what is it? Rats? Mice? Some lower order vermin with eight legs and fangs?"

The people wouldn't answer.

"What's the matter with you? Why this shyness? Lots of perfectly fine towns have trouble with pests. It is no reflection on your nobility. What is bothering you?"

Mr. Darling stood up. He flustered for a moment before speaking. "You see, sir, what is bothering us is—" He almost stopped here, and looked back down to his chair. Then he seemed to brace himself, closing his eyes and tightening his fists, as if he were about to strike someone. "The dead," he gasped. "The dead are what plagues us."

The Pied Piper stared back at him for a moment, trying to decide if this was a joke. He decided it was. "Well, now," he said with a smile, "that can be troubling. I find the trick is to bury them, and then they won't bother you anymore."

"They walk the streets," Mrs. Darling said, her expression grave. "They—seek our children in the night."

The Pied Piper looked at the other faces in the crowd, finding a mix of eagerness and fear.

"This is... no joke?" he asked, looking around the room. The sincerity of the townspeople's expressions, even on the old grandmothers hugging the banisters in the corners, led him to believe that they was serious. These people really believed they were haunted by the dead.

Which could be very lucrative.

He clasped his hands together and gripped them hungrily, his smile returning with more teeth displayed than before.

"All right then," he said, turning from one face to another. "I've handled worse. Now, what kind of dead are these? Phantoms? Ghouls?"

"They are the walking dead," an old man from the corner said, his voice raspy. "They walk the streets seeking human flesh, and aim to increase their ranks."

"They stole my baby!" shouted a female voice from the back.

"A bite will make you one of them," a youngish woman wearing a scarf added. "My Timmy was fine and healthy, and then a small bite on his wrist changed him within a day's time. He's one of them now."

"A bite?" That's quite imaginative, the Pied Piper thought. But then, he had visited villages that thought sprites were hidden among the leaves of their gardens, ruining their crops. It turned out to be crows, but the Piper collected double pay for his supernatural exterminations. Yet he had never heard of anything like this, like these walking dead.

"And you say they're after you're children?" he confirmed.

"They *are* our children," a bereaved father said, and then dropped his head into his hands.

Ah, the Pied Piper realized. Hooligans. Youth gone wild, and all that. Probably startled the old ladies in the marketplace, wearing masks or howling like demons so no one would notice as they plucked a few apples from the stands. He smiled again. If these folk were that gullible, he was going to make a killing.

He turned to the crowd and raised his hands for silence— a totally unnecessary gesture as the crowd was already silent and giving him their complete attention.

"Now," he said, "let's discuss the method of payment."

Mr. Darling spoke for the group. "We'll pay whatever it takes. You have our word. Even if your mission fails, we will compensate you for the attempt. We are that desperate."

The Pied Piper smiled.

"Fine men and women," he said in a booming voice, "have no fear: the Pied Piper is here. And from this day forward, your children will never be in danger again!"

*　*　*

Wendy stared at Peter.

She wondered how he kept warm in his short sleeves and—what was he wearing? It looked like leaves. She looked up into his eyes, and he looked back at her, his face white and his hair wild. The reflection of the fire's last dying embers glowed in his boyish eyes, and his mouth twisted up into a smile, revealing a row of baby teeth.

Wendy put a hand out to unlock the window.

"Wait!" John called, running forward. He put his hand on hers, and took it off the lock. "Remember what Mother said? We're not supposed to let anyone in."

"But it's *Peter!*" Wendy exclaimed. "She couldn't have meant to keep *him* out."

John glanced at the boy in the window, and his shoulders dropped. "Actually," he whispered, "I'm pretty sure that Peter is exactly who she meant."

Wendy slapped him away. "Pish posh!" she said, and threw open the window.

The night air sent a chill into the room immediately. The children were all wearing thin nightgowns, and clutched their arms over their chests, trying to keep warm. Peter was bare armed, but he didn't shiver or have goosebumps. He didn't even seem to feel the cold.

The children stepped back, and Peter jumped down to the floor. He stared at them in the darkness, his smile growing wider, and his eyes growing narrower.

"How did you get up here?" Michael asked, waddling up and taking Wendy's hand. "Did you fly?" Wendy looked to Peter, curious about his answer as well.

Peter's gaze moved to Michael, his eyes unblinking and wide as he smiled at the toddler. Michael took a step back behind Wendy.

"Is it true," Wendy asked in a whisper, "that you don't age? That you will remain a child forever?"

The boy shifted his gaze to her. His small teeth glinted in the moonlight, and his expression reminded Wendy of a jackal. He did not blink, not even once. Then he nodded slowly in answer to her question, and Wendy felt hope flutter inside of her.

"I don't want to grow up," Wendy said. "They're making me leave the nursery. I'd rather stay a child forever, if you can do that."

She took a step forward, away from her brothers, as if presenting herself to Peter. The boy's smile grew even wider, so that all his teeth seemed to show, top and bottom.

Wendy braced herself. She would be brave. Death might be painful, but it would be worth it to avoid ending up like her parents. She held her breath and closed her eyes.

Peter shoved her to the floor, and she opened her eyes to see him jump on her baby brother.

Michael screamed out in surprise. Peter picked him up like a small dog and took a bite out of his throat. Blood sprayed out, staining the wood of the nursery, and Michael's little body went into spasms. He made a bubbling, choking sound, like he was coughing underwater, and then his head fell onto his shoulders.

Peter tossed him to the ground, and fixed his gaze on John.

"No!" Wendy cried, and rose to her feet. "Take me!"

Peter didn't even turn in her direction. He stumbled across the room toward the retreating John.

John's face had gone white from watching the death of his little brother. He backed up toward the fireplace, and felt behind his back for the iron poker. "Keep your distance," he said with a shaky voice. Meanwhile, Wendy had gone to Peter, and was pulling on his shirt from behind.

"I'm ready!" she said. "Do me first!"

Peter turned back to her, the bloody smile on his face dropping slightly as he looked at her. She held his gaze with urgent eyes.

"I don't want to grow up," she whispered. She pulled the hair away from her neck, and bent her head so that he'd have easy access. Peter looked at her for a moment, and then turned back to John.

"Wendy!" John yelled, the poker raised in the air. "Save me!"

But Wendy was too upset to help. Before she had collected herself, Peter had jumped, and rammed John against the brick of the fireplace. John swiped the poker at the air as they both sank to the floor, but Peter fixed his hands around the boy's neck. As he strangled him, he also bit into his flesh greedily.

"Wendy," John wheezed, looking at her as she stood there. And then he was dead.

Peter stepped away. John's eyes were still open, and there were red half-moons in his nightgown where Peter had bitten him. He didn't move at all, looking like a ventriloquist's dummy with no one to animate him.

Wendy decided that when Peter bit her, she wouldn't fight. That would only make it take longer. "I'm ready," she said, and waited.

Peter looked right past her to the open window. Then he bent down and picked up John, throwing the dead boy over his shoulder. He stomped past Wendy to the window, and threw the boy out.

Wendy gasped. She knew her brother was already dead, but when she heard the crunch of his body against the cobblestones below, she couldn't help but to cringe.

"Courage," she whispered to herself. "It will be worth it. Anything would be worth it."

Then Peter turned to Michael, and lifted his little body by the feet. Michael's limp arms flopped to the floor, and Peter started to climb over the windowsill, holding the boy with one hand.

"Wait!" Wendy called, rushing forward to stop him. "Where are you going?"

Peter didn't wait. He jumped to the beam above the window, his feet dangling in the open window frame. Then he pulled himself up.

"Come back!" Wendy cried, and ran toward the window. She nearly slipped in the puddle of Michael's blood on the way, and caught her balance on the windowsill. She stuck her head outside and bent to look up.

Peter was climbing up the side of the building. He had Michael by the back of the neck, holding him in his mouth like a mother cat with a kitten as he scaled the outer walls.

"Wait for me!" Wendy shouted. She started to climb on the windowsill. The cold night air blew her hair, and felt like ice on her skin through the nightgown. She glanced down, and saw the ground three stories below. It might as well have been ten, it looked so far away.

And she saw below as her brother John's corpse was being lifted by a gang of children to be carried off into the night.

THE CURSE OF PETER PAN

"No!" she cried. Tears were forming in her eyes. "Don't leave me."

She held out her arms and gripped both sides of the window frame, and then turned to look up for Peter again. She caught a glimpse of his shadow along the edge of the roof. Above, the full moon lit up the sky, and the stars glittered at an impossible distance away.

They didn't want her. She had been left behind.

There was a shout from down on the street. Someone was calling her name. She looked down to see her parents running toward their house. A strange man was beside them. But Wendy barely registered that fact.

She had been abandoned.

Her breathing grew more ragged as she considered what life would be like for her now that her brothers were gone. She would be left with her parents. She would never get to play again. Her eyes flickered back toward the ground below, and suddenly the idea of jumping didn't seem so bad.

Better to die, she thought. Better to have it all over with.

She had a moment's hesitation though. She was afraid of heights. She looked down, and the ground seemed so far away, like she could go on falling forever. She shook her head, and looked up at the stars.

No, she decided. Not falling. *Flying.* She would fly to her grave.

She lifted one foot from the windowsill, still holding onto the sides with her fingers. Then she let go.

She felt her body lean forward into the night.

But instead of falling out the window, she was pulled back inside.

"Let me go!" she screamed. It was her father that had pulled her back in, and she looked into his eyes with as much rage as she could muster. She started to struggle, clawing at his arms and trying to struggle back to the open window.

"Be sensible, girl!" her father shouted, and slapped her heavily across the face.

Wendy's body crumpled in defeat. Her shoulders rose and fell with her heavy breathing, but she did not fight. There was no point now. Peter was gone. Her mother ran around her and locked the window. She lit a candle, and then seemed to notice the blood on the floor for the first time.

"My babies!" she cried. She bent down to Wendy, and shook her by the shoulders. "Where are they? *Where?*"

"With Peter," Wendy answered, her spirit deflated. "He took them away."

Mrs. Darling looked up with horror. "You have to find them," she commanded, and Wendy looked up to see that the stranger had entered the room. He bowed to Mrs. Darling, but his eyes expressed a nervousness that conflicted with his graceful gesture.

Wendy stared at his strange ensemble. He was dressed like a child might pretending to be an adult, but one that didn't really know how adults were supposed to dress.

Her father stood up, leaving Wendy on the floor. "Go downstairs," he said to his wife, "and make us some tea. I need to speak to our guest first alone."

Her mother looked down at the blood on the floor, then left the room obediently. Her father took the strange man by the arm, and led him over to the fireplace.

"I will pay you double what we promised if you find my boys," he said. He was trying to speak in private, but Wendy could hear him perfectly.

"Double?" the stranger asked, running a finger over his curled moustache. He seemed to recognize the inappropriateness of his glee, and his tone became more serious. "What are the terms?"

"If they are alive, you are to bring them back. If they are not, you are to eradicate them and every member of their group. No more children must join them."

Wendy felt a wave of nausea at the thought of Peter Pan's death. If he died, she would never become one of them.

"I can help," she offered, and sat up from the ground. The stranger met her glance, and gave her a little bow.

"No," her father ordered, looking at her now. "This is not your task. I will not have you trudging about in the dark, and risking your life. At least one of my children will grow up to be old." He turned to the stranger. "Let's go downstairs."

And without another word, they went out the door. Wendy stood up to follow, and she heard the door lock from the outside.

Wendy screamed out in frustration and stomped her feet on the ground. She had to get out. She no longer wanted to die—not in a way that wouldn't bring her back, not if she could still find Peter—but she had to do something soon, or else this stranger might kill whatever chance she had at being young forever.

Perhaps if she warned Peter, he would be so glad that he'd make her one of them after all. Yes, it was worth an effort. And if she failed, well, there would always be a window to jump out of later.

She waited until the sounds of her father's footsteps had disappeared, and then turned back to the bedroom. She didn't have much time.

She looked around for anything she could use, and settled on the sheets of the bed. She rushed forward and ripped them off the mattresses, knocking the pillows to the ground, and started tying the ends of the sheets together. She tied several knots along the way, so that she'd have something to use for leverage, and then tied the end of the rope around the foot of the bed. She gave it a good tug, and then went toward the window.

Before opening it, she listened again. She couldn't hear her parents. She carefully slid back the bolt of the window, pausing when it made a click, and then slowly, carefully pulled. The cold air numbed her fingertips, and as she stood looking out at the cold night beyond, she decided to return to her room for a coat. She slipped it right over her night-gown, and was about to find some shoes when she heard the front door open below.

"Rest assured," said the stranger's voice, "I will find your boys, or my name isn't the Pied Piper!"

Wendy crept up to the windowsill, and peeked over to see him bow and then turn away into the street. Their front door closed, and the Pied Piper started walking away on the wet cobblestones.

No time for shoes, Wendy decided, and stuck her feet into a pair of slippers. Then she took hold of the rope, and squatted on the windowsill, her back to the outside. She summoned up all her bravery, refusing to look down, and hopped backward out the window.

The rope brought her back toward the building, and she slammed her feet into the brick. She was grateful for her slippers, because her hard-soled shoes would have made noise to alert her parents. She waited a moment, catching her breath, and then started climbing down the rope. She slid down quickly past her parents' bedroom on the second floor, just as her mother had started to open her door. They hadn't seen her. She slid down to the end of the rope, and jumped the final few feet to the front stoop of their house.

She had done it. A sense of accomplishment warmed her. She had started her own adventure.

But then she remembered the Piper, and looked up to see the street empty. She ran immediately in the direction he had gone, her slippers slapping against the cobblestones.

She turned a corner, and saw the Pied Piper only a few steps ahead of her. She had to duck back, barely hiding before he turned around. She heard him take one step toward her, then stop as if reconsidering, before his footsteps clapped in the other direction with greater speed.

She followed him, sticking to the shadows, as he led her through the empty marketplace, until he finally stopped outside the door of the tavern inn.

*   *   *

He needed a few things. He passed through the dark tavern where the barmaid was asleep on the counter, and went up the stairs to his room. He was staying on the second floor, with a window facing toward the street. He peered out through the foggy glass and couldn't see anyone. Then he pulled the curtains shut. He didn't need any witnesses.

He traveled lightly, all except for a formidable chest that he kept locked at all times. In this trunk were all his secrets, and he wasn't about to let some common thief expose his ways to the crowd.

He was a charlatan. He had never really ridden a town of any pests or plagues. But there was good money in pretending, and above all the Pied Piper considered himself a type of actor. In his chest were his various costumes and props, some used only once, and some used repeatedly from town to town. He even had an assortment of items pertaining to witchcraft: tarot cards, black candles, and even a pirate's flag. He dug through the pile until he found what he was looking for: a genuine silver sword. He stood, and swiped it through the air for practice.

It was a real sword. If you're going to be a fake person, you needed real props. And this seemed like something that would scare the children of the town.

After all, he didn't really *believe* the town's children were walking the streets as the living dead. He wasn't a fool. But if pretending to fight the dead was what it took to earn his paycheck, he would play along.

He fit a belt around his waist, and slid the sword into the scabbard.

*   *   *

Wendy saw him emerge a few minutes later. He looked absolutely ridiculous, and she wondered how he had ever tricked the parents of the town into paying him anything. Any child could see that he was a fool.

The man stepped out onto the street and threw back his cape with a flamboyant gesture. His sword glimmered in the inn's torchlight, and the man smiled.

A flutter of anxiety passed through Wendy. Although she didn't consider this man sensible, the fact that he had a weapon was troublesome. If anything, it was *more* troublesome because he was such a fool. Would he even remember who she was? Her father had instructed him to kill her brothers. What if he killed her, too, without realizing she was no threat?

The man finished his display, and started to head west through the marketplace. None of the streetlamps had been lit. Here and there a square of blue moonlight landed, but the rest of the space was dark. Wendy could hear his footsteps just fine, though, and it would be easier for her to follow in darkness anyway.

She took a step, and her slipper slapped against the ground. She froze, and saw the Piper turn in her direction. He peered into the darkness, but he couldn't see her in the shadows. After a moment, he went on.

Wendy stepped out of her slippers and held them in her hand before continuing. She cringed at the cold cobblestones, but knew it would be quieter this way, and she did her best to follow the man in silence.

She soon realized he was following streaks of blood in the lane. It was the trail from her brother's corpse. As the blood became less frequent, the Piper's posture seemed to lose some of its confidence.

At the edge of the town, the man stopped. His body was

black against the black shadows, and then in the next moment there was a white spark, followed by a blaze of light. He had lit a match, and then a torch, and held it up above him to see his way better. It created a halo of light around him as he went over the stone bridge out of town, and continued down the path as it turned from stone to dirt.

Wendy waited until he got a little ahead into the trees before she approached the bridge. She had never left town by herself before, and had never left town even with her parents at night. She could still turn back. She was still within the safety of the town.

But then she had an image of what she was returning to: she pictured herself in her mother's place, wearing her mother's tight-fitting clothes, and pretending to laugh at her father's jokes as her mother did. No, Wendy did not want to return to that. She scurried across the bridge, and accepted whatever there might be waiting for her in the darkness.

She could see the glow of the torch ahead, and tried to keep it far enough ahead of her that she wouldn't be seen in its light, but close enough that she never lost sight of it. She had put back on her slippers, as they didn't sound against the soil, but it was an odd feeling, being out in the darkness of the woods in her pajamas. She felt incredibly vulnerable. The thick trees blocked the moonlight here, so that everything seemed black and invisible in the darkness. It was like being blind in a dark room, and having to feel your way along the walls. Only these walls had occasional thorns. And perhaps she wasn't alone in the room.

She followed the man for what felt like an incredibly long time. As she got farther from town, there were more patches of snow from the last storm. The air had grown colder, and Wendy was shivering, glad she had had the foresight to bring a jacket. Her nose was running, and she had to fight to keep her teeth from chattering.

Then, to Wendy's surprise, the torch stopped moving.

She remained still for a few minutes, in case this meant that the Piper was about to turn around, but when it became clear that he had definitely stopped, she allowed herself to creep forward to investigate. And it was a good thing she did, because in the next moment the flame was put out.

It took Wendy's eyes a moment to adjust to the darkness. The flame had burned a dot in her vision, and it seemed to leap through the blackness as she looked in different directions. She could see the dim outline of the Pied Piper ahead on the path, and the blackness of the trees on either side of him. She was maybe ten steps away from him now, and kept to the edge of the trees. As she stared in his direction, she saw the fading dot of the flame's afterimage start to glow brighter. She blinked, confused, and the dot of light multiplied. She was beginning to think there was something seriously wrong with her vision when the multiple lights all started moving on their own, and Wendy realized that what she was seeing was not inside her mind, but outside, in the woods.

These mysterious floating lights must have been what had prompted the Pied Piper to put out his own flame, and surely enough, Wendy could make out the man stepping off the path and into the trees in the direction of the lights. She took a few steps into the trees in parallel with him, keeping a distance between them.

They both approached the borders of a circular clearing, the Pied Piper at the nine o'clock position, and Wendy at six. In the face of the circle were the dancing lights, floating through the air like a swarm of fireflies. Only they were too large to be fireflies.

"*Fairies!*" Wendy said to herself, moving her lips but not making any noise. She had found fairies! She took another step forward as silently as she could, and pulled back the leaves of a branch to see that there were children dancing with them, and the orbs of light were—

Matches?

Each child in the circle had a long match with a white sparkling flame, and each spun it in the air as if casting a spell with a magic wand. Their movements were stunted and labored, but obviously joyful. The dirty faces of the children were smiling, their eyes looking up toward the sky as they circled a pile of leaves in the center of the clearing. They looked like witches at a midnight Sabbath, and the air smelled of smoke and death.

Then from the far side of the clearing appeared Peter Pan himself. He was not dancing, and the other children turned toward him, clearing a path and bowing as he passed. He walked directly to the center of the clearing, and Wendy realized how silent the night had become. The only sound she heard was Peter's feet crunching the leaves as he walked.

Peter spread his arms wide, as if casting a spell into the night. Then he bent down and started pawing at the ground like an animal, making guttural noises and groans. The other children reciprocated, making moans of their own that sent chills down Wendy's spine.

Still, she was curious, and leaned forward, trying to watch what Peter was doing.

He swiped at the leaves, and Wendy realized he was un-covering something. He knocked his fist against the dirt, and then a moment later the ground in the center began to bulge and quiver. Peter and the other children stepped back, and from the black soil erupted two little demons. It wasn't until they stood up, and Wendy saw their smeared pajamas, that she recognized the pair as her brothers. Peter handed each of them a lit match, and pulled them toward the other chil-dren, who had begun circling again. Her brothers caught on, and started to stumble around in the dark as well, the dirt falling off of them in clumps.

Wendy couldn't help but feel a little jealous of this. Why hadn't she been buried in the dirt and invited to the dance? Why had Peter left *her* behind? She had thought at first that he was being unfair, that maybe he only invited boys to play with him. But here in the circle were other girls among the dead, dancing and playing with the rest. Wendy felt ready to cry, crossing her arms under her coat, and feeling very silly for tracking all this way in the dark in her slippers.

She was about to turn back, to cry privately in a corner somewhere, when she saw the Pied Piper step out from his covering in the woods. His whole posture had changed. He was no longer walking with a confident strut, but came out with hunched shoulders, holding his sword in front of him. Wendy followed his concentrated gaze, and saw that the Pied Piper was headed right toward Peter. The other children were too caught up in their game to notice as the Piper raised his sword, barely a step away from stabbing Peter in the back.

"No!" Wendy shouted, running out from the trees. The children froze and looked up toward her. "Behind you!" she called to Peter, and pointed to the Piper. Peter turned, and was able to jump away as the Piper heaved down the blade of the sword. It lodged in the earth, and as he was trying to pull it out, Peter pounced on his hand.

Even in the darkness, Wendy could see the blood. Black splotches of it sprayed on Peter's face, and he snarled as he dug his teeth into the Pied Piper's wrist. The Pied Piper let go of the sword completely, and tried to push Peter off, but the boy was locked on him like a shark. The Piper screamed, and the worst part was that even from a distance, it looked like Peter was smiling.

The man fell backward and the other children crowded around, blocking him. Wendy took a step closer, both horrified and curious. She could see over the heads of the children, as she was taller than any of them. Some of the children had their matches, but most had thrown theirs aside to the pile of leaves in the center of the clearing. The leaves had caught fire, the wild flames lighting the scene in a hellish light, sending their long shadows dancing on the ground and against the trees surrounding the clearing.

Peter let go of the man's wrist, and spread out his own arms, pushing the other children away. He wanted the Pied Piper for himself. He stood up, blood dripping down his chin, and pulled the heavy sword from the ground. Meanwhile, the Pied Piper was scrambling to his knees, unable to get free of the children.

"What *are* you?" he screamed at them, and Wendy realized this man must never have believed a thing the townspeople told him. Not until it was too late.

He turned back to Peter, and looked into the boy's face as if looking at Death himself.

"Please," he whispered. "Let me go."

A gust of air left Peter's throat—the dead boy's version of a laugh—and it sprayed the Pied Piper with his own blood.

Then Peter brought the sword down, and chopped off the man's hand in one blow.

The Pied Piper screamed out, clutching his stump with his good hand. His eyes were wide with panic as spurts of blood sprayed out, sparkling in the light of the fire. The other children leapt on his severed hand, and several were tugging at it between them, fighting over it. A little girl in grey rags that Wendy had seen on the streets selling matches won the prize, and ran off to chew on it by herself. The other children turned toward the Pied Piper with hungry looks in their eyes.

Peter let out a growl, and stepped forward. This was his prize.

The Pied Piper looked at the boy, at first with fear. Then a change came over his expression. The side of his lip curled up, twitching his moustache, and the fear heated to rage in his eyes.

In one swift movement, he reached under his cape and pulled out the piece of wood he had used as a torch. He stumbled away to the fire, and stuck it in the flames. There was black pitch on the end of it, and it caught ablaze at once. The Pied Piper's eyes were wide and crazed as he rose to his full height, swiping at the air with the torch.

"Back!" he cried. "Or I'll burn you all!"

The children didn't seem very threatened, but they kept their distance regardless. The Pied Piper took his opportunity, and backed out of the clearing, holding his bleeding stump to his chest. When he reached the edge of the trees, he turned and ran into the night. Peter made a move to follow, and then turned back toward Wendy, remembering her for the first time since she had called out. The other children followed his lead, and Wendy soon found herself with her back to the fire, surrounded by a circle of dead children.

She bent down, and picked up the sword from the ground. She held it high, and looked down at Peter.

"Peter Pan," she said, keeping her voice steady. She made sure not to flinch or show any emotion whatsoever, not even when he took a step forward.

He caught her gaze, and peered at her. She looked him right in the eye, and said, "Make me one of you."

*   *   *

The Pied Piper stumbled back to the path, feeling his strength drip out of him. Once he was sure he was not being followed by the demon children—as he now believed they were—he stopped, and held his bloody stump in front of his face.

Blood was flowing freely, and he had no way to stop it. Even if he had some sort of bandage, he lacked the articulation to wrap it securely. The flame of the torch sizzled by his ear, and he knew what he'd have to do. He would have to cauterize the wound.

He held his stump in front of him, and brought the flame

of the torch level with it, but a short distance apart. He knew it was best to just get it over with, and even in this moment's delay the fear was building up inside of him. He clenched down his teeth, and shoved his stump into the flame.

A sound emerged from his throat as his tender flesh cooked and bubbled under the fire. It would have been bad enough to put his hand under a flame, but the open wound was even more painful.

"One," he grunted. "Two. *Three*."

His vision blackened, but he held his stump resolutely in the fire.

"Four... five!"

With a gasp he pulled himself from the fire and waved his flesh in the cool night air. Steam rose from the stump, and blisters were forming all over his forearm. The smell of cooked meat rose to his nose, and he felt nauseous and suddenly very dizzy.

But he knew the children weren't far, and even in his half-blind state, he forced himself to stumble forward along the path. As he walked, blasts of pain shot through his arm into what felt like his fingers. He had to look down to be certain his hand was still gone. It was, of course; but these phantom sensations flashed repeatedly as he walked on.

When he finally reached town, the sky was already beginning to turn blue-grey with dawn. He threw aside the torch, and shuffled over the little stone bridge into town. He felt a sense of relief at being free of the woods. He was hurt, but he was not dead. And now he was back among people that could help him.

But the town looked different in the light. He had arrived the day before under the cover of darkness, and hadn't seen the blackened facades of the buildings. Some sort of fire had ravaged this town, and recently, judging by singed furniture that still remained inside of the broken windows.

Not seeing a single person, he stumbled onward until he

reached the marketplace. At least from here he could reach the inn. He knew there would be someone there.

The marketplace looked different in the daytime as well. The stalls were abandoned, their canvas overhangs torn. Bodies were piled along the edges of the streets. He had seen the forms of these the night before, but had just assumed they were sandbags to—well, he wasn't sure to what purpose. He dragged himself forward, looking at the rotted corpses, at their faces melted away to the bone with decay. This town was worse off than anyone had led him to believe.

He reached the inn. As he pushed open the door, the innkeeper pushed it back shut.

"Help me," cried the Piper. "I've been attacked."

"You're not coming back in here," the innkeeper shouted through the glass. "You've got the plague."

"Plague?"

"You're as good as dead," the innkeeper said. "So you might as well keep away, and spare the rest of us."

"But my hand—"

"Not our concern."

The Piper backed away from the door, and as he stepped into the morning light, he caught sight of his reflection in the glass. His hair was wild, and his eyes were dark in his abnormally pale face. He looked down at his arms, and saw his blood blackened in his veins. The stump itself had turned black entirely, and the blackness was crawling up his arm in thin, root-like spirals.

He clutched his arm with horror, and backed away into the marketplace. He looked at the piles of the dead, and a terror filled him as he pictured himself becoming one of them. How many of them had been like him, hired by the town to fix their problem?

Just then he saw someone passing at the end of the lane. He looked up, and newfound hope made him weak in the knees.

"Mr. Darling!" he cried, stomping forward. Mr. Darling turned in his direction, and then started to hurry away. "Wait!" cried the Piper. "I found your children."

Mr. Darling stopped. He waited in place until the Piper had struggled to make his way across the market.

"Well?" he said impatiently. "Where are they? Is the girl with you?"

"They're in the woods," the Piper gasped, feeling faint from exertion. "Get me to a doctor, and then I can take you to them." He reached out to rest his weight against Mr. Darling's shoulder.

Mr. Darling stepped back. "And just how do you expect to pay for a doctor?"

"I found your children," the Piper said. "Even the girl. Pay me my fee, and I will take care of the rest."

Mr. Darling scoffed. "Pay your fee? For what? So you can go off on another lark?"

The Piper's eyes went wide and he held up his stump. "They bit off my hand!"

Mr. Darling shook his head. "No payment."

"But you promised! The whole town promised." He was already feeling weaker, and could barely stand. "Please," he begged, "without a doctor, I'll die." This last plea had taken all the energy he had left. He stumbled, and reached out again for Mr. Darling. Again, the man stepped back, and the Piper fell to the ground.

"Well," said Mr. Darling, "at least dying is free." And with that, he walked away, leaving the Pied Piper in the street.

Even in his sickened condition, the Pied Piper had enough pride to drag himself to the dark shadows rather than to die in the open. He crawled to the nearest stand, a fisherman's booth, and fell among the dried and brittle fish heads.

"No payment," he whispered to himself, growing delirious. "No payment?"

His vision darkened, and a crazed smile spread across his face.

"But you must pay," he croaked. "You *must* pay the Piper."

And with that thought on his mind, he sank into the rotten fish, and died.

* * *

As the sky began to lighten with dawn, Wendy was practically sleepwalking on her feet. She had been following the dead children through the woods for hours, and she had the feeling that they were walking in circles. She tried to tell herself that this was all part of some elaborate game, the rules of which the voiceless children couldn't explain to her. But another part of her was afraid they were simply trying to wear her out, so that it would be easier to overpower her and take the sword away.

She followed the line of children through the brush, and when she emerged on the other side, the sound of flowing water drew her attention. It was a stream. Wendy recognized it as the river that led into town, although she had only been this far along the trail maybe once or twice with her parents in all her life. The clear water flowed through the small riverbed, and farther ahead, joined the greenish muck of a small bog.

She looked at the water, and felt an overwhelming desire to take a drink. She ran up the line to Peter. "Do you mind if we stop a while?" she asked, finding herself out of breath from the long excursion.

Peter paused and turned to her. His eyes looked at her for a moment as if he had forgotten who she was entirely. Then his mouth opened in a dark grin, his small teeth exposed. He reached out and took her hand. His fingers were cold and silky, and he pulled her away from the stream.

"No!" Wendy snapped. "I'm thirsty!"

She rushed toward the stream before he could stop her. She bent down at once, setting the sword by her side, and started to rinse the blood from her hands. She took a drink. Then she scooped up some water to rinse her face and neck. It was incredibly refreshing, and she felt not only more awake, but more alive afterward. She had just dunked her legs into the water, watching the blood and grime swirl away in the water, when she heard a splash to her right.

Her mouth opened with astonishment. She stood up, making sure to pick up her sword, and took a few steps toward the bog.

There were women in the sludge, wading in the bog with their shoulders exposed. One lifted a muddy arm from the muck, and motioned for Wendy to come closer.

"Mermaids," she whispered. She turned to the other children, to see if they shared her amazement, but she couldn't tell how they were feeling from their blank expressions. They all stayed a good distance back, and did not follow.

Wendy crept closer to gaze upon these women. She had always believed in mermaids, just as she had always believed in witches, goblins, and fairies. But when she got near the edge of the bog, she started to notice the women's long tangled hair, and the wild, animalistic looks in their eyes. Since they were in the mud, Wendy couldn't tell if they were wearing any clothes at all, and the idea of swimming in that dreck naked seemed absolutely beastly.

She turned back to the other children, seeing John and Michael in the crowd. They were the only ones wearing white. The rest of the children's outfits had become stained from being in the woods, brown with dirt and grime. Already there were some scuffs on the legs of her brother's pajamas. And, of course, there were long slashes of dried blood as well. Why hadn't they gone to wash like she had?

She turned back to the bog and saw the women standing up, the mud of the bog slopping off of them. And when they stood, she saw that they weren't really mermaids, but had legs like anyone else. The closest one opened her mouth, and she let out a long, guttural moan. As she did so, more mud came out of her mouth, and oozed down her breasts.

Wendy reached for her sword. "Stay back!" she yelled, but they didn't seem to hear her. The group of mud women lurched toward her, and Wendy stepped backward, feeling something crunch under her feet. She glanced down to see small bones littering the shore of the bog. They looked like children's bones.

"Peter?" she called, clutching the sword for her life. She turned her head—and the children were gone. "Peter!" she called, her voice filled with panic.

The swamp women stepped up to the shore. Wendy backed away, swiping at the air in front of her with the sword, but there was no way she could take on so many. There were four women on the shore already, and more and more kept popping their heads up from the bog, drawn by the noise. She backed up to the trees, and pressed her back against a gnarled grey tree trunk.

She had just wanted to play with her dolls and to be left alone. And now she was about to become a meal for these swamp hags. Her body was shaking with fear, and the women seemed to delight in it, staggering toward her with increased fervor.

A hand closed in around Wendy's heel from behind, and she shrieked. She turned around toward the tree, instinctively raising the sword, and looked down to see Peter smiling at her from a nook in the tree trunk. Then his head popped back into the tree, and he was gone.

There was an opening in the tree, its borders smeared with blood. Wendy crouched down immediately, and started to shove her feet into it. They fell below into an open space, and she realized it was some kind of tunnel. But there was no time for caution. She shoved her legs inside, and backed up into it, using her elbows to push herself backward along the ground. The swamp hags doubled their efforts, seeing she was trying to escape. The closest one let out a growl of rage, and lunged toward her.

Wendy pushed herself back, the woman's claws inches from her face, and fell into the dark tunnel. She slid down the mud, unable to get a grip to slow herself, and twisted around a curve in the tunnel into pitch blackness. She fell, the walls disappearing on both sides, and landed in a muddy pile of what felt like rags, leaves, and dirt.

She stood up, her feet sinking into the muck, and opened her eyes wide, unable to see a thing. She wiped at the mud she felt on her face, and flicked it to the ground. She could still smell it in her nostrils, and she started to gag.

There were sounds around her. She was not alone.

"Peter?" she whispered, her voice trembling.

There was the strike of a match, and a moment later she saw Peter's grinning face floating before her in the darkness. The blaze of the match lit the wick of a candle, and a flickering light illuminated the space.

Wendy glanced around, as if expecting something to jump out at her. She was in an underground chamber, a bubble of open space in the mud and dirt. The walls and ceiling were lined with thick tree roots, and the ground was wet and sloppy. The air smelled thick and sour, and Wendy noticed with a gasp that the pile she had fallen into was made up of decomposing limbs. She tried not to think too closely about that as she pulled her feet out of it, leaving her slippers behind. Then she turned back to Peter.

He had the sword. A lump of dread formed in Wendy's throat. She was cold and tired, and covered with wet filth. "Are you going to kill me?" she asked, unable to stop herself.

Peter just smiled. He stepped aside and lifted the candle to an opening in the wall behind him. Then he pointed the sword, first toward Wendy, and then toward the opening.

She stepped forward, trying to tell herself that Peter had just saved her from the mermaids. Why would he save her just to kill her a moment later?

Unless he was saving her for himself.

The next room was longer, and she was able to stand without crouching. Peter followed her with his candle, and set it on a small table. One of the other children, the little match girl, started lighting candles throughout the room.

There were coffins here, a row of them along the ground. Wendy's breath quickened, realizing she was in some sort of ancient burial chamber. The walls here were muddy stones, and large cobwebs fell in sheets from the rounded ceiling. She heard something to her side, and saw a large wooden barrel. The top was on, and from inside she could hear a slithering sound, as if something alive were inside. She reached out a hand toward it, and Peter nudged her forward, away from it. Her bare feet landed in muddy puddles until she reached the center of the room, where Peter gestured for her to sit on the edge of one of the coffins.

She sat.

"Why have you brought me here?" she asked. She no longer thought there was any chance of being turned into one of them. He had rejected her back in the nursery, and he had never changed his opinion on the matter. Her eyes scanned the room for an escape.

Peter sat down on the coffin opposite her, pulling his legs up to sit with them crossed in front of him.

"Are you going to kill me?" Wendy asked, and Peter shook his head. "Then why am I here?"

Peter's smile widened. He gestured to one of the other children, and a little boy came forward. He must have been down in the chamber the entire time, for Wendy would have remembered his grotesque appearance.

His face was sewn together in loose stitches, the skin along his cheeks separating. His ankle was nearly severed, and he carried one of his arms in his hands, a few black strands of thread trailing from the end of it. He stumbled past Wendy, to the coffin behind her, and pushed off the lid.

Inside was a corpse lying on a bed of skeletons. The skin was shriveled away from the face, but from the apron and maid's uniform, Wendy could tell it had been a woman. She shivered, and watched as the boy struggled to rip off the dead woman's apron. Then he shambled back to Wendy, and dropped it in her lap. When she just stared at it, the boy lifted it toward her with his one hand, pressing it against her until she realized she was supposed to put it on.

Wendy picked it up, and held her breath as she pulled the bands of the apron over her neck, and tied the strings around her waist. She was more confused than ever, and it intensified her fear. She forced herself to turn away from the open coffin, and back to Peter. He was still smiling, seeming even happier now that she had the apron on.

It was silent in the chamber, all except the weird slithering sound that came from the barrel by the doorway. She turned toward the blank expressions of the children, who were all staring at her with their darkened eyes. "I don't understand," she said. And she didn't. She had the feeling that they had brought her here to replace the dead woman whose apron she now wore, but who had this dead woman been to them? A maid? A slave? "What do you want from me?" she asked out loud.

Peter leaned forward. He opened his mouth, and made an effort to inhale, his chest filling with air. Then his eyes squinted in concentration as he manipulated his lips.

He spoke. It was more of a growl than a word. But Wendy understood it perfectly.

"*Mmmothhhur.*"

Wendy shook her head. "But I don't want to be a mother, not to anyone. I want to stay a little girl."

Peter's expression grew rabid, and he pulled back his lips

in a snarl. The other children started to snarl as well, even Wendy's own siblings, John and Michael. They came closer to her, and Wendy looked behind her to the dead woman in the coffin. Had she refused to be their mother? Or had she agreed, and this is what became of her anyway?

"Okay," she whispered, bowing her head. She had no choice. "I'll be your mother."

The children stopped snarling and started jumping around the room, making sounds like horses being strangled. They were giggling.

As they put a rag into Wendy's hand, she kept her head down. She wiped away the mud on a little girl's face, but the entire time she kept her eyes on the sword in Peter's hand.

She would have to fight. That was the only way to leave this hell. If she won, she could get back to town, where she could be safe. There were adults there to protect her, and they would know how to fend off the monsters. She just needed to get back to town, and then everything would be fine.

Or, at least, she told herself so.

*   *   *

The Pied Piper opened his blackened eyes.

He sat up, the scales of the dead fish falling off of him onto the marketplace stones. His coat was stained with blood, and he held up the dried stump in front of his face.

The memories came back—jumbled, but trustworthy enough. He remembered he was owed a debt. That the town had not paid.

And he knew it was time to collect.

He pushed himself up from the ground, and looked around at his surroundings. It was disorientating, like waking up from a dream into a stranger's bed. Then his eyes glanced down at the fisherman's stall in front of him. And there, hanging before him like an upside-down question mark, was a silver fisherman's hook.

Hook, he thought to himself. Yes, a hook would do.

It was covered in grime, but that only let him grip it better as he wriggled it free of the wood plank of the stand. He tugged it out, and then pressed it into his blackened stump, the rotten flesh oozing out the sides like pudding. He used his good hand to test its strength, but it was loose. He needed something to lodge it into the bone.

He looked around for a hammer. The stands were all bare around him, and there was nothing close that would work. He turned until he had made a complete circle, and found himself facing the wall of the nearest building. It would do.

He punched the wall with his hooked stump, driving the silver into his forearm, until he felt it split the bone and lodge within it. He backed away, and slashed through the air to test it. Then he stumbled back to the fisherman's stand, and raised his arm. He lunged his hook down, and it split the stand in half, right down the middle. The hook didn't even wiggle. It was like it had become a part of him.

He lifted his eyes at the sound of footsteps.

It was the innkeeper. He worked his way across the marketplace, heading toward the tavern inn. The Pied Piper stood up, hiding his hook behind his back, and when the innkeeper saw him, he stopped.

"Piper," he called out. "Keep your distance!" The innkeeper ran to his residence, and took out a ring of keys from his pocket. His hands were shaking so badly that he dropped them.

The Pied Piper walked to him. He found that his legs were stiff, and he couldn't move with his former speed. By the time he got to the innkeeper, the man had already picked up the keys and inserted the correct one into the lock. He had just opened the door and taken a step inside when he made the mistake of looking back over his shoulder.

The Pied Piper swung an uppercut blow, piercing the end of the hook through the underside of innkeeper's chin. It ripped through his mouth and skull, until the tip of the hook poked out between the innkeeper's eyes. The innkeeper fell. The Pied Piper slid out the hook, and licked off the hot gore.

He staggered into the tavern, scraping his hook along the wall as he walked, scratching through the wallpaper. When he had gotten to the stairs that led up to the rooms of the inn, the barmaid was coming down with a tray of dirty dishes. Her eyes opened wide when she saw him, and she dropped the plates. They shattered on the steps, and she raised her hands to protect herself as he brought the hook down on the crown of her skull, splitting it in two.

He stepped over her body and made his way up the stairs.

Every room was full. He could practically smell the flesh walking around inside, unaware. Trapped.

He knocked with his hook on the first door he came to. It opened at once, the man inside probably thinking it was more room service.

He was wrong. It was time to pay his dues.

*   *   *

Wendy had patiently waited for her first opportunity to rebel.

She had wordlessly agreed to clean the little chamber—as much as it could be cleaned. She was mostly just rearranging the dirt from one location to another. But the task had had one benefit: it had given her an idea.

She was wiping off surfaces toward the entrance, trying to peer around the corner to the anteroom she had tumbled into originally. There had to be an easier way up to the surface than the tunnel she had used, and she was trying to discover it while mindlessly running a rag over the broken chairs and shards of china along the far wall. While she was doing this, two children—a brother and sister, from the looks of them—had shambled up to her as quickly as they could. They took her by the wrist, and pulled her from the doorway.

At first she had thought she was caught in the act, but then she realized the pair wasn't looking through the doorway, but to the closed barrel next to it. Wendy had gotten close to it without noticing. Whatever was in there, making that horrible slithering noise, the children were afraid of it.

And if they were afraid of it, it might be of use to her.

Wendy sat back down on one of the coffins, and she began her next task: sewing up the boy with the loose stitches. She worked the needle through the split flesh on his face, her mind still considering the barrel, and pulled tight the black thread. At having his face restored, the boy seemed relieved. He gave a small smile, and then tossed his severed arm into her lap. Then he turned to offer her his shoulder, and waited patiently.

Wendy continued nervously, breathing through her mouth. The boy, like everything else in the pit, smelled terrible. She glanced up at Peter for a moment, and saw he was still sitting at the end of the room, the sword in his lap. He had his gaze fixed on her.

It was now or never.

Wendy jumped up, throwing the boy in the middle of the path behind her. She ran, pushing down the little match girl, and jumped over the coffins to the corner of the room. She could hear Peter scurrying behind her, but she didn't stop. She got to the main entrance, and her brothers were there, blocking her path.

The traitors, she thought, and jumped out of their grasp and to the corner with the barrel.

As soon as she laid her hands on the lid of the barrel, everyone in the room froze. Even John and Michael froze, although Wendy was certain they had no idea what was in the barrel, having never been here before either. Wendy untied the rope that secured the lid.

She looked at Pan. There was a look of utter rage on his face, and she almost laughed. Until he lifted the sword. She dug her fingers into the side of the lid as Peter charged down the room toward her. He threw the sword toward her with all his might, aiming right for her face. Wendy plucked off the lid of the barrel, and held it in front of her as a shield.

The sword thrust its way into it, the blade poking through the back of the lid only a thimble's length from her eye. She lowered it, and saw the children backing away. Then she turned toward the barrel.

At first it was hard to see in the darkened chamber. The first impression she got was of albino snakes, lacing their fat bodies over and through one another. But then she saw miniature fingers and fat little toes attached to the snakes, and her mind struggled to put the confused image together in a way that made sense. It wasn't until the first baby raised its face over the side of the barrel, its translucent skin pulled back into a fat smile, and its black eyes fixing hungrily on her, that she realized what it was:

It was a barrel full of dead babies.

They were hideous and hairless, like naked mole rats with apelike intelligence in their eyes. Whatever change happened to adults and children when they were turned into the walking dead, it didn't happen in quite the same way for infants.

For one thing, they could move much faster.

The first infant jumped toward Wendy like a spider. She still had the lid in her hands, and barely had time to lift it to block the baby's attack. She felt its weight on the shield, and then a moment later its fat fingers curled around the top of the lid. Wendy was startled to see that it had sharp black fingernails that were almost an inch long. She shook her head. What was wrong with these babies?

She dropped the lid, and the baby looked up at her like a

shaved rat. It was about to scurry toward her, when there was a clap from the other side of the room. Wendy looked up, and saw that all of her former captors were huddled against the far wall, their eyes open wide and their expressions stretched with terror. Peter had his hands together. The baby turned to him, and he clapped again. He was as scared of the baby as the rest of the children, but this was apparently some way to control the creature.

The baby laughed—a husky, demonic chuckle that made even Wendy do a double take. It crawled on all fours toward the children, but not as a baby would, on its palms and knees, but as an insect might, on its long black fingernails and toenails.

Wendy lost no time. She stood on the barrel lid with both feet, and pulled the sword out of it. Then, with all the strength she could muster, she pushed over the entire barrel. The babies swarmed out, climbing up along the walls and racing along the ceiling, their long nails clicking against every surface. She heard Peter let out a moan from across the room, but she didn't let herself become distracted.

She ran back out into the anteroom, and saw her brothers staring back at Peter and the other children. They were obviously trying to decide what they could do to help their friends—but without getting too close. By the time they registered Wendy, she had already made it halfway around them. Michael, who barely came up to her waist, reached out for her.

"No!" she yelled, and grabbed her brother around the middle, and threw his little body back toward the main chamber. He landed on his back, and just as he was sitting up, a cloud of babies covered him.

Wendy ran. She was right, there were other openings in the walls. She chose one of the larger ones, and elbowed her way inside, working as fast as she could to climb the tunnel. She made it up around a bend within a minute, and climbed out behind a bush, back into the woods.

She could still hear the clicking below, echoing out through the tunnel, and didn't wait around. She ran, stumbling over a tree and finding herself back by the small stream she had washed in earlier. She looked back, and saw the mermaids in the mud. They were submerged up to their noses, watching her like crocodiles, but they must have considered her too much work to follow. Plus, she still had the sword.

She ran along the stream, knowing it to lead back to town. A path might have been faster, but she didn't trust herself to find one in these woods. The light was already fading, and she couldn't tell exactly what time it was. What little she saw of the sky through the trees looked grey and dim.

Her feet were numb with cold when she had reached a part of the woods that started to look familiar. Only then did she stop long enough to peel off the filthy apron from around her neck. She went on, reaching the bridge that led over the stream and into town, and rushed across it, not stopping.

She knew the babies would stop Peter and the other children for some time, but she didn't think the babies could kill them. For one, the children were already dead. And for another, they had obviously overpowered the babies once before, or else how would they have gotten them into the barrel in the first place?

Wendy's home was on the other side of town, and the fastest way to reach it would be to cut through the market-place.

She had started out running, the sword heavy in her hand, but when she got to the open square, a chill passed through her. Street traffic had grown lighter over the last few months, but this was the one space in town that you could almost always count on seeing at least one person.

But it was completely empty. And before dark, that was not normal.

She crept forward, her bare feet feeling the rounded edges of the cobblestones as she made her way past the mounds of bodies that encircled the market, and past the empty stands that had once been busy with activity. She hadn't been out to the town much since the fires. Was it really like this all the time now?

She had made it nearly midway through when she saw the first body, and she wouldn't even have noticed it if it wasn't coated in bright red blood. She froze, glancing around her, and then made her way as quietly as she could forward.

It was the innkeeper. She peered into the tavern behind him, and saw the wooden floors drenched with blood. There was a body on the stairwell, but Wendy was too scared to investigate beyond that. She broke into a run, and got away as fast as she could.

As she passed through the streets, she saw more bodies. Fresh ones. These weren't plague victims, as far as she could tell. They lacked the pale skin and dark circles that had become so familiar to her. These just looked like murder victims.

Something had happened while she was away—was *still* happening, as far as she knew—and she didn't feel safe exposed on the streets. She turned a corner, and saw her house around the bend. She waited a moment, watching to make sure there wasn't anyone hiding that might jump out at her, and then she ran across the street and to her front door.

It was open. She went inside, and slammed it shut behind her, throwing down the latch to lock it. She was in such a panic that it didn't even strike her as odd, the fact that the door was left open in the middle of the day. She might not have considered it at all, if she hadn't turned around.

"Oh!" she cried, putting a hand over her mouth.

There, at the base of the stairwell, was Nana. Well, most of Nana. Someone had made off with her head.

Wendy crept forward, forcing herself to step over the dog to climb the stairs.

"Mother?" she whispered, straining to listen to any sounds. "Father?"

She still had the sword. She was suddenly so grateful that she had bothered to carry it with her all this way. She clutched it by her side, and used her other hand to steady herself on the banister.

The old stairway creaked at every step. There was no helping it. Wendy forced herself to continue, stopping briefly on the second floor. The room to her parents' bedroom was open, and she had to bend to look inside without putting herself in danger.

It was dark, and as far as she could tell, empty. She went on to the third floor.

Ahead of her she could see the door to the nursery. It was shut. But from under the door, she could see a flicker of light. Someone had lit a candle inside. The chance of seeing someone familiar melted all caution. Wendy ran forward, and threw open the door.

Sitting in front of the window was her mother. Her mouth was slack, and there was a gaping hole in the middle of her forehead.

Wendy stumbled backward. "Mother," she whispered, and then she heard a shuffling noise from the corner of the room.

Whipping around instantly, she lunged the sword toward the sound. It found its mark, and she looked up from the hilt—to see it was her father.

He looked down at the sword, and then up toward Wendy. "Run," he gurgled, blood spluttering out of his mouth. He fell to his knees, and Wendy pulled the sword out.

She bent down, and put a hand on her father's back. "I'm so sorry," she said. "I didn't know it was you."

Her father looked up at her, his face going pale. "Run," he whispered again, and then he fell over.

Then she heard it: a dull thump from below on the stairs. Then another heavy footstep. Then another. And as the person walked up the stairs, he dragged something along the wall.

Wendy jumped up at once and slammed the door of the nursery. She looked around for something to block the door, but all she kept finding were her parents' bodies. Desperate, she slid under her bed, bringing the sword with her.

The door flew open with one blow. Heavy boots stumbled into the room, and from the lurching way they walked, Wendy knew that the killer was one of the dead after all.

He stopped by her father's body, and Wendy could practically hear the man thinking. She wondered if her father had been hiding this whole time. Had he hid under the bed like she had? Did he watch his own wife get murdered, and do nothing about it?

The killer turned away from her father, and she heard him take a deep inhale. He was sniffing the air. Could he smell her? Was that possible? And then Wendy realized she probably stank. She had spent all that time in the muck of the woods, and down in that underground chamber with all those dead bodies. They could probably smell her from a block away. The boots of the man turned toward the bed, and Wendy put a hand over her mouth so that the sounds of her breathing would be muffled. She kept her other hand on the hilt of the sword. She didn't think she could kill the man from this angle, but she might be able to slow him down.

He took two dragging footsteps toward her. The light from the candle sent his shadow across the floor, and Wendy saw the outline of a sharp hook where his hand should be. She realized with a weapon like that, he could pull her out from under the bed and rip open her guts before she'd have time to lift the sword. He took another step toward her, and started to bend down toward the bed.

Just then, there was a knock at the window. The killer stood up and looked—Wendy could tell this from his shadow—and then let out a fearsome growl. He stomped away from the bed and to the window, and Wendy heard him bang his hook against the glass.

Wendy scuffled to the other end of the bed, away from the window, and peeked out.

Peter was at the window, looking surprised and amused. Wendy recognized the killer as the Piper at once, but it was hard for her to think of him now as anything other than the Man with the Hook. He threw her mother to the side and shattered the glass, but couldn't manage to open the window with his hook.

Wendy slid out from the end of the bed, hoping that Peter wouldn't give her away. She silently rose to her feet, and raised the sword above her head. Then she heaved it down, using every muscle in her entire body, into the man's back.

It slid between his ribs, and Wendy exhaled. She felt like she had been holding her breath the entire time. But as soon as she let go of the sword, the man started to turn around. He didn't seem hurt at all.

Wendy saw him lift his hooked arm, and she cringed in anticipation of his blow.

It didn't come.

She looked up, and saw Pan struggling to keep hold of the man's arm through the broken window.

"Oh!" she cried, and saw the Man with the Hook turn to Peter with all his fury. As he did so, the sword in his back swiveled around toward Wendy again.

She knew an opportunity when she saw one.

Wendy pulled the sword from the man's back, jumped up on her bed to match his height, and said, "Hey, Hook!"

He turned toward her, and she pierced the blade through his eye. He reached a hand toward her, and she leaned her weight into the blade until it skewered his skull. Then he crumpled to the floor.

Peter Pan smiled at her from outside the window. He reached his hand through the broken window in an attempt to undo the latch.

"No!" Wendy cried. She pulled the sword out of the dead

man's head, and slapped the blade against the window. Peter whipped his hand back outside. He looked up at her, his expression uncharacteristically thoughtful.

"Stay out!" Wendy yelled, holding up the sword.

Then Peter smiled his dangerous smile. From down below, Wendy could hear a crash against the front door. The other children were already trying to get in. She was trapped.

But what was she to do? Wendy bit her lip. If she let Peter in, he'd take her back to be a mother. And even if she could defeat him and remain in the house, then what? She would stay alive, grow old, and become—a mother?

Wendy shook her head. She didn't want any of that. She never did.

She looked at the bodies on the floor. Then she had an idea.

She smiled. "If you won't turn me," she said to Peter, "then I'll do it myself."

It was common knowledge in town at this point that a bite or a scratch could infect you with the plague. Even Wendy knew this, and her parents barely told her anything. She dropped to the floor, and picked up the lifeless hand of the Man with the Hook. Then, fumbling with his fingers, she scratched herself across the arm.

Was that enough? she wondered. Or did it take more?

Peter, growing suspicious, began to fiddle with the window again. Wendy stood up and tried to stab him with the sword.

"I said, 'Stay out!'" she cried. Then she was back on her knees, and turning the man onto his side. He was heavy, and his eye dribbled out a black ooze that was thicker than blood should be. She pried open his jaws with the sword, and then shoved her wrist inside his mouth.

She stared down at him for a moment, and then slapped her free hand on the base of his chin. He bit into her like a nutcracker, and Wendy shrieked in pain. She pulled her arm away, and huddled with it against her chest. Blood was flowing now onto her nightgown, and the wound stung terribly.

Peter was still trying to get in. She could see him motioning to the children on the street, and below she heard a crash as the door was knocked down. Then a moment later there was the pounding of the children's feet running up the stairs. She looked up at Peter, and he smiled back at her.

"No," Wendy said, and struggled back to her feet. "I'm not leaving. I refuse."

She heard the children running up the steps, and then saw their forms as they approached the final few steps to the nursery. Wendy pressed herself against the man's corpse, and reached back for his hook. As the first of the children—her own brothers!—were running through the nursery door, Wendy dragged the bloody hook across her throat.

The children stumbled, and Wendy fell over, the blood gushing out from her neck and onto the floor.

She smiled in triumph.

*　　*　　*

For Wendy, death was like flying through a dark night, a cold and starless abyss removed from the concepts of time or age. It was so relaxing to be dead, that after sailing through the blissful nothingness, she was almost surprised to find herself back in the nursery.

The first thing she noticed was that, although it was dark, she could see perfectly well. What's more, the colors of the room seemed more vibrant than they had ever been when she was alive.

Was she not alive?

Wendy's mind worked to catch up to where she was now. She went through the memories of the nursery, of climbing out the window, the Man with the Hook, and Peter Pan.

She had killed herself.

Wendy sat up. She tried to speak but no sound came out. She lifted her hands to her neck, and felt the gashes in her throat. They didn't hurt, but they scared her. Her nightgown was covered in dried blood. She opened her mouth, attempting to speak again, and a husky wheeze of air came out. She sucked in air, and—

Food.

She looked at the ground, sniffing the air and tasting the scent of blood in it. Then she saw that someone had left her a pile of organs.

She crawled over to it, and began eating greedily, too hungry to chew. It tasted so good that she finished the whole pile.

Then she looked up, still licking the blood from her hands, and saw Peter standing outside the window.

She didn't know how to feel about that. He couldn't hurt her anymore. *No one* could hurt her anymore. And she didn't need him at all.

She crossed her arms over her chest, and tapped her foot. It took more effort to do this than she liked, but the message got across nonetheless.

Peter smiled. He motioned for her to come closer, and then he pointed down below to the street. Keeping her eyes on him, Wendy took a step forward. She peered out through the broken window, and saw the dead children playing in the dark street. If there were any adults left in the town, they weren't trying to stop the hordes now. The children were safe to stay children.

Peter waited for her response, and she recognized that he was inviting her to join them.

But after all she had been through, Wendy didn't really feel like being around Peter Pan right now. She shook her head, and turned back to her dark room.

She felt Peter watching her as she stumbled across to the fireplace, and then as she pulled out the remains of a blackened doll. Wendy pulled it to her chest, and sat down with it in her lap.

So what if she looked silly, a girl of fourteen—*forever fourteen*—playing with dolls in a dark corner alone, covered with her own blood? She was home, and she was in her nursery, and no one could make her grow up now. Not her parents, not the Man with the Hook, and not even Peter Pan.

Wendy smiled, thinking of this, and ran her fingers through the doll's charred hair. She rocked it back and forth, and started to hum.

She might never leave the nursery again.

THE LITTLE MERMAID OF DEATH

Ariel was given the signal to move forward. The attack on the palace had begun.

The morning was grey, but the women didn't feel the cold. They were already dead, their naked bodies smeared with dirt and slime from the swamp. No one stopped them as they slipped, one by one, through the broken gates of the palace.

Food had become scarce. Back when the women of the swamp were the only dead around, it seemed like some unlucky traveler fell into their clutches almost every day. But in the past few months, the town's population had dropped to zero—or close to it, anyway. And Ariel and her sisters were starving. The last guaranteed meal large enough to feed a horde of their size was within the palace walls.

But for Ariel this mission would give her more than food; it would feed her soul. Because—much to the embarrassment of the other swamp hags—Ariel *loved* humans. She loved their creations, their architecture, their fine clothing. Ariel herself had no memories of her former life, and that made the humans all the more fascinating.

She moved forward with the horde, a smile forming on her ragged face. She had a good feeling about this raid.

*   *   *

Inside the palace, a quiet circle had gathered around the dying king. He lay in his bed in the royal chamber, barely able to move or speak. His body was covered with black and red burns, giving his skin the appearance of molten rock.

Bowing next to his bed was a young man wearing a loose-fitting white shirt, and sitting behind him was a stern-looking young woman in a floor-length purple dress. A single candle burned on his bedside table.

"Your Majesty," the woman said, "we came as soon as we heard." She forced a smile. It was easy for Ursula to smile looking at the King's burns, even if her brother Eric seemed grieved by the man's pain.

The King looked at her blankly for a moment, and then motioned for her brother to come forward.

He took Eric's hand. "My son… is dead," he wheezed, as if it were a revelation. Ursula turned away to roll her eyes. "My kingdom… in ruins. As my sister's first-born son, that makes you… my heir."

Ursula snarled internally. She was the first-born child, and her mother was still quite alive. But as long as *one* male heir remained, they would never gain control of the kingdom. Her lips curled as she looked at her brother's back, bowed before the king.

Eric was broad-shouldered, handsome, and utterly devoid of what Ursula considered the appropriate disposition to rule. He was pleasant but not witty; clear-thinking but not resolute; and far too trusting.

Worst of all, he never seemed to get how offensive it was that *he* would be the next in line for power when Ursula was so much better suited for such a position. He didn't consider her at all, which was a mistake.

She was ruthless, and a leader. She would never have let the kingdom get to this point. Overrun by the dead? How weak do you have to be to let your kingdom fall to walking skeletons?

"You have… my blessing," the King said, putting a blackened hand on Eric's shoulder. "The kingdom will pass to you as soon as you settle on a wife. It cannot wait until my death. It is important…" His eyes lost focus for a moment, and he made a choked sound, deep in his throat.

"My King?" Eric asked, leaning forward. Ursula leaned forward as well. Was it possible? she thought hopefully. Could he be dead already?

Then the King coughed, and tears spilled from his eyes and ran down the blistered and blackened skin of his face. "It is *important*," he continued, "that our line continue. That we survive this time."

Ursula leaned back in her chair. She might as well have been invisible as the King mumbled on. She thought about how if she were next in line, she wouldn't sit there, kissing the King's ring. No, not at all. She would press his pillow down on his face, not wavering as his arms flapped against her like a flightless bird. He would die, and, just like that, she would be queen. Her eyes narrowed, looking at her brother. *He* would never do that, she thought bitterly. And yet *he's* next in line. What a waste.

And she wondered, what had *really* happened to the last prince? She had liked him much better. He at least had a sense of humor. Yet she could never get a straight answer out of anyone of what became of him. Which was too bad, because he was quite charming.

"My son," the King said, and it drew back Ursula's attention, "could never produce an heir. Don't make that mistake."

Eric nodded, as if he had just been told the secret to the universe. Ursula had had enough.

"Look," she said, reaching a hand inside the pocket of her gown. The King glanced to her, not amused that he had been interrupted. Eric just looked at her placidly.

"What is it, sister?" he asked.

"I have a gift for Your Majesty," she said, and pulled out a bright red crab. She stood and set it on the King's stomach with both hands. He looked at it, confused and worried, and then slowly lifted his blackened hand to touch it with his dirty fingertip. The crab did not move. He nudged it again, and it fell over, its legs jutting out stiff in the air. The King looked to Eric for an explanation.

"It is preserved," Ursula said, taking back the center of attention. She picked up the crustacean and set it on the King's side table, and turned it so that its dead black eyes were facing him. "There. Now you will always have a friend at your side."

"It looks... so *real*," the King said with fearful admiration.

"Yes," Eric said. "My sister has a gift. She once left a snake preserved in a position of attack in my bedchamber. It was... very lifelike."

"I can do all sorts of things," Ursula bragged. "Dogs, turtles, mice. There was even a mother in our village who lost her child at a young age, and since it was no larger than a cat, it fit quite easily into my jars and—"

But before she could finish, there was a crash in the hallway outside their room. All three looked up in alarm. They heard the yell of a guard, and the unmistakable groaning of the dead.

"They're here," the King whispered, sitting up in panic. "They've come back to finish me off."

Ursula looked at him, surprised by this bit of news. He had told her that his burns were the result of an accident, not an attack. Were the dead really that powerful?

"Sister," Eric said, shaking Ursula's shoulder, "hide! I will protect the King."

It took all of Ursula's control to not laugh at her brother's statement. Protect the King? He would get himself killed.

But rather than showing her joy, she nodded sincerely, and said, "God be with you."

Eric stood in front of the King, spreading his arms over him, and Ursula hurried behind a changing screen in the corner of the room. She ducked down just as the double doors to the chamber were thrown open.

Through the mesh fabric of the screen, she was able to see as the creatures outside the room chased the guards down the hall. Then one of the things came to their doorway, and stopped.

It was a woman. Or at least, it once had been. She was naked, although her body was coated with so much mud and grime that it was almost like clothing. She walked into the room with uncertain steps, and turned her gnarled face upon the King and Eric. Her mouth opened, and a groan came out from between her sharp, rotted teeth. Then she turned, and closed the doors behind her.

Eric held his place in front of the King, and the woman took a step forward into the room. Ursula could smell the creature, and she had to bury her face in the folds of her gown to keep herself from gagging. The woman came forward, stepping between Ursula and the bed, and momentarily blocked the view of her brother.

This is it, Ursula thought. This will be the death of all the men ahead of her. She stared at the back of this woman, noticing the deep sores within her flesh and the muddy tangles of her hair, and willed the woman to attack.

But she merely stood there, staring down at the men.

"What do you want?" her brother asked, and Ursula could not help but to shake her head at the fool. You don't bargain with the enemy; you strike them down. How could he be so stupid?

The woman didn't answer. She lifted an arm, and pointed at something. Ursula leaned to her side, trying to peer around the woman's back to see what she wanted, but it was no use.

"This?" her brother asked. "But—well, I suppose it would be okay." He handed her something, and then she shambled back to the doorway. As she opened it, the groans of her companions could be heard. The woman stood in the doorway, blocking the view of Eric and the King, and when her friends came near, she made a pointing gesture down the hall to distract them. Then she shuffled out and closed the doors, leaving the stench of her presence behind like a foul perfume.

Ursula emerged from the screen. She took a look at her brother and the King, saw that they were both unharmed and unfortunately alive. She went up to the four-poster bed, and tugged against one of the posts. Her brother looked at her dumbfounded, but she didn't bother to explain. She ripped off the post, and ran across the room to the doorway. There she shoved it through the loops of the door handles, and secured their safety in the room.

She let out a sigh, and looked back to the bed. The bed curtains had collapsed, and her brother was working to lift them off the struggling King.

Just then, there were sounds outside the doorway. The doors buckled in toward the room, and Ursula pressed her shoulder against them. Her brother merely stared, staying by the bed. But between the brace formed by the bedpost and her own strength, Ursula was able to hold the doors shut on her own. It wasn't until she felt the doors relax and heard the things outside moving on that she turned to her brother.

"Eric," she said, "why didn't that thing kill you?"

Her brother shrugged. Next to him, the King was still looking around the room, trying to catch up with what was going on.

"I honestly don't know," her brother replied. "She seemed to be interested in something else."

"What?"

Eric looked down, embarrassed.

"She took the crab."

*   *   *

Ariel heaved the sack of treasures over her shoulder, and followed her sisters down the hill from the palace. The rest of the horde carried the fresh kills of the day, either slung over their muddy shoulders, or by dragging the larger corpses by the legs through the dirt. There were a few screams that could be heard from farther ahead in the line, meaning that some of the prisoners were still alive. This kept them fresh as long as possible, although no one really lasted more than a day or so at the swamp. The temptation of live flesh was too great.

Ariel tried to see around the gnarled hair of the sister in front of her, curious as to what objects the living might still have on their person, but the front of the line had already passed the first trees and into the woods. She could see very well in the dark, but today there was a thick fog in the woods. No luck in finding out what treasures these strangers might be carrying. She pressed onward, holding her place at the end of the line, and followed the screams into the woods.

Her sisters were moving at a brisk pace, and for once, there was no fighting between them. The whole tribe was overjoyed at the promise of food, and those lugging sacks of flesh were practically dancing with delight.

Ariel was excited, too, but for a whole different reason. She couldn't wait to get back to the mud, and sort through everything she had found. After today's haul, her collection of human artifacts would nearly double.

As they walked, the smell of the trees started to become familiar, and before long the horde had reached their bog. It was in a small clearing at the end of a stream, a muddy circle deep within the woods. The trees sunk toward the bog with gnarled roots, but nothing grew beyond the border of the brown and green sludge.

The line of women stepped through the muddy shore,

327

and descended into the muck with relief. The bodies they carried sank down with them below the surface. Those with living cargo stayed by the shallow shores, their humans screaming wildly now as they began to understand their fate. A few of the victims were already missing limbs, their wounds staining the shores with blood.

Ariel glanced at the humans as she reached the water. Her eyes scanned their outfits, but she didn't see any necklaces or jewelry that interested her. Nothing to rival what she had found at the palace. She turned back to the bog, and dunked below the surface.

She had to admit, there was some comfort in being hidden from the world. The surface of the bog was covered with a thick layer of green slime, and when the women entered as a group, it stirred up the mud floor and made the water thick and clouded. But as the women settled into their underwater nests, the mud settled, and the bog water had some visibility again.

Ariel crouched down to her nest of rocks and bones, and held her sack to her chest. She looked around, fearful of being watched, and was relieved to see the other women completely absorbed in their meals. The water, which was never crystal clear, was blotted with explosions of blood, seeping outward in small pockets like red ink from the nests of her swamp sisters. It was as if a curtain had been drawn around her, and Ariel was glad.

In her privacy, she removed a stone near the base of her nest. There was a hollow underneath, about the size of a tree stump, that she used to hide her treasures. She opened her sack, and the contents tumbled out into her lap, floating down in slow motion.

Sinking down at once were a pocket watch, a few pieces of silverware, a pearl comb, and a candlestick. A leather bound journal hovered in front of her, and the little crab, still filled with air, started to float up to the surface. Ariel took it in her hand, watching the bubbles rise from its shell, and waited until she felt it fill with water.

She looked at it, her eyes wide with wonder, and her hair undulating around her skull like seaweed in a mild current. She opened her mouth, and more bubbles rose to the surface from between her sharp, rotted teeth.

She liked this crab. It was dead, so it wouldn't swim away like the snakes that also lived in the bog. She set it down on the side of her nest, and admired it. Then, feeling playful, she patted it on the back of its shell before turning to the rest of her newly acquired treasures.

The journal, she was disappointed to see, was not meant to be underwater. The ink was already washing off, and the pages were starting to clump away. Still, as an object from the other world, it was valuable. She closed the book, and wedged it on the shelf between two mechanical tin soldiers she had looted from a deserted toyshop on a previous outing.

She looked at the silverware in her lap with some confusion. Objects like these lacked a definite purpose. They seemed to be in every household, in one form or another, and Ariel was pretty sure they were some kind of weapon. But they were so small. Perhaps they were used for fighting babies?

Dead babies were actually quite formidable, and since Ariel had no memory of living babies, she assumed that human infants were the same. She picked up a fork, and tore into the mud outside her nest, imagining it to be the soft shell of a baby's head. It might work, she decided, although it would do nothing to protect against their claws.

She placed the fork inside her nook, and then began to admire her other newfound curiosities. She was handling the pocket watch, which confused her more than the silverware, when one of her sisters crashed into her back and knocked her treasures flying in all directions.

Ariel snarled, and the mottled skin of her face wrinkled with anger. She swam after the other hag, slicing her sharp fingernails into the flesh of her legs. Her sister didn't feel the pain, of course, but turned around in annoyance at being slowed. Ariel recognized this wench—an older woman, whose face was completely skinless, so that only the sinews and pulp of her muscle surrounded her clouded eyes. She was weaker than Ariel, and was unable to free her legs from her grasp. The faceless woman pulled, reaching out toward something at the surface.

Ariel looked up to see a pair of bare feet flapping in the middle of the bog. This old woman's prey had gotten away from her, and was poking his head through the layer of muck in the middle of the bog. The other swamp hags had all turned toward him now, hungry with the promise of a fresh kill.

The faceless woman started squirming in desperation, and Ariel let her go. But the old woman was too slow. The other women passed her by, working to surround the man, and then coming at him from all sides digging their fingernails into his soft flesh. The sounds of his screams filtered down through the water, and his blood spread out in red clouds under the surface.

Ariel swam toward the group. She hadn't fed with the others before, having been too distracted by her treasures, and at the sight of the man's struggle, her hunger had awakened.

The women dragged the man to the shore, taking small nips out of him along the way. With live meals, they liked to extend the pleasure of the kill as long as possible. On the mud, he coughed up water, then turned toward the women, holding up his hands.

"Please," he begged, "I don't want to die." His wet black hair was dripping into his eyes, and the flesh of his chest was rising and falling with his breathing. The women salivated, and a few let out wet chuckles as they stepped closer to the man.

Ariel took a step forward herself, and was about to reach

her hand out to scoop a chunk of flesh from the side of his gut, when one of the other women dragged a fork along the side of the man's neck. Ariel's eyes went wide. A fork? How had she gotten that?

She turned back toward the bog, and saw a jumble of her treasures floating on the surface. Ariel let out a terrified groan, and stumbled back down the shore and into the water. As she was descending, the old faceless woman was stepping out. The old woman looked at her, and the muscles on her skull pulled up into a smile as she shook with laughter. Water sprayed out between her teeth, and splattered off the sagging flaps of her wrinkled body.

Ariel's face crumpled with despair. She jumped into the water, and frantically tried to collect the remains of her collection. She picked up the arm of her toy soldier, a broken piece of a ceramic dish, and a few pages floating by from the journal. The old woman had destroyed everything. Her secret nook was empty. Even her nest had been torn up, the bones scattered and the rocks displaced.

Defeated, Ariel slumped down to the floor of the bog. She let the pieces of her collection fall out of her arms.

It wasn't fair. She just wanted to know some part of the life she had lost, and now she felt as if she had lost some part of herself as well. She slumped down into the muck, losing what little hunger she had. She turned away from the feast on the shore and closed her eyes.

She had to get out of the swamp. Even if it would be dangerous to venture out without the safety of numbers, and even if she had no idea where she would go, she had to leave. This life was killing her. Determined, she opened her eyes, and there before her, untouched by the faceless wench, was the dead little crab she had stolen from the palace. It rested on a smooth rock, and Ariel was sure the only reason it had survived the hag's vengeance was that she mistook it for a living creature, and not part of her collection.

Ariel brightened a little, picking up the crab and pushing away from the floor of the bog. She swam to the shore, and walked past the horde of women feasting on the man. The smell of blood was in the air, and although her stomach churned with hunger, she walked on through the mud. One of her sisters was sitting on a log by the border of the trees, tearing into a hunk of red flesh in her hands. She looked up at Ariel, as if thinking she were crazy to walk away from such a comfortable life. Ariel ignored her, and pushed through the bushes, away from the groans and snarls of the horde's celebration.

She stood on the brink of the woods, and stopped to stick the dead crab into the mud on her shoulder. It wasn't much of a companion, but it was more welcome than the deceit and treachery of her swamp sisters. She could hear them digging into the man, his last screams in the distance, and walked farther into the woods to be clear of them.

Once she was beyond the noise of the swamp, her sensitive hearing picked up the sounds of something approaching in the distance. She stumbled forward, and could see she was a few steps away from a dirt path that ran through the woods. The galloping of horses was coming up swiftly, and she felt the pangs of her hunger once again.

Quickly, she tossed a few stray branches into the middle of the path, and then retreated behind the tree line, ready to pounce out from the shadows.

The carriage came around the bend, and the driver brought the horses to a halt. Ariel was surprised to see that the driver was wearing a metallic suit of armor that covered every inch of his body. It even had a visor that covered his face. And on either side of him were two other armored men, each facing outward with heavy axes. The carriage, too, was armored, its sides plated with metal and bolted together without any seams. Ariel couldn't help but to admire the ingenuity of their defenses.

One of the armored men climbed down from the front of the carriage, and started to clomp over to the branches. As he walked, a side window of the carriage rolled up, and a man stuck out his head.

"What's going on out there?" he called.

"Keep your window closed, Prince Eric," the driver responded, sounding somewhat frightened. "We will be moving in a moment."

The human called Eric turned toward the trees, and peered into the shadows. He had bright blue eyes, soft black hair, and a handsome face with lighthearted, compassionate features. Ariel did not move. She could have easily taken the two steps forward and grabbed him by the throat. She could have probably eaten half of him before the soldiers had a chance to stop her. But somehow, looking into his soft understanding eyes, she found she wanted nothing more than to keep on staring.

A moment later he pulled down his window, and the soldier was climbing back onto the carriage. They had cleared the road, and at once they slapped the reins and were galloping down the lane.

Ariel emerged onto the path, taking a wistful step in their direction.

That man—Eric—she could still see his eyes in her memory. It was as if everything inside herself that was empty was made full again by those eyes. She cannot lose him. Desperately, she stumbled forward, already hearing the sounds of the carriage fading into the impossible distance.

There was still the faint trace of his scent on the wind. Without pausing a moment, she trampled after it, away from her sisters and her life at the swamp, and off into the unknown, with the dead crab still on her shoulder.

*   *   *

Ursula could not listen to another word. Her brother had been talking nonstop since they left the palace. If that weren't bad enough, Eric had chosen as the subject of his obsession the desire to find a bride, so that he could start producing an heir at once.

"It will be my duty," he said, ignoring the way Ursula pressed her fingers to her temples. "Our family line is almost all dried up as it is. Once our uncle, the King, is dead—which could be any moment now—that only leaves me."

Ursula gave him such a withering look at this comment that even Eric picked up on it.

"You know what I mean, Sister," he said, putting a hand on her shoulder. "But you have to admit, our family is growing smaller. There's only us left." He paused for a moment, thinking. "And Mother, of course. Although she hasn't been in a mental state fit to rule for some time."

It was true. Their mother lived alone in a castle a few miles from their village, and spent most of her time and all of her funds on miracle beauty treatments.

"Have you heard of her latest fad?" Ursula asked.

Eric nodded. "Virgin blood."

Their mother had taken to daily baths in the fresh blood of virgins. The last time Ursula had visited, her mother was espousing her belief that they would keep her young forever.

"But who knows how long that will last?" Ursula said. "She'll feel restored for about a day, and then some young maiden will pass, and she'll get twisted with jealousy all over again."

Eric nodded. "You're lucky she doesn't consider you a threat in that regard," he said. "Otherwise you would be dead already."

Ursula grimaced at her brother's words. It was intended as a compliment, but how could she be grateful that her mother didn't consider her attractive enough to be competition? Her mouth formed a hard line, and her eyes narrowed.

"Yes," she said through her teeth. "Lucky."

They rode in silence the rest of the way. There were no more roadblocks, and they reached their own village before nightfall. They unlocked their doors when the driver called to them that they were home, and Ursula sat waiting for an attendant to open it for her. But when she saw that Eric's door had been opened first, as he was now ahead of her in hierarchy, she grunted in exasperation and pushed open her own door. It was unladylike, but Ursula was tired of being a lady. She wanted to be treated like a man.

Their own estate was much smaller than the King's palace, and smaller even than their mother's ramshackle castle. It was a white building in the Italian style, with plastered walls, arched windows and doorways, and red-tiled roofing. Green vines crawled up the sides of the building, and large open windows looked out to the garden, which was mostly bare at this time of year. Ursula walked behind her brother through the main entranceway, wishing she could shoot fire from her eyes. They parted without words, going in opposite directions to their rooms within the estate.

Ursula washed her face and stared at the mirror in her bedchamber. She couldn't go on like this. She needed a plan to get rid of Eric, but what could she do? The easiest way to kill him would be through poison, but she would be suspected of that in a moment. She would really be suspected no matter how he died, so it had to be in a way in which she was completely blameless.

True, her mother would be the first to inherit the kingdom. But the populace would probably think of Ursula as a saint if she brought about her mother's death. That would be no trouble.

But Eric... what to do about Eric?

She spent the rest of the evening locked in her room, dismissing plan after plan, and growing incredibly frustrated as the day worn on. When it was dark, a servant knocked on her door to alert her to a late supper. Ursula dragged herself to her feet, and trudged down the hallway with a sneer.

Her brother was already seated at the table, and looked up at her entrance with smiling eyes. She sat down across from her brother. He looked ready to burst, he was so pleased.

"And what are *you* so happy about?" she asked, inclining her face forward.

"Babies!" he shouted. "I keep thinking about babies."

"Babies?" she asked, although at once she wished she hadn't. It started a long, passionate outpouring from Eric about his desire to have children, "enough to populate the entire kingdom!"

Ursula listened, stabbing at her food, and grinding her teeth together as she chewed. If he had children, her chances of moving up in line would be ruined. Even a female child of his would rank above her.

Finally, when Eric started dividing off the rooms of their estate to his forthcoming brood, Ursula could take no more.

"If you'll excuse me," she said, standing up, "I must retire. This meal has given me indigestion."

"That's okay, Sister," Eric said, not bothering to stand himself as she rose. "We can continue this discussion tomorrow morning. I want you to help me pick out a suitable vessel."

Ursula held her tongue. He was talking about finding a fertile wife. She nodded, unable to trust herself to say a word, and hurried away from the room.

Once out of his presence, she let out her breath at once. "Oh!" she muttered to herself, unable to form coherent thoughts in her rage. *"Oh!"*

She lit a lantern and ran out the back entrance of the estate to her cottage. Although she slept within the main house, she had usurped a guest cottage on the grounds to use as her personal taxidermy space. Eric didn't mind, as her hobby was a fragrant one, and Ursula spent many days and nights locked inside perfecting her craft. It was her own private kingdom, and she was possessive about it, keeping it locked at all times from the outside world. Even the servants weren't allowed to see inside.

She was midway across the lawn when she stopped, noticing a trail of mud dragged along the path. She held up the lantern, and followed the trail with her eyes out into the darkness, where it seemed to lead to the stone well at the back of the property.

Ursula stepped off the path and walked to the well, the light of the lantern swinging before her. The well had mud stained over the sides, as if a body had been dragged from the house and dumped below. She held the lantern over the edge and looked down, seeing nothing but the reflection of the flame in the dark underground stream below. She stepped back, and held the light up to the stones of the well, and then down along the base. She gasped.

A footprint was still fresh in the mud. It was of a bare foot, and the toes were pointed away from the well. If Ursula didn't know any better, she could have sworn someone had climbed *out* of the well.

But that was impossible. Anyone would surely drown in the attempt. They would have had to crawl through the small river from downstream, entering from the sewer pipe outside the village walls. No one could hold his breath that long.

Yet there was the footprint.

She followed the trail back across the lawn, and found herself facing the window of the dining room. Eric was still at the table, with a servant standing behind him with his back to the window. And outside the house, stepping on the flowers of the garden, was a filthy woman looking in at them. She was naked, with green sores on her skin, and mud splattered along her body. Even from a few steps back, Ursula could smell her rank odor. That, more than anything else, told her that this woman was dead.

Ursula didn't move. She was still taking in what she was seeing. And the dead woman hadn't noticed her at all. Very slowly, Ursula lowered her lantern, and turned a knob on the side to reduce the flame.

If it were a living enemy, she would have looked for some weapon, and taken care of him herself. But the dead— the dead weren't such a threat when there was only one of them. Ursula was sure she could outrun this woman, if it came to that.

And then there was the dead woman's placement. She was aimed toward Eric. If Ursula walked away, and just let this little scene take its course, all of her problems might be solved. This might be the solution she was searching for.

"I can let you in," she said, after taking a precautionary step backward.

Any living person would have jumped with surprise at her words, but the dead woman didn't react at all, not at first. When she did, she turned toward Ursula with an expressionless look on her dead face.

Ursula's breath caught at the sight of her. This woman was hideous. The skin of her face had been scratched and torn, and her hair had fallen out in patches, leaving bald spots on her grey scalp. Her mouth hung open, revealing sharp, broken teeth. She stared at Ursula, and it wasn't clear if she was actually seeing her or not.

"If you're hungry," Ursula said quietly, "I can give you a chance to eat him."

The dead woman stared at her for a moment, then very slowly, but unmistakably, shook her head in refusal.

"Why not?" Ursula snapped. "I thought your kind *loved* to eat humans." She narrowed her eyes. "Why else would you be staring at my brother? What is your purpose?"

The dead woman struggled to lift her hand, and then placed it over her naked breast, right above her heart. Then Ursula noticed for the first time the little crab the girl had on her shoulder. It was darkened with mud, and tangled with bits of her hair, but naturally Ursula recognized it.

"It's *you*," she said. "The woman from the palace. The one that wouldn't touch my brother."

She stared at her for a moment, considering.

This changed everything. If the woman wasn't here to kill Eric, if she was here because of some demented crush, then she was of little use. Eric would see her and order her killed in an instant, just from the sight of her.

Although, if he somehow could be fooled, if the creature could be placed with him in a setting without guards... Surely the dead could not withstand their violent nature very long? This woman would have to feed eventually, no matter how much she cared for Eric. And even if he wasn't killed out-right, if Ursula could get this creature to make Eric like her, *marry* her, the public shame might be enough to ruin him.

Ursula turned toward the dead girl with a poor attempt to look sympathetic. "You want to be with my brother, don't you?"

The dead woman nodded.

"But you know, my dear, you can't gain his affection looking like that." Ursula gestured toward the dead woman, and pointed from her head to her toes. "He is a prince, and he expects his women to be beautiful. You—he would not like you as you are."

The dead woman's head dropped. She looked down at herself, and then turned back to the window. Her face was as expressionless as before, but her inner state was obvious.

Ursula smiled. "I, for one, always felt like members of your kind were misrepresented." The dead woman looked back to her, and Ursula was encouraged. "Poor unfortunate souls like yourself deserve a chance at Eric's hand, just like anyone else. After all, I *desperately* want my brother to be happy. And you seem like a girl with a gentle nature." Her eyes flicked involuntarily to the slash marks on the dead girl's skin before regaining her calm smile. "It's a shame you couldn't be a part of his world. Perhaps," she said, taking a step closer, "perhaps we can strike a deal?"

The dead woman didn't move. Ursula held her helpful expression, and then finally the dead woman tilted her head, motioning for her to continue.

"If you agree to make Eric into one of the dead like yourself, I will make you appear to be one of the living in order to get close to him."

The dead woman stared at her, her face forming a rare expression of disbelief. She opened her mouth, and a garbled mumbling came out, along with a fantastic stink. Ursula held up her hand for the creature to stop.

"You seem to doubt my abilities," she said calmly. "Yet you admire them." She pointed to the crab on the dead woman's shoulder. "That is my work. It was dead, and I restored its appearance to one of life. True, it is not alive, but it was not as you are to begin with." She looked at the dead woman another moment, and then saw a flicker of movement behind her in the window. Eric was standing up. "Quickly," she said, motioning for the dead woman to follow. "We must start at once. Do you agree to my bargain? Your life for his? Your beauty in exchange for making him one of the walking dead?"

The woman hesitated for a moment, and Ursula thought that she had been stupid for trying to reason with the dead.

But then the dead woman took a step forward. She nodded her head, and looked intently at Ursula.

"We must move," Ursula said, glancing back at the window.

And then as quietly as she could, Ursula led the dead woman through the yard and back to the little cottage. She unlocked the door, and invited her victim into the workshop.

* * *

Ariel was not sure what to make of this. Her heart was full of excitement, and—honestly—that made her sort of hungry. She wished she had eaten something back at the swamp celebration, but it was too late for that now.

"There," said the strange woman, closing the door to her cottage. "I don't think anyone saw us."

Ariel looked around the small, dark room in amazement. There were large animals posed on shelves all along the walls: cats in crouching positions; piles of mice and sparrows and wild birds; the head of a lion, its mouth open in a frozen snarl; snakes, turtles, and frogs; and a great assortment of animals of all kinds and sizes. Not an inch of space was empty, and even the edges of the floor had animals spilling over. The strange woman stepped over a stuffed fox, and worked her way to the back wall. Ariel ducked under an eagle hanging from the ceiling with its wings extended, and followed.

Along the back wall was a series of musty jars of clouded liquid, and a low table was set in front of them with specialized knives and tools. In the corner of the room was a large black cauldron. Seeing the cauldron, Ariel started to think of this woman as a witch. Who else but a dabbler in the dark arts could have a collection such as this, of all these creatures paralyzed in a moment of time?

The witch set the lantern down on the table, and reached out to a large jar without searching. She used both arms to set it down on the table with a clink, and then slapped the side of the glass, looking at Ariel with pride.

Ariel was utterly confused.

"This is how you will trick my brother," the witch said. "This is who you will become."

Ariel looked back at the jar. Inside was a tangled mess of red hair. It swirled around, still unsettled from being moved. Then Ariel saw that there was a head in the jar. Its face turned toward her, and Ariel opened her mouth in surprise.

Inside the jar was the head of a beautiful woman, perfectly preserved. The head had been severed at the neck, but if Ariel hadn't known better, she would have sworn the woman was still alive.

"Our little village has gotten a bit ruthless with its criminals lately," the witch explained. She was smiling openly now. "They've taken to beheading with any pretext they can find. This poor creature must have been in the wrong place at the wrong time." She looked at the face in the jar, her smile fading. "They'd better be careful about that. Eventually Sleepy Hollow will come up against someone who doesn't like being headless." She shook herself. "But that's no concern of ours!"

She let go of the glass and took a good long look at Ariel. "Hmm," she said, "we're going to have our work cut out for us." But there wasn't a note of complaint in her voice; it was merely an observation. She lifted a finger to Ariel. "Excuse me," she said, and poked into the side of Ariel's stomach.

It squished against her touch, and when she pulled back her hand, there was a strand of slime sticking to the end of it. The witch shook her head.

"I'll have to do the full body. A face alone won't fool anyone. Plus," she said, lighting another candle and waving the smoke from the match in the air, "you smell of the dead. Even if we could make you look right, you'd have to *smell* right, too. Yes," she said, nodding, "this will be my most challenging project yet."

Ariel watched as the woman set out her supplies, and started to grow a bit nervous over what this transformation would entail. The witch took out scalpels, pinchers, long needles, and several glass bottles of liquid with skulls and crossbones on the labels. She seemed to be digging out everything she had, going so far as to burrow into a trunk of clothes, slinging out old garments and ladies' gloves and even a frail little umbrella.

"We'll be going in stages," the woman explained. "And I'm afraid each stage will be more painful than the last."

Ariel shrugged. She didn't feel pain anymore, so it didn't make any difference to her.

"Okay," said the witch. "Let's get started."

The first thing she did was to direct Ariel into a large cauldron in the corner of the room. Ariel climbed inside, and the witch pushed her down by the shoulders so that she was folded within the iron basin, with her legs over her shoulders. Then the witch started dumping one jar after another into the cauldron, and Ariel's skin started to sizzle. The smell was salty and sulfuric, and the witch opened the shutters of a side window to let in the night air. She instructed Ariel to remain still, and then made a trip to the well and doused Ariel with water, filling the pot to the brim.

Ariel was used to being underwater, so this didn't bother her so much. But this was no ordinary water. She felt her skin tightening and shriveling, and the elixir was soaking in through the gashes in her side. It went up her nose and into her mouth, filling her with the taste, feel, and smell of the chemicals. As she soaked, the flavor became less sulfuric, and more briny, as if she were being pickled.

She was just starting to daydream about the man in the window—Prince Eric, she remembered—when the cauldron was turned over, and she fell onto a metal grating. The liquid seeped away down a gutter carved into the wall of the building, and then the woman snapped for Ariel to stand.

She inspected Ariel's skin closely. "Hmm," she muttered. "Your flesh is stubborn."

Ariel wasn't sure how to feel about that. She waited for the witch to continue.

"But I think we may have stopped some of the rotting, at least for a few days. We'll have to do something else about the smell. It seems to be coming from *inside* of you. Normally, in cases like these, I'd just hollow out the entire animal and fill it with sawdust." She looked at Ariel for a minute, as if contemplating this. Ariel shook her head, and the woman frowned. "I suppose we could do a seaweed wrap. Then a layer of bandages."

And that's just what they did. The witch had a jar filled with bright green seaweed, floating in brown swampy water. She shook each leaf out, and then wrapped it around Ariel's limbs. She worked her way up from her ankles, keeping the bindings tight, and didn't stop until she reached the neck.

The bandages were worse. The witch had several long rolls of white cloth, and started wrapping it around Ariel like a mummy, again leaving her head bare. Then she used a needle and thread to tie the bandages together. Afterward, she leaned in close to Ariel's stomach, and took in a deep whiff of breath. Ariel may not have been in pain, but she felt terribly embarrassed.

The woman shook her head. "I can still smell you. It's faint, but you don't smell the way a person smells." Without another word, she went back to her worktable, and began mixing several items in a bowl. It was a white gloppy sludge of glue and cooking flour, into which the woman dunked an entire vial of potent perfume. She turned back to Ariel with the bowl tucked under her arm, and a brush in her free hand, and began to paint the mixture over the bandages. She skipped Ariel's knees, elbows, and joints, and in a few minutes Ariel began to understand why: the mixture was hardening as it dried. It had crusted over her like scented armor, and she moved her arm experimentally, testing her new exoskeleton.

"Don't move," the woman ordered. "While you dry, I will prepare the face."

She carefully lifted the head from the jar, and placed it on a tray. Then she sat with her back to Ariel, her hand reaching to the side periodically to select a scalpel or knife as she worked. At one point the woman had to get up from the table to get a pair of scissors, and Ariel caught a glimpse of the half-skinned head. The skull was bare and surprisingly bloodless, and the lip of flesh was pulled back on both sides and pinned down within the tray.

The witch came back and worked an hour or so more. Ariel stood obediently still the entire time, in the way that the dead can hold one position without feeling strained, or inclined to itch or scratch. She thought again of Eric, and looked down at herself, having doubts about the witch's plan. How could this fool anyone?

When the witch had finished skinning the head, she tossed the leftover innards back into the jar. She turned back to Ariel, the face held in her hands with the inner side of the skin turned up. It looked rubbery and dead, but Ariel said nothing as the witch held it up to her dead face to measure it. Then she set the face down in the tray, and turned back, stroking her chin with her finger thoughtfully.

"It's time for the second step," she said. "I need to remove your skin."

Ariel opened her mouth, and the witch spoke faster.

"Otherwise your face will be too bulky under the mask. Also, just so you know," the woman said, hesitating a bit, "you won't be able to move your face again after the mask is on. Otherwise it will tear. This means you won't be able to open your mouth. I know you can't talk, but this also means you won't be able to feed."

Ariel stumbled backward.

"It's the price you'll have to pay," the witch insisted. "And it won't be long. Since the new skin has not be treated—it would have been too obviously a mask if it wasn't kept fresh—it won't last more than a day." When Ariel still hesitated, the woman added, "If you want to be with Eric, this is what you must do."

She had been warned it would be painful. Just the thought of going without food for any length of time sent her stomach churning. She had the wild urge to eat the witch now, so that she would have a meal before the trans-formation. But if she ate this woman, there would *be* no transformation. Ariel would have to swallow nothing but her fear, and volunteer herself to starve. She stepped forward.

"Good," said the witch. She pulled a chair toward the cauldron. "Sit down—*carefully*."

Ariel did her best to lurch over to the chair, and as soon as she had fallen into it, the woman leaned the chair back until Ariel's neck rested against the rim of the cauldron. Then, with a pair of gloves on, she picked up a trowel from the worktable.

"This will only take a minute," the witch said, and then began to scrape away Ariel's skin.

It didn't hurt; that was the only part for which Ariel was thankful. But it was disconcerting to feel her skin tugged off of her face, to feel it tear and separate from the soft flesh underneath, and hear it plop into the empty cauldron below. She tried to be brave, to focus on the eyes of the woman bent over her. This stranger had such a look of concentra-tion that it calmed Ariel somewhat, if only for giving her the assurance—how ever ill-founded—that this woman knew what she was doing.

The witch tore away the flesh of Ariel's cheeks and chin, cut off the end of her nose, and peeled away the flaps of her ears and the skin of her forehead. Ariel felt quite naked, star-ing up at this woman. She imagined that she must look like the faceless woman back at the swamp, with wide eyeballs looking desperately from a grey-muscled face. Her lips were gone, and she felt the night air on her tongue. She wanted to hide, frightened of what people must think, but forced her-self to do as she was told and remain exactly still during the deep exfoliation. She wanted to be pretty for Eric.

"This next step is a wax," the witch said. She was already mixing something in a small pot raised above a set of candles on the table. "This will act as the seal between your flesh and the mask." She was about to lift up the steaming pot when she looked down at Ariel's face, noticing something. "Hmm," she said, and Ariel felt her confidence drop with the sound. "I forgot about the eyes."

She put the pot back on the burner, and started shifting through a shelf of small jars above the worktable. Ariel felt ashamed. She had seen the eyes of the dead, and knew that hers must be the same: clouded and yellowed. Even the most beautiful woman in the world would look hideous with her eyes.

"Aha!" the witch cried, pulling down a jar. Inside were eyeballs, swirling about like olives. She popped open the top, and used a spoon to fish out two eyes. Then she moved the lantern closer, and Ariel strained to see what she was doing, but was afraid to sit up and potentially ruin any part of the process.

The woman set down the scalpel, and then turned to Ariel with a smile. She held up two eyes in her palm with emerald green irises. They had been chopped in half and hollowed out into discs. The pupil, to Ariel's surprise, was clear.

"Now hold still," the woman said, and stuck one disc over each of Ariel's eyes. It was a bit uncomfortable, like she had something stuck in her eyes. She tried to blink, but found that the woman had cut off her eyelids when she had scrapped off the rest of her face.

The woman inspected the eyes for a moment, and then she nodded in approval. Without skipping a beat, she picked up the small pot of boiling wax. Ariel watched as she poured the pink wax onto her throat, easing her way up her chin and mouth, and stopping at her nose. It seeped between her teeth, and sealed her mouth shut. Then the witch placed two coins over Ariel's eyes, and poured the rest of the wax over her eyes and forehead.

It was hot; Ariel could tell that, even if she couldn't feel the pain. And she felt pressure on her face as the woman spread out the wax with a spatula. Then, delicately, Ariel felt something pressed up against her mouth and nose, and then over her entire face. It was tucked under her chin and over her throat, and then pulled back past the sockets where her ears had been.

The coins were pulled through the mask as the wax was cooling, and Ariel saw the woman's concentrated expression once more. "Turn," she said, the sound of her voice muffled by some wax that had gotten into Ariel's ear canal. "Face down." Ariel spun onto her stomach and held her head over the side of the cauldron. As the witch poured more wax onto the back of her scalp, and folded down the flaps around the nape of her neck, Ariel waited, staring at the shreds of skin that were once her face on the base of the cauldron.

The wax cooled, and the woman moved Ariel back upright in the chair. She looked at her for a minute, her face expressionless as Ariel eagerly wondered what she looked like now. The corner of the woman's lip raised in a sneer of disapproval, and Ariel looked up at her, feeling more buried under the layers of disguise than she had at the bottom of the swamp.

"The expression is wrong," she said, as if Ariel weren't alive underneath the mask. She reached out and started morphing the face with her fingers, shifting up the cheeks and pinching at the lips. The wax was quickly hardening, and she did what she could until it had solidified completely. "It's a little better, but still somewhat blank. Honestly, he'll probably think if you don't react to things strongly that it means you're more of a lady."

Ariel tried to store away this knowledge of Eric's preferences. She had so many questions about him, and about the world she was soon to enter. She didn't want to ruin this chance.

The witch worked on the mask's hair next, washing it

with fresh water, and smothering it with oils and creams. She dried it with a towel, and then spent what felt like an hour brushing it out, and teasing the strands into delicate curls. Ariel could see some of her new hair hanging down around the edges of her vision, and it looked so clean and alive that she longed to smell it as well. But her nose had been plugged up with the wax, and she couldn't smell anything at all.

When it was time for her makeup, the witch literally painted it on Ariel's face, using a thin brush and a palette of colors. Ariel thought this was smart. If she happened to get wet, this would stop the makeup from washing off, and prevent her new skin from returning to the rubbery grey of the severed head.

When she was satisfied, the witch started to rummage through the different outfits. She pulled out an elegant pale-blue dress that nicely complemented the hair color of the mask.

"You'll wear gloves," she explained, laying out a pair of long silk gloves on the table. "Only your face will show. The rest of you will be covered at all times. No one must help you with your clothes, do you understand? I will come into the guest bedroom myself at the start of each day."

She laid out the outfit on the floor, placing the gloves and shoes where the hands and feet would be. Then she turned to Ariel.

"Now for the third step: the weapon to fulfill our bargain."

She walked over to a shelf and pulled off a stuffed badger. She flipped it upside-down, and pulled out a hidden dagger from its belly.

"This," she said, holding up the blade before Ariel, "is what you will use to murder my brother."

Ariel tried to open her mouth, but couldn't.

"First, we must coat it with your own infected flesh," the woman continued. "To do this, it must be hidden within you." She raised the dagger over Ariel, clutching the hilt. Ariel trembled, and the witch laughed. "But don't you want to make him one of the walking dead? Don't you want to be with him *forever?*"

Ariel tried to nod, but found her neck too stiff to complete the gesture. She settled for a slight bow of her entire body. Then she sat up straight, and the witch lunged the knife down into her chest. Even without the pain, the shock of the penetration shook Ariel, and she looked up to see the witch struggling to place the knife in deeper. She wedged it inside of her ribcage, until Ariel felt the blade stabbing directly into her heart.

"There!" the witch said, falling back. "Now the first chance you get alone with Eric, you must reach inside yourself to remove the dagger, then use it to pierce his heart. And remember," she said, holding up a finger, "you must do this before the mask begins to rot. Otherwise, your disguise will be up, and he will discover what you really are."

Ariel gave a half-bow to show she understood.

"Good. Now let's get you dressed." The witch looked out through the window. "It's almost morning. We can have you finished in time for breakfast."

Ariel stood up, ready to get into costume. She had no idea what she looked like, and doubted she'd see before she had to walk into the grand house.

She could only trust that this would work.

* * *

Ursula left the girl in the shadows of the entryway, and went in to find her brother.

"Sister!" he exclaimed, rising from his seat at the dining room table. He met her in the middle of the room, and squeezed her around the middle in an embrace neither sibling particularly enjoyed. Ursula pulled away with a gasp and composed herself. She smoothed out the folds of her purple dress, grateful that her brother never noticed what she wore, and wouldn't ask why she hadn't changed since yesterday.

She smiled. "Brother," she said, her hatred thinly concealed, "I have a surprise for you."

Eric raised an eyebrow. "Another… preservation?" he asked tentatively.

Ursula's smile became real. "Better." She turned toward the doorway, and called, "Come in."

Eric looked up, and Ursula felt her breath catch in her throat. Had she acted too rashly? Maybe she should have checked the girl one last time? She had been staring at the face for the last few hours, with no sleep; she might not have been able to judge if she looked alive or not. But there was only one true test, and that was Eric's reaction. He would either fall in love—or run from the room screaming.

The girl stepped into the doorway. The morning light fell upon her vibrant red hair, forming a halo around her soft and immobile face. Her pale-blue dress had frills that seemed to float in the air around her, and her gloved arms were rigid against the sides of her waist as she walked into the room. Her face had been painted meticulously, with a hint of green shading on each eye, blood red lipstick, and white powder on her face.

Her face—Ursula couldn't help being unnerved by it. It looked so different than the dead girl underneath. Even the eyes seemed false somehow, staring at her as if from behind a painting with peepholes instead of eyes. Except they were looking at Eric. And the woman's expression—it was one of calm amusement. Polite attention. But devoid of life or personality, as if she were a walking doll. Ursula felt her stomach sink with disappointment. The girl looked completely artificial. What had she been thinking?

Eric bowed before the mannequin woman. She did not react. He leaned forward, took her gloved hand, and kissed it.

"It is a pleasure to make your acquaintance," Eric said regally. He looked up at the living doll, waiting for her to make the appropriate response.

Still, the girl did not react.

A moment passed, and then Ursula remembered.

"Oh!" she cried, stepped forward. "I'm afraid our guest is a mute." Eric turned toward his sister, confused. "That means she can't talk," Ursula explained. "Although she can understand everything that you say to her."

It took a moment for this to sink in. Then Eric's smile returned. "Well," he said to the living doll, his voice comforting, "I've always thought a girl who gossips is a bore. Won't you join us for breakfast?"

Ursula had to speak up again. "Our guest," she said, drawing the attention back to herself, "will not be able to dine with us. She has a *special* diet by doctor's orders. Nothing serious, but she will be eating alone in the guest chambers." She lowered her voice and said directly to Eric, "I hope I wasn't being presumptuous, but she has traveled a long way to see you, and I invited her to stay with us."

Eric nodded, still staring at their guest. "Of course," he whispered.

There was a moment of silence as the three stood looking at one another. Then Eric asked, "Is she going back to her room now?"

Ursula gave a strained smile. "No, she will sit with us."

The three walked together to the dining room, where Eric held out a chair for the living doll. He then took a seat at the head of the table, and let Ursula seat herself across from their guest.

Eric finished his breakfast in silence. To Ursula's annoyance, servants remained in the room throughout the meal. An older male servant with a beaked nose kept staring at the dead girl, and the room itself filled up with such a stink that Ursula had to ask him to open a window. Even with all the layers of seaweed and perfumed cloth, the dead girl still stunk like what she was. There was no getting around that.

When the servants cleared away the dishes, Ursula turned to her brother. "If I might, could I have a word with you in private?" Eric nodded, and Ursula, to be polite, asked the dead girl, "Could you excuse us for a moment?"

The girl made no reaction, and Ursula shuddered internally. It was hard to think of her as a person; she looked as dead as any of Ursula's other preservations.

Ursula stood up and took her brother by the arm, pulling him away from the table and into the doorway of the neighboring hall. He was still staring at the girl in the next room. Ursula coughed, and he turned to her.

"What do you think of our guest?" she asked.

Eric shrugged, his expression bored.

Ursula spoke quickly. "She may not seem like much, but she comes from a noble and highly reproductive family. She is the twenty-first born of twenty-one children."

"How many were male?" Eric asked, suddenly attentive with a matter of business.

"Eighteen," Ursula said without missing a beat. "And her mother still lives, even after all those births."

Eric nodded in approval. "Are they all mute?" he asked.

"Only the women."

"Acceptable."

He didn't ask about the dowry, which was a relief for Ursula. She could easily lie about an amount, but if Eric required it before any serious considerations, there would be no way for her to provide it.

"Who is her family?" Eric asked.

Ursula had forgotten about names. She closed her eyes to concentrate. "Incognito," she blurted. "She comes from the family Incognito, a noble line from a distant land. Her parents want her to wed as soon as possible, as does the girl."

"Why the rush?"

"She wants to be a mother many times over. For that she must start at once."

Eric was silent for a moment. He turned toward the living doll, who was still sitting in the next room and not moving a muscle. She looked like a statue. Eric stared at her, his expression unreadable. Then he asked, "Will the family need to travel to attend the wedding?"

"They will be unable to attend."

Eric nodded. He seemed relieved by this, probably because there would be much less expense without having to entertain such a large extended family. "And you can vouch for her?"

Ursula smiled. "I can assure you, I know this girl inside and out."

Eric didn't reply, and Ursula grew nervous.

"Well?" she asked. "Would you like to spend some time with her? See if you two get along?"

Eric waved her thought away. "No need for that. She'll do."

"She—she will?" Ursula was too surprised to censor herself. Eric had seemed completely uninterested throughout the entire meal.

Eric shrugged. "She can bear children, she looks appropriate, and she won't ever contradict me. What else is there to know? Make the arrangements."

Ursula stood blinking at her brother. She opened her mouth, her sleep-deprived mind unable to come up with a suitable response. It wasn't supposed to be this easy.

"Don't you think," she said, her mind working quickly, "that you should propose to the girl first? In private. *Alone.* Just the two of you?"

Eric didn't seem to care one way or another. "Sure," he said. "If you think that's best."

"Oh, I do," Ursula said, allowing some of her excitement to show through. She was allowed to be excited about her brother's engagement, as long as only she knew that it was an engagement with death. "Why don't you go into Mother's old room and pick out one of her rings? I will sit with our guest in the meantime. Does that sound acceptable?"

Eric waved a hand in a gesture to show he couldn't care less. "Whatever," he said, "as long as I end up a father." He turned down the hall, walking away without even looking back toward the dead girl that he was intending to marry.

Ursula went back to the girl. She had not moved from the table. "Listen," she said, leaning down toward her, "I've arranged it all." The girl shifted and looked up at her. It was odd knowing there was another set of eyes peering out from behind the artificial ones, and for a brief moment, she thought she saw the demon lurking within. Ursula shook the thought away, and continued. "Eric will be back in a moment and you two will be left alone. I will make sure every servant has been removed, and that the doors are closed. This is our best chance." Ursula turned toward the hallway, and then leaned in close to whisper. "Now, the perfect time will be when he's down on his knees. Then you take out the knife, and stab it into him just as he's about to propose."

The dead girl's shoulders twisted sharply. Ursula stepped back, and watched in horror as the skin stretched along the lips, and then parted in a wide crack that ran up the side of the left cheek.

"Your face!" Ursula gasped. "You've split your face!"

At her exclamation, a servant rushed into the room, and Ursula held up her arms.

"Out!" she yelled. "Out!"

She grabbed the dead girl by the hand, and rushed her out of the dining room and through the back door, tugging her back toward her cottage.

* * *

Ariel hadn't meant to smile. But when she heard that the handsome Prince Eric wanted her to be his bride—*her! Ariel the swamp hag!*—she was so overwhelmed with bliss that she couldn't control herself.

"Relax your face," Ursula ordered. Ariel, who had picked up the witch's name during the meal, tried to do as her future sister-in-law commanded.

But it was not easy.

All throughout the breakfast she had been convinced Eric didn't care for her. She had felt foolish for thinking she could be good enough for him, that any amount of enhancement would be enough to hide her true form. But when Ursula came back into the room and told her of Eric's true feelings, it was such a surprise! She couldn't help it, and thinking back on it, she smiled all over again.

Ursula slapped her across the face. "Do you want him to see you like this? Concentrate!"

The thought of Eric seeing her without the mask sobered Ariel in an instant.

"You're only going to have one chance at this," Ursula continued. They were back in the witch's cottage, and Ursula was filling in the cracks of the mask with thick putty. "Do you still have the dagger?"

Ariel pointed to her chest, not wanting to nod while the witch worked on her face.

"Good. Use it. Because if you fail today, I don't know what we're going to do." She painted some concealer over the putty, and then waved her hands to dry it, biting her lip with anxiety. "This mask is already starting to show signs of wear," she muttered, reaching for the powder, "and it's only been a few hours. We don't have much time at all."

Ariel waited as Ursula patted down her face and neck with a thick coating of powder, and then held still as she brushed out her long red hair. Ursula stepped back when she was done, and even she seemed impressed with the result.

"You look the image of health and beauty," she said, and then helped Ariel out of the cottage and back to the yard. As they walked, Ursula kept up a constant stream of instructions.

Ariel tried to listen, but she forgot everything as soon as she saw Eric again, standing in the back doorway with a bright white shirt that showed off his savory tan. She took his hand, and excitement fluttered within her as he led her into a private sitting room, and left her to sit on a high-backed couch. She looked back at Ursula, whose face was tense with concern, and raised a gloved hand to wave to her as Eric shut the doors of the room.

Eric turned to her. He gave her a weak smile, and then came forward to take her hand. Ariel could barely feel his touch under all the layers of silk and gauze and seaweed. He bent to his knees, and looked up into what he thought were her eyes.

"My dear," he said, his eyebrows raised, "will you do me the honor of taking my hand in marriage? To be the mother of my children, and the caretaker of my home?" He produced a ring from his pocket. Ariel leaned forward, marveling over it. It was a gold band inlaid with glittering jewels, with a diamond on the top as large as pea. She had the inconvenient urge to run back to her swamp to hide it away in her nook. He must have felt her silence. She looked up at him and nodded with a half bow.

Eric was pleased. He reached up, and started tugging at the end of Ariel's glove in order to place the ring on her bare finger. Ariel whipped back her arm, and felt the resistance of the wax as her face tried to snarl.

She calmed herself, and held forward her gloved fingers, holding her wrist with her other gloved hand, so that he would understand that the gloves were not coming off.

To his credit, Eric went along with her request without a word of complaint. He squeezed the ring past the knuckle, and turned the diamond to face up squarely in the middle of her ring finger. "There," he said, "you'll all set, my dear—dear—hmm." He looked up at her. "By the way, what is your name?"

Ariel instinctively tried to open her mouth, and felt at once that it was sealed shut. Since Eric couldn't see her inner struggle, she raised her hand to her throat.

"Ah," Eric said, remembering her condition. Then he waved it away. "It doesn't matter. The important thing is that you'll be my bride."

He leaned down, and kissed the tips of her fingers through the silk. Ariel looked at the back of his strong neck, and sat forward to see him better. As she did so, the dagger in her chest pressed in deeper, piercing through the rim of her heart.

She didn't even think of removing it.

When they emerged from the sitting room, Eric leading the way, Ursula's expression was one of utter bewilderment. She patted Eric's arm absentmindedly as he told her the good news. Then Eric ordered the servants to start the preparations for the wedding, which would be held the next day.

The rest of the afternoon was a flurry of activity as the servants rushed about cleaning the house, running errands, and asking both Ursula and Eric a multitude of questions. Ariel sat between them in a daze. If anyone did ask her a direct question, either Ursula or her new fiancé would answer for her, so that she was free to let her mind wander. She stared at the ring on her finger, and kept imagining what it would be like to live in the grand estate forever.

It wasn't until the evening, when Eric had gone to bed early, and Ursula led Ariel outside into the darkness of the yard, that she even remembered her mission.

"What happened?" Ursula snapped. "Why didn't you do it? Is the dagger still there?"

Ariel gave a half-bow.

"Then why? That was our bargain!"

They walked farther away from the house. The crickets and creatures of the night were stirring in the yard, and the women stepped into the shadow of the little cottage. Even if she could talk, Ariel had no answers. She shrugged.

Ursula paced back and forth, her hands pressed against her temples. "Okay," she said after moment. "Okay. All is not lost. Tonight, while my brother sleeps, I will call away his guard saying I heard a sound down the corridor. His door does not have a lock, he is so confident in his safety. When the way is free, you will sneak inside, and stab him in the heart. Then you can disappear before he is discovered in the morning."

A growl came from deep within Ariel's chest, and she stepped away from the witch. Very deliberately, she shook her head in refusal.

Ursula looked up at her, startled. "What do you mean, 'No'? What possible reason could you have?"

Ariel held up her hand, and pointed to the ring. Ursula still wasn't getting it.

"You can keep the ring. I don't care."

Ariel pointed to the ring again, and then put her hand over her heart. She held the position, waiting for Ursula to comprehend. After a moment, Ursula's eyes widened with understanding.

"You can't be serious!" she shrieked. Then she realized the secrecy of the conversation, and lowered her voice to a fierce whisper. "Don't be daft, dead one. Your face is crumbling as we speak. It may not even last until tomorrow, no matter how much we patch it. Do you really think he's going to want you when he sees what you are?"

Ariel turned away. If she could cry, there would have been tears coming from her second set of eyes.

Ursula followed, and kept herself in front of Ariel. "The wedding is tomorrow," she said, as if talking to an especially stupid child. "Do you have any idea what happens afterward, on the wedding night? My brother is obsessed with having children. Do you think he won't notice that you're *dead inside?"*

Ariel didn't care. She just wanted to stay with Eric and to be in his world so much that she was willing to believe there must be some way to fix things. Maybe if she made herself pretty enough, they could steal some children from the village, and he would never need to know. She looked down at the ring. It was the most beautiful thing she had ever seen.

"He doesn't love you!" Ursula continued. "The moment he finds out, he's going to order you thrown out and killed. You're not meant to *be* here. Don't you understand? You're a disgusting, filthy, foul-smelling monster, and he's a royal—"

Ursula's words were choked off with a gasp. Her eyebrows raised in confusion, and then her eyes lowered down to her chest.

Ariel had pulled out the dagger and stabbed it through Ursula's heart. The witch's hands went weakly toward the blade, and Ariel twisted it in deeper. The witch opened her mouth to speak, and blood dribbled down her chin. Ariel pulled out the dagger, and Ursula dropped to her knees. Then Ariel drove the dagger into the witch's back, again and again, not stopping even after the woman had stopped fighting back, stopped moving, and stopped breathing. She hated the witch, and hated everything that she had said.

No, Ariel thought, it's not true. I *will* be happy with Eric. And she's not going to stop me.

She lifted Ursula's corpse under the arms, and dragged her over to the well. Then, with one swift movement, she dropped her down into the depths. She heard the body splash, and looked down to see the current carry her away.

She stumbled back to the dagger on the ground. She wiped it on the grass, and then slid it back into the groove inside her chest. Her dress was ruined, splattered with blood and dirt. But it didn't matter, because in a moment she would go inside and change into white. She turned back toward the house, determined and vicious.

No one was going to ruin her special day.

*   *   *

By the time the sun rose the next morning, Ariel had already shredded off her blue dress of the day before, and struggled into a sheer white gown she found within the witch's cottage. But it wasn't until the servants woke that the wedding day preparations really began.

Ariel was assigned a number of women to help her prepare for the ceremony. They had apparently been instructed beforehand of her mute condition, as they asked her no questions, and spoke especially loud whenever they spoke to her, as if she were deaf as well.

She was brought into a formal boudoir and seated in front of a counter spread with cosmetic supplies. A large mirror with three panels stood against the wall of the counter, the glass angled so that she could see herself from all sides at once. It was the first time Ariel had gotten any kind of look at herself after her transformation. She had a smooth young face, full lips, and glamorous eyes. Even her hair was dazzling, its long red strands teased and styled to frame her face perfectly. She was beautiful. She looked like someone that belonged in her environment.

Staring at herself, her mouth moved to drop open with awe, and the effect was terrible.

The wax stopped the worst of the movement, but Ariel saw in the mirror as little rips formed down her cheeks. Even after she shut her mouth as tight as she could, the rips remained, like slashes in a curtain. She glanced at the maids behind her in the mirror, and saw they were too busy opening a heavy armoire of clothes to notice.

Ariel reached out for the cosmetics, applying some at

random, and scrambling to dab the rips with the powder puff she found on the counter. The newly applied makeup stood out against her mask in dry clumps, and the powder didn't blend like it had when the witch applied it. It looked like she had been sprinkled with sifted flour. The maids turned back, and their expressions were horrified for one terrible moment before they remembered their place, and went back to their neutral visage.

"Allow me, miss," said one, reaching forward for a bottle of pink cream. "We're best off removing it all and starting fresh."

Ariel snapped forward and clamped down a gloved hand on her wrist.

"Ow!" the maid cried with pain. "Please, miss! You're hurting me!"

Ariel let go reluctantly, and the maid didn't reach for the cream again.

The maids decided to skip the makeup, and they started fitting Ariel in her wedding dress. Again, they tried to remove her gloves and coverings, and Ariel slapped their hands away. She wouldn't even take off her shoes.

"Let it be," said the oldest of the maids. "It will all be covered by the dress anyhow." She turned to Ariel with a kind smile. "A bride is allowed to be modest."

When Ariel didn't return her expression, the maid turned away with discomfort. They cracked a window and worked steadily after that, lacing up the frills of the dress, and finding the biggest, thickest veil possible to cover Ariel's face. They might as well have been dressing a statue. They did remove the ring, explaining to Ariel that she would receive it again from Eric at the alter.

Once they were finished, Ariel opened the door of the small chamber for them to leave. The maids hesitated, and looked to the oldest among them. "It is tradition," she said to Ariel, "for the maids-in-waiting to *wait* with the bride."

But Ariel stood firm, her hand on the door, until the head maid dropped her head in a bow.

"As you wish," she said, and started out the door with the line of maids following. Ariel slammed the door behind them, and stumbled back to sit before the mirrors. She lifted her veil, and leaned in close to the mirror to inspect her face.

It was worse than before. Her skin looked like the cracked ground of a desert after a drought. She lifted a finger to a flap of skin on her cheekbone that had torn away. She pressed it back up to her face, and it dropped away completely along with a chunk of wax, revealing grey muscle and bone underneath.

Ariel picked up the pink cream, and smeared it over the exposed flesh. The color didn't match the rest of her face at all, but it was better than her skull protruding through her mask. She fumbled with the other items on the counter, and dabbed a little red lipstick on her bottom lip. But she applied too much pressure, and now her lips were smashed out of shame and uneven. She tried to push it back with her fingers, but the effort just made it worse.

She threw down the lipstick in frustration, and looked at her blotched face in the mirror. The mask was starting to discolor as well as crack. The witch had been right; she wouldn't make it much longer. She pulled down the veil again, glad for the covering, and was suddenly grateful for the tradition of the groom not seeing the bride before the wedding.

She sat looking at herself covered with the veil in the mirror. If she didn't move, if she remained completely still, then her face could not deteriorate.

She was in control, and soon she would be Eric's wife.

She felt a little better after telling herself this. She was even starting to believe that everything would be fine.

As long as she didn't have to move.

* * *

The midday sun sparkled on the filth streaming out of the black drainage pipe. It emptied into a pond of sewage on the outskirts of the village, in a particularly rancid and fly-ridden neck of the woods. Between the reeds of the pond the dragonflies dipped down, hopping on the water, and sending out concentric ripples to the shore, where a woman's body was sprawled facedown in the mud.

She might have stayed that way longer if not for the crunch of footsteps approaching her.

Ursula was hungry. And at the sound of a potential meal, her body woke before her mind had realized where she was or what she was doing. She pushed herself up, the mud slopping down from the front of her tattered dress, and she set her darkened eyes on the trees along the swamp. Her mouth was open in a toothy sneer, and her hair was wild, sticking out in dirty spikes.

She saw the forms in the shadows and knew at once that they were not alive. They lacked the vibrancy of life, and their smell was dry and rotten. She pushed herself to her feet, and the dead things noticed her for the first time, pausing to turn toward her. Then, seeing she was dead, they turned away with disinterest, and went on with their hunting.

Ursula opened her mouth to call to them. Her memories were returning with a blinding speed, even if she found they weren't as ordered as they once had been. Rather, she had the impression of events, and the leftover emotions that surrounded them. She remembered the dead girl she had disguised, and she remembered being killed because the dead girl was in love with her worthless brother. They were back at her home now, where they did not belong. The estate should be hers. It should *still* be hers, and when she opened her mouth, that was what she was trying to explain to the fellow creatures.

A gurgle came out, nothing more.

Ursula raised her fingers to her neck, unable to understand. She tried to speak again with no result. Frustrated, she seethed in air through her lips, and let it out again in a violent roar. The figures in the woods stopped and turned back to her. Ursula stumbled forward out of the pond, and waited.

After a moment, the two figures stepped into the light.

They were women. Or at least, they had been. These creatures were even more rotted and vile than the one Ursula had transformed, but they seemed to be of the same ilk.

Ursula was at a loss of how to communicate what she needed. She pointed toward the drainage pipe, her arm heavy with fatigue. She was incredibly weak with hunger. But the creatures didn't know what she meant, and they started to turn away. She gave another growl, this one more desperate than the one before, and started to lift her fingers toward her mouth, chewing the air as if she were eating.

The creatures stopped, curious.

Ursula repeated the mime, and then pointed again to the drainage pipe. One of the dead women stepped forward, keeping her eyes on Ursula as she passed, and made her way to the drainage pipe. She leaned down into it, and inhaled deeply, smelling the air. Then she turned back and looked at her companion, and pointed to the pipe.

The companion, instead of stepping forward, turned back toward the trees. Ursula thought she had failed, but then the creature let out a roar into the wilderness. To Ursula's surprise and satisfaction, more creatures came out of the woods, an entire horde of them. A good number were like the other rotted women, but there were others among them, even children.

Ursula remembered the raid on her uncle's palace, and the way his town had been emptied of life. These creatures had run out of their easy meals, and were ready to find a new source of nourishment. They staggered forward, desperate and vicious, and Ursula pointed to the pipe.

Then, pushing the first rotten woman aside, Ursula

crawled in herself. She wasn't sure if the message had gotten across, if the others understood that there was food on the other side.

But in a moment she heard them behind her, and knew, whether they believed her or not, the horde was hungry enough to follow.

* * *

A knock came to Ariel's door. She didn't get up from her seat, and the knob turned. A maid stuck in her head.

"It is time."

Ariel held out an arm, and the maid rushed inside to help her to her feet. Ariel wobbled. She was feeling exceptionally weak; she hadn't fed in days, even with all her activity, and the heat coming from this tender maid was almost too much for her. Instinctively, she sniffed in the air to smell her prey. The wax had been pried loose in her nostrils, and she was able to inhale the smallest amount of air.

The maid—she smelled *so good*.

Ariel shook her head. The white dress, she reminded herself. She couldn't get this woman's blood on the white dress. She had to wait a little longer…

The maid, who seemed to guess at the conflict inside Ariel, decided to interpret it as wedding day jitters. "Now, now," she said, "it'll be all right. The hard part's over, my lady. All you have to do is walk down the aisle and say, 'I do.'" The maid flushed. "That is, nod your head. The meaning will come across. And then it'll all be over, and you can cut the cake and enjoy the banquet."

Banquet? Ariel pictured all the guests ripping into the flesh of the dead meat, tearing at it with their teeth, and sucking the juices out before swallowing it down. She growled, unable to stop herself, and the maid froze in mid-step.

With every last bit of self-control she had, Ariel forced

herself to keep moving. They made their way through the darkened hallway, and out through a side entrance to the yard.

Ariel was stunned by the transformation that had taken place while she was sitting immobile in her dressing room. A large canopy had been erected in the middle of the yard. A minister stood in the center of it in a long black robe, and he was flanked by bushels of pink flowers. Next to him, with his back toward her, was Eric, dressed in a regal white coat with long tails, black pants, and black boots.

Guests were seated in rows of chairs in the yard, about forty or fifty in all, none of whom Ariel had ever seen before. A frenzied maid ran up to her, and shoved a bouquet of red roses into her hands, and then ran off again. Then the first maid led her along through the back of the crowd, whispering into her ear.

"You walk down the aisle and stand by His Grace and listen to the little speech. They'll tell you what to do from there."

Ariel would have nodded, but she was too worried about splitting her face in two with the effort. A moment later music erupted from behind the canopy, and the maid pushed Ariel forward.

Everyone stood to look at her as she walked down the aisle. She was thankful for the veil, and wondered how the crowd would react if they knew what she looked like underneath. She looked at the calm faces of the older men and women, and pictured their faces twisting with rage as they all ganged up to tear her apart.

She made it to the end of the aisle and tried to catch a glimpse of Eric's face, but he barely glanced at her before returning his attention to the minister. Ariel listened to the man's words for a few sentences, but she couldn't concentrate on them; they were meaningless to her. So instead she concentrated on not moving at all, at saving what little remained of her disguise.

It wasn't until the minister spoke directly to her that she

woke up from her daze. He asked if she would take Eric until they were parted by death. She found that an odd phrasing, but carefully leaned forward to show she agreed. Eric slipped the ring onto her finger again, this time not even attempting to take off the glove, and then he smiled at her. She could just make out the glimmer of his teeth through the white mist of her veil.

"You may kiss the bride," the minister boomed, raising his arms.

Eric lifted the veil.

If he noticed anything peculiar about Ariel's face, his expression did not betray it. They leaned toward each other, and he pressed his lips against the dead skin of the mask. Ariel, who could not close her eyes, saw his incredible nearness, and could smell the flavor of his flesh through the mask. Eric leaned back, a calm expression on his face, and opened his eyes.

The color left his face at once. Then his mouth opened, his lips quivering, and his eyes grew wider. He was going to scream; Ariel could tell that much. The minister, turning toward her, soon lost his own expression of gentle amusement. He made the sign of the cross on his chest, and took a step back.

Slowly, and not without her own feelings of horror, Ariel raised her gloved hand to her face. She could barely feel anything under all the layers, but when she pulled her hand away, the bottom lip of the mask was stuck to her fingertips. He had kissed it right off.

Ariel reached out a hand toward him, wanting to tell him it was okay, that she was still the girl he had loved a moment ago. She opened her mouth, straining against the wax sealing it shut, and felt her jaw open with a smack. The skin of the mask split horizontally in a line from ear to ear, and she saw the wax crumbling away from the corners of her vision. She sucked in air to speak, and lurched toward Eric.

At the gesture, Eric stumbled backward, bumping into the minister, and knocked them both to the ground. There were gasps in the crowd, but Ariel refused to be diverted. She was more concerned with Eric.

She took a step toward him, no longer trying to be careful, and felt the seaweed bindings snap loose on her legs. Ariel groaned, unable to articulate anything more than a wounded moan.

Just then, there were screams in the crowd. Men and women were jumping up from their chairs, and running in all directions. Ariel turned behind her, and was surprised to see that she did not seem to be the source of the panic. No one even looked in her direction. Eric and the minister were realizing this as well, and all three turned to look toward the back of the yard.

The dead were climbing out of the well like ants from a burning anthill. One after another, Ariel's dirty sisters climbed over the stone, and instantly took off running in the direction of the guests. Ursula was among them, reanimated and lurching forward with slanted shoulders. Her purple dress was torn and wet, whipping in the wind around her feet like tentacles. She stumbled forward, and locked eyes with Ariel.

"Why have you done this?" Eric shouted at his new bride. "Why have you brought them here?"

Her face was slipping away, and she wiped at it with her hand. Didn't he understand? She had nothing to do with this. All she wanted was to be with him. To be like everyone else. To be beautiful.

And now the witch had ruined it all.

Ariel screamed, the cry coming from deep inside her chest, and reverberating through her entire being. But Eric didn't hear her pain. When she looked at him, he only backed away.

She was about to take another step toward him, hoping

to explain this to him somehow, when across the yard she saw Ursula lower her head and start to charge. Ariel stood in front of Eric and braced herself, digging her heels into the ground. The seaweed dropped under the train of her wedding gown, and she ignored it. A moment later, the witch had rammed into her.

They both rolled to the ground, clawing at each other and snarling. The witch tore away what remained of Ariel's face, and threw her scalp of red hair behind them. It landed in Eric's lap like a deflated dog, and he jumped up, swiping at his pants as if it might bite.

Ariel rolled onto her stomach and furiously tore off her gloves. The wedding ring popped off, and when she looked to see where it went, Ursula slammed a fist into her head. Bits of seaweed that had been stuck to Ariel's skull fell off, and she snorted out the wax in her nose before rolling onto her back, and throwing Ursula off onto the grass.

Ursula saw Eric trying to back away, and scrambled toward him, pulling herself along the ground with her fingers. Ariel hopped on her back, and bit down into the witch's neck, twisting her broken teeth into the bitter and rotten flesh. This didn't stop the witch, of course; she couldn't feel bites anymore. But it slowed her down enough for Eric to slip away. He dodged the men and women and creatures in the yard, and made his way back into the house, slamming the door behind him.

Ariel pushed Ursula away and stood up. She felt the air on her skin, her true skin, and could smell the taste of chaos on the wind. She looked at the men and women running in fear around her, and felt the intense craving of the hunt taking hold of her soul. She was starving—ravenous—but what she wanted most was more than flesh. What she wanted was her man.

Before Ursula could stop her, Ariel shambled across the yard. When she reached the house, she threw herself shoulders-first through the window of the dining room. She wondered, landing in the glass on the hardwood floor, if she should have just barged in to begin with, the first time she saw Eric. Chances are, it couldn't have turned out any worse. She pushed herself to her feet, and shuffled through the hallways of the house, seaweed and bandages falling off as she walked.

Eric was trying to be quiet, she could tell that. But she could also smell him. Following his scent was as easy as following a trail of breadcrumbs through the woods, and it wasn't long before she was standing outside his bedroom door.

It had no lock.

Ariel pushed her way inside, and breathed in the scent of her new husband. However he may have reacted, she would forgive him. That was what good wives do, and she didn't want to fight. After all, this *was* their honeymoon.

The room was almost bare except for a large, four-poster bed in the center of it. The curtains of the bed were drawn back, and the bed itself was empty. Ariel shook her head at her husband, choosing a room with only one obvious place to hide.

She bent down, and he was shocked to be found so quickly under the bed. He tried to scuttle back, but she grabbed him by the boot, and dragged him out into the room. He looked up at her, his body shaking, and she bent down over him. She didn't want any barriers between them now. She had shown her true face, and he would have to see it. She reached up, and took out the only part that remained of her costume: the halves of the eyes from the jar. Eric screamed when she peeled them off, and she realized he probably thought she was plucking out her own eyes. She ran her hand along his face to say, 'No, no. I'm okay.'

He looked up at her, keeping his eyes locked with hers, and inched up toward her. Ariel realized he was leaning up for a kiss. He must have forgiven her. Perhaps he was still eager to get the children he desired.

She lowered her head toward him, and she felt the blade slide out of her. Even without the pain, the shock of having the dagger pulled from her chest with such force caught her off guard.

"Die!" Eric yelled, and shoved the blade into her side with the power of a punch. She was thrown to the floor, too confused to chase after him as he ran across the room. She had only just turned to him when she saw him open the door.

He pulled it open, his body leaning forward to run, and was blocked by Ursula in the doorway. Eric stumbled back, standing between the women. He looked at his sister with shock, at her face smeared with blood.

She hissed at him, and he backed up against the wall and into the corner. Ariel was still so confused by the stabbing that she didn't even stop to think about what it meant. She saw that Eric was in danger, and jumped up to protect him. She stood in front of him, and held her ground facing Ursula.

The witch smiled. Then she backed out of the room, and shut the door.

Ariel was dumbfounded by this quick retreat. She turned to Eric, and leaned against him in the corner. He struggled against her, beating his fists on her shoulder. She felt him reaching around, trying to grab the dagger that was still lodged in her side. She took hold of it first, pulling it out of herself and throwing it across the room and out of his reach.

She shook her head. She loved Eric, but he was not bright. How could he think that he could kill her by stabbing, when he had found the knife he was using inside of her to begin with?

And why had Ursula left?

Then Ariel realized the witch had never actually entered. She had been blocking Eric from leaving.

She must be helping them to be together.

At the kind gesture, Ariel felt such gratitude. She threw her arms around Eric, and hugged him. They could be together now. He had seen her true form, and although he had yet to accept it, in time he would learn to love her. She could live with him at the estate as his wife, and she would never have to return to the swamp again.

Ariel was feeling so generous that she wouldn't even mind if her sisters wanted to live in the house. Or Ursula. Or the dead children. Eric had always wanted children anyway. And they could all live together in this new village, feasting as they liked, with her husband as their ruler.

And then when this village was empty, they could move onto the next town. And the next, and the next. Until they had spread their love to the entire world.

She turned to Eric, overwhelmed with joy. She wanted to tell him how much she loved him, how it had all been worth it—the transformation, the starving, the deception—if it meant being here with him now. He was still struggling, trying to get away, but she decided she could be happy enough for the both of them. She pressed him against the corner, and gave him a kiss, her bare teeth pressing against his lips.

He smelled so good. She licked the flesh around her mouth, and could taste him. Suddenly, she wanted him inside of her more than anything—but she restrained herself.

No, she thought, looking at his wide eyes staring back at her. This was her love. This was who she fought to protect. She would be good to him. They could have a life together. They could live happily ever after.

She leaned forward and kissed again, intending to stop.

But she was just too hungry.

THE HEADLESS HORSEMAN

A rock was thrown through the window of the Sleepy Hollow schoolhouse. Mary, the schoolteacher, startled out of sleep. It was night, and she was alone in the building. She must have dozed off while grading papers.

She stood up, leaving the papers in disarray on her desk, and crept her way forward in the dark, keeping her head behind the wall in case anything more might be thrown through the broken glass.

"I can hear you out there!" she called, edging her way forward.

Mary Van Tassel had been the Sleepy Hollow school-teacher for going on a year now. She was a young teacher, barely more than a student herself, but the work had hardened her, like a soldier after a year of war.

She couldn't stand the children. They didn't want to learn; they didn't even want to be nice. Lately, pranks had begun: little things at first, like pins on her chair, and foul words written on the blackboard. Then the pranks escalated to bigger crimes, like setting small fires outside the schoolhouse door.

And now this—*vandalism*.

She heard the sound of footsteps outside, and Mary lost

her temper. She rushed back to her desk, picked up the lantern, and raced to the door. She threw it open, a look of accomplishment on her youthful face, and saw—nothing.

It was dark. She stepped out, her bonnet lopsided, the wind tickling the strands of her blond hair that stuck out. She held up the lantern, and felt incredibly vulnerable not being able to see beyond its circle of light.

"Who's there?" she asked, still trying to hold the authority in her voice. "Answer me!"

Surrounding the schoolhouse were low shrubs and bushes, and a long dirt path that led down to the isolated buildings in the village beyond. The cold night air tickled her fingers, and she heard an owl hooting in the distance.

After peering out a moment longer, she turned back into the schoolhouse.

But as soon as she had, there was the snap of a branch breaking behind her. She spun around, and saw the limbs of a nearby bush quivering.

Mary clenched her fists. "Show yourself!" she cried, stomping over to the tree line. "Show yourself now, you little hooligans, or you'll be sorry!"

She heard more footsteps, only these she recognized as the thudding of horse hooves. They came forward from the darkness, and a moment later she was knocked back by the hooves of a great black stallion.

She looked up, seeing the beast rearing before her, and had to dart aside as the massive legs crashed back down.

"Watch where you're going!" she snapped.

Her eyes traveled up the legs of the rider on its back, taking in his black boots, his billowing cape, and his black leather coat. He held a sword at his side, the blunt tip catching the light of her overturned lantern.

She looked up into his face—and he didn't have one. The rider didn't have a head at all.

Mary was too stunned to move. She huddled back with

her mouth open, and the Headless Horseman rushed toward her, slapping the reins against his steed, and lifting the shining blade of his sword in the air.

As the flash of the blow came toward her, Mary had one distinct thought:

This was the children's fault.

And then the blade passed through her neck, and sliced her head clean off.

* * *

It was a rare sunny morning in Sleepy Hollow, but the light itself was colorless and cold, and did little to brighten the grey dwellings and muddy lanes of the village.

Or so it seemed to Katrina Van Tassel as she made her way into town. She lived with her father in a farmhouse outside the border of the town, and chose to walk the mile into the main village rather than take a carriage. She needed to think, and it was easier to think when walking.

Both sides of the pathway were lined with tall fences, so that it felt like she was walking down a long hallway rather than through the woods. The fences were one of the many changes that had occurred in the past few months, after the plague of the dead had ravished the much of the kingdom.

The pathway opened up at a fork in the road. To her right she could see the road leading to the old covered bridge that led into the woods. There were armed guards here, and she nodded to them as she passed, even though she didn't think they could see her.

The old bridge was where most of the dead tried to get in, now that the walls had been constructed around the borders of Sleepy Hollow. It had been torture to construct the barriers during the dead of winter, but no one wanted to be overrun like the town by the palace, or like Eric's estate beyond the hills. The threat was real, and everyone—Katrina included—aided in the construction. And she had to admit, she rested much easier at night knowing she was safe.

At least, she had—until her sister's death.

She shook the thought away and continued into the village itself.

The moment she entered the narrow band of shops and houses, she felt everyone's eyes upon her. She was used to attention. Katrina was the most beautiful woman in the village, and the daughter of the richest man. Her form was shapely, and filled out her mourning clothes with curves that made the men turn their heads. And her face was sweet and youthful, with blond hair, blue eyes, and pink lips.

But people were looking at her differently after her sister died. Their gazes were filled with a mixture of pity and distrust. No one understood how her sister had been murdered when the village was supposed to be secure. And the way she was murdered—it didn't appear to be the work of the dead. The body was left untouched, with only the head missing. Katrina could feel the suspicion looming over the village like a fog.

Someone had killed Mary. And that someone was most likely still among them. Katrina took in a deep breath, straightened her back, and continued down the dirt street.

Her thoughts were interrupted by a shout ahead of her.

She looked up to see Brom Bones holding a man up to the side of a building, with a flank of his followers around him. Katrina let out an exasperated sigh, and made her way over.

"Enough!" she called out, trotting up to the group. Brom looked over his massive shoulder, and reluctantly let the man down. He gave her a sly grin, and then a wink. Katrina was surprised to find she felt nothing at the expression. She felt nothing for this man whatsoever.

That might not have bothered her, except for the fact that Brom was her fiancé.

The bullied man, who was someone Katrina had never

seen before, fell to the ground. A moment later he bounced back up, brushing the dust off his clothes. Katrina stared at him. He was strange-looking, inordinately tall and lanky, like a scarecrow brought to life. His slight figure was further exaggerated by standing next to the bulky mass of man that was Brom.

"I must apologize for your treatment," Katrina said, bending down to pick up the books and papers that had been scattered on the ground.

"Don't you pick up his things," Brom boomed behind her. She narrowed her eyes, and continued what she was doing. When she handed the books over, she looked up into the stranger's face.

His cheeks were red with embarrassment. His sandy brown hair was tussled from the fight, and he reached up his thin hand to swipe away his long bangs from startling, pale-green eyes. He looked like a scared little boy, and Katrina felt an overwhelming urge to comfort him at once.

But she didn't want to embarrass him further. She let the stranger stand without helping him up, and then turned to Brom with a flutter of her eyelashes.

"Brom, dear," she said, ignoring their company, "would you deliver a message to my father for me? Tell him I'll be by for lunch shortly."

Brom opened his mouth to object, and Katrina leaned in to plant a kiss on his cheek to stop him.

"Wait there for me, will you?" she added.

He nodded, and was about to walk away when one of his followers let out a laugh. Katrina turned and recognized Mr. Blackstone, a short straw blond youth with a gap between his teeth. "Who's the *man* in your relationship, Brom?" he jeered.

Brom's eyes filled with rage. He turned on Katrina and Ichabod with his shoulders lifted, like a bull about to charge.

"Brom is the man," Katrina said in a tired voice. She didn't have the energy for a fight today.

For a tense moment, Brom looked like he would hit her for interfering. Then all his anger seemed to melt, and his face drained of all expression.

"Yes," he said softly. He looked back at Mr. Blackstone, and then turned to walk down the lane without another word. Slowly, his crowd of devotees dispersed, and Katrina let out a sigh of relief.

She turned to the stranger. He was standing now at full height, and she had to look up to meet his gaze.

She smiled an uneasy smile. "My name is Katrina. How do you do?"

He bit his lip. "Not well, actually. I'm late."

She ignored his coarse manners. If anything, she found his lack of decorum fascinating. It wasn't every day that she met someone who wasn't instantly enamored by her. "Where are you headed, Mr. ...?"

"Crane," he said absently. "Ichabod Crane. I'm the new schoolmaster."

Katrina's mood dropped. "Oh."

Here was the man who would replace her sister. The reality that her sister would never return knocked the wind out of her.

Ichabod stared at her with curiosity, and Katrina steeled herself against tears. "It's right this way," she said. "I can escort you, Mr. Crane."

"I'm Mr. Crane to my students," he said, a small smile forming on his lips. "Call me Ichabod."

She felt a flutter at this, and turned at once to lead him through the village. They walked in comfortable silence down the thin dirt path, and Katrina felt a swell of pride as the newcomer took in her childhood home.

"Where are you from, Ichabod?" she asked as they strolled down the main street of the village, a sleepy little row of shops and eateries.

"The town beyond the woods," he said.

There passed a moment of silence that was decidedly un-comfortable. As far as Katrina knew, there were no more survivors left from the town beyond the woods.

"I see. Are you staying in our village alone?" she asked, and he understood her meaning even through the polite phrasing.

He nodded. "My mother is gone. She was the only family I had left." He turned to her, and gave her the saddest smile she had ever seen. "But something tells me you know about loss yourself," he said, and gestured toward her black clothing.

"My sister," Katrina said. "She was murdered."

Ichabod opened his mouth to respond, but his words were interrupted by a scream. They both looked up ahead, and saw a heavy-set woman rush out into the lane. It was the baker's wife.

"Help!" she cried, and ran up to them. "Help!"

"What is it?" Katrina asked, taking the woman's hand.

"A body," she gasped. "In the alley."

Katrina and Ichabod ran after the woman, who led them into a little nook between the bakery and the barber. They saw the body at once: a man's corpse in workman's clothes, crumpled against the wall, and missing a head.

"Oh!" Katrina gasped, putting her hand over her mouth. She turned away, but the image of the neck, the bloody stump, was burned into her vision.

After a moment, she turned back, keeping her eyes on the wall instead of looking directly at the body. Ichabod had bent down, and was searching the pockets for a clue to the man's identity. By now a little crowd had formed around the scene, already whispering among themselves.

Ichabod pulled out a sheet of paper from the man's vest pocket. "It looks to be a receipt for horseshoes," he said, and flipped the sheet over to see if there was anything on the back. "I can't make out the signature."

"The blacksmith," the baker's wife whispered, and then repeated it loudly for the crowd. There were gasps.

Ichabod turned to Katrina for explanation.

"He was young," she said in a daze. "He had—*we* had—" Her eyes filled with tears. "He had asked me to be his wife once. Before Brom."

Ichabod looked at her with empathetic eyes. "You need some air," he said, and stood up to take her hand. Katrina nodded in thanks, leaning against the new schoolmaster for balance as they started to walk away from the corpse.

As they were passing through the gathering crowd, an old man stepped forward. He was thin and hunched, with only sparse teeth left in his sunken mouth. "It was the Horseman," he cried, both to Katrina and the crowd. "I saw him with my own eyes. It was the Headless Horseman."

Katrina and Ichabod stopped in their tracks.

The old man continued, encouraged by their reaction. "The blacksmith was waiting on the corner near to midnight, pacing worried-like. Then there came a black rider from the mist, as if materializing from Hell itself. He rode to the man with demonic speed. The blacksmith turned—and the Headless Horseman used a glowing blade to slice through his neck. He picked up the head, and rode off into the night."

Ichabod stared at the man. "And how come you are just saying this now? Why didn't you inform anyone of what you saw, instead of waiting for someone else to stumble on the body?"

"I didn't figure it was any of my business," he said with some shame. "Besides, I was sleeping until just now. Sleeping off the night's entertainments."

Ichabod looked ready to spit, he was so disgusted with this man. "Come, Katrina," he said, and led her off from the crowd. After they had gone some distance, he slowed, and Katrina reflected on the scene.

"That's not possible, is it?" she asked. "A headless man?"

Ichabod grimaced. "I've seen stranger things these past few months."

"But this has nothing to do with the plague," Katrina insisted. "This is *murder*. Someone is just using the plague as a distraction." She shook her head. "Besides, the dead can't even get into Sleepy Hollow. We've taken precautions. It *can't* happen here."

Ichabod looked at her as if she were a child. "A year ago," he said gently, "I would have agreed with you. It could not happen here. But then, I would have said the same thing about my own town." He stopped for a moment, staring into space. "This plague is like nothing you have ever seen before. If it could get Mother, a kindly old spinster who never had a hard word for anyone, then no one is safe."

Katrina scowled, refusing to be convinced. "In your town," she asked, "did they *behead* the victims?"

"Well, actually," Ichabod said, straining his memory, "there were rumors of beheadings at Bluebeard Palace."

Katrina was deeply troubled by this. They continued walking, and before long they found themselves climbing the base of a small hill. The wooden schoolhouse towered above them, and Katrina felt a chill, knowing she was walking over the ground where her sister's death had occurred. Her sister's *murder*.

"Do you really think it could happen again?" she asked in a whisper. "That those *things* could have gotten my sister?"

When Ichabod didn't answer, she looked up at him, and was startled to see him looking at her with an expression of intense concentration, as if he were trying to decide something about her.

Finally, he asked: "Who *is* Brom Bones to you?"

Katrina's face flushed. She saw that Ichabod was holding his books, some of which were still stained with mud from when Brom had bullied him. She looked away, unable to meet his eyes, and said, "He's my fiancé."

She peeked up to see Ichabod give her a look of pity mixed with disgust. Then his features softened, and he let out a tired sigh. "I suppose," he said with the utmost charity, "that sometimes we see things in the ones we love that others cannot. It was that way with Mother and me."

Katrina felt relief and appreciation pass through her. "Do you miss her?" she asked.

"Not a day goes by that I do not think about her," Ichabod said without missing a beat. "She was more than a mother to me. She was my best friend."

And at his words, Katrina felt a deep connection to this newcomer. Then her face dropped, thinking of how he and her sister would have gotten along. That they might have made the perfect couple if she were still alive.

"Ichabod," she said, reaching out to touch him, placing her delicate hand on his thin arm and looking up into his eyes. Looking at him closer now, he was more handsome than she had originally given him credit. His eyes were deep green pools of complexity and sensitivity. She felt herself falling under their spell. "Ichabod," she whispered, leaning up toward him. He bent his head to hers.

A line of children coming up the path interrupted their moment. The boys and girls hadn't noticed anything, and raced up the hill, lunging into Ichabod on their way. They giggled as they knocked his books and papers to the ground once again, and scampered through the door of the school-house screaming.

"You shouldn't let them treat you like that," Katrina advised as she bent to help him pick up his things, yet again. "You have to be firm with this group. Otherwise, they'll walk all over you."

Ichabod gave a patient smile. "They're only children," he said, not an ounce of hurt or anger in his voice. "They're people, too, you know. We must give them respect first, if we ever expect to receive it in return."

Katrina stared at him, as if he had claimed he could fly to the moon. She looked up ahead through the open door of the schoolhouse, and saw the children running within, throwing up papers and pencils as they continued their riot.

"Well," she said, "good luck."

She turned down the hill, and thought that between Brom Bones and the schoolchildren, Ichabod didn't stand a chance.

* * *

Katrina spent the rest of the afternoon mulling over the events of the morning. She still hadn't decided how she should feel about Ichabod. Really, she shouldn't feel anything at all, but there was just something about him that struck a chord with her. He was the first person she'd met since her sister's death whose grief seemed to match her own. Even her father's sadness was lacking. And Brom didn't seem to react at all.

At lunch, she could barely meet her fiancé's eyes at the table. When he noticed, she tried to play it off that she was still angry with him.

"Over the schoolteacher?" Brom asked. "Let me tell you, Katrina, I've met a lot of men in my life. I *know* people. That schoolteacher isn't worth a handful of beans."

"He's just... sensitive."

"No, he's lazy and afraid and not nearly as smart as he makes himself out to be. What's he even doing here? He couldn't find some other village to settle in? I don't trust him."

Katrina sighed, frustrated with Brom's instant hatred. "What about you?" she asked, turning to her father. "Have you heard about what happened in town?"

Her father paused with a corncob raised to his mouth. He set it down on his plate, and said, "Yes. I wanted to talk to you about that." He took a sip of wine before continuing.

"From now on, I want you inside this house by nightfall, Katrina. Do you understand? And you are to be attended by Brom, whenever possible. I won't have you going off alone—or with *strangers*," he added, meaning Ichabod.

"But Father—"

"No excuses! I won't lose another daughter because she has a desire to be headstrong. I don't want you going out alone!"

"So I'm supposed to stay here, locked up in some high tower, never to see another person again?"

"Katrina," her father said, shaking his head. "You're a Van Tassel. When you want to see people, they will come to you. Have a gathering, if you must. A get-together."

Katrina nodded. "All right. This Friday, we'll throw a party."

"Just don't invite that *schoolteacher*," Brom said, stuffing his face with mashed potatoes. "He's odd."

"He seemed perfectly ordinary to me," Katrina said.

Brom looked to her father, and rolled his eyes at the simplicity of women. "Katrina," he said, turning back to her, "nobody is *that* innocent. How well do you *really* know this man?"

Katrina was silent. She looked at Brom and then her father. And she wondered, How well did she really know anyone?

* * *

The next morning, Katrina rose at dawn and sat down to her desk at once. She made a list of all the guests, finishing by the time the servants brought her breakfast. By the time they brought her lunch, the invitations were done. She kissed her father on the cheek on her way out, and—per his insistence—took a horse and carriage for the mile ride into town. She felt it was silly of him to require her to be protected in the middle of the day, but it was either that or not send the letters at all.

When she got into town, she spent a good amount of time visiting and calling on various friends and notable merchants. She had slipped Ichabod's letter to the bottom of the stack on purpose. Not only was he still in the middle of his lessons at the school, but she didn't want to be rushed away from him. She felt like she had something to ask him, even if the question itself hadn't yet materialized in her mind.

She was so far lost in her thought that it shocked her when the baker's wife, whom she invited along with her husband, leaned over to whisper, "The Horseman has struck again."

"Where?" Katrina asked. They were standing on opposite sides of the store counter, and the baker's wife had smears of flour on her apron.

"On the streets, same as before. Except this time there were two."

A customer came in, needing six eggs and a loaf of bread, and their conversation was paused until the transaction was complete. The baker's wife was still smiling thanks and waving the customer out the door when she leaned close to Katrina and whispered, "That old man, the one that spoke out yesterday." She dragged her finger across her neck and made a *squick* sound. "Dead."

"But why would anyone kill him?" Katrina asked. "He was harmless."

"He was a witness," the baker's wife corrected.

Katrina considered this. "Has anyone else seen the Horseman?" she asked.

"If he has, he's keeping his mouth shut," she said, and waddled back around the counter. "I would, too. Not safe to be pointing fingers."

"But how could someone without a head even recognize a witness?" She shook her head. "How could he move at all?"

The baker's wife inclined her head and said ominously, "The dead have their ways."

Katrina had to fight not to argue. Trying to change the subject, she asked, "Who was the other victim? You said there were two."

The baker's wife nodded. "The other was young Mr. Blackstone, former friend of your very own Brom Bones."

"Mr. Blackstone!" Katrina exclaimed. He was the straw-haired man from Brom's gang. And then she remembered the look Brom had given him after being insulted.

"And what's more," the baker's wife added, taking Katrina's hands in her excitement, "my husband heard from the executioner that all his heads went missing."

"His... heads?"

"After the beheadings," she explained. "They collect the guilty heads in a basket, and then toss them in the grave with the bodies after. Only at last weekend's execution, the basket went *missing*. Someone stole it—along with all the heads!"

Katrina recoiled at the enthusiasm of the baker's wife when delivering this news. "So let me get this clear," she said, collecting herself, "a Headless Horseman has been going around at night, with four victims to date?"

"Four *known* victims," the baker's wife corrected.

"Right." Katrina didn't want to dwell on that. "But the victims—my sister Mary, the blacksmith, the homeless fellow, and poor Mr. Blackstone—they were all killed *at night*. And last time I checked, the executions were held in the daytime."

"Bright and early, first thing in the morning," the baker's wife agreed. Then she frowned, realizing the discrepancy. "Do you think," she asked, "that there could be *two* villains on the loose?"

"I think whatever this is, it's more complicated than we imagine. But I wouldn't be surprised if it was all connected."

"Everything is connected, dear," the baker's wife said earnestly. Katrina found this statement a little worldly for an illiterate woman with flour in her hair, but she held her tongue.

"Well," Katrina said, pulling her hands away, "I will see you Friday?"

"If the Lord allows," said the baker's wife, nodding like a drowsy turtle, her eyes half-closed. "If the Lord allows…"

Katrina left the shop more confused than ever. Two more murders? And what about the basket of heads? What was happening to her town? The only comfort she had was that it didn't seem to have anything to do with the plague of the dead that haunted Ichabod's former town. A murderer could be caught, but if this were related to an uncontrollable plague, there would be no solution. Her village would be lost.

She made her way down the lane and turned off toward the schoolhouse. She had often come at this time of day to visit her sister, and—as if by routine—she had started to prepare what she was thinking in her head, getting ready to tell it to Mary.

And then she remembered Mary was dead.

"Oh, Mary," she said aloud, but could think of no way to finish the thought.

When she climbed the hill, the first thing she noticed was how quiet the schoolhouse was. She was sure she had come at the right time. Perhaps Ichabod had let the children out early for the day?

Or maybe they were too much for him. There were days, Mary had said, when she felt like walking out the door and never coming back.

Katrina stepped off the path and walked to the side of the building, choosing to look through one of the windows before knocking at the door. It had been so quiet that when she didn't see an empty classroom, she let out a gasp.

The children all sat in their seats, bent over their little books and copying out long lines of text onto their parchments. Not one had eyes that strayed from his or her work, and the room itself was cleaner than Katrina had ever seen it. The blackboard had been washed, the items on the teacher's desk were straightened, and even the children themselves looked cleaner.

At the front of the classroom was Ichabod, leaning against a stool and casually reading from a book. He wasn't even watching the children! They were behaving on their own.

Katrina stood there, absolutely stunned. A moment later Ichabod happened to glance up and see her there. He pulled a watch from his pocket, and said to the class only one word: "Dismissed." The children got up silently and started collecting their things. Katrina walked back to the front of the schoolhouse, and out walked the children in two quiet lines.

When Ichabod joined her in the doorway, she expressed her surprise. "What's your secret?" she asked.

"No secret," he said. "Just as I told you: I treat the children as I'd treat anyone else, and they respect me for it."

Katrina couldn't speak. She looked at the children.

There was something off about them, something beyond their good behavior.

The last girl in line, a blond child with chubby cheeks, scurried down the steps of the schoolhouse so quickly that she tripped. When Katrina moved to help her up, the girl flinched and scuffled away. She ran, looking back over her shoulder at intervals to make sure she wasn't being chased.

"The children," Katrina said, "they seem frightened."

"Naturally," Ichabod replied, and Katrina turned to him. He smiled and said, "With everything that's been going on in Sleepy Hollow, we've *all* been frightened."

Katrina hadn't considered that. She looked up and caught another glimpse of his remarkably green eyes. She had to force herself to look away, scared of repeating the moment from the day before—and without the chance of interruption.

"I'd better be going," she said, and it wasn't until she turned away that she remembered the invitation. "Wait!"

she called, and reached into her pocket to retrieve a sealed envelope. She handed it to him. "It's an invitation," she explained as he opened it. "I'm having a gathering at my house. I'd like it if you could attend."

He looked down at the invitation. "This Friday?" he asked. "Do you think that's wise?"

Katrina blushed. No one else had questioned the propriety of having a party so soon after her sister's death. Probably because the others in town were used to the Van Tassels throwing parties, rain or shine, all throughout the year. But Ichabod thought it was odd.

She kept a smile on her face. "Yes. Will you be there?"

After a moment, he nodded. And then he went back into the schoolhouse and shut the door without another word. Katrina stood for a moment, finding his behavior especially odd. Then she turned and walked down the hill, taking out the last invitation in her pocket. It had been addressed to Mr. Blackstone.

She sighed, and was about to tear it in half when she noticed the date on her invitations. She was in such a daze this morning she hadn't even realized it.

Her party would be held the night of Friday the Thirteenth.

* * *

The next few days brought no solace to Sleepy Hollow. It was now typical to see both men and women walking about in groups, and casting suspicious glances to whomever was unlucky enough to be out alone. The defense against the dead on the bridge had been doubled during the day, and abandoned completely at nightfall.

There were more murders, too. The baker had been found dead outside his shop, his neck sliced and head missing just like the rest. His wife insisted that his attack had happened not more than an hour before dawn, as he had gone out to enjoy a smoke in between batches of bread.

"I never let him smoke around the dough," she said when Katrina had seen her. "You could taste it in the product."

Katrina herself was spending more time at home, growing depressed whenever she made her morning rounds of the neighborhood. She hadn't seen the schoolteacher since she had invited him to the party, and she wondered if he still planned to attend.

The only person in town, as far as Katrina could tell, who wasn't affected by the murders was Brom. He came by their house for lunch as usual, and was loud and boisterous and crude at the table.

"Aren't you upset?" she asked him finally. "Don't you even care that one of your friends has died?"

Brom chewed on a hunk of meat, and then swallowed it down. "Not everyone can be as sensitive as your little schoolteacher."

Katrina's face turned red. "You leave Ichabod out of this! He wouldn't hurt a fly!"

"Yeah, well," said Brom, taking a loud sip of his ale, "he's got it coming to him. The only reason the Horseman hasn't gotten him yet is because he's hiding under his bed all night."

Katrina didn't respond. As far as she was concerned, hiding indoors was the only reason *any* of the village folk were still alive—Brom included.

"You can't possibly want him to die," she said eventually.

Brom laughed. "That fool? I'd chop off his head myself, if I got half the chance."

They didn't speak another word for the rest of the meal, and Katrina retreated into her own thoughts.

For the hundredth time that week, she wished her sister were here. *She* would know what to do. But as it was, Katrina didn't know what to think.

And now this assertion that Brom wanted Ichabod dead?

Did he really mean that? And how did he know that Ichabod hadn't been out at night?

But Brom as the Headless Horseman? Her own fiancé? She couldn't imagine that. He could never have killed Mary.

But try as she might, Katrina could not shake the feelings of mistrust. And the more she thought about it, the less she knew.

*   *   *

The morning of the party was dark and grim. When Katrina stepped out of her carriage, she looked at the villagers passing by her with unease. The day was overcast, and none of the trees or flowers had started to sprout. The air was cold, and it felt like winter would never end. Perhaps that was all the mystery had to it: they were doomed.

Judging by the hurried pace and narrowed eyes of the people she passed, the villagers had all come to the same conclusion.

There was a crowd outside her first stop, the bakery. She needed to pick up the bread and rolls for her party that night. It still amazed her that no one had refused her invitations. If anything, she had a stronger attendance than usual. She could only guess that in this time of crisis, the people were desperate for a night of cheer.

She pushed through the little crowd of gossipers and made her way into the shop. The baker's wife was behind the counter, staring at the wall vacantly. She was wearing black under her white apron. Her eyes were red, and Katrina felt pity for her.

But when the baker's wife saw her, her expression became hardened. "I suppose you're here for your rolls," she said with loathing, "for your *party*."

"I'm sorry for your loss," Katrina said softly. "You must know I lost my sister in the same way."

"Hmph!" said the woman, shoving a paper bag into Katrina's hand. "Same way? You mean by Brom's hand?"

Katrina nearly dropped the rolls. "Brom?" she whispered. "Why do you say that?"

"It's what everyone's saying," the woman continued with scornful glee. "No one would say that to his face, of course, for fear of getting their head chopped off. But who else could it be? He's always been a bully, and now everyone who's ever had a quarrel with him is falling off."

"Your husband had a quarrel with Brom?" Katrina asked in surprise. This was news to her.

"Most definitely. Mr. Brom Bones owed quite a bit to my husband—may he rest in peace."

Katrina was confused. "He didn't pay for his bread? How much could it be?"

"Gambling debts, Miss Katrina. Cards. Brom's got a passion for the cards, but lacks the skill to match it. Or didn't you know?"

"I wasn't aware," Katrina whispered.

"How else do you think he can afford to buy you such pretty things? He's in desperate strains to become the Lord of your estate." The woman's expression darkened, and her mouth lifted into a sneer. She reached behind the counter, and took hold of a long chopping knife. "But if *he* thinks he's getting out of what he owes to my family," she growled, "Bam!" She drove the knife into the counter with such fierceness that it made Katrina jump. "I'll chop off his head myself!"

Katrina backed out of the bakery, and the baker's wife only smiled at her fear. By the time she passed through the door and back to the street, she could hear the woman cackling back in her shop, and shouting curses after her.

Katrina was spooked. She kept her head down and tried not to engage in any more conversations as she collected the last few items for her party. She looked at everyone around her with caution, and began to grow paranoid. She passed the butcher, chopping bloody meat in his window with a savagery that bordered on inhuman; she passed the men that usually trailed after Brom, now absent of their leader; and then she came to the gallows outside the courthouse on the edge of the lane. The executioner was speaking loudly to a gathering of men.

"He stole my heads," he grumbled. "I'll see him hang for that. If that don't work, I'll chop him to bits and use him as firewood."

Katrina rushed past and up the dirt lane that led to the schoolhouse. She felt suffocated by the village, at the transformation in her community. She had dealt with her own private grief with dignity and solemnity. Now that others shared her pain, she had expected a bond to form between those who had been robbed of their loved ones. But instead their thoughts had turned violent. Yes, she wanted to stop the Horseman as much as the rest, but their almost euphoric bloodlust held no attraction for her, and made her feel even more alone than ever.

She turned the corner, and saw another circle of adults assembled outside the schoolhouse. She ran up the hill, averting the crowd, and went around to the side windows of the schoolhouse. It was dark inside. She pressed her face to the glass, and called out, "Ichabod? Are you there? Ichabod?"

Then she remembered the circle of people out front, the way they had been gathered inward, as if looking down on something. "No," she whispered, "not him." She walked with weak legs back to the front of the schoolhouse, trying to peer through the bodies and legs of those that had gathered. Unable to see, she had to push herself between the men and women, and looked down to see a body covered by a thick canvas sheet. It looked to be sitting up underneath, and where the head should be there was a stain of blood.

"No," she whispered again, and bent down to the sheet.

She heard the others shout to her, and saw the men reach out their arms to stop her, but she could not control herself. Her fingers clasped the rough canvas, and she threw off the sheet.

Underneath were the headless bodies of five children, all sitting with their backs to each other in a circle. They were dressed in their grey school clothes, their collars stained with blood. The stumps of their necks were still bright red. Fresh.

Katrina backed away with her hand over her mouth, and one of the villagers replaced the sheet covering the bodies. Katrina recognized at once that the circle that had gathered were the children's parents, and she looked at the faces in the crowd, and saw their expressions marked with thinly concealed hysteria.

School must have been cancelled, she realized. Ichabod was not among the parents gathered, but as far as she knew, he was not among the dead.

"Is the schoolmaster here?" she asked one of the mothers.

The woman turned to her. She was a middle-aged woman with hard lines on her face, and a high-forehead wrinkled with anxiety. It took her a moment to process Katrina's question, but the moment she did, all the muscles in her face tensed.

"Leave this place," she spat. "Go plan your party elsewhere."

There wasn't much Katrina could say in reply. She nodded, unable to make eye contact, and walked back down the lane with the feeling of being watched.

She found her way back to her carriage, eager to be away from the village and back to the safety of her father's house. As she walked through the row of shops back to her carriage, she found herself as edgy as the rest of the populace.

She had had doubts about holding a celebration in the face of such tragedy before, but after hearing how Brom was suspected by so many to be the killer, to call off the party now would be like an admission of guilt.

She took one last look at the people she had known her entire life, and as the carriage rolled away, she had only one clear thought:

The killer could be anyone.

*   *   *

Evening fell with quiet relief. As the sun lowered in the sky, and the landscape turned golden with the dying rays of the sun, Katrina waited by the front door, looking out at her father's fields. She had spent the day decorating along with the servants, eager to keep her mind distracted from the fact that she had not heard from Brom all day, and that her father had not emerged from his study.

Only the idea that she would be safe at her own party kept her going.

She looked up as the thud of horse hooves announced the arrival of the first carriage. It was a small uncovered buggy carrying the butcher and his wife. Behind him were several others, who had apparently decided to travel together, and Katrina couldn't say she blamed them for this.

She stood at the door and began the greetings. The loud cries were a welcome change from the silence that had surrounded her most of the day, and the only point of discomfort was when the butcher's wife looked down at her clothes for a moment too long.

Katrina had decided to forego the black of mourning for the sake of the party. It wasn't that she was over her sister's death—far from it—but she felt hypocritical wearing shades of despair at a festive gathering that she initiated. Besides, for just one night, she wanted to have fun. She put on dark lipstick, curled her hair, and wore a frilly sky blue dress that hugged her curvy figure—and had a collar that dipped down as far as decency allowed.

"You look lovely," the butcher's wife said, once she had

recovered herself. Katrina took her by the hand and led her inside, and showed her where the refreshments were laid out, where they could hang their coats, and, pointing to the guest house across the yard, where they would be spending the night. Then she went back to the front door, and did the same for the rest of the guests as they arrived.

Before the sun set, the house was full of life and noise. Even the baker's wife came, although she did little more to prepare than throw off her apron. When Katrina gave her a kiss of greeting, she could still smell the flour in her hair. But everyone seemed to let out a collective breath of relief upon entering. It had been a hard week for the small community, and they basked in the safety of numbers. There was the delight of having something normal and familiar like one of the Van Tassel parties, and the feeling that, no matter how unknowably cruel the world became, there would always be safe pockets for good people to gather. Even the children—or what was left of them—were brought and consigned to a little room to themselves, locked up and safe.

Katrina felt lighter, too, but she didn't let her guard down even as she held her smile. The killer might be here tonight, and she eyed each guest carefully, as if with skillful observation her gaze could penetrate through to their souls.

Ichabod arrived at nightfall, riding up on the sorriest excuse for a horse that Katrina had ever seen. It was an old grey mare, with cataracts on its eyes and patches of fur missing. Ichabod climbed off awkwardly, and a servant flared his nostrils when taking the apparently smelly beast to the barn.

"I'm sorry I'm late," Ichabod said, bowing before Katrina. He kissed her hand, and she felt a wave of excitement pass through her.

"I was starting to worry that you wouldn't show," she said softly, and their eyes met. Ichabod gave a shy grin, looking like a little boy who ate all the cookies.

"There was work to be done at the schoolhouse, and I

didn't want to disturb any of the parents earlier in the day." He looked away from her, wanting to change the subject, and gestured to the party. "It looks like just about everyone from town is here."

Katrina looked at the darkness outside, and then forced herself to turn inside with a host's smile, and reluctantly shut the door.

Brom had not arrived.

"If you'll excuse me, Ichabod," she said putting a hand on his shoulder, "I must find my father. Make yourself at home."

She walked away from the music and bustle of the party, and through the twisting hallway back to her father's study. The Baron had not yet made an appearance at the gathering, and that was unusual in itself. Katrina was sure some of the guests had noticed, even if they hadn't yet had the opportunity to ask about it.

She knocked on the doors to his study. "Father?" she asked. There was no reply, and after calling again, she pushed the doors open slowly.

Her father's study was one of the areas in the house Katrina had almost never been in. It was dark, with no windows to the outside, and a large fireplace on the back wall.

Her father was slumped in a high-backed leather chair. The fire was out behind him, and a thin candle on a table by the wall provided the only light. Katrina ran forward and shook him, with the odd fear that his head would roll from his shoulders and land on the floor.

But her father woke. He pushed her away, sneering at her touch. "Leave me alone," he growled.

"Father," she said, dropping to her knees before him, "the party has started, and Brom is nowhere to be seen. I'm worried he may be out there on the streets by himself."

The Baron sat up straight. "Brom? Alone?" He looked down at his daughter, his expression alert. "What time is it?"

"It's after nightfall."

Her father nodded seriously. "Katrina," he said, taking her hands, "I am going to ask you a question, and I want you to answer honestly."

She was surprised by this sudden shift in her father. His eyes burned into hers, waiting for her response. "Yes, Father?" she asked.

"Do you love Brom?" He shook his head. "I mean, do you *really* want him to be the one for you?"

Katrina blinked. She had not been prepared for such an intimate question. And the truth was, she hadn't ever really considered this. The other men in town had always seemed so inferior to Brom that there was never any doubt he was the best among them. That is, until she met Ichabod. But by then it was too late.

"Yes," she said, after a hesitation. "I want to be with Brom."

Her father stared into her eyes for a deep moment before letting go of her hands.

"All right," he said, and walked toward the wall. "Then I will bring him back for you. Even if it means taking down the Headless Horseman myself." He reached up for a sword that had been lodged on a plaque, and tugged it off the wall. He started pacing back and forth, swiping it through the air.

"Let me come with you," she asked, and he looked at her as if he had been slapped.

"No," he said. "You will be kept safe. If Brom and I can't hold our own against the Horseman, there's no chance that you can help."

"I could keep watch. Or maybe we could gather some of the other guests?" She was thinking of Ichabod, although she realized that his help would be as useless as her own.

"Not a chance." He walked up to her. "I want you to promise me, Katrina, that you will not leave this house, for any reason, under any circumstances. I cannot lose you as well as Mary. Do you promise?"

She was quiet. She wanted to go, but she also knew that her father would not leave unless she promised. "Yes," she whispered, "I promise."

He kissed her cheek, and stormed out of the room. He turned in the hallway toward the stables, and didn't stop when there were calls to him by the guests of the party.

Katrina stood in her father's study. The room smelled like the bad habits of men: cigars, whiskey, and sweat. This was the first time she had ever been left alone here, and the temptation to look around was too strong for her to resist. Her father had always been a secretive man. What secrets did his private quarters hold?

She took the candle from the side table, and walked along the bookshelves. She let her eyes fall upon the titles— volumes on agriculture, on finance and law—until she came to a shelf with a gap between the books. There was a clean mark in the dust. A book had been removed recently.

Katrina turned toward the darkened fireplace, and saw a low table by the hearth. A book lay open, piled on top of a second, and she made her way to it. The candle shined upon the first book, and Katrina gasped.

It was an illustration, a detailed engraving in stark chiaroscuro, of a naked man holding his own severed head like a lantern. The setting was a pit of Hell, with tortured souls huddled in a pile beneath where the man stood, their skin torn and limbs severed.

The caption read: *Betran de Born, the Baron.*

Katrina shuddered, and flipped through the book at random. The drawings were horrific, of beasts and creatures and dark suffering. Why had her father taken this book out? But the answers in her head were none that she could accept, and she lifted the book aside, hoping to find something to soothe her suspicions.

Underneath was the Bible. This was not a good sign. Katrina's father had never been a religious man, as far as she knew, and she hesitantly brought the candle close to see what he had been reading.

He had circled a passage with red ink. She read it aloud.

"And I looked, and beheld a pale horse. And his rider's name was Death." She knew the passage; it presaged the apocalypse, and the time the dead would rise.

She backed away, the candle shaking in her hand. No wonder her father had been spooked the last few days. No wonder he hadn't felt like joining the party. He obviously thought the end of the world was nigh. Perhaps the plague in the next town, and the Horseman, had set his mind at work and convinced him—or perhaps he had already been convinced. Had her father gone mad? Was it possible that he was the Horseman?

Katrina turned, ready to get out of the study and back to the party, and knocked into someone standing right behind her. She screamed, nearly dropping the candle.

It was Ichabod. He must have followed her into the room. And she couldn't help it: she felt instantly relieved that he wasn't her father.

"Oh, Ichabod," she said, and set down the candle to immediately throw her arms around him. He seemed surprised by this, but in a moment his body relaxed. His hand reached down, and he laced his fingers through her hair, gently stroking the nape of her neck.

"I didn't mean to startle you," he apologized. "I saw your father rush out, and I didn't see you anywhere, and—" he paused, embarrassed. Katrina stepped back and looked up at him. He continued, unable to meet her eyes. "I thought something had happened."

"He's going out to look for Brom," she explained.

Ichabod nodded. "That must be a relief to you."

"It was," she said carefully, "at first. But then I found these." She took Ichabod by the hand, and led him over to the books she had found. His face became serious as he flipped through, reading the passages in the Bible as she had. Then he stood back up to his full height, his face unreadable.

Katrina couldn't take his silence. "You don't think…?" she prompted.

He wouldn't meet her eyes. "What your father is reading is no different than what everyone in town has been talking about. You will hear similar stories of the apocalypse and theories of the Horseman if you stand around the punch-bowl. This may not mean anything."

He was being too kind. "Talk to me like a man," Katrina insisted. "Do you really think my father could be capable of such things? Of—*beheadings?*"

She had expected—and hoped—that Ichabod would instantly refute her. But he turned to her, and his eyes were filled with sadness. "If there's one thing I've learned recently, it is that there are horrors in everyone's soul. I myself have had to do things I would never have imagined myself capable of, and I'm not half the man your father is."

"But *why?*" Katrina asked. It didn't make any sense to her.

Ichabod shrugged. "Perhaps your father thought he could protect you by killing those that he viewed as threats. If I believed I could save my mother by killing others, I would have done it. Without hesitation."

"But my sister!" Katrina exclaimed. "Why would he kill his own daughter if he was trying to *protect* us? Unless—unless he was only trying to protect me?" She remembered how her father had reacted when her sister had insisted on being on her own, outside of his house. Did he think Katrina would follow? Did he kill Mary so that she would know it was not safe to leave him?

Ichabod put his arms around her. "The things we do for those we love are often the cruelest, most unspeakable acts of all."

She breathed in the smell of his shirt, and felt tears in her eyes. "Oh, Ichabod," she whispered, "if only you had lived here from the start. You would have been spared so much, and we," she sniffled, "we could have been together."

He pulled away, and reached down to hold her face. "No," he said, "you wouldn't have loved me then." Before she could object, he continued. "You can only love me now, after my suffering. What bonds us is our grief."

At these words, she pulled him back toward her, and kissed him.

His lips were warm and gentle, and she felt sparks of emotion throughout her body, like she was a fuse that had been lit on fire. It felt safe and warm and right, in a way she never felt with—

Brom!

"Katrina!" He was standing in the doorway, staring at them in shock. Then he looked to Ichabod, and snarled, "You!"

"Brom, wait!" Katrina cried, trying to protect Ichabod by putting her arms in front of him. Brom didn't even see her in his rage. He came forward, and shoved her to the ground. She looked up to see him push Ichabod against the book-case by his throat.

"Schoolteacher," he growled. Ichabod tried to squirm out of Brom's grasp, but he was defenseless to stop him. "Look at me," Brom commanded with unsettling calm. Ichabod looked up, as if raising his eyes to face a pistol. Brom spoke quietly, and slowly, but there was no hiding his temper.

"I want you gone," he said. "Out of the party, out of Sleepy Hollow, and out of our lives. If I ever see you again, if I ever so much as *hear* about you again, so help me, I will snap your neck in half and feed you to the dogs. Katrina is *mine*. Is that understood?"

Ichabod managed to squeak out a "Yes," and then Brom threw him to the floor. He scrambled up, and ran out of the room. Katrina watched him until he disappeared around the door, and then she looked up to her fiancé.

"Brom," she began, not knowing where to start.

He turned to her with a look of utter rage, and she edged back. But at the same time she could see in his eyes that a part of him was broken. "Not a word, Katrina," he said through clenched teeth. "I don't want to hear a word."

Then he stomped out of the room, and slammed the door behind him.

Katrina fell back against the wall, her mind racing. Ichabod couldn't leave now. Even if it weren't for the Horseman, she couldn't lose him now. She had barely gotten to know him, barely discovered the hints of their potential.

And where would he go? He couldn't go back to his old town. He would have to set out somewhere new. And once he did, there would be no telling which way the wind would take him. If she didn't get to him now, she would lose him forever.

And Katrina knew he had to go back to the schoolhouse before he left for good. That was where his things were, and where he slept, in the little room in the back that held his cot. If she could make it there before he left...

She got up to her feet and left her father's study. The music hit her in the face as soon as she walked out; she had forgotten all about the party. Several guests turned toward her. She plastered a fake smile on her face, more to avoid suspicion than from any concern about the party's success, and hurriedly weaved her way through the crowd.

Scanning the room revealed neither Brom nor Ichabod.

"Looking for your man?" slurred a bitter voice. She turned to see the baker's wife, holding what could not have been her first glass of punch for the evening.

"Do you know where they are?" she asked, ignoring the sour look the woman was giving her.

The baker's wife took a long sip, and then smacked her lips. "It's a shame when a woman doesn't know where her fiancé is," she sneered. When Katrina refused to respond, she rolled her eyes. "Brom left in a rush, chasing after the schoolmaster."

"Thank you," Katrina said, and started to turn away.

The baker's wife caught her wrist. "He's trouble."

Katrina wasn't sure which man she meant, but didn't care to ask. She pulled away, took one last look through the guests, this time looking for her father and not finding him, and then slipped out through the kitchen to the back door.

It was full dark now. An orange moon hung low and fat on the horizon, like a disembodied head floating across the sky. She stepped through the grass to the stables, and found it full of horses due to the party. The stall of her father's horse was empty, and as she went looking for a steed to borrow, she found herself staring eye to eye with the pitiful creature Ichabod had arrived upon.

What did that mean? Had he taken another horse? Or was he really going back to the village on foot, completely vulnerable?

And right past the bridge?

She selected a fast-looking palomino. This would be stealing, she realized. "No, only borrowing," she whispered aloud. But the truth was, she wasn't sure if she'd ever return. She led the horse by the bridal out of the stable, and as she crossed the lawn, she took one last look at the house.

The windows were alight with a warm glow, and she could hear the band inside, along with a melody of friendly voices. There was a small crowd gathered behind the house on the opposite side, and their carefree laughter echoed into the night.

She had promised not to leave the safety of the party. And leaving her guests alone would make her a bad host.

But her father was out there, and Brom, and Ichabod. They were the three people left in the world that she cared about. If she stayed at the party, she might survive the night, but she would have nothing left to live for.

She walked quietly with the horse until she reached the path leading back to town. There, she hopped on the strange horse's back, and hoped it was trained. She kicked her heels into its ribs, and the horse took off into the night at once.

The schoolhouse, she thought, clutching onto the horse's neck as the wind whipped against her ears and sent the curls of her hair flying behind her like a flag. She must get to the schoolhouse. She kicked again, refusing to notice the growls and moans coming from beyond the walls of the path. She rushed past the bridge, and in a few minutes reached the darkness of the village.

It was silent here, and the lane was empty. Not a single candle was lit in any of the windows, and no one had bothered to light either of the village's two streetlamps. Memory guided her, and the light from the full moon, but as she continued she found that fear made her move slower.

She reached the end of the village shops, and turned up toward the schoolhouse. The horse was wheezing, and she patted the side of its thick neck as thanks for its efforts. They continued up the rural path, and Katrina kept her eyes wide, alert to every sound.

She heard the croaking of frogs, and the chirp of crickets. The wind rustled the dry branches all around her, and the sound of the horse's footsteps seemed hollow and empty as she went along the path. The smell of soil was strong, and she could picture the worms and insects churning up from the ground as if rising from their graves. There were no human sounds, or human sights, and for a moment, Katrina thought that this must be how the world sounded before mankind had settled the landscape. And maybe this is what it would sound like again after they were all gone.

She turned the corner to the schoolhouse, and saw the structure looming over the night like a crouching giant. She edged her horse up the path, and nearly jumped out of her skin when there was a snap in the branches next to her. She swung the horse in the direction of the noise, and gasped when she saw a man standing in the brush.

"Katrina," he whispered, and she recognized the voice.

She edged the horse backward. "Brom," she said, and he hushed her. She asked more quietly, "What are you doing here?"

He looked in either direction, and then stepped out onto the path. His face was splattered with blood. It looked black in the moonlight.

"I was waiting for the Horseman," he said, not noticing her reaction. "Your father and I both were."

She looked past him, and saw that his own horse was tied to a tree just beyond the path. But she didn't see any sign of her father.

"Where's Ichabod?" she asked, not taking her eyes off of him. He didn't have a weapon. At least, not one she could see.

He looked confused. "How should I know? Listen, Katrina, you need to get back home. It isn't safe here. The Headless Horseman could be here any moment."

"Why are you covered with blood?"

He looked down at himself, as if realizing it for the first time. "It must be your father's." He looked up at her, and saw her startled expression. "We were attacked by the dead," he explained. "Your father was injured."

He took a step toward her, and she flinched. "Stay back," she said.

"Katrina?" His head tilted, and the blood dripped down the side of his cheek. "If you're upset about earlier, we can talk about it when we get home. But right now you need to—"

He took another step forward, this time with his arms out to grab the reins of the horse, and she screamed. Her cry split through the night like a bolt of lightning, and sent a flock of birds into the air, cawing with annoyance at being disturbed.

Brom froze, his eyes wide.

"You shouldn't have done that," he whispered in a voice dead of tone. "He'll have heard it. He'll know we're here."

Then in the distance, a mad shout of laughter vibrated through the night. Katrina turned, fear filling her soul. The laughter had come from the village, and seemed to be moving in their direction very quickly.

"Into the woods!" Brom said, and before Katrina could stop him, he was pushing against her horse and backing them into the trees. He stopped and looked up, and that's when Katrina heard it:

Horse hooves thudding through the night. They were coming up the path, barely farther than around the corner.

"Your father is on the bridge," Brom said, rushing through his words. "Lead the Horseman there. That was our plan, to ambush him. Your father's hiding on the other end of the bridge."

"Brom?"

"The *bridge*, Katrina. Once the Horseman passes, get to the bridge. It's your only chance."

He helped her push her horse back into the trees, and then barely had time to return to the path before the Horseman rounded the corner.

Katrina put her hand over her mouth. Until now, she hadn't believed it. But at the end of the path, there was a man riding on the back of a giant black stallion. He had a long black cape, a shining silver sword, and no head. In her astonishment, Katrina had the detached thought that, if he didn't have a head, how did he laugh a moment ago? How was that possible?

The Headless Horseman charged up the lane toward the schoolhouse, passing Katrina in the trees, and went chasing after Brom. Brom was running up the hill at full speed, but he wasn't fast enough to beat the horse. The Horseman swiped his sword, and in one swift movement Brom's head was severed and rolling down the hill. The Horseman turned his black beast, and skewered the head with his sword. Then he shoved it into a canvas satchel tied around his waist.

It was only then that Katrina shook from her trance. The bridge, she remembered. Without a moment's hesitation, she kicked her heels into the horse, and turned it on the path back toward the village.

She prodded it to run faster, faster, and swerved between trees and around the bends of the path. When she neared the sight of the shops, she chanced a look behind her, and saw that the Headless Horseman was barely a house-length behind her, and gaining.

"Please," she whispered, "let him be at the bridge."

She didn't know what she'd do if her father wasn't there. It was too far back to her home; she would never be able to outrun the Horseman. Her palomino was already wheezing and foaming at the mouth from exhaustion.

Finally, she reached the end of the shops and turned on the fork in the road. Then she saw it: the bridge.

It was an old, rickety structure. The wood itself had turned grey with age, and even though she was being chased by a headless man, the sight of the bridge filled her with such fear that she had trouble not steering the horse away from it. The bridge had been associated so strongly with the walking dead that she had come to believe the structure itself was dangerous.

But she didn't turn. Closing her eyes and bending her body down toward the horse, she charged into the mouth of the bridge. The wooden planks thumped underneath her, and a moment later she heard the footfalls of the Headless Horseman behind her.

She felt the horse step off the wooden planks and onto the dirt of the path, and opened her eyes just in time to skid the horse to a stop before it entered the dark woods.

She looked back. Her father was indeed waiting behind the end of the bridge. She saw him lunge out, and stab the

Horseman's stallion through the muscle of its front leg. The horse let out a cry and stumbled, knocking the Horseman off and throwing him through the air. The horse tumbled over itself, and landed on top of its rider, crushing his legs.

"Katrina!" called her father, rushing toward her in surprise. He had a limp to his walk, and his face was sweaty and pale. "What are you doing here? Where's Brom?"

"Dead," Katrina answered, and jumped down from her horse. "The Horseman killed him."

They turned toward the man. He was flipping back and forth, trying to dislodge himself from the horse's weight. His sword was on the ground at the border of the trees, far from his grasp.

Katrina didn't bother to go after it. She was distracted by the Headless Horseman himself. She took a step toward him, and her father reached for her to stop, but she evaded his grasp. "Look," she said, and pointed to the man.

In the violence of the fall, the Headless Horseman's cape had flipped up, and Katrina could see a second set of shoulders beneath the ones of the coat.

"It's a disguise," she said, and her father came forward as well, drawn by his curiosity.

Katrina pulled on the cape, and the top half of the Horseman's torso—the fabricated part—slid away. And underneath was a normal man. He looked up at Katrina, his brown hair falling into his piercing green eyes.

"Ichabod!" she gasped. "You're the Headless Horseman?"

"So it's not a demon," her father said, coming to his own realization.

"Why?" Katrina cried, dropping to her knees before him. "How could you do such a thing?" Her eyes filled with tears, realizing the man she thought she loved was someone else entirely. He was a murderer. He had killed Brom. He had killed children.

He had killed her sister.

Katrina stood up, her face losing what little confusion and sorrow it held. "You killed Mary," she said without feeling. She looked at the sword the Horseman had dropped in his fall, and took a step toward it. "Brom was right about you all along."

Ichabod followed her gaze, and his eyes grew wide. "Please, Katrina! It's not what you think."

Katrina didn't care to listen. "I risked my life to save you," she said with a snarl. "I thought you were out here, defenseless, vulnerable. I thought you were *sensitive!*" She shook her head. "You drove my father half to madness, and killed everyone else I cared about. You deserve to die."

She took another step toward the sword, but before she could reach it, there was movement in the trees. A woman stepped out, only she was nothing like any woman Katrina had ever seen before. Her face had been scraped away to the bone, and her skin was mottled and covered with dirt and grime. Around her torso were the last tatters of what looked to have once been a wedding dress.

Katrina recoiled, stepping back toward her father and Ichabod. And the dead woman stepped out.

"They're back," her father gasped. He turned to his daughter. "There's more where she came from. You must run, Katrina. You must get out of here."

"What about you?" she asked, not taking her eye off the woman.

Her father pulled up the sleeve of his coat, revealing an open gash on his skin. "I've been bitten," he said. "I'm as good as dead anyway."

More of the creatures were stumbling out of the shadows now, drawn by the noise and the smell of blood. There seemed to be no sense to the grouping: men, women, and children traveling together like a pack. The children bothered her the most, especially one little boy covered in green leaves with a ferocious smile on his face. For a moment,

Katrina thought she preferred dealing with the Headless Horseman.

"Get out of here! Back home!" her father yelled, and he pulled Katrina away from the walking dead and toward her palomino.

"Wait," gasped Ichabod. He reached down into his coat pocket, and took out a ring of keys. "Go to the schoolhouse. You won't make it to your house. They've set the walls of the path on fire."

Katrina looked up to her father. He thought about it for a moment as the creatures stumbled forward out of the shadows, and then he nodded. He bent down to Ichabod and tore the keys from his hand, and then threw them to Katrina.

"Lock yourself in," he ordered. "I'll hold them back until—"

A little dead girl in rags jumped on his back before he could finish, and he let out a cry, forgetting Katrina entirely as the girl bit into him.

Katrina took a half step forward to help him, but Ichabod yelled at her. "Go!" he cried. She turned and hopped up on her horse, and kicked it harder than she meant to. It reared up and whinnied, and the creatures gathered closer.

Katrina pulled the reins, and kicked again. This time the horse understood, and went galloping across the wood of the bridge. They ran through the night to the fork in the road, and Katrina saw at once that Ichabod had been right: there were dead everywhere along the path back to her farmhouse, illuminated by the flames of the burning wall. They shuffled closer, and she turned the steed back toward the village.

But not before she heard the screams of her guests at the farmhouse echoing into the night.

She turned the horse, and went at full speed through the

dark town. She didn't stop to knock on any of the windows or warn anyone that might be sleeping that the town was under attack. There was no time.

It was when she rounded the corner at the end of the village that the horse gave out. It stumbled over its feet, and Katrina felt its body shake as its heart collapsed from the effort. She was so alert from fear already that she had the foresight to jump off the horse before it hit the ground. She skidded on her elbows in the dirt, landing painfully on her hip. The horse fell on the other side of the path, and Katrina was grateful she hadn't been trapped as Ichabod had.

She pushed herself up, not letting herself feel her scratches, and patted her pocket to make sure the keys were still there. They were. Then pulling up the front of her dirt-smeared dress, she ran up the hill to the schoolhouse. She could hear one of the dead shaking the branches of the trees as she passed, and she didn't stop to look. She reached the door, jammed in the key, and pushed herself into the schoolhouse. As soon as she was in, she slammed the door shut behind her, catching a glimpse of a woman dressed in a torn purple dress lurching after her.

She ran around the room, pulling the shutters closed on the windows, and bolting them down with the latch. After she had secured the last window, she hunched over and heaved in breath after breath, unable to make her heart stop thrashing in her chest. Sweat poured down her face, and she was glad for the cold air in the schoolhouse.

Then she realized how dark it was with all the windows closed. She felt her way forward to the teacher's desk, where she knew there was a candle, and patted the worn wooden desk until she found a match.

Once she had some light, her sense of relief increased considerably. The things outside were scratching against the doors and the windows, and Katrina's mind worked quickly. She set the candle down on the desk, and then went to work pushing all the desks against the door of the schoolhouse to form a barricade. She couldn't do much about the windows, but at least they were high enough on the wall that not more than one of the dead could climb in at a time. She could handle that, if she had to.

And then when morning came, she would be saved. Even if everyone back at her house was dead now, there were still people in the village. And even more in the villages beyond. She could run and keep ahead of the creatures.

She pictured this, in her head, but instead of seeing herself, she just saw Ichabod running from the dead that had infested his old town. They had simply followed him here. There was no escape.

She shook her head. But that still didn't explain why he had posed as the Horseman. Why had he killed? Was he insane? If he was, he was the most sensible insane person Katrina had ever met.

She heard another scratch at the window, but tried to ignore it. Instead, she walked around the front of Ichabod's desk. Maybe there would be something to help explain his actions. Despite seeing him unmasked with her own eyes, she still had trouble reconciling the sensitive schoolmaster with the violent Horseman.

She thumbed through some papers, seeing nothing more than assignments. She was about to put them back, when she noticed a drawing in the corner of one. A skull and cross bones drawn in black, and underneath it read:

Bad children lose their heads.

She shuddered, and shoved the papers away. She had figured out Ichabod's disciplinary practices, if nothing else. No wonder the children had been so terrified, so obedient.

She stood up, taking the candle with her, and pushed open the small door that led to the teacher's quarters. It was little more than a booth with a cot and a small basin to wash. Underneath the cot, Katrina could see a bloody bundle poking out. She leaned down to check, but stopped herself.

What if her sister's head was in the bag?

But then as the thought settled in of her sister's head being shoved like garbage into a dirty old bag, she knew she had to take it out.

She bent down, and pulled out the bag. She dumped it out right there in the little room. Bones clattered out, fragments of skull and jaws. She looked down at them, confused. These were the remains, as she had expected, but they had been—it looked as if they had been *licked* clean.

There was a scratch along the floor in the schoolroom behind her. She turned with the candle, and there in the center of the floor was one of the dead. Katrina's eyes darted to the windows and the door, but they were still closed. She stood up, her back to the little room, and held up the candle toward the creature lurching toward her.

It was an old woman. She was dead, her skin grey and rotted away, but great care and attention had been paid to the rest of her. Her white hair was freshly curled, and her dress—a loose-fitting gown with a flowered pattern—was clean and freshly pressed. She even had on a pair of slippers.

She took a step toward Katrina, her mouth open and drooling. Katrina had never seen this woman before, yet there was something familiar about her... her body frame, her thin face, and—her green eyes.

Mother.

"Of course," Katrina whispered. Ichabod must have been hiding her here from the start, taking her with him even after she died, unable to let go.

This was why he collected heads. Because Mother was hungry. Katrina looked up at the dead woman coming toward her.

Apparently, Mother was still hungry.

Katrina backed into the little room, her shoes crunching on the skulls of her sister and countless others.

She thought of Ichabod, how he had used his last ounce of strength to send her here, knowing full well what would happen after.

And as the old woman leapt in the air, her teeth exposed and eyes wild with hunger, Katrina knew that if she had been in Ichabod's place, if the only way to keep her sister alive was to hunt down strangers and behead them, she would have done it, too.

She understood completely. You do what you must for the people you love. And as the old woman bit down into her arm, she felt a wave of regret.

Not that she would die.

Not that the world was doomed.

But regret that she would never know a life with someone as devoted as Ichabod. She loved him. Even as his mother's teeth ripped into her skin, she couldn't deny this. She loved Ichabod.

She just wished Ichabod had loved her this much in return.

SKULL WHITE

A line of naked girls was brought into the dark chamber, their hands tied behind their backs and their bare feet slapping against the stone floor.

"Some fine choices today," the Royal Physician said, holding their ropes like a leash as he shut the chamber door. He stood fully dressed in a shapeless black cloak, admiring his procurement. He had a beaked nose, bushy white eyebrows, and a bald, wrinkled scalp.

In the center of the room sat the Queen. She was a regal woman, middle-aged, with her hair hidden under a tight hood. Her eyes were narrow, and her expression blank. Next to her chair rested an empty white bathtub.

She stood up, and came to the girls. They set their pleading eyes on her, and some were making bovine moans as they tried to talk through their gags. But that's not what the Queen noticed.

She turned to the Physician. "You can't be serious. These girls are hideous."

Waxy skin. Dull eyes. Asymmetric eyebrows. She went down the row, each face more hideous than the last.

The Physician turned to the girls. "They look fine to me."

The Queen shook her head. "That's because when you

look at a face, all you see are the generalities: eyes, nose, mouth. You have no appreciation for subtleties."

How could she explain it to one so unbeautiful as the Physician? He had probably never looked at a face for more than two seconds at a time, not even his own.

She took hold of a girl's chin between her fingers, and held the face toward her. "When I look at a face," she explained, "I see every detail. I see each individual pore. Each individual strand of the eyebrows. The way an earlobe hangs." She pushed the girl away from her. "I look the way an artist looks, noting the actual proportions, the actual details. Not just the names—nose, eyes, mouth—but the real *shape* of things."

The Royal Physician blinked. He turned his bald head back to the girls. After not more than a full second, he said, "They still look fine to me." He smiled at a plump girl, maybe thirteen, with tears running down her cheeks. "Very fresh."

The Queen sighed. "That's because they're young. Youth is its own kind of beauty. You have to learn to see past it, to see them as old women."

"Your body will only accept the beautiful," the Physician reminded her. "Just as it only takes the nutrients from the foods that you eat, and discards the rest."

She supposed that was true. Besides, the entire reason for this emergency bath was because of Lord Valiant's approach. This was to be the first gentleman caller in over ten years.

Men pretty much stayed away after they learned she had her previous husband executed. But now that her brother, the King, was on his deathbed, and her own children had perished in the plague of the dead, she was next in line to command, and suddenly the men were returning.

But it would do no good if they suspected she was too old to produce an heir.

"Besides," the Physician continued, "these are the last of the young in the kingdom. They will have to do."

The Queen bit her lip. Then she nodded. "Bring them to the tub."

The Physician tugged on his leash, and brought the girls forward. They were fighting more now, whimpering and twisting their shoulders in an effort to get away.

"Down!" the Physician ordered, shoving each girl to her knees, facing the tub. "There's no way out so don't even try!"

Meanwhile, the Queen walked to a corner of the room, and took out a heavy black leather glove. It had been outfitted with long silver claws over each fingernail, like a vulture's talons. The Queen put it on, and sliced at the air.

Then the Queen stepped up behind each girl, threw each against the tub, and dragged her razor-sharp talons across each young neck. Red blood drizzled down the sides of the white ceramic tub, and soon a healthy puddle formed in the center of the human fountains.

She was almost done. Most of the girls were too shocked to do anything but die, but the last one in line seemed to think she had a chance. When the Queen came up behind her, she kicked her foot out like a donkey.

The Queen smiled and grasped the girl by the scruff of the neck. "Tsk tsk," she cooed. "Don't you know? The more you struggle, the faster you die." And she pulled her talons across the girl's neck slowly, savoring it, holding the girl down as her body flopped in revolt. Blood surged out from the broken dam of her neck, until finally the girl's body relaxed, and fell limp. She didn't seem so defiant now. Without her fight, she seemed smaller, like a deflated blow-fish. She was maybe seven years old.

"Feisty this time," the Queen said, pulling off her glove and whacking it into the Physician's stomach. "I suppose that's worth something."

She slid off her robe, and handed that over as well. Then, naked, she raised a foot over the edge of the tub, and kept her hands on the side of the basin as she lowered herself in.

The girls were still trickling and sputtering warm blood, and the Queen closed her eyes and felt the droplets like warm rain on her face. She let out a sigh through her nose, and felt her bony shoulders unclench as all her muscles relaxed.

There was nothing as refreshing as a hot bath.

She was just drifting off to sleep when trumpets sounded deep within the castle.

"What is that?" she asked, sitting up. Blood dripped off her face, her hair, her breasts.

"He must be here," the Physician said, looking toward the sound and listening carefully.

"Lord Valiant? He was not supposed to be here until nightfall." She looked up at the girls, their eyes blank now, but their necks still dripping into the tub. "Quickly!" she cried, and began splashing the blood on her face and rubbing it into her cheeks. "I need to soak up the essence!"

"It won't do much good when you're stressed," he chastised, but he helped rub the blood into her hair nonetheless. They continued until the blood cooled. Then the Queen stood up, and moved into a second chamber, where a more traditional bath had been prepared. She rinsed her hair and body of the blood, scrubbing in annoyance, and then rushed back to her grooming quarters to begin slathering on every lotion and ointment she had.

This might be her last chance to find a mate. She had to make sure everything about herself was perfect.

"Bring the mirror!" she shouted to the Physician.

The only mirror in the entire kingdom that the Queen trusted was her golden floor-length mirror. The glass was flat and reflective enough to alert her to the faintest smudge of her makeup, while at the same time, its golden hue was extremely flattering, and bolstered her confidence.

Two servants entered behind the Physician and set the mirror down carefully on its stand in the center of the room. The Queen waited until the two had left before approaching the glass.

"Oh, mirror," she whispered, and caressed the gold as if stroking the face of a lover. "Mirror, mirror, you are the only one honest enough to tell me if I am still beautiful." She tilted up the glass, and peered into her own face.

When the Queen looked in the mirror, she didn't see what others saw. Others might expect her to see her stately face: her thin nose, high cheekbones, and regally arched eyebrows. They might look at her trim body and luscious black hair, and think she looked suspiciously good for her age. But when the Queen looked at herself in the mirror, she saw nothing but an old woman whose face was full of faults.

Her expression grew grim, and she pressed forward until her nose almost touched the glass.

There were new wrinkles around her eyes, a deep one on her left eye that curved down like a hook. She grimaced, and then almost cried at the multitude of lines this expression created. Dispirited, she was about to turn away when she saw *it* out of the corner of her eye.

"No," she gasped. "No, no, no, please no!" She gripped the side of the mirror, and turned her head to the left just to be sure. "Ah!" she cried out, and slumped to the ground in shame.

The Physician ran up to her, his eyes wide with alarm. "What?" he asked. "What is it?"

The Queen looked up at him with spite. "This!" she snarled, and grabbed a hunk of her hair. *"This!"*

And there, among the dark folds of her hair, was a single grey hair. It stood out like an albino snake in a nest of ebony.

"Well, we can pluck that," the Physician said calmly.

"That's not the point!" the Queen screamed. She let go of her hair, and turned back to the mirror. "The point is that all these beauty treatments haven't been working. I'm getting older by the minute!" She pushed her cheek up to the side of the glass. "It's hopeless. I might as well be a corpse!"

The Physician's soft voice asked, "Would you like to send Lord Valiant away? Make up some excuse?"

The Queen pulled away from the mirror. "No, of course not." She blinked, quickly regaining herself. She turned to the Physician, and squeezed his hand. "But these baths aren't working. We need to do something more."

The Physician looked away. "This is not my fault. Our stock is limited in today's world. If we still had access to the town, to a never-ending supply of young maidens, these treatments would still work. But our well has run dry."

The Queen looked at him. "Be straight with me," she said. "I can tell you are holding back. I don't know why. Did I shrink away when you suggested bathing in the blood of virgins? No. I went out that evening and filled up my first tub."

"Yes, Your Majesty. It's just that the next step is more—*unseemly.*"

The Queen scoffed. "There's no need to pussyfoot with me." She straightened her back and forced him to meet her eye. "Talk to me like a man, Physician. I have the stomach for it."

Little beads of sweat had formed on the Royal Physician's bald head. "That is an especially apt phrase, my Queen. For the only other remedy in my books is to consume the organs of the healthy."

The Queen's eyes went wide, and the Physician hurried his speech.

"It's an old remedy, a dark one, for what it calls for is the heart, lungs, and liver as fresh as possible from the source. The ingredients should be boiled in salt water, and eaten before the sun rises the next morning." The Physician lowered his voice. "It is said that this will cure any disease, heal any ailment, and restore the patient to the full bloom of youth and beauty."

The Queen laughed. "Perfect! Perfect!"

"But," said the Physician, cringing as the Queen turned to him, "there is one limitation."

"*Yes?*"

"The patient will only be as strong, or as healthy, or as *beautiful* as the one from which she has consumed."

The Queen's smile fell. There was a silence between them. They both knew perfectly well that she had already drained every fair maiden within their grasp. They had already taken the last of the young.

The trumpets sounded again, and the Queen shook away her thoughts.

"What are you doing sitting here?" she snapped. "Get me my crown. Its sparkle should distract him enough for now."

The Physician scurried out of the room, and the Queen turned back to the mirror. She stared at her reflection, as if facing an enemy, and took the grey hair between two fingers.

"You will not win!" she declared, and tore the strand from her scalp.

But who knew how long she would last before another replaced it? And another? And another?

* * *

Lord Valiant waited with his son for nearly three hours before the Queen made her appearance. She was wearing an elaborate emerald green gown with nearly twenty pounds of fine fabric within its billows. The fabric itched terribly. Her waist had been squeezed into a girdle barely larger than the size of an orange, and every inch of her—from her high collar to the train of her dress—was covered with sparkling jewels. The largest diamond was in her crown, and the Queen was pleased to see Lord Valiant's eyes uncontrollably drawn to it as he approached her to bow.

"Your Grace," he said, kissing her fingers. He had a square chin, determined eyes, and a sharp, businesslike smile.

His son also rose and bowed, but kept his distance.

She could feel her makeup clump as she smiled. "Please," she said, "sit."

They took their seats in the windowless dark chamber. She sat next to a small fireplace. It lit her good side at the perfect angle from below, and left the rest of her form in shadow.

"I hope you are comfortable here," she said, trying to scratch her side without drawing attention to the motion.

He nodded. "It seems especially secure."

"This is perhaps the safest location in the entire kingdom," she agreed. Men always found fortifications admirable. "The main entrance is only accessible by drawbridge, which we keep up; we have our own inner courtyard with a garden and natural spring; and, possibly most impressive of all, every window has been walled-up with stone."

She did not mention that the structural changes were made years before she or anyone else had even heard of the walking dead. It was merely coincidence that the Queen's desire to avoid unflattering natural light had made her castle into an impenetrable fortress.

"Very impressive," Lord Valiant said with a smile. "Although there is talk about evacuating what is left of the kingdom, and walling off this entire area, abandoning it to the dead."

The Queen laughed. "What fools are talking about that? Don't they realize how large the kingdom is? How far this plague has spread?"

"I believe," Lord Valiant said carefully, "it was your brother, the King, who proposed this."

The Queen sneered. "My brother? Is he still alive? I would have thought he was dead by now."

"Very close, I'm afraid. But he still holds some sway with public opinion, even if—" Lord Valiant stopped himself.

"What?" The Queen leaned closer, and fluttered her eyes. "You can tell me."

Lord Valiant looked confused by her gesture. And the Queen suddenly felt very foolish for flirting with him. Even in the dim light of the chamber, she could tell how much younger he was than her. She felt twice as insecure just looking at him. And she would only get older.

But he was here to see her, and she wasn't about to let any weakness show. She searched her mind for an abrupt change of topic. Then her eyes landed on his son. "And who might this be?" she asked, her eyes growing wide. The child shrank down.

"This is Phillip," Lord Valiant said, ruffling a hand through the boy's brown hair. "My son."

"Oh," the Queen said. "Are you a widower?"

"Unfortunately, I am," he replied. Then he smiled. "But being here in your radiant presence, it almost makes it worthwhile."

The Queen nearly fell over with delight. She was about to make a comment about second chances when the door to the chamber opened, and a veiled servant woman entered, holding a bowl of apples.

The Queen allowed the older servants to wear veils, not so much because she was worried about their beauty competing with her own—there was no one left she hadn't drained that even came close—but because she didn't want herself associated with anyone unattractive. Plus the servants seemed more comfortable not having to look her in the eye.

The servant set the bowl down on a table before the chairs, gave a small bow, and turned to leave. But a corner of her sleeve had caught underneath the bowl, and as she turned, she sent the bowl crashing to the ground.

The Queen jumped up and took the servant by the arm.

"Stupid woman!" she shrieked, and slapped the servant across the face, knocking off her veil.

The Queen gasped.

Underneath the veil was the most beautiful girl the Queen had ever seen. She had blemish-free skin, soft as new fallen snow; raven-black hair that shined with health; wide, uncomplicated eyes and a small upturned nose. She also had the reddest lips in the kingdom, as if she had blotted them with blood. This girl had features that were the exact perfection of every possible trait. The Queen was awestruck.

And struck with hunger.

"What is your name?" the Queen asked.

"Sn-Snow White," the girl said. Her voice was like the cooing of pigeons.

"How come I've never seen your face before?"

The girl looked down, and she was innocence and beauty made flesh. Venus, Eve, Mary—they were but pale imitations of this girl's perfection.

Snow White pressed her red lips together. "My mother keeps me locked away. But she was sick today, and unable to go about her tasks. I'm sorry, Your Majesty."

Lord Valiant laughed, and the Queen woke from her daze. She looked up at him with malignity.

"All is forgiven," he said to the girl. He could not keep his eyes off of her. "Accidents happen."

The Queen nodded with a stony expression, and got back into her chair reluctantly. She scratched her hips miserably. If only she had been alone when she had seen this girl! Now she would have to wait for another opportunity. For she knew that although she had no problem with consuming the hearts of the young, Lord Valiant might not share her practicality.

The girl, this Snow White, plucked up the apples from the floor, her perfect snowy hands placing them back into the bowl. When she set them back on the table, the Queen caught a whiff of her fragrance. She smelled like strawberries and fresh linen.

The Queen looked over, and saw that Lord Valiant had his eyes closed, savoring the flavor of the girl as well.

"That's enough!" she snarled.

Snow White bowed her head, and backed out of the room.

But even after she left, her presence seemed to linger in the air. And neither the Queen nor Lord Valiant could manage to restart the conversation, nor had he any interest in trying.

*　　*　　*

"She saw you?" her mother gasped, sitting up in her bed.

"Please," Snow White begged, "it's nothing to worry about." She tried to push her mother back down by the shoulders, but the woman threw her legs over the side of the bed.

"We must flee." Her eyes darted to her coat hung in the corner, and she made a grasping gesture toward it. "Help me gather our things. We must leave at once."

"Mother!" Snow White said, not moving. "What are you talking about? And flee *where?* We are in the safest place in the world."

Her mother pushed past her, threw on her coat, and started placing items at random into a basket. "Not anymore. The woods. We'll have to face the woods."

"But the dead!" Snow White trembled just thinking of it. "We wouldn't last a day out in the woods with *them.*"

"You don't know the Queen. Why do you think I've kept you hidden? Why do you think you're still alive?" Her mother started to explain further, but at the next word she doubled over with a coughing fit. Snow White stood up and patted her on the back. "No time," her mother choked. "The veil. Put on your veil."

Snow White shook her head. "You are barely fit to walk. This is insanity."

Her mother wiped the back of her hand across her mouth, and then reached up to attach the veil over Snow White's face. "There is a back entrance to the castle. If we hurry, no one will stop us."

There was no arguing with her mother, so Snow White helped her gather the last of their belongings into the basket, took one last look at their cubby-hole of a room, and shut the door behind them. Her veil covered her face, and she still wore the grey gown of the servants.

Even being in the dark hallways of the castle was an adventure to Snow White. For the past few months, ever since the outbreak of the dead, she and her mother had been posing as one person within the castle. In order to keep up the charade, Snow White had been forced into confinement in the little chamber, with no one to talk to, and nothing to do but wait until the plague had exhausted itself.

And now, running like scurrying mice through the twists and turns of the castle, even with the danger, she felt such relief and excitement at the prospect of being free. Even if the woods were dangerous, she would rather run in the open air than hide in the dark.

After a set of twisting stairs, they emerged before a small wooden door. It had been reinforced with a heavy metal beam, and Snow White's mother worked to pull it off.

"Help me," she whispered, and Snow White helped to lift the beam and shove it against the wall. Her mother laced her fingers around the handle—and paused. "Snow White," she said. Her voice was hoarse. "I can only imagine that it has gotten worse on the outside. Whatever happens, you are to keep running. The dead are slow; stay ahead of them, and *do not* let those things bite you."

Snow White nodded. She put her hand over her mother's, and together they pushed open the door.

The light outside was blinding. After months of nothing but candlelight, direct sunlight made them both wince and recoil. Snow White held her hand over her eyes as a shield, and squinted into the distance as her eyes fought to adjust.

This was indeed a back entrance. Snow White and her mother had entered through the front gates, where a long drawbridge guarded massive doors. But here there was nothing but a small clearing on the border of the walls, and then the thick darkness of the woods. The ground sloped down at a precipitous angle, but it looked manageable, at least on the way down.

Snow White unhooked her veil and took in a grateful breath of the fresh air. She turned with a smile to her mother.

Her mother's kind face smiled back from under the hood of her coat as a shadow appeared behind her in the doorway. Snow White opened her mouth to warn her, but it was too late.

The Queen had found them.

She was still in her finery from earlier, and seemed to jangle as she reached for Snow White's mother. Snow White screamed, and lifted a hand to save her, but her mother called out, "Run! Don't let her get you! She'll—"

The Queen raised her other hand, and she was wearing a glove, almost a hunter's glove, with sharp metal talons on each finger. She drew the razors toward Snow White's mother, and again the woman called out to her daughter, "Go! Go now!"

Snow White stumbled backward, and saw a grim-looking bald man step forward from behind the Queen. It was the Royal Physician. Even Snow White had heard of the tortures he inflicted on young women.

"Get her," the Queen ordered, and the man gave a leer as he looked at Snow White.

She turned and ran falling down the side of the clearing toward the trees. She heard her mother let out a scream and wanted to turn back, but the Physician was at her heels, and she didn't dare slow.

It was when she neared the trees that the first of the dead emerged. They shambled out from the darkness like shadows given life. There was a blonde woman in a sky blue dress, the fabric ripped and muddy. Her arm, covered with old bites, reached toward Snow White. The girl backed up, and smacked into another body. It wrapped its arms around Snow White, and she screamed.

It was holding her, and the dead were coming thicker now from the trees. Men and women, some dressed for a party, others for bed, all covered with dirt and dried blood, their eyes hazy, their jaws clacking, as they stumbled forward toward her.

She screamed again, and a voice came gruff in her ear. "Quiet, you fool. You're drawing them nearer." Snow White turned her head to see that it was the Physician that held her. He was struggling to pull her back to the castle.

But if Snow White had to die, she decided it would be better to die here, in the sunlight, than in some dark pit of the castle.

"No!" she cried, and stomped on the Royal Physician's foot. He yelped and loosened his grip. Not missing a beat, Snow White ran toward the trees.

She did not stop running as her mother screamed out in pain.

She did not stop running when her mother's screaming stopped.

*   *   *

The girl was getting away! The Queen was furious. She tried pushing the girl's mother aside, but the woman wouldn't let her pass.

"Don't be a fool," the Queen hissed. "You're no match for me."

She lunged at the mother with her razor talons, and

ripped at her chest, through the fabric and into the skin. The woman shuddered with shock, but kept looking out toward the trees, toward her daughter.

Frustrated, the Queen pointed two fingers, and stabbed the talons into the woman's eyes. She screamed out, but would not let go.

The Queen looked up from the castle doorway as the Royal Physician caught the girl. The dead were emerging from the woods, but the Queen smiled. The girl didn't stand a chance.

"It's all over now," she whispered. "She's mine now."

But then the girl managed to break free and steal away into the woods.

"No!" the Queen cried, and threw down the girl's mother, running after Snow White herself. The woman screamed out like a siren, and the Queen knew that every one of the dead within a mile would be drawn to the castle by the sound.

The Queen was so fixated on the image of Snow White descending into the woods that she didn't notice the Physician until the dead had lifted him up into her path. She stumbled to a stop a few steps in front of him, looking for a way around, but the dead bordered both sides.

They swarmed the Physician. Several had a hold of his limbs, and were pulling at his arms and legs as the Physician's eyes went wide. He screamed a shriek of pure terror, but the creatures kept pulling, until all at once, the Physician snapped apart like a party cracker. His stomach split, his entrails spilling out to the ground, and one of his arms was pulled off entirely.

Somehow, his eyes were still open, although his scream was muted now. He looked up at the Queen, and then down to his stomach as the dead rushed forward to scoop up his insides. They soon blocked the Queen's view of him entirely.

Beyond this pile of the dead were the woods, where Snow White was visible no longer. Instead, even more of the dead were coming. The Queen realized the girl's mother was still screaming, and she turned to see a few of the dead leaning down and nipping at the blinded woman.

The dead blocked the woods. If she waited any longer, they would block the castle. Already some of the dead were looking up from the Physician, their mouths dripping gore, and pushing themselves up toward the Queen.

She took a step backward up the hill. Then she turned, and ran with all her speed toward the open doorway. The dead around the mother reached toward her, brushing against her legs as she hopped by them. She had placed a foot onto the stone of the castle when her dress caught on something from behind, and she nearly fell. She clutched onto the door for balance with her clawed hand, and turned to see a woman in black, her face nearly disintegrated with rot, clawing at the length of her garments, trying to keep hold.

The Queen brought her talons down on the woman's head, piercing through the decayed bone, and collapsing her skull into her brains. She pulled out her talons, coated with filth, and kicked the woman in black away. Then she pulled herself forward through the doorway, and slammed it shut behind her. Hurriedly, she dropped the beam into place just as she heard the dead banging on the door from the outside.

The door held, and she collapsed in front of it, letting out a sigh of relief. She felt her heartbeat thudding in her chest, and her breath wheezing in and out, slowing now. Sweat made her gown sticky and uncomfortable. Without thinking, she scratched an itch on the side of her waist, and gave a yip of pain.

She looked down and realized she was still wearing her talons. A bladed finger had ripped through the fabric and into her skin. She held her hand closer to her face in disbelief.

A drop of her own blood dripped down from the tip of the talon. The rest of the blade was still smeared with the dead woman's gore.

432

She tried to tell herself that it was probably nothing, but already her itch was turning into a burn. She used her other hand to rip the fabric on her side to see the wound—and gasped.

It was a small cut, almost a pen mark, on the side of her white flesh. But underneath the surface of her skin, she could see little black wisps spreading outward, like ink dispersing into a bowl of milk.

*   *   *

Snow White had no idea where she was going. Even before she had been confined to the castle with her mother, she had never spent much time in these woods. There was no path here, and the sun wasn't visible through the trees. But she didn't really care if she was going north, south, east, or west. There was only one direction she cared about: away from the castle.

She ran until her lungs burned and her thighs were on fire. She reached a clearing and stopped in the middle of it, bending over and seizing her chest. The air was chilled but she was sweating terribly. She tore off her cloak and tossed it onto the ground. The fresh air felt wonderful against her skin, and she brushed her hands over her dress and her hair.

She knew she'd have to put the cloak back on in a moment. Her pale yellow dress was too conspicuous in the woods. It had a royal blue corset and poofs at her shoulders, while the arms were bare. Her mother had made it for her. And she wondered if her mother was still alive.

She didn't want to think about it.

She heard a groan in the distance, maybe three hundred yards away, and decided it was time to move on. She pulled back on the grey cloak, held the veil in her hands for a moment, and then threw it on the ground. It was too uncomfortable.

Besides, the Queen had already seen her face. There was no point in hiding it now.

The woods darkened as she made her way deeper and deeper into the trees. She moved like a deer, stopping in her tracks whenever she heard even the faintest hint of a sound, and would either flee or hide until she was confident it was safe to move on. Her shoes dug into her heels, and once when hiding behind a bush, she looked down to see that she had scraped away the skin where her shoes met her feet. She found a leaf and placed it between her heel and the shoe, but it began to sting with every step. Still, she had to keep moving.

The trees seemed to grow more feral the deeper she traveled into the heart of the woods. Instead of shooting straight up to the sky, their trunks bent at odd angles, twisting between each other in strange knots, so that she could no longer pass between the trees, but had to climb over the trunks and duck under branches. She had the feeling that she was entering a space that wasn't meant for the living, a strange new world inhabited only by monsters and witches. She was boiling under her cloak, but she pulled it tighter around her as she emerged onto an incredibly dead section of the woods.

The trees were completely bare, and their branches looked burnt. She could see through to the grey sky, but it gave her no clue to her whereabouts. She stepped over damp rotted leaves, and couldn't hear a sound. Not a bird, none of the dead, barely even her own breathing. All the colors and sounds were muted, as if she were underwater.

Then, in the distance, she saw the dim outline of something square through the trees. She stared at it, waiting for it to move, and then started toward it cautiously when it didn't. As she grew closer, she could make out more of it, until she finally stepped out from the trees in front of it.

It was a horse cart, abandoned on a path.

She almost didn't trust it enough to be real. To come across something man-made this deep in the woods gave her chills. But morbid curiosity forced her to examine it.

Logs of wood were piled in the back. Two of the logs were on the ground. They had been there long enough for plants to have grown and died over them. There were dark stains on the wood paneling of the cart. She knew it was blood.

She forced herself to lift up a log and check in the front of the cart, to see if anything useful might have been left behind. But she didn't find anything.

Snow White left the cart and traveled in the direction it pointed, which—as far as she could tell—was also the direction away from the Queen's castle. She had barely walked ten steps when she heard a sound behind her. She looked back.

Standing in front of the cart were two children, a boy and a girl, holding hands. Their clothes were as colorless as the woods, and their black eyes floated in their grey-skinned faces.

They didn't move at all. Not even to breathe.

Snow White took a step away from them, and turned ahead, making sure the path ahead was clear. She continued on, glancing back over her shoulder as she went around a turn through the woods. But the children hadn't moved. They were still there the last she saw, their empty eyes fixed upon her. Watching.

She quickened her pace to a slow jog. Her heel was bleeding again, but there was nothing she could do about it. She debated leaving the path to hide in the woods, but she knew she could travel faster on the path, and speed was her only defense against the dead.

The sun was setting, and it made the shadows of the woods flatter. The branches and the earth drained of color until everything became a barely indistinguishable grey. It was at this time of twilight when she turned another corner of the path, and came up to a small dwelling standing alone in the woods.

It was nothing but a poorly constructed hut, the roof sagging and the front window dark. She looked around and, not seeing any sign of people, went forward to the window. She used the sleeve of her cloak to wipe away a circle of dust, and stuck her nose against the glass.

Chairs had been overturned. There was a table in the center of the room with bowls covered with cobwebs. An unlit fireplace was in the corner, and against the opposite wall was a small bed, with a loft above it. It was filthy and dark, but to Snow White, it looked wonderful.

She went to the front door—it was wooden with gaps between the boards—and tried the handle. It gave at once, and the door crept ajar with a creak.

"Hello?" Snow White whispered into the crack, feeling like an intruder. She looked back over her shoulder, and she could have sworn she saw something moving from the shadows, something that froze when she turned her head. Without another moment's hesitation, she slipped inside the little hut, and shut the door until it latched. She glanced around for something to secure it with, and found a little hook on a chain. It didn't look secure, but she fastened it nonetheless.

It was almost too dark to see, and it was as cold inside as out, so the first task that Snow White decided upon was to light a fire. She tiptoed over broken bowls and dolls with cracked faces, and came to the fireplace.

It was dusty from disuse, but there was a pile of logs next to it and she threw a few into the fire, working to layer them properly to allow the air to circulate.

There was a bundle of matches spilled on the floor, and she picked them up and put them into the pocket of her cloak. Then she looked around for something that would burn to start the fire. She had to waste a match to help guide her search, and she drew the light over the floor and table, finding nothing. Then she went over to the bed, and found a Bible on the nightstand, next to an overturned candle.

She glanced around again, just to be sure there was nothing else, and then took both the Bible and the candle over to the fire. She lit the candle and flipped through the book, stopping at the first page to read through the family names.

Most of it was in a scroll that she couldn't make out. She followed with her finger down the lines, and came to the latest generation. Judging by the dates, they were just children. Hansel and Gretel.

She shook her head, not wanting to think about what had happened to this family, and flipped through to the end of the book. She had never been very fond of Revelations, and tore out a few pages. She crumpled them up and set them under the logs, and then used the matches to light them.

The heat was almost immediate. The flames licked up the logs and spread across them. Snow White peeled off her cloak and huddled close. The fire lit up her pale skin, and warmed her throbbing fingers. There were scratch marks all over her hands from the woods, and she was just about to bend down to check on her feet when there was a *thunk* on the window.

Snow White spun around and screamed. Pressing their faces against the glass were three creatures of the undead— children. And as soon as they saw her, others began pounding on the front door and groaning wildly. Snow White screamed again. But when one of the dead threw itself against the door, she came to her senses. She jumped up, dragged the table to the doorway, and put it on its side to block the front door.

"Leave me alone!" she screamed, and the children in the window made wheezing noises that Snow White recognized with a chill as attempted giggles. This was a game to them.

She looked at them closer now. One was a little girl in a red hood, her smile coated with blood. Another was a boy with stitches across the middle of his face. And the third was a peasant girl with limp blonde hair, her face dirty with soot.

There was a thump on the roof. Snow White looked up, and heard little feet scurrying. She followed the sound with her eyes and came to the chimney.

The fireplace!

Snow White jumped up and threw more logs into the fire, sending up a wild blaze and heavy smoke into the air.

The footsteps stopped. She turned to the window and could see nothing but darkness outside. Slowly, she got to her feet and crept to the door, listening.

Had she scared them away? Would they leave her alone?

The sun had just gone down, and there was no way she would find anywhere safer to spend the night.

"Please," she begged. "Let this be the end. Let it be okay from here."

But as soon as she said that, the footsteps were back on the roof, and something was being thrown down the chimney.

* * *

By nightfall, the Queen's wound only grew worse. The blood in her veins had darkened, and her eyes were shadowed and red. She slathered on some eye shadow to cover the discoloration, but there was no hiding the exhaustion in her features. The lines on either side of her mouth were especially prominent, but she didn't even think about going to bed for her rest.

She knew sleep wasn't what would restore her. No, the only thing that could help her now was in the chest of that degenerate Snow White. And where was she? The Queen had no idea.

She cancelled dinner with Lord Valiant. Part of her fretted over what he must think of her, barely giving him any attention during their greeting, and then ignoring him the rest of the night. But she would have to remedy that later. For now, she needed to take care of herself.

She took a case of wine from the kitchen, and made her way to her grooming chamber.

Staring at herself in the mirror, and sipping from her bottle of wine, the Queen grew more and more depressed. She couldn't tell anymore what wrinkles were from the illness and which had been there all along. She started applying more creams and powders to her face, layer upon layer, trying to make herself beautiful again.

She finished the first bottle of wine and moved onto the second.

By the third bottle, she had used up the entirety of her concealer, all of her mascara, her lipstick, and even her powder. It had gotten into her hair, making it look grey and brittle.

She set down the powder, and leaned in close to her reflection. Reflexively, she posed with a smile—and it was the saddest thing she had ever seen. She looked hideous, dirty with makeup; and even with it all, her eyes still looked tired, her mouth shriveled and sneering and *old*.

She was so tired of pretending.

She took out her swabs and cloths, and a fresh basin of water, and methodically wiped her face clean. She even pulled back the hood of her cloak, and untied her hair, letting it fall down to her shoulders, dry and limp. There were more white strands now. Worry had aged her overnight.

She looked at her face, plain and aged—her true face—and started to cry.

"Why did she have to run?" she blubbered, watching herself as she cried in the mirror, noting how unattractive the tears made her but forcing herself to stare anyway. "It's all her fault! She did this to me!"

Her shoulders dropped. It was no use. Soon she would be all used up. She should have jumped on the girl the instant she saw her, Lord Valiant be damned, and dug out her heart then.

It wasn't that she really believed that the heart could cure her disease. Nothing could cure the plague, she knew that. But rather, that if she had to die, she didn't want to die ugly.

The idea of being placed into a coffin, shriveled like a raisin, and having everyone look at her and think, "Oh, that's how she must have *really* looked all along"—it scared her more than death itself.

But worse yet was another idea. What if Snow White came back once she was dead?

She pictured Snow White, perfect and young, standing over her coffin. She could hear the whispers of everyone making comparisons between them. And she was jealous of all the attention this girl would receive at her own funeral.

No, the Queen decided. If this was the end, it was going to end *her* way.

She stood up, and wobbled down the hall to a darkened stairway. She dragged herself up the spiral steps, having to pause several times from lightheadedness, and eventually made it to the highest turret of the castle, the lookout tower.

It had long been deserted. Everyone already knew they were surrounded, and there wasn't much point in alerting everyone that there was no change in their situation. The Queen stepped out to the round, open-air tower with triumphant grace.

The cold night air felt pleasant on her hot forehead, and the billows of her black evening robe billowed in the wind. She walked to the edge of the tower and clutched the railing.

Down below, she could see into the castle's courtyard. There was a small garden there, and surrounding it were the halls and quarters of her staff. It was clean and maintained, an oasis of life in the dark forest that surrounded them. Beyond it was the drawbridge, without a single torch lit. She could barely discern it in the blue-grey light of early dawn.

As she was about to lift herself over to jump, she looked down at her hands clutching the stone banister of the tower.

They were shriveled and knobby, like an old hag's hands. And she thought of the corpse she would leave behind in the courtyard. She shook her head. Better to land outside the castle walls.

She turned in the other direction, where the dawn was breaking over the horizon. The great expanse of trees stretched out like a dark ocean in all directions. Snow White could be anywhere.

"It's not fair," she said, looking at the sunrise. Why should Nature be allowed an ageless beauty, but not her? Why should the sky get to be eternally serene, free of any blemish—

Except a little trail of smoke in the far distance, creating a black stain rising from the trees.

Smoke.

The Queen's eyes widened, and her heartbeat accelerated. "Smoke?" she said aloud, and then again, "Smoke!" and laughed to herself.

No one had been alive in those woods for months. The far kingdom was dead; everyone knew that.

There was only one person that could be out there, stupid enough to light a fire that would draw everything for miles around right to her.

The Queen cackled, her face stretched in an exhausted grimace, and she turned to ran back down the stairs.

But how would she get through the woods? The dead were thick. They would try to attack.

Yet Snow White got through. Yet Lord Valiant got through.

"Yes," she muttered to herself, "his carriage." The Lord had arrived in an armored carriage, the way all the nobility traveled nowadays. The dead could not break through. "Yes," the Queen was nodding as she made her way down through the castle.

When she reached the armory inside the front gates, she clapped her hands together to wake up the sleeping guards.

"The carriage!" she shrieked. "Prepare the carriage!"

The men woke up with a start, blanching at her appearance. But they knew better than to question their Queen.

"And bring me some armor!" she cried.

As they worked, her eyes went wide, thinking of herself riding like a knight through the dead woods, following the smoke until she found the girl, the sweet, unsuspecting girl.

She snapped her teeth.

She was more than ready to take a bite.

* * *

Snow White huddled facing the fireplace, ready for the next attack. Her eyes were bleary from exhaustion and tears, her face covered with soot, and her arms aching. Still, she remained vigilant, and didn't lower her guard, not even when the dawn brightened the woods outside to a dull grey.

The cottage was in a sorry state. The furniture was gone. It had been dismantled, and thrown into the fire, piece by piece, in order to keep the flames high. Broken rubbish littered the floor, and there were scorch marks at odd locations on the walls and floor, especially in front of the fire.

There were footsteps on the roof. Snow White threw in a beam—the last of the bedframe—and raised the blanket in front of her, ready for the attack.

Then she heard the screeching up above, and a moment later, a raven's caw echoed out of the fireplace as the poor creature smashed into the logs of the fire. Its black wings fluttered, and then it launched itself at Snow White, confused and panicked. She threw down the blanket, but she was too slow, and the bird—now a flaming fireball—flew past her and slammed into the wall by the window. It fell to the floor, and she hopped on it with the blanket, smothering the flames.

"I'm sorry," she whispered to its body twitching under

the fabric. It was still fighting her, but at least the flames were out.

It wasn't dead. Some of the other animals the children had thrown down had died almost instantly. But this poor creature was in pain, and there was no way Snow White could help it now. She gritted her teeth, gathered up the ends of the blanket, and slammed the bird inside to the ground. Then, before it could regain consciousness, she ran it over to the fire, and turned away as it burned on the pile of blackened bones.

The children giggled overhead, and Snow White didn't know how much more she could take of this. The worst part was that she was getting hungry, and that this time, the smell of roasting flesh didn't disgust her as much.

At noon, the sun broke through the clouds for a moment, and by the time it was gone, the last of the fire had died out.

Snow White watched the last wisps of smoke twirl up, and then fear filled her at once. She had hoped to be rescued by now. By whom, she didn't know, but it couldn't end like this. Not for her.

She turned and looked back at the cottage. Her eyes darted up to the small loft above the bed. The ladder was hammered into the wall. She had already tried to dislodge it for firewood earlier in the night. She might feel a little safer in the loft, but once the children got in, they could climb up and get her. Could they climb? Maybe they wouldn't be able to follow?

Then she heard footsteps on the roof, and felt incredibly stupid for forgetting that they could climb, probably better than she could. She was just tired. And even the bad ideas were better than no ideas.

Maybe if she ran out the front door?

No, there were the children out front, waiting for her. She couldn't be sure how many of them there were, but she was definitely outnumbered. And now she had nothing to defend herself with, except a smoky blanket.

She heard their wild groans from the roof, and the ones at the window began banging against the glass.

"Leave me alone!" Snow White cried, putting her hands to her face and dropping to her knees. "Please, I didn't know this was your house. I would have never come in here if I had known. I just—" she was openly bawling now, "I just want to go home. I want—I want my mother."

The banging stopped.

It took Snow White a moment to raise her face. She looked toward the window, and saw the children drawing away. On the roof, their footsteps scurried off and down the sides of the walls. No one was pounding on the door.

Snow White sniffled, and wiped the tears from her eyes.

She was so exhausted, she wasn't sure what had happened. Did they finally listen to her? Was that all it would have taken? To ask?

She climbed shakily to her feet, and sniffled again, edging closer to the window.

Outside, in front of the house, the children had formed a line. They were turned away from her, looking out toward the path.

They were facing a hunched old woman with long grey hair and a black cloak.

They were facing the Queen.

*   *   *

The little brats had formed a line of defense against her. The Queen smiled. As if that would do them any good.

The smoke that had been her beacon through the woods had fizzled out to a thin white line from the chimney. For a moment she worried that the children had killed the girl. But then there was movement from inside the window, and the

Queen knew that Snow White was still alive. That her heart was still beating.

She stepped away from the armored carriage, keeping her hands inside the pockets of her cloak, one hand holding a short dagger, and the other inside the taloned glove.

She counted seven children in all, an odd mix of boys and girls. Their leader seemed to be a boy standing in the middle of the group, slightly ahead of the others. He wore a green outfit that looked as if it were made out of nothing but dead leaves and filth. She met his eye and addressed him alone.

"I'm only going to ask once," she said calmly. "Move aside."

He snarled at the Queen.

She kept her face blank. "Fine."

Then, before the children could do anything, she walked the five steps across the path to the boy in green, took out the dagger from her pocket, and stabbed him in the head. He fell to the ground with his skull split down the middle, and she pulled the dagger out as he fell.

The other dead children were so shocked that their response lagged even for the dead. Only one girl with pigtails, wearing a child's nightgown that she had long since outgrown, bent down to the fallen boy, taking him in her hands.

The Queen turned to the rest.

"I'm not playing games here," she snarled. "Get out of my way!"

To prove her point, she lunged at the boy nearest her, one that must have been injured in life, as his face and limbs were covered with stitches. She clutched his arm, digging in with her talons, and the boy's mouth opened letting out a foul gasp.

"I'll kill every last one of you if I have to," she said, and raised the dagger.

The boy tugged as she dug into his arm, and then there

was a rip, and the Queen fell back slightly. She looked up to see the boy running away, his arm still twitching in her hand.

The rest fled. Even the girl in pigtails left, dragging the boy in green toward the trees, unable to let him go.

When they had all gone, the Queen turned to the little cottage. She took in a deep breath, and knocked on the door.

After a moment, a shy and feminine voice called through, "Are they gone?"

"Yes, my dearie, I've saved you," said the Queen, trying to hide her excitement. "Now come out, and let's go back to the castle together."

The door didn't open.

"What's the matter, dear? Don't you trust me?"

Silence.

"If I didn't care for you, *why* would I risk my life to come here? Did I not chase your tormentors away? Did I not bring an armored carriage to escort you back?"

Snow White came to the window. There were bars across the rippled glass. The Queen thought that if she had to break them, and tear them off one by one, it might eat up too much time. It might be too late.

The girl looked out. Her face was as perfect as in the Queen's memory. A poor night's sleep had given her slight shadows under her eyes, but on her face, they only added to her charm. She looked like an angel after a storm.

She looked out, and then past the Queen. "Where's my mother?"

The Queen smiled. "Back at the castle, of course. She is not well. I would not let her endanger herself."

"She said you were going to kill me."

The Queen cackled. "Me? No, never. She had a fever, my dear. She was delusional." The Queen twisted her face in an exaggerated display of grief. "She may not have long left. And she's waiting for you, asking why you aren't at her bedside. Don't you want to see her before it's too late?"

Was this too much? Would the girl believe it? The Queen kept talking, trying to use up any opportunity for the girl to think, to rationalize.

"Quickly!" she shouted, looking back to the woods. "I think I hear more of them coming!"

"Oh!" Snow White yelped, and left the window. There was a heavy sliding sound from behind the door, and then the metal tinkling of a chain. The door opened inward, and the weakened Snow White stood in the doorway, the soft white light of the day illuminating her pale complexion. The Queen's shadow was at her feet, and it rose up, swallowing her stomach and chest, as the Queen took a step closer.

Snow White looked up into her eyes. "Your Majesty," she gasped, "you don't look well."

"Not to worry," the Queen said merrily. "I know just the thing that will cheer me up."

And she lunged her taloned hand into Snow White's chest.

The girl gave a scream but was too overcome to do more than take a half-step backward. The Queen held her in place with her left arm, placing a solid hand on the girl's back, and shoved the fingers of her right hand in deeper. Never breaking eye contact with the girl, she pushed her fingers through her ribs, and twisted them around the girl's beating heart. The Queen paused for a moment, breathing heavily and luxuriating in the fact that she was touching the very life of the girl. Snow White's eyes fluttered.

"Stay with me, girlie," the Queen said. "This is the best part."

She removed her left hand from the girl's back and placed it on her stomach, pushing the girl backward while keeping a grip on her heart with the other hand. There was a wet snapping sound, and then Snow White fell to the ground. Her arms spread out on the floor, and her eyes stared up at the roof, unmoving.

In the Queen's hand, the bloody heart gave one final beat. The blood splurted out over the Queen's pointed talons, and started to dribble down onto the floor.

"No!" the Queen cried, "we mustn't waste a drop!"

And she leaned her head sideways and began licking the hot blood from her talons, getting it on her wrinkled lips and chin. She didn't bother to wipe it off. There was no time. She hobbled back to the carriage and found a metal box she had brought with her. She placed the heart inside and shut the lid, and then went back to the cottage, licking her palms.

She took Snow White by the ankles, and dragged her through the dirt to the carriage.

The heart was the important organ, the Queen knew that. But the Royal Physician had said she was to eat the liver as well, and possibly the lungs. Nothing must go to waste.

The Queen shoved the girl's corpse in the carriage, shut the door, and then climbed onto driver's seat. She took the horse's reins and gave them a healthy smack, and then they were on their way back to the castle.

* * *

Young Philip watched from behind a statue as the Evil Queen—as he had come to think of her—rolled back into the castle in his father's carriage. He knew for a fact that she had not asked to use it, and what if she had gotten attacked? Or it had been damaged? Then they would have no way to get around the monsters.

She clanked as she climbed down, and he realized from the bulkiness that she wore armor underneath her cloak. He thought that strange, not that she was wearing armor—it would be reckless not to wear armor outside—but why would she try to hide it?

She looked very different than the last time he saw her

the day before. Her face was paler, and her hair was down. It was grey, too, and scraggly like an old man's beard. She had a hunch to her walk, and seemed to struggle as she pried open the door to the carriage.

Out fell a young woman, her chest bloody and arms limp. She was dead, and the Queen was dragging her out onto the ground like a sack of potatoes. Philip had to put his hand over his mouth to keep from making noise. She pulled the woman to a cage along the far wall. Cages like these had become common at the entrances to buildings or towns. They were used to quarantine suspicious newcomers until everyone could be sure it was safe to let them in. This cage was square and tall, like a standing coffin, and the Queen slammed the door shut and turned a lock.

She's a murderer, Philip realized. Otherwise there wouldn't be so much blood.

The Queen rummaged in the back of the carriage until she found a small metal box. She left the entry chamber then, clutching the box to her chest, and went up a flight of steps. Once he was sure she was gone, Philip emerged from his hiding place, and tiptoed over to the girl.

He looked through the bars, and saw the young body slumped down, with a pale arm hanging over the head. The legs were twisted together, and the fingers stiff. Philip bent down to look at her face, and saw that it was the servant girl from the day before.

He remembered the Queen's rage. Had she killed the girl just because she dropped the apples?

Philip jumped up. He had to warn his father. He ran out of the chamber, through the dark hallways and up the stairs, until he came to the guest quarters. He pushed open the heavy door, and whispered, "Father? Father, are you awake?"

A groan came from the bed, and his father sat up and stretched his arms. "What is it, Philip?"

"The Queen murdered a girl," Philip said at once, running to the side of the bed. "She trapped her in a cage downstairs."

"She what?" His father gave a deep yawn. "It was probably just a bad dream."

"No!" Philip insisted, and tugged on his father's hand. "She stole our carriage to do it. I can show you."

His father's face grew serious. "Philip. Are you sure you know what you're saying?"

"Come *on*," he cried. "Downstairs!"

Philip waited, tapping his foot and pacing as his father laboriously dressed himself and straightened his hair in the mirror. When he was done, he walked slowly down the hallways, and refused to act like he was in a hurry. "If something *is* wrong," he said, "we'd be fools to act as if we knew we were in danger."

Finally, they made their way to the front chamber of the castle, by the drawbridge where the carriages and armor were kept.

"See!" whispered Philip, pointing to the cage.

His father stopped mid-step. His eyes narrowed. "Get in the carriage, Philip."

"But—"

"Go!"

Philip ran to their carriage. The horses were still in their harnesses, their faces and bodies covered with thick armor of their own. He opened the door to the carriage, and found the inside coated with blood. He looked back out at his father, and saw him staring at the girl inside the cage. Then his father's hand went to the lock of the cage, and opened the door. The girl's body spilled out.

"No!" Philip shouted, but his father ignored him. He leaned down and examined the body, and then touched its face with his hands. Philip couldn't watch. He covered his eyes with his hands and shrank back around the corner of the carriage door. He was trembling, and nearly crying when his father picked up the girl, and brought her back to the carriage in his arms.

"What are you *doing?*" Philip asked, backing away from the dead woman.

"Look at her," his father said. "Look at her face. There's no sign of infection."

"But she's dead!"

His father shook his head. "Her fingers are twitching. And when I went over, I saw her eyes move toward me. We can't leave her here."

Philip stared at the bloody cavity in her chest. "She's one of them."

"Nonsense. She's too beautiful to be one of them."

Philip retreated against the wall of the carriage. "She's one of *them*," he repeated. He couldn't help it; he started to cry. "She'll hurt us."

"Fine," his father said. "I'll put her up front." He carried the woman up to the driver's seat. Then he came back around, wiping the blood on the sides of his pants. "Now you stay inside while I open the drawbridge."

"We can leave?" Philip asked. He hadn't expected it to be this easy. "What about saying goodbye?"

"I'd rather get out of here," he said, looking off toward the castle. "This place doesn't feel right. And besides, the Queen isn't really my type." He sneered. "Too *old*. You need a younger mother."

Philip nodded, even though he didn't agree. He didn't want a new mother. But he did want to get out of there as soon as possible.

He watched from inside the carriage as his father heaved on the great crank that lowered the drawbridge. As the light from outside came in, brightening the dark chamber, Philip let out a breath of relief.

They were going. They were going away from the Queen. Once the drawbridge was down, his father came back, dusting his hands. "We'll have to hurry before the dead notice—" He stopped, blinking. He was looking at the driver's seat of the carriage, beyond Philip's view.

"What is it, Father?" he asked, his panic returning.

"The girl," he said. "She's… gone."

Philip stared at his father, framed in the doorway of the carriage. His father's gaze shifted back to Philip, and he smiled at the boy, and gave a weak shrug.

"I guess she—"

Then there was a blur of movement from the right that knocked his father down. It was the woman. She was alive. She was biting him. She was biting his father.

A torrent of blood sprayed against the side of the carriage, and young Philip backed farther inside, his eyes wide, and started to scream.

*   *   *

She had already put the pot on the boil and added the salt when her work was interrupted by a scream.

The Queen looked up. She was in her beauty chamber, and her head burned with a terrible fever. The heart lay on a side table, resting on a white platter, and the edges of the room were lined with black candles. The mirror was on the far wall.

She looked back at the pot, considering going on, but then there was that scream again, and she knew she had to see what it was. She was glad she hadn't yet bothered to remove the armor under her cloak.

A minute later she was in the front chamber. She took in the scene with calm eyes. The drawbridge was down. There was a bloody husk of a man on the ground outside the carriage. And—of most importance to the Queen—the cage was empty.

"Fools!" the Queen shrieked, running forward. "Imbeciles! Who would let her out?"

Along the front wall were lines of weapons. She pulled down a heavy axe, and held it in front of her chest. Then, with her lip curled in a snarl, she stomped over to the carriage.

She pulled at the door, but it was locked. There was another scream from inside. A child.

"Open the door!" she bellowed. "Open the door, or I'll chop you to bits!"

She jiggled the handle again, her fingers slipping on the blood, and then gave up. The girl wasn't inside—she would have eaten the boy—but the Queen was so furious she couldn't contain herself. She kicked the side of the carriage in her rage, thwacking at it with her axe. "You think you can hide from me?" She chopped at the corner, and the axe made a small cut. She put her eye to the fresh opening, and saw the little boy hiding in the dark. "I'm going to eat your heart, you little brat," she screamed into the carriage. "That will teach you!" She lifted the axe, and slammed it down again.

Then she heard the groans. She turned to the drawbridge, and saw the outlines of the dead against the sky. They had heard the screaming too.

She ran over to the drawbridge controls, but they were too heavy for her to lift. Frustrated, she ran back to the carriage, hoping to send it out to distract the dead. She slammed the back end of one of the horses with the side of the axe blade. It reared up and shunted forward, circling wildly in the small chamber and setting its eyes on the exit. The Queen was right behind, smacking on the carriage to scare it, and sent them out through the gate and over the drawbridge. The dead jumped onto the side, and the horses pulled them and the carriage into the darkness of the woods.

When she turned around, Snow White was in the chamber. She had been lurking on the other side of the carriage, biding her time. Her corset and dress had been smeared with blood, but her face was clean. The Queen looked at her, and felt a moment of awe. She was beautiful even in death.

"How did you come back?" she whispered. "You weren't bitten."

And then the Queen looked down at her hand, at the taloned glove that had ripped out Snow White's heart. Whatever had been on the blades had infected both of them. The girl was one of the dead now, although since the sickness had had so little time to ravage her looks, she was still as beautiful as when she died.

"It's not fair!" the Queen shouted. "Even in death you are beautiful!"

There was only one way to solve this. She would have to chop the girl up and put her in a stew.

She raised the axe. "Come here. I need to eat you while you're fresh."

She took a step toward the girl, and Snow White took a step back to the wall.

"Now, now," the Queen clucked. "Even your mother put up more of a fight than that, before I plucked out her eyes and threw her to the dead!"

Snow White snarled, and launched herself at the Queen, knocking them both to the ground.

"That's it! Fight!" the Queen shouted, and started to cackle. "Fight so you can lose!" She and Snow White rolled on the ground, struggling with each other. The axe fell to the ground, and they rolled away from it.

The dead were starting to come into the castle again. Their groans filled the air, and they shuffled past the Queen and Snow White to feast on Lord Valiant's remains.

The children from the cottage scurried inside, edging along the sides of the walls, keeping their distance from the Queen. They looked at her with cold, dead eyes, and then disappeared down the dark hallways.

The Queen threw off Snow White, and scooted away on the floor, backing up to the axe. She drew her face into a pitiful expression. "See what you've done? The castle is lost now. It's all lost." She held out her arm. "You might as well finish me off, I've got nothing left to live for."

Snow White's mouth twisted up, and she dragged her feet forward, her fingers pinching the air. She reached out and clutched the Queen's arm, and then sunk her teeth into it.

She bit down against metal under the cloak.

"You always were too trusting," the Queen said, and then raised the axe and hacked through Snow White's neck with one clean chop.

The body fell limp, but the head kept biting. It held onto the Queen's arm even as she dragged the girl's headless body back to the cage and slammed the door. Then the Queen twisted her fingers into Snow White's hair, and ripped the girl from her arm.

She turned the head to the body in the cage. "That's so I can save the rest of you for later, without worrying about these others getting to it first."

Then she walked across the chamber to the stairwell, not breaking her eye contact with the stairs even as she hacked the skulls of the few dead that dared block her path.

She went back to her beauty chamber and slammed the door, throwing down the bolt. Then she set Snow White's head down on a side table, facing out to the room. The pot was boiling now, and the Queen went over to stir it.

"Just right!" she cried, and turned back to Snow White's head. The girl was quite conscious, and followed her with her eyes, and even snarled a little when she drew nearer.

"And here," said the Queen, "is something you might recognize." She picked up the heart with her hands and held it before Snow White. Bubbles of rage foamed out of the girl's mouth, and the Queen held up a finger. "Sorry, my dear, but there isn't enough to share."

The Queen dropped the heart into the pot, stirred the mixture for thirty seconds, and then took the heart out and plopped it back onto the plate. Then she pulled up a chair directly before Snow White, and used a knife and fork to slice up the heart.

"It's very chewy," she said, talking through her first bite. "But rare! I like it rare!" And she laughed.

She ate the entire heart as Snow White watched, unable to do a thing. Then she placed the silverware down on the plate with a clatter, and tapped her lips with a napkin. A small burp escaped her lips, and she smiled. "Excuse me."

Then she let out a loud sigh, and got up to stand in front of the mirror, looking at herself.

"Hmm," she muttered, pulling at the limp skin around her eyes. "I do have a little more color, but I can't see any difference otherwise." She shook her head. "Maybe I'm not used to looking at myself without makeup?"

Then, whistling as she worked, she used what remained of her beauty products to even out her complexion, cover the wrinkles, and smooth out her hair. The entire time she could hear the screams of the castle residents as the dead made their way inside. There was banging on her door. She didn't get up, pursing her lips as she applied lipstick. She was occupied, and they'd have to take care of themselves.

She looked better at the end, but she was completely exhausted. The fight had taken all her energy, and the promise of youth was all that had kept her going. She sat, staring at the mirror, struggling to breathe. Her hands were shaking, and her vision was blurring. She turned to Snow White, intending to prod the head for information, but the movement threw her off balance, and she fell to the floor.

Crumpled, feeling her heartbeat slow in her chest, she knew she was dying. She used the last effort of her life to turn her face toward the mirror.

She died staring at herself, a triumphant grin on her face.

* * *

The next morning she woke again. The dizziness was gone, replaced by an overwhelming hunger. It was harder to move, her limbs unresponsive and unfeeling, as if her entire body were numb.

The fire had gone out, but she could still see well enough to find the matches, and lit a candle. Its flame lit up the room like the sun.

She turned to the mirror instinctively, and went close to look at herself, touching her face in disbelief.

She looked good. Maybe not perfect, maybe not alive, but the makeup was still in place. She looked better than any of the other dead. And she had only eaten the heart, she remembered. There was still an entire body left to revive her.

These encouraging thoughts were running through her mind when she saw the head behind her in the mirror. It was staring at her from the side table, with Snow White's eternally youthful skin and flawless features exactly as before. Mocking her. Making her look old in comparison.

Snow White was still more beautiful.

No, the Queen thought, hobbling forward. We'll just have to change that.

She lifted the head off the shelf, and dragged the chair before the mirror, sitting down with Snow White's head in her lap.

She set the candle down next to her, and began to stroke the girl's hair. She opened her mouth to speak, but found her tongue unresponsive.

The girl would have to watch and catch on.

The Queen still wore her talons. She flicked them in front of Snow White's face, making sure the girl noticed them. Then she pointed the head toward the mirror, making sure Snow White had a good look at herself before she jabbed one of the talons into the girl's forehead.

She spun the head around, dragging her talon and peeling off Snow White's face in one long ribbon, as if peeling the skin of an apple. She held the end of it over the flame of the candle, and waited until the fire had shriveled it up to nothing. Then she stood up, and dunked the head into the pot of water that she had used to cook the heart.

Once it was clean, she sat down before the mirror again. The living skull in her lap still had eyes, and it stared at itself, unable to talk, unable to fight. The Queen gave a husky laugh, more of a wheeze than a cackle, and patted the bare white skull with her fingertips.

That's right, she thought. Take a good look at yourself, because now there is no question. There is no changing it.

The Queen smiled.

Now *she* was the fairest in the land.

SLEEPING BEAUTY WAKES IN HELL

Philip eavesdropped from behind the wall of servants. He was a small boy, twelve years old and wiry. In the past week, his entire world had been destroyed, and it was all because of *them*.

Them. The monsters. The dead.

It was them the King was discussing. His staff had brought everything to him in his bed, because he was too weak to walk.

The King was an old man before the plague had begun, his life spent. Now his legacy had been destroyed as well.

"That's no good," he said, slamming his hand down on the charts. "They've already invaded farther than that." He pointed at something. "They're past those woods. They've been in Sleepy Hollow. They've been to my sister's castle. You'll have to expand the circle wider."

"But, Your Majesty," said an advisor, "that will demolish what's left of the kingdom entirely."

The King sat up, an expression of rage on his gnarled face. He grabbed the advisor by the collar and screamed, "Don't you understand? The Kingdom is *already* lost! What we're fighting for now is our lives. Our *children's* lives." He let go, and fell back to the bed breathing heavily. "Yes," he wheezed.

"I decree it. The entire kingdom. Surround the entire king-dom in a ring of fire, and work your way in. Wipe out everything, everything that moves." His voice lowered, and became bitter and hoarse. "It's time to end this madness."

Philip edged away from the room, his head whirling.

Attack the dead? Was it possible? But if the King had decreed it, it must be so. He had to find Aurora and discuss this with her.

They lived in a crumbling stone fortress at the border of the kingdom. The King had been moved here after his own palace had been abandoned. Philip had arrived a week ago, after his carriage had been found by a soldier.

His father was dead, killed by the creatures, and Philip had barely escaped himself, fleeing in the armored carriage into the woods. After countless hours of outrunning the dead, the horses were dying from exhaustion. One of the king's soldiers found the carriage, pulled Philip out of it, and rode the boy to safety.

He was an orphan, but nobody seemed to notice. Every-one here had lost somebody. He was also one of the only children at the fortress, so it didn't take long for him and Aurora to find each other.

She was his age, with blonde hair and a gentle disposition. She had said her parents were dead, but that they turned out not to be her real parents after all. Her real father was the King, but he had kept it secret from everyone until now be-cause her mother wasn't his wife. But now he was so desperate for a child, he didn't care if she was a bastard or not.

That was the word she used. Philip would never say that about her.

He ran through the fortress, his shoes sinking into the muddy floor. There were torches lit on the moss-covered stones, but the entire place still seemed full of dancing shadows. He passed bare rooms with men and women huddled together on straw like animals, their stink worse than any barn. He turned a corner, and stomped up a set of broken stairs. He met a wooden door and pushed it open without knocking.

"They're building a wall," he sputtered before freezing with his eyes wide.

Aurora's bare back faced him, her thin shoulders being slipped into the sleeves of a simple dress. She held her long curls up in her hands, and turned her head to look at him, a coy smile on her lips. On her right shoulder was a birthmark in the shape of a rose. "Just a moment," she said in her singsong voice. "I've just had a bath."

He looked at a tub of stale water in the corner of the room. A wet rag hung over the side.

A servant woman laced up the back of the dress, and Aurora let go of her hair. She thanked the servant, and then jumped down from her stool and met Philip at the door.

In the fortress that smelled of damp mud and snot, Aurora smelled like fresh roses. Nothing seemed to touch her here. Philip breathed in her scent, and then looked over his shoulder at the servant distrustfully.

He whispered, "They're building a wall made of fire. That's how they're stopping the dead."

She took his hand, and then looked back at the servant herself. The old woman nodded, and Aurora took Philip out into the hallway.

"A wall of fire? But how will that stop them? I thought they didn't feel pain?"

"They can still burn," Philip said. "I've seen them set on fire. Their brains melt out their nose."

Aurora nodded. Neither child recognized the image as gruesome. It was a way of life to them.

"But how long can they keep it burning?" she asked.

"I think they're going to build a real wall, too."

"It would have to be a million feet high. And deep, or they might dig under."

"Can they dig?" Philip asked.

Neither knew the answer.

"I want to see it," Aurora said suddenly.

"Them digging?"

"The wall of fire." She took his hand, and looked right into his eyes. She had bright blue eyes, round and wide. "Will you take me? We'd have to sneak out."

Philip stepped back. "I don't know. That's kind of dangerous."

She rolled her eyes. "There will be guards. And we won't go near the dead. I just want to *see* it."

Philip didn't want to see the dead ever again. He had seen his father ripped apart by one of them. He still had nightmares about it.

"*Please*," Aurora begged. "Won't you be my prince, Philip?"

His heart fluttered. She was technically a princess, no matter how illegitimate. And to be *hers*...

Before he could decide, she leaned over and kissed him on the lips.

This was Philip's first kiss, and certainly his first kiss with Aurora, but there was something oddly familiar about it, as if he had dreamed this kiss many times before.

Aurora stepped back, giggling at his flustered expression. "You'll do it?" she asked, and he gave a weak nod. She laughed and took his hand. As they continued through the mud of the fortress, he kept sneaking glances at her carefree face.

She seemed so confident, so resolute. Maybe he shouldn't be worried at all.

But every time he tried to relax, an image flashed in his mind of his father, the look of surprise on his face as the dead woman eagerly disemboweled him. That moment had seemed stuck in time as well. Even now Philip could see the awful way his father looked when he died: so lost, so removed from the world, as if he were drowning beneath a surface of ice.

Philip looked back at Aurora. He held her hand tighter, and forced himself to smile back at her as she skipped along next to him.

But something still felt wrong.

It felt as if they were sliding into a nightmare.

*   *   *

The next day, when the army filed out of the fortress, Aurora and Philip hid in a trunk together in the back of the King's procession. The road bumped underneath them, and even in the darkness Philip could feel Aurora smiling with excitement. Anticipation seemed to radiate out of her like the sun, and it made Philip feel edgy and uncomfortable.

They didn't have a plan, other than to sneak out and see what they could see. If they kept their distance, Philip told himself, they would be safe.

When the procession stopped, they remained perfectly still as heavy footsteps and gruff voices came from outside the trunk. Then, much to their surprise and alarm, they felt the trunk shifting, and heard a groan as two men were lifting them into the air. Neither Philip nor Aurora dared to make a sound, even as they were tossed from side to side as the trunk was being carried.

The longer they were being transported in this manner, the more frightened Philip became. What did these men think was in the trunk? Did they know there were children in it all along? He searched his memory, but couldn't remember the odds and ends that he and Aurora had shoved out before climbing inside.

The trunk dropped out from under them suddenly, and then crashed into Philip's knees as it crashed against the dirt. The gruff voices bellowed, and then grew quieter as they walked away. A moment later, Aurora whispered to him.

"Do you think it's safe to go out?"

"I don't know," Philip answered. Part of him wanted to just stay in the trunk until it was time to go home.

"I'm going to look."

"Aurora, wait!"

But before he could stop her, the girl was pushing up the lid of the trunk and peeking out.

The day, which had turned to evening, seemed bright after the darkness of the trunk. Philip sat up and peered out of the crack under the lid.

The first thing he saw was the King's army in the distance. The procession of chariots and carriages were huddled together like sleeping cattle, and surrounded by milling soldiers. Small tents had been erected, and campfires had been lit.

The trunk itself had been heaved onto the top of a great pile of rubbish: broken chairs, suitcases and shoes, tree limbs and dead leaves. The pile extended into the distance and curved to the left like a wall.

Then suddenly everything started to become brighter, just as the sun had dipped below the tree line. A glow formed over the ground and the distant camp, and the soldiers turned to face the pile of rubbish.

"They've seen us!" Aurora gasped, and she ducked back down.

But Philip didn't think so.

"Why's it getting so bright?" he muttered. There was a sound too, like waves crashing against a shore. Were they by the ocean? But that was impossible. They hadn't been traveling that long.

And then Philip smelled it.

Smoke.

"Aurora!" he shouted, throwing open the lid of the trunk. He turned, and behind them rose a great curtain of fire, drawing closer as if pulled along the hill of rubbish. Aurora shrieked, and they tumbled forward out of the trunk.

"The wall of fire," Philip said, taking her hand and running forward on the top of the pile. "We're on the wall of fire!"

"We'll have to jump," Aurora said, and Philip nodded. But when they looked down, on both sides of them were legions of the dead, moaning and extending their arms up to them. To make matters worse, many of these creatures were on fire themselves, like flaming candles.

"Oh!" cried Philip. He looked ahead to the soldiers, where there was a clear area of the wall. "Come on," he said, and took Aurora by the hand. Together, stumbling over the crumbling wall, they scurried along, waving their hands and shouting.

Finally, one of the soldiers spotted them, and alerted the rest.

The soldiers fought against the burning dead, stabbing them and hacking at their skulls, working through the horde. The two children stood huddled together on the edge of the wall as the fire grew closer and closer.

The dead were ahead of them, trying to climb over the wall to freedom before the fire spread. And the dead behind them were trying to clutch at their feet, as flames boiled the tongues in their gaping mouths.

"Hurry!" shouted Philip as the flames grew hotter. He could feel the heat on his skin, like standing too close to an oven. Aurora was in tears, holding onto Philip as if he could fly them to safety. The flames were closing in from the other direction now too, eager to join in the middle where they stood.

The soldiers hacked away at the dead, and were just clearing a path as the flames came within ten feet on either side. The hair on Philip's arm sizzled and burned, and he knew they didn't have a choice.

"We'll have to jump," Philip said. Aurora nodded, and they bent forward toward the soldiers just as they had reached the wall themselves. A broad-faced man in black armor reached up and took Philip under the arms. He set him on the ground as his companions hacked at the dead around them. Then the soldier turned back to Aurora, and had just placed his hands under her arms when she let out a scream.

There was a hand reaching over from the other side of the wall, clutching at her ankle.

Aurora screamed hysterically, kicking at her foot, and the soldier tugged on her arms to pull her to safety. Philip grabbed him around the waist to help.

They pulled Aurora forward, but in the process, lifted up one of the dead to stand on the wall.

It was the Evil Queen, the dead queen whose actions had led to the death of Philip's father. Her face startled Philip so much that he let go of the soldier, and the soldier lost his grip on Aurora. In a flash, the Queen scooped up Aurora, and held the struggling girl to her chest.

"No!" Philip screamed. It was all happening again. The Queen, who wore a tattered black robe and what looked to be armor underneath, locked eyes with him. Then she took a step back, with the girl in her arms, just as the flames closed in on either side of her. As they sealed the gap, the Evil Queen fell back to the other side of the wall, and Philip lunged forward, his hands extended toward the flames.

But the soldier held him back.

"Let me go!" he shouted, tears running down his cheeks. The soldier threw Philip over his back, and ran with him back to the camp. The fierce battle with the dead flashed by upside-down on either side of Philip as they ran, and he beat his fists against the soldier, saying, "Go back, go back," through his sobs.

When they were among the others, the soldier set Philip onto the back of a carriage, standing guard to make sure he didn't jump off and run back into the fire.

"What were you doing here?" the soldier asked, but Philip couldn't concentrate enough to answer his question.

"You have to save her!" he sobbed. A group of soldiers had gathered around them now. "She's on the other side, the Queen's got her!"

The soldier gave him a pitying look. "I'm sorry," he said. "She's gone."

"No!" Philip shouted. "She wasn't bitten! She's—the Queen has Aurora!"

At the name, the soldiers perked up. "Aurora?" asked one of the soldiers. "The King's daughter?"

"Yes," Philip said in exasperation. "The princess! She's on the other side of the wall!"

At this, several of the group ran off at once. A messenger was sent to the King, and as Philip sat, huddled on the side of a dark carriage, word spread throughout the troops that the princess had been captured.

It wasn't until hours later, after the fires had been burning long into the night, that anyone thought to bring Philip to the King.

"His Majesty requests your presence," a servant informed him. Then Philip was escorted by a guard to a gilded carriage at the head of the procession. The rear door opened, and a waft of moist and sour air emerged. The King looked up from his small bed, crimson blankets pulled up over his stomach, and started coughing at once. A soldier pushed Philip inside.

He related to the King how he and Aurora were friends, and how they came to be on the wall as it was set ablaze. When he got to the part about the Queen, the King stopped him.

"My sister? Are you sure?"

"Yes," Philip said quietly. "My father and I were staying at her castle when it fell. I was the only one to make it out alive."

"And she was one of the dead?"

Philip nodded. The King was silent, and the boy looked

at the old man. He was nothing like his sister, or anything like the other royal family, from what Philip had heard of them. And he wondered how such a disparate group of people could be expected to rule a kingdom together. If their family had been happier, would the dead have been able to overthrow them so easily?

Their silence was interrupted by a troop of men, rushing up to the King. One among them was carried on the arms of his friends, his skin pale but dirty with soot, and his neck splattered with blood. His fellow soldiers explained that he had made it over the wall, through the flames and into enemy territory. He had seen the girl.

"She's alive," he gasped. "The Queen had her, but wouldn't let the other dead touch her. The Queen—she kept the girl alive."

The King sat up, his eyes wide. "Aurora is safe? Where is she?"

"I couldn't reach her, Your Majesty," the soldier said, his eyes lowering to the floor. "The Queen wouldn't let the dead touch the girl, but she didn't stop them from attacking me." He coughed, blood spilling over his chin. "I've been bitten," he gurgled. "I've been bitten, Your Majesty."

The King ignored him, locking eyes with another soldier, their leader. "Send another troop over the wall at once. I want my daughter brought back alive."

"Yes, Your Majesty."

Then the King looked back at the infected soldier. "And as for him," he said softly, "make sure he doesn't come back as one of them." The other soldiers nodded, and carried the infected man away.

Philip was taken to an empty carriage, one meant for livestock, and locked inside so that he wouldn't try to cause more trouble. He huddled in the hay, unable to sleep, and when the morning came, he was among the first group brought back to the fortress.

They had been successful in their mission to place a barricade against the dead, but failed in their attempt to save the kingdom.

* * *

The King spent the remaining months of his life assembling one campaign after another in the unsuccessful effort to rescue his daughter. He was convinced she was still alive, beyond the borders of the wall, and would not be deterred from his belief, offering huge sums of gold and land to anyone that might bring her back—or prove that she was dead, once and for all.

But he died without finding her, and the kingdom was left without an heir.

His last royal decree before closing his eyes upon the world was this:

Whoever found the girl would win not only her hand in marriage, but the rights to the entire kingdom as well. Until Aurora could be brought back from the land of the dead—or proven to be one of its undying inhabitants—all citizens would be ruled by a royal council of landlords and judges, able to tax and revise the laws as they saw fit, all except for his dying wish.

The King was buried outside of his homeland, in the royal tomb that had housed generations of his ancestors, and life in the displaced kingdom moved on.

Over the next decade, the newfound council grew rich and corrupt, leeching what little resources the common folk were able to muster. The new cities were shadows of the towns the people had once known, and even the successful merchants were barely able to feed themselves and their families—or what was left of them. But no one dared question the council, as it was the council who kept them safe from the dead. It was the council that used a portion of the taxes it collected to maintain the wall, and ensured the plague of the dead would not erupt again.

Plus, as any official was quick to add, anyone that was unhappy with their situation in life could improve it, if they were brave enough. Anyone was free to go over the wall to try to rescue the princess with the rose birthmark. Anyone—man, woman, or child—had the opportunity to be the next king or queen, if they weren't lazy about it. And in this way, the council kept their control.

Anyone that actively disagreed with them was sent, whether by choice or by force, over the wall. And anyone sent over was never heard from again.

Over the years, the citizens began to lose hope that the princess was still alive. Faith in her actual existence was questioned by the young, and for many she became nothing more than a legend, an abstract symbol of potential wealth. Little by little, those who knew her forgot about the *real* Princess Aurora, about the girl with blonde curls who smelled like roses.

They all forgot about her, all except one.

*   *   *

Philip woke with a start. He had had the dream again.

He sat up in bed, and immediately started shivering. He could see his breath in the air, and pulled the thin blanket back over him.

It was winter, and it was colder than it had been in years.

He had grown from a wiry young boy into a wiry young man, handsome like his father, with neat brown hair and hopeful, haunted eyes.

He had dreamed about *her*. They were dancing. She was older now than before, but what happened was the same: he spun her around, and then brought her close. They kissed. As he looked into her eyes, there was a snap in the branches behind him. And then the dead came out, and ripped her away from him. They dragged her away, Aurora looking at him with the same helpless look his father had when he was killed. And when Philip tried to scream, tried to run after her, he was frozen in place like a statue. Powerless as a child.

He combed his hair down with his fingers, and took his jacket from the bedknob. He slept in his shirt and trousers, and even still had his socks on as his slid his feet back into his well-worn boots. He left the small room, barley a cupboard, and went into the main room of the shop, where his master was lighting the fires for the day.

He worked as an apprentice to the blacksmith, and his apprenticeship was nearing an end. He had no idea what he'd do when expected to go out on his own. He had only landed this position in the first place because the blacksmith felt sorry for him, after his own apprentice had been killed recently back in his hometown. But Philip's heart was never in the profession, and he couldn't help but remember that if his father had lived, he might be a prince by now. That is, if he wasn't orphaned by the dead.

He bid good morning to his master, and then went out through the back door with an empty pail. The settlement outside the wall was hastily built, and it seemed unfinished even after all these years. Mismatched panels and roofing made up the squat buildings, windows were crooked, and the roads were muddy and full of apple cores and flies. Philip's first task in the morning was to fetch water from the well in the center of the settlement, to help cool the instruments after being in the fire. He trudged along the muddy streets, looking up at the heavy clouds, and he wondered if *she* were looking at these clouds right now from the other side of the wall.

He was so lost in his thoughts that he didn't hear his friend shout, and knocked right into him in the middle of the street.

"Jack!" he said, picking up his pail. "Sorry, I—my mind was elsewhere."

Jack smiled at him. Jack was older than Philip, and broader across the chest. Most men were intimidated by him, as he had a reputation of being one of the fiercest killers of the dead when he was only a teenager. He's been living off that reputation since the plague ended, having strangers buy him drinks and food at bars as he told his tales. Like Philip, he was an orphan. It was rumored that Jack's parents were killed by the dead, and that this trauma had fueled his later killings. But Philip had never heard Jack speak of his life before the plague, or of his family at all.

Jack smiled at him, his teeth white under his blond beard. "I've got someone for you to meet," he said, pulling at Philip's arm.

"I've got work," Philip said. He couldn't return Jack's smile. He kept thinking about the dream.

"There's a man at the bar who has been asleep since before the plague," Jack said. Philip stopped, and Jack continued. "He hasn't even *heard* of the walking dead. He thought we were making it up. Took the wall to convince him."

"Where's he been?"

Jack threw up his hands. "Asleep! Got thrown from his horse and hit his head on a rock. Last thing he remembers. Then he wakes up, and some old lady is looking after him, some old hermit in the woods. He woke up, and she tried to *kill* him, she was so surprised. He's been sleeping over ten years." Jack shook his head. "Can you believe it?"

"Hmm," muttered Philip. "Not really."

He went forward with his pail, and Jack chased after.

"Don't you want to meet him?"

Philip looked straight ahead. "I've got work to do."

"Oh, *work*," Jack said with disgust. "Look, Philip, you can go up and down a hill with a pail of water all day, it won't

472

get you anywhere. *Believe* me." He lowered his voice to a whisper. "This guy has *gold*."

Philip kept walking. "That must be nice."

"He wants to find out what happened to his family."

"I bet."

"And he's got gold. Are you listening? Enough to lead an expedition... over the wall."

Philip stopped. He turned to Jack. "I don't have time for your games."

"It's not a game," Jack said quickly, his face serious. "He already knows all the risks. Doesn't care. Says he *must* know. This is your chance, Philip. This is your chance to find Aurora."

When troop after troop had been sent over the wall never to return, eventually men could no longer be coerced to go out of sheer patriotism. Wealth was required to pave the way to hell, and Philip was poor. He had the distant hope of saving up enough once he became a blacksmith, cheapening the costs by making his own weapons and armor, but that was still far out of reach.

"Have you talked to him?" Philip asked. "I mean, *explained* to him the risks? That he'd be throwing his money away?"

"He knows," Jack said, his enthusiasm growing. "He's crazy with the idea of it. Honestly, I'm not sure all his wits lasted through his sleep, if you know what I mean. But I told him all about it. I told him about *you*."

Philip stood in the middle of the road. He looked down at his pail.

"He wants to talk to you, Philip."

"All right," Philip said, giving up. He held up a finger. "But only for a minute."

Jack leapt into the air, and together they turned down a bent lane to the settlement's tavern.

It was unusually crowded for this time of morning, and Philip saw that most of the men stood huddled in the corner, blocking the view of the stranger. Even the bar was empty, the bartender among the throng around the man.

"Make way," Jack shouted ceremoniously, and a few heads turned in his direction. They pushed through the crowd, and Jack pushed Philip in front of him, so that he was face to face with the strange gentleman.

He was old. Philip wasn't prepared for how old he looked. He had a face covered in wrinkles, and a long beard, silky and white, that hung down to his stomach. He wore modest clothes in earth tones, and had a bewildered expression on his face, as if he had just woken up in someone else's bed. Which, Philip realized, the man had.

Philip introduced himself, and after a moment's hesitation, the man took his hand.

"A pleasure to meet you, young man. I am Rip Van Winkle." The man's hand went limp in his shake, and he looked away. "Or at least, I was." He smiled in shame, his eyes saddened. "So much of who we are depends on others. I used to be Rip, loving husband and father. Am I still? I would like to be." He looked Philip in the eye. "I hear you lead troops over the wall?"

Philip looked at Jack, who smiled and shrugged.

"That is who I would like to be," Philip answered.

Rip nodded.

"I understand, vaguely, that you have your own motives."

Philip looked at Jack again, and Jack had the decency to blush this time.

The old man continued. "That is very well. I have no interest in the kingdom. That can be your reward. As for the other men we require, I can pay them handsomely."

"Pay their families," someone in the bar murmured, and the old man heard it.

"Whomever they wish," he said. "I only have two requests."

Philip's stomach dropped. He caught Jack's stony expression out of the corner of his eyes, and knew that this was news to him, too.

"The first is that we leave at once. I am an old man, and I am not getting any younger. I cannot wait until the spring."

Philip nodded, and relaxed a little. "That can be arranged."

"The second is that you may pick all your own men—but one." The old man sat back, a pleased expression on his weathered face. "That is all."

Jack shook his head. "What is all? Who is the man?"

"Why, me, of course," the old man said. "You must take me with you. If any of your men make it back without me, no one gets paid."

"You can barely walk!" Jack shouted. "You'd kill us all!"

Rip didn't move a muscle of his expression. "Those are the terms."

Jack took Philip by the sleeve. "Come on, let's get out of here."

But Philip didn't move. He stood staring at the old man's eyes, not looking away.

"All right," he said. "I'll do it."

*   *   *

Philip returned to his master's shop with the bucket of water, and told him of the offer.

"You may go," his master said. "But if it's all the same to you, I'll hold on to your remaining wages until you return."

Philip agreed, and the pair spent the next week preparing weapons and armor funded by the old man's gold. Meanwhile, Jack went to every bar within hiking distance in search of men in debt who could fight. This proved not to be a challenging task, and by the time the armor was ready, they had a small fleet of able-bodied men to fill the helmets.

The night before they were to depart, Rip, Jack, and Philip met to discuss the journey at the tavern.

"This was the most current map I could find," Rip said, spreading out a scroll on the table. They all hunched over it.

The land of the dead was surrounded by walls all around, and was shaped like an egg on its side. Rip pointed to the east end.

"This is the entrance here," he said, "near where we are. Just beyond is the palace and its surrounding town." He moved his finger toward the west. "Farther on, you must cross through the woods, until you reach Sleepy Hollow. North of that is the estate of Prince Eric, and south is the castle of the Queen, on the border of the lands."

Philip studied the map, committing it to memory. "If Aurora is anywhere, she's most likely at the Evil Queen's castle." He looked up at Rip. "But if your family is any-where, it's in the town by the east entrance. If that is so, you are to take half the men and return to the gate at once."

Jack looked up at him, but kept his mouth shut.

"The men that go with me," Philip continued, "are to be paid double. But I am only telling this to the men I have chosen to escort me, should we split."

Rip nodded. "Fair."

They rolled up the map, and went over the financial ar-rangements once more before calling it a night. Philip went back to his little room in the blacksmith's shop, intending to sleep but unable to close his eyes all night. He didn't even need to dream; he could picture Aurora with his eyes open.

Apparently, he wasn't the only one who couldn't sleep, for when the sky had barely turned from black to grey, there was a knock at the door. Philip left his room at once, and made his way quietly to the door of the shop. Standing outside was Rip Van Winkle, his eyes heavy and his shoulders slumped.

"She's dead," he said without preamble. "My wife is dead."

Philip looked back over his shoulder. He could hear his master stirring, and stepped outside into the cold, shutting the door behind him.

"What are you saying?" he asked.

"I had arranged for a meeting last night," the old man said, his eyes unfocused. There was alcohol on his breath. "A man who had lived in the same town I had. An acquaintance. He made it out before the town fell, but he was there long enough to see what became of them."

Philip was silent. As much as he felt sorry for this man, the primary emotion he felt was utter disappointment. The trip wasn't happening. He would not be able to find Aurora.

"When I disappeared, my wife had no way of maintaining our lodgings. She and my daughter were pushed onto the streets." He sniffled. "In the cold. They were there in the cold. And this gentleman said—well, he didn't say it directly, but he alluded to the fact that, in order to eat, to provide nourishment for our daughter, my wife had to—had to sell herself. It was in the streets that she died, run over by a horse cart."

"Did the man," asked Philip after a moment, "mention what became of your daughter?"

Rip looked up, his eyes watery. "No. She was left on the streets, he assumed. He doesn't remember seeing her. There were a lot of children on the streets toward the end."

Philip couldn't keep eye contact. He looked away at the sky, at the clouds lightening as the sun rose behind them. He let out a long sigh. "What shall I tell the men?" he asked.

Rip wrinkled his forehead. "Tell the men?"

"They won't be happy about not getting paid."

"Who said they won't get paid?" The old man was getting angry. "What are you talking about?"

Philip looked back at him. "I just assumed, that since you had your news, there would be no need for the expedition."

"News? I have no news!" the old man yelled, his voice echoing into the chilled air. "No one found my daughter! I can't leave her in there, especially now that I know she's without a mother. What kind of father would I be? How could I leave behind my little Ada?"

In a guilty sort of way, Philip had to fight the smile from his face. "Of course," he said. He looked again at the dawn. "Well, no use in trying to sleep now. Let's prepare what we can."

Together they packed the bags and double-checked the supplies before the men arrived. By then, a small crowd had formed to see the men off, and a cheer went round when it was time to head to the gate.

Philip led the party, in silver armor with his sword on display, followed by their ten recruits, and Jack at the rear, leading a black horse by the reins. On the back of the horse, in armor and with a grey blanket wrapped around his shoulders, was Rip Van Winkle.

The team of thirteen made their way to the end of town, where members of the council stood in wait. The eldest gave a short speech, and Philip could barely follow, his mind was so distracted. He kept thinking back on Van Winkle's wife. He hadn't realized until this moment that her death, no matter how long ago, seemed a bad omen for the start of their trek. His doubts were put on hold, though, when someone spoke to him directly.

Philip looked up at a grim-faced man, working through a set of keys on a chain. "Are you the leader of this mission?"

Philip nodded.

"Very well, follow me. I am the Gatekeeper."

As the men entered the trees, the noise of the crowd became a memory, and it was suddenly very clear that they were actually doing this, and that their last walk through the outside world may already be behind them.

The trees parted, and a great wooden wall rose before them. At the base of the wall, directly before them, was a heavy wooden door. It was twice as tall as any of the men, but at the same time, so narrow that Philip worried the horse may not be able to squeeze through.

"We keep it just a crack as a precaution," the Gatekeeper

explained. "If there ever were a break-out—which there won't be—it'd be easier to stop them if they came out one by one."

The group approached the wall and huddled close. The Gatekeeper worked a crank to lift a massive beam from the front of the door. Then he went forward, under the beam, and took out a small black key. As he unlocked the door, a chill went up Philip's spine. He half expected to see the dead on the other side, hungry to escape.

But the door opened outward, revealing a narrow passage within the wall. Philip took a step forward, and the Gatekeeper stopped him.

"When you enter," he said, "you will wait to open the second door, do you understand? Not until the first door is completely sealed. The double doors are for our protection, not yours. You will not open the second door; we will do that for you. After you are through, it will be locked again from behind."

"How do we get back?" Philip asked, and the Gatekeeper smiled as if Philip had made a joke.

"We have a man on the tower. Signal to him, and he will unlatch the second door with a lever. If you can get into the passage without any of the dead following, and shut the door behind you, we will open the first door again. But, you should know, that is our process in theory only. It has never needed to be tested in practice. No one has ever returned, and most understand that to walk through this door is to abandon all hope of doing so. Through here is the way to certain death." He smiled, and then stepped aside. "You may enter."

Philip took a breath, perhaps his last breath of free air, and made the first step into the stone passage.

"All the way down," the Gatekeeper ordered. "It'll be a squeeze with all of you in there, but you'll be out in the open soon enough. Perhaps sooner than you'd like."

Philip walked to the end of the dark passage, and stood

beside the outer door. It had a bar placed over it as well, tied to a rope that ran through a crack in the ceiling. By the time all the men and the horse had made it into the passage, Philip was shoved against the door and barely able to breathe.

The Gatekeeper peered at him with a smile from outside the passage. His hand was on the door.

"Last chance," he taunted. "You can still turn back."

There was a loaded moment of silence as the men contemplated this, which Philip was forced to interrupt with a shout, "Close it. We're ready."

The Gatekeeper shut the door, and the men were trapped in the darkness. The key scraped against the lock, and then there was a boom as the beam was lowered back into place. Then there was a tense, immeasurable period while they waited in the pitch black, pressed up against each other, waiting to be freed. No one spoke. No one could move. And Philip wondered if this was what death felt like.

Finally, there was a scraping sound from above them. A gear was turned, and Philip felt the beam he was pressed against pull back along the wall. He reached down, and turned the handle, and at once they all spilled out into the cold air again.

When everyone was outside the passage, Philip closed the door. A moment later, he heard the beam slide down on the other side. It was an awful sound, like the sound of a lid being dragged onto a coffin. He turned around, forcing himself to hide the fear he felt, and faced his men.

They were in the land of the dead.

Philip looked to Rip on his horse. "Which way?" he asked. The old man pointed west.

"It shouldn't be more than a mile to town," he said. His words seemed muted, as if the air itself were dead here, too.

In silence, the men commenced, two of the paid recruits in front of Philip as they followed the path.

The trees on either side of them were nothing but

stumps. Their mass had presumably been used for the wall, and their absence allowed the men see ahead of them for some distance. The earth was grey, and covered with ash leftover from the fires of long ago. As they walked, their feet kicked up the dust into the air, and it swirled down among them, landing like snowflakes on their shoulders.

There were no animals that they could hear. Silence met their ears in all directions, and if it weren't for the muffled sounds of their footsteps, Philip might have sworn he'd lost his hearing completely.

It might have been a mile to the town, or it might have been ten. Everything they passed looked so monotonous that distance and time were in limbo, and Philip found himself both wanting to speed up and slow down at the same time. More than once he had the urge to turn around, to bellow out to the Gatekeeper to let him back to the world of the living. He might have, too, had it not been for the other men with him, and for his role as leader. It was his job not to give up.

As eerie as the landscape of tree stumps had seemed, when they entered the woods, the silence was overbearing. Philip was sure they'd have seen something by now. He remembered his own encounters with the dead as a child, how they sought out anything that moved, and how the herds had followed his carriage, trying to eat away at him. Where were they? Where were all the dead?

"There!" Rip whispered. His voice made all the men jump. Philip pulled his sword, and turned to see where the old man was pointing.

He was seated calmly on the back of his horse, one hand holding his blanket over his shoulders, and the other pointing limply into the distance.

To the left of the path, on a high hill, loomed a large structure.

"The palace," Rip said, and lowered his hand. Philip

nodded, and the troop continued onward, the path widening until it became a road. The stones of the pavement were so covered with dust that it blended into the dirt of the woods, and there wasn't a single footprint to be seen.

They took this road up the hill, watching the shadows of the dead trees surrounding them, and waited for something to jump out at them.

"Where *are* they?" Jack muttered. Philip didn't like this at all, and he couldn't fight the feeling that they were walking into some sort of trap. But wasn't that why they were here in the first place? To come face-to-face with the dead?

"This road leads right to town," the old man urged. "We're almost there."

But no one went any faster. If anything, the longer they traveled without seeing anyone, or a sign of anyone, the more cautious they became.

When they reached the palace, the men paused for a minute outside the broken gates to marvel at its dilapidated grandeur. Philip tried to imagine how this structure might have looked in its prime—the ornamental flourishes, the sparkling white marble walls. Now the walls were blackened with smoke, and overgrown with weeds. It was dark inside the windows, and a tower had collapsed on the far side and lay across the lawn like a fallen dinosaur.

The road curved along the front gates. There, outside the gates, was the uniform of a royal guard, with its arms spread out to the sides and legs twisted, as if running in place. The front of the jacket was torn open, but nothing remained of its owner, nothing but dust.

The town below was covered with a dense fog, with only the peaks of rooftops showing above the surface. Continuing down the hill, Philip could almost hear the tension buzzing in his ears, the alarm of his nerves telling him to stop. But he went dutifully forward, thinking of Aurora, and stepped down into the mist.

Once their line was submerged, Philip looked back at the other men. They gripped their weapons with twitchy fingers, their eyes wide and darting to the sides. Even Jack seemed unnerved, taking timid steps forward as he held onto the reins of the horse like a magical talisman. Only Rip Van Winkle's face betrayed no fear. The old man was leaning forward even, his beard hanging over the horse's neck, and he seemed ready to jump off to meet his daughter at a moment's notice.

Through the soup of the fog they were able to make out the charred remains of the buildings, their facades sliding to the ground, the lettering on the signs faded away to nothing. They passed the remains of a church, and then found themselves in the center of what looked to have been the marketplace.

"Oh God," gasped one of the men, and the entire party jumped. Philip turned to see that it was Jack, his face white as he stared at something near him.

Philip took up his sword and came toward him. "Is it them?" he whispered through his teeth.

Jack shook his head.

Next to him, and encircling the entire marketplace, were piles of skeletons. Some still wore their clothes, their white skulls poking out from colorless jackets. They were all sizes— men, women, children. And there were hundreds of them.

The history of death surrounded them, and any attempt Philip made to try to see the town before its demise was futile. It was like trying to picture Atlantis before the waves came crashing down, trying to forget how many people had died in that very spot.

"Let me down," called the old man. The men looked to Philip, and he nodded his approval. "We have to search all these houses," he said once his feet were on the ground. "She might be in any of them."

Jack looked at Philip, and there was no question what

he was thinking. He was thinking the same as the rest of them: How could anyone be alive here? But Rip would not be deterred.

He kept looking up at the buildings and shaking his head. "I can't believe it. I just can't believe it."

Jack edged his way over to Philip. "How long are we going to humor him?"

"We came here to look," Philip said, although he wanted to get out of the open as much as the rest of his men. "Stay together. We'll go building by building."

"The fastest way to do it would be to shout out," Rip said, coming up to Philip.

"No way," Jack said, holding up his hands. "It'll draw them all toward us."

"Draw *who*?" countered Rip. "We haven't seen a single person this entire time. Frankly, I have trouble believing the stories I've heard. The dead rising? It's fantasy."

"It happened," Philip grumbled.

"Oh, I admit *something* happened," Rip continued, looking around through the open windows along the marketplace. "That much is obvious. But what I think is that these people must simply have been very sick, in a state of madness. Panic and fear created your stories of the dead."

"You're paying these men an awful lot to protect you from fantasies," Philip grumbled.

Rip had the good sense not to argue that point, and instead went forward to peer into the different shop windows. When he came to a store that was completely boarded up, he stopped.

"Here," he said with certainty. "This used to be the toy-shop. It was Ada's favorite place in the entire town. If she's anywhere, she's in here."

Philip looked at the building with skepticism. But then he noticed something. "The boards," he said, stepping forward, "they're not burnt. This was boarded up *after* the town fell."

SLEEPING BEAUTY WAKES IN HELL

And it was true. The fresh planks were like pale bandages against the blackened façade.

"I told you!" Rip said, clapping his hands together. "She's in here, I know it." He went forward to dig his fingers under a board nailed across the doorframe.

"Wait," Philip said. "Let's leave the door blocked. If there are dead inside, I don't want them spilling out. We'll take the beams off the windows, one at a time, and go in that way after we can scope it out."

"Good thinking," Jack agreed.

So together they pried off the boards of the window, leaving the nails in place on the planks so that the opening could be closed quickly. As the gap grew wider, the daylight landed on broken toys, overturned shelves, and layers of dust. But they didn't see anything move, and there was no inkling of the dead.

Philip climbed through first, his boots landing on something that snapped like a broken twig. He paused, waiting, ready to leap back through the window. When nothing happened, he stepped all the way inside, and motioned for the old man to follow. After him, Philip ordered two of his men inside to act as guards. The rest were to wait outside with Jack.

"This used to be such a happy place," Rip commented, looking upon the rows of dusty toys. He stepped forward, eyeing a stuffed bear, and then become transfixed by a bloated baby doll, covered in cobwebs. "The dolls were her favorite. It seems such a waste to just leave it here, when Ada would enjoy it so."

He reached his withered hands toward the shelf.

"Don't touch anything," Philip hissed. "Let's search the upstairs and get out."

"Don't be silly," Rip said, and put both hands around the middle of the doll.

It happened so fast that if Philip hadn't been hyped up

with panic already, he might have missed it. As soon as Rip squeezed the doll, it snapped forward around his arm like a mousetrap. It had long black fingernails that it dug into his armor, and Rip was so surprised that he immediately whipped the infant off of him, flinging it across the room. This might have been a good strategy, except that one of the hired men was in the direct path of the infant's flight, and it smacked into his head and latched on, digging its claws into his ears.

He screamed as it bit into his face, his voice distorted but thunderous.

"The doll came *alive!*" Rip said with a gasp, backing away to the wall.

"That's no doll," Philip yelled, raising his sword. "That's a dead baby."

But before he could strike, a rumbling began on the floors above them. It sounded as if a million rats had suddenly been let out of their cages, their tiny claws clacking against the wood in a mad rush to freedom.

"Out!" Philip screamed. "Out, now!" He took the old man by the shoulder and shoved him to the window. "Pull him out!" The men outside yanked the old man through, and then Philip felt himself being pushed by one of the men behind him. He landed outside, and turned around to grasp the arms of the hired man.

Behind the man, Philip could see the first hired man fighting against the thing on his face, knocking against the shelves of toys and sending the items crashing to the ground. Movement drew Philip's gaze away from him and toward the staircase, where a wave of babies were descending, spilling over the steps and climbing over the side of the banister, climbing even on the ceiling like spiders and dropping down into the middle of the shop in their wild scurry toward what must have been their first meal in ages.

They swept over the man with the baby on his face, and

rushed forward to the window. "Ah!" the other hired man cried out as the infants ran up his legs, tearing into his flesh with their blackened nails,

"Close the gap!" Philip screamed, letting go of the hired man's arms. "Put the boards back!"

"No, wait!" cried the man. "Don't leave me!"

As they pounded the last board into the window, the babies were throwing themselves against the barriers. They tore at the walls, and pounded against the door. The wood creaked, and all the men stepped back.

"We need to get out of here," Philip said, and no one disagreed. He looked to Jack, and then at the empty horse behind him. "Where's Van Winkle?"

The men turned to see the old man standing alone at a distance in the street, looking away.

"Rip!" Philip called. "Get over here!"

But the old man wouldn't budge. Philip rushed over to him.

"I thought I saw something," the old man said, looking into the mist.

"We have to leave." Philip reached down for the old man's wrist. He tugged on it, and then noticed a dark line across the old man's hand. He dropped it with a shudder.

"It got you," he whispered.

Rip looked down at his hand and pursed his lips. "It's only a scratch," he said dismissing it, and then went back to looking ahead.

Philip went back to the men. He had heard of this dismissal of infection before. It's part of how the plague spread so fast to begin with: those with wounds wanted more than anything to believe the rules didn't apply to them, and in their stubbornness, doomed an entire kingdom. "We have to leave him."

"Well, we can't leave without him," Jack said. "The men know they won't get paid if we return without him."

He took Jack to the side and whispered, "He's been scratched."

"I'm not sure if—" He trailed off, and Philip looked up to see what had distracted him.

Ten feet in front of Rip stood a child in the mist.

"Ada!" he exclaimed.

He took a step forward before anyone could stop him. The child didn't move. It was a girl dressed in grey rags, with limp blond hair and an unmistakably dead slant to her posture.

Philip stepped forward. "She's dead, Rip," he said, edging closer to the old man.

"What do you mean dead? She's right here."

"Look at her. She's a little girl."

"Yes. It's Ada. *My* little girl."

"Think about it, Rip. You've been gone how many years? She shouldn't be little anymore."

The old man was beyond reason. He stepped forward, and embraced the dead girl. Philip took a step back, and as he did, more little figures seemed to materialize out of the fog. Boys and girls, all of them dead, and looking at Van Winkle with hungry eyes. There was another thump on the door of the toyshop, and Philip knew their time was almost up.

He retreated to the remaining men as the dead children closed in the circle on Ada and Van Winkle. The old man let go of his embrace, and noticed the other children for the first time.

"Ada," he asked, "who are your friends?"

The children, as if in response, jumped on him, knocking him to the cobblestones and tearing off his armor. He let out a scream that echoed through the town, and to Philip's surprise, instead of joining in with her friends, Ada was trying to pull them off her father. Finding no success, she took a step back, reached into her pocket, and pulled out a match.

She lit it, and there was a smile on her face as she bent down and touched the flame to Rip Van Winkle's beard.

The blaze erupted in a fireball, and encircled the old man's head. The dead children jumped back, and Ada held up the lit match in triumph as her father writhed in pain behind her. Her stance was unambiguously territorial. It said he was hers, and if she couldn't have him, nobody could.

So the children turned instead to Philip and his men.

"Run!" Philip screamed. "Out of the town, into the woods—as fast as you can!"

As soon as the first man made a move to retreat, the children spread out and attacked. A small boy and girl who looked to be siblings jumped onto a man with an axe; he swung it wildly through the air, hitting nothing until he was brought to his knees. Another boy, his face torn and stitched back together, climbed up the side of another man, and this man panicked all together, running straight into a pile of skeletons. The horse reared on its hind legs, and Jack tried to calm it so that he could climb on its back.

Philip found himself with his back to the wall of the toyshop, feeling the thudding of the infants inside as they threw their small bodies against the boards. A dead girl on the street was watching him, not moving forward. She looked older than the others, but with childish pigtails, and she wore a green cape over the tatters of her nightgown. The cape looked to be made of leaves.

She took a step forward just as there was a crash to Philip's left. The babies had broken the barrier, and they were hopping out like crickets onto the street. They took down another of his men without even slowing their pace. The dead children looked up from their slaughter, their faces coated with gore, and dropped their victims. At once they ran back into the mist, some of the infants following after, the rest scurrying forward on their black nails over the cobblestones to attack the men.

"Come on," Philip said, grabbing Jack by the sleeve. He pulled Jack down a lane, the horse and a handful of the luckier men behind them. They ran through the streets, dodging the dead that had been drawn to the noise, and weaved their way to the woods on the west side of town. They paused for a moment to catch their breath.

"They'll be coming now," Philip said, bent over and wishing his armor were lighter. "All that noise, and the smoke from the fire."

Less than a moment after his statement the first of the dead came out of the trees. It was a group of women in muddy ball gowns, with a woman in a shimmering blue dress at their center. The horse reared and ran off into the trees, but there was no time to fetch it. The men formed a semi-circle, and as the dead came at them, they slashed and hacked at them. When one of the men fell, the women pounced on him, tearing off his armor like peeling an egg.

The rest of the men retreated farther into the trees, keeping their backs together as they faced out into the shadows. Philip could feel the shoulders of the others on either side of his own. Jack was shaking, and then he bent over, and vomited.

"I thought you were a famous killer of the dead," mocked one of the other men. Jack merely looked at him with a seasick expression, and wiped off his chin.

Then the ground began to rumble. Dust fell from the empty branches above them. And in the air sounded a distant roar, as if the earth itself were being torn in two.

"It's them," Philip said. "It's the dead." He looked around for somewhere to hide, somewhere to protect them, but they were alone in the woods. Then he looked up. "The trees! Quickly!"

And as fast as they could, the men ascended the tree trunks, and made it as far up as the branches would hold them. Philip climbed out onto a thick branch, hugging the frozen wood with his arms and legs, and looking down below as the dead began to emerge in earnest.

It was as if some great dam of hell had burst, and sent all of the dead flooding outward at once. The bodies below Philip were so thick that he couldn't see an inch of ground between their shoulders. The sound of their groans was deafening, while their smell was overpowering, stinging his eyes and making him gag. He held a hand over his mouth to stop his coughing, and looked up to see the remaining men transfixed by the sights below their own trees.

Like a mighty river, the dead swept away everything they passed. The smaller trees snapped and fell underneath them, and Philip's tree was bashed and rammed. It was strong though, and did not fall. The other men were not so lucky. One man made the mistake of climbing a sapling, and it was trampled down by the masses, sending him screaming to the ground.

At once they were upon him in a fit of cannibalistic fury. They pounced on him, poking their fingers into his flesh and tearing away skin as they pulled him along with the current of the crowd. The men in the trees watched in impotent silence as their friend was reduced to meat and pieces in a matter of moments. Splatters of blood rose like a mist as the dead fought over the last remaining scraps, snapping their teeth at each other and arguing over the smallest morsel.

Then the fight was over. The dead moved on, and it was as if their friend had never existed.

It was dark before the dead thinned enough that the men even thought of going down. Even then there were stragglers, and not just men anymore, but animals, too. Undead wolves sniffed out the leftovers, led by a small child in a red cloak, her face covered by the shadow of her hood. But these were nothing compared to the herd that had passed earlier, and Philip found himself falling in and out of sleep as he waited for a chance to descend.

At dawn, the earth was finally clear. Philip motioned for the other men to stay put, and he shimmied down the trunk of his tree. He landed on his feet and drew his sword, turning in each direction before motioning to the others that it was safe to follow.

Of their original party of thirteen, there were only five left: Philip, Jack, and three of the hired men.

"What do we have left?" Philip asked.

Their supplies had been lost, all but one bag of dried fruit, and both Jack and one of the men had lost their helmets. Philip found that he was the only one left with a proper weapon.

Jack scratched his blond beard and stared at the rising sun in the east. "If we go around the town, heading southeast, we might be able to dodge the herd."

"We're going west," Philip said, turning over clumps of dirt on the ground with his sword. "If we hurry, we can make it by sundown."

"West?" Jack asked. "But the gate—" He stopped himself, looking at the hired men. "Philip," he said, taking him by the shoulder and stepping out of earshot, "you can't be serious about continuing now. You saw what we're up against. We won't make it."

"It's why we're here," Philip said through gritted teeth. "The old man wanted his family; he got it. I want Aurora."

"But all the dead," Jack whispered, "you can't possibly think she could survive all these years among that?"

"I don't know. But we're here now, and I'm never going to get another chance like this." Philip smiled. "Besides, I've got the most experienced fighter on my side. How can I lose?"

Jack bit his lip. "Listen, Philip. Don't be mad, but all those stories about how I fought twenty or thirty of the dead at the same time, single-handedly, and won—they're just stories."

"I'm aware that you exaggerate."

"No," Jack emphasized. "I'm not a fighter at all. When

the dead knocked down my parents' door, I ran to the basement and locked myself in. They ate my parents and my sister Jill; I ate our food stock until I was rescued. No one would give charity to an orphan, so I started to say whatever would work to let me eat. And then, as the years went on, I sort of learned to tell my stories better."

"You're not a fighter?"

Jack shook his head. "To be honest, this is the first time I've actually *seen* the dead. I'm not going to walk up and kiss them, like that senseless old man, but I didn't know—I didn't realize what I was getting myself into. Everyone believed that I could kill thirty of those things in one blow. I thought that meant someone could. I mean, how was I supposed to know the dead could be so... deadly?"

Philip growled. "Has *anyone* in this crew been around the dead before?" He turned away, brewing over what Jack had said.

Was he being as blind as Rip Van Winkle? He couldn't tell. The old man died going after what he wanted, yet that seemed better than returning to the settlement, always wondering what might have been. And Philip knew that if he went back now, he might as well have died out here. There would be nothing left to live for. No, he had to go on, for Aurora, and for himself.

As for the other men—well, their families would be rewarded.

He rejoined the group, and pointed west. "This is the way I am going. It is west, toward the castle where the princess is held. I cannot force any of you to follow me rather than retreating for the gate, but I do suggest you consider these three facts. First, the old man is dead. You know his rule: if anyone comes back without him, their reward is nulled. Second, if I rescue the princess, I will inherit the kingdom, and I swear that any who have aided me in the process will be handsomely rewarded. And third, between you and the gate are the herds of the undead, hungry for their next meal, and I am the only one left among us with anything resembling a weapon."

He looked at each of them in the eye, including Jack—*especially* Jack—and then turned to walk away into the woods, to the west.

The men remained silent for a moment. Then, as one, they all came running after.

*　*　*

They lost three more on the way.

One was lost as they were crossing a swamp. His legs sank down into the muck, and when they tried to pull him up by the arms, several swamp hags had already latched onto him from below, tearing into his side. They were forced to leave him.

Another they lost while resting by a garden of rose bushes. Two of the dead emerged from the shadows without warning: a woman with brown hair, and her companion, a beastly fellow who used his fists like front paws as he walked. They seized one of the men, and tore into him together. The rest of the men retreated behind a bank of trees, and watched in horror as the two dead lovingly brought handfuls of gore to each other's mouths, as if feeding each other the first bites of a wedding cake.

The third they lost outside Sleepy Hollow, a town with its own set of dilapidated walls, which had done little to protect it in its time. By now the company was down to Philip, Jack, and the last of the hired men, and the three gazed in exhausted dread at a series of heads along the top of the wall. These had been placed at equal distances to each other, like holiday decorations, facing outward to the woods. Some of the heads were decayed skeletons, while others seemed fresh—aside from a layer of dust—with skin and eyes intact. The hired man took a step toward the wall to gaze up at one of these fresher ones, a portly man's head with a beard, when the head suddenly reanimated, his nostrils twitching and the eyes opening wide as it tumbled itself forward over the wall. It landed on the hired man's shoulder, biting into his neck and then falling to the ground, munching on the bit of bloody skin it had stolen.

"Please," the hired man begged, looking up at Philip from the ground, "help me."

Jack made a movement to step forward, but Philip held him back. A dead woman had been lured by the sound from behind the wall.

She tottered over to the hired man, wearing a frilly sky blue dress, faded with time and tattered at the hem, and in her hands she held a shining sword. She swung it like a lasso above her head as she walked, all the eyes of the heads on the wall upon her. But the hired man didn't notice as she stepped up behind him. She lowered the blade with a thrust, and sliced through his neck with one blow, sending his head tumbling into the dirt.

As Philip and Jack turned south toward the woods, she was picking up the heads that had fallen, and replacing them on the wall.

They walked in silence through the woods that remained between them and the Evil Queen's castle. Philip saw Jack's nervousness from the corner of his eyes, the way the man jumped at every sound, how his face had gone pale with fear, his eyelids twitching and breathing fast and shallow. But Philip felt no such nervousness himself. In fact, with each step he felt more and more resolved to find Aurora in the castle. If he died, he died. What would be worse would be returning to his safe but meaningless life. Better to hunt in hell than drift in heaven.

The trees began to thin at their sides, and the path widened to reveal the way ahead. Philip felt his breath catch as he caught sight of the castle on the hill ahead. Dark clouds circled above, but underneath, much to his consternation, thick briars twisted like a moat around the castle base.

Who had planted these? Philip wondered. Had the Evil Queen become a farmer in order to protect her treasure? But that was nonsense. More likely, these briars had been here all along, but tame, and continually cut back. And in the intervening years had been allowed to grow free and overrun the gardens surrounding the castle. Yes, that was more likely. But at this point, nothing seemed to be in his way by chance. Philip took out his sword, and hacked into the briars, forming a path and thinking the entire time that he was thwarting the Evil Queen's attempts to stop him.

He had formed a small nook in the briars when he turned to Jack. "Stay close behind, we'll make it through."

"Actually," Jack said, scratching the back of his neck, "if it's all right with you, I'm going to wait out here."

Philip turned to him, his forehead sweaty. "What?"

Jack was looking up at the dark castle. "I can't go in there. I'll stay out here, where it's safe, up in a tree."

Philip didn't think it was any safer up a tree than inside the castle, but he nodded in agreement, mostly because he felt that Jack might slow him down. Also, part of him wanted to find the princess alone.

"Stay safe," he said, and then gave his full attention to the briars.

It was darkening again by the time he had cut a tunnel to the castle bridge. His limbs were aching, and under his armor his skin was cold with sweat. He made his way across the silent bridge, mist circling his ankles. A bitter cold sank through his skin to his bones.

He had crossed this bridge before, as a boy. Had Aurora passed this bridge as well? Was she waiting for him on the other side of the castle wall? Would she even recognize him?

He reached the mouth of the castle. Stepping through, he

recognized the entryway. This was the armory. Holding his sword at the ready, he passed the cage that had held the dead maiden, and the empty spot on the ground where his father had been ripped apart. It almost felt as if he had never left, that he was a boy walking back into the same room again, except that now he was here alone.

At the end of the entryway, the door to the castle was locked. After a moment's hesitation, he pulled on the heavy handle. He pulled again, leaning back with all his weight. The door didn't even creak. Philip glanced around for another entrance into the castle—to have come this far only to be thwarted now, by a door, by a *door!*—but he found only another locked door at the top of a small stairwell.

He sank to his knees, going over his options in his head. It was growing dark, and the moon sent a blue beam through the mouth of the castle, making his armor glimmer like the scales of a fish. He let his eyes follow the light up, and was surprised to see it came not from the mouth of the castle, but from a crack in the ceiling. There were cracks and missing bricks all around him, letting in the moonlight like the light peeking through the leaves of a tree. He sat up, his eyes squinting against the darkness, and turned to the wall before him, running his fingers along the cold stone.

It crumbled at his touch. He let out a quiet laugh. The doors were solid, but the walls were crumbling.

Working diligently, he worked the tip of his sword around a large stone toward the bottom of the wall, digging out the dry mortar until he had unearthed it enough to dig his fingers into either side. He paused a moment, wondering what horrors he might be unleashing, and then tugged out the stone.

It landed with a soft thud at his feet. The dust of the walls crumbled down the dark opening it created. It was just large enough for him to squeeze through. He bent down, and looked to the other side.

It was a hallway of the castle, bathed blue in the moonlight. There must be cracks in the ceiling throughout the ruined stronghold, he realized.

He waited a moment to see if any of the dead would rush the hole, sticking their dead arms through to grab him, but nothing moved or made a sound, so he bent forward and tried to squeeze through. Trying to go headfirst and finding himself unable to fit, he tried again with his feet but found that his waist caught on the edges. The armor was too bulky. He climbed back out, and started to dig at the mortar on the wall, when a stone above dislodged an inch, making him fear that if he continued, the hole might be closed up altogether.

There was only one option. Reluctantly, Philip stood up and stripped himself of his bulky armor. He set each piece down carefully on the stone floor by the opening, and arranged them in a small pile, one that he could pull through piece by piece when he got to the other side. He would carry his sword through the first trip, just in case he ran into any of the dead. It would have to work. He couldn't see another way about it.

He crawled through the hole on his stomach, inching through like a worm with his sword held out in front of him. He was nearly through when his thigh accidentally knocked against the side of the opening, and the stones of the wall began to shudder. Panicked, he tumbled forward pulling his legs free of the gap, and heard the stones slide behind him.

A mouse might be able to fit through the hole that remained, but Philip would have to find another way out. He stood in the blue hallway, holding his sword at the ready, and felt completely naked without his armor. He stood in his workman's clothes, his plain brown work boots and loose carpenter's shirt, and for a moment was more worried about meeting the princess like a commoner than about the dead being able to bite freely into his skin. He had wanted to be her knight in shining armor. Now how would he look? What if she didn't want him?

He would have to put this out of his mind for now. There were other details that needed his attention.

A thick layer of dust coated the hallway floor. Ancient lanterns were mounted on the walls, covered with sheets of cobwebs. Philip was grateful for the moonlight, which made the cobwebs glow white, and everything else shine with an otherworldly blue light. But even if he wasn't blind, he was still lost. Where was the princess? He took a step forward, trying to remember the geography of the castle from his childhood.

He followed the hallway around a bend, and there it led past a large chamber open to the sky. Philip stayed at the edge of the first archway into this room, and peeked around the corner.

It was the castle courtyard. Every plant within it was dead now, and great cobwebs covered the benches and tree limbs. Philip kept to the side of the hallway as he passed this opening, stepping lightly but quickly, as he noticed figures standing and sitting among the dead trees.

The dead, only they were unmoving. Perhaps there were mere corpses, not the reanimated dead? They were too far away to be sure, and Philip kept his distance, practically jumping into the dark of the hallway once it turned back into the castle.

Here he met a spiral staircase. It led up, and was completely dark within its turns. He looked up into its black obscurity, unsure if he should ascend or try to follow the hallway in the opposite direction. But part of him didn't want to have to face that open courtyard. He had a better chance of defending himself against an attack in a narrow hallway, where they wouldn't get a chance to surround him. So, telling himself that he could always go back down again if he needed to, Philip went blindly up the stairs.

He was never so aware of each individual step. Unwilling to take either hand off his sword, he had to feel each new step with the toe of his boot. It was dark and it was silent as he made his careful way. The air smelled stale, as if he were the first person to breathe here in a thousand years. And he wondered, if Jack was still alive outside, would the man ever come after him if he failed to return? And he knew at once that Jack wouldn't. If Philip didn't return, there would be no rescue, no reward. If he never made it out of this darkness, it would be as if he ceased to exist.

Had this been what it felt like for Aurora? Did she know people had tried to rescue her? Or did she think she was abandoned without hope?

The stairway finally let out to an upper floor of the castle. Ahead he could see the moonlight again, and Philip made his way through the darkness, recognizing nothing. He had the irrational fear that he had somehow entered the wrong castle, and had only been confused when he thought he had recognized the entryway. He edged forward, becoming more and more convinced that he had been mistaken after all, that he should retreat, when he came upon the throne room of the Queen.

He was on the far side of the long room. Moonlight spilled through the crumbling walls, sending an iridescent beam directly onto the throne itself, where the Queen still sat. She was motionless, with her hands on the arms of the throne, and her head staring forward into the empty room. She wore a long black cloak, and a Viking warrior's helmet on her head, with two long horns that were dark and twisted with time. Around her sat what Philip assumed was her staff. They were equally frozen in time, covered with as many cobwebs as the castle walls. They seemed dead, utterly dead.

Still, Philip thought it best not to walk through that door. The hallway led around the room and to another stairway, and he felt it would be best to get as much distance between himself and the Evil Queen as possible. He crept on tiptoe down the hallway, stopping only at the stairwell, and here he stopped absolutely.

The dust had been broken here. Everywhere he had been before, his footsteps had been the only marks in the layers of dust in the castle. But here, in a slash before him and leading up the stairwell, was a trail that had been walked clean. His eyes darted up, following the trail into the darkness. Then, with dread, his eyes followed the trail in the other direction, across the path before him, and into the throne room. There the path led to the feet of the Evil Queen.

She hadn't moved since he saw her last. She was still facing forward, away from Philip, but the trail was evidence that she could move—*had* moved—and might move again.

Philip's heart began to beat with anticipation. Where, he asked himself, would the Evil Queen go? What would be the *only* thing to entice her up these stairs? Without the calm he had before, Philip went up the black stairwell, as quickly as he could without seeing, and for the first time since this all started, he felt like he was getting closer to Princess Aurora.

He followed the trail around the labyrinthine bends of another set of hallways, his pace quickening, sweat forming on his back and neck in his excitement. He wanted to shout to Aurora that he was near, he wanted to sing it at the top of his lungs, but he had to remain silent, or else he might wake the dead. Then, after another turn, he found himself in front of a closed doorway. The dust trail led underneath, and even the handle had been shined by frequent use.

This was it. He knew this had to be it.

Delicately, as if it were made of glass, he lifted the handle. The door creaked inward, and he found himself within a turret of the castle. A high window let in a stream of blue moonlight, and it flickered down the walls and spilled into the center of the room, pooling around a woman lying on a bed of straw, her body bound in ropes.

He gasped with wonder, and choked on the smell. The room smelled worse than any pigsty he had ever had the displeasure of passing, and he coughed into his elbow, taking pains to breathe through his mouth instead of his nostrils.

He took a step toward her, and saw that her eyes were closed.

She was blonde, and impossibly thin. He looked down on her emaciated face, smudged and frail, and tried to see the girl he knew within it. She was deathly pale, but he wasn't sure if she appeared so because of the moonlight or her natural pallor. The coarse ropes began under her bony shoulders, and twisted around her arms and torso like angry serpents, all the way to her thighs. Her legs were bare, and her feet blackened from dirt.

Philip stared at her, dumbfounded. She was a mess. This woman conflicted with how he had pictured Aurora all these years. Her hair was in tangles, her face aged prematurely from her hard life, and her smell offensive and overwhelming. To be honest, he wasn't entirely convinced she was still alive. How could anything be alive in here?

He bent to his knees before her, and listened.

At first nothing. Then, after a moment, the faintest escape of breath.

Philip sat back. The dead don't breathe, do they? He couldn't remember. Then, to be sure, he reached out his hand and placed it on top of the ropes above her heart.

Then he felt it, the kick of her heartbeat. It thundered in her chest, ushering her warm blood to her extremities, and proving once and for all that his Aurora was in fact alive. Philip felt something inside him blossom, and he looked down at her face again. This time he saw her delicate features through the grime, her thin nose and her proud cheekbones. How could he ever doubt her? How could he think of her as anything but beautiful?

All the feeling that had been buried in him during these

dark years came to the surface, and he was overcome with emotion. Suddenly, all the death and loneliness and bitterness of his life seemed justified, worthwhile even, if it led to this moment. He looked down at her beautiful face, his eyes filling with tears, and he had to express his gratitude. He had come here to rescue her, but it was she who had saved him. He bent down, unworthy, and pressed his trembling lips to hers.

He kissed her. And his kiss woke her up.

"Arghhh!" she howled, and before Philip could back away, Aurora lifted her head and bashed her teeth into his face. He tumbled backward, the cut smarting on his cheek, and looked up with wide eyes to see the woman sitting up. Her arms were still wrapped by her sides, but she looked at him, baring her teeth and snarling.

Then, struggling within her ropes like a caterpillar trying to escape its cocoon, she backed away against the far wall, not taking her eyes off of him.

She bit him. Philip put his hand to his check, feeling the wet blood. He was done for. All it took was one bite, a single scratch and—

But wasn't she alive?

He looked up at her, and saw her shiver with fear at his glance. Then he realized where she was, how she had spent all these years. He must be the first living person she's seen since she was a child.

"I won't hurt you," he said quietly, and at the sound of his voice she gasped. "I came here to rescue you," he continued. "I'm going to bring you home."

She stared at him, her mouth open.

"Aurora," he said, "don't you remember me? It's Philip." He pointed to his chest. "Philip."

Aurora moved her lips in imitation of the sound, but said nothing. Then, remembering her ropes, she started struggling against them again. Philip stood up, reaching for his sword to cut her free, but at his movements she stumbled backward and started hissing again, so—as a sign of peace—he set his sword down on the floor between them.

Without his help, she wiggled free of her ropes, first twisting on her back, pushing them down to her waist to free her arms, and then standing up to push them past her legs to step out of them, as if removing an especially uncomfortable pair of pants. She had obviously wriggled free many times before, and was only in the ropes now as some sort of pretense.

Now it was Philip's turn to be shy. Aurora was standing in front of him completely naked, with apparently no qualms about her nudity. Philip politely looked away, but not before the image of her starved form burned its image into his vision. Her body was nothing but ribs and skin, her stomach sunken and her hips sharp and protruding. Philip bowed his head before her, ready to lunge for his sword if she tried to rush him.

"We must find you something to wear," he said, and allowed his eyes to search the rest of the room. In one corner was a broken spinning wheel, useless now, but along the wall hung a long tapestry. He could drape it around her.

He stood up and walked over to it, but as soon as he placed his hands on it she waved her hands to stop him.

"But why?"

She was panicked, and came toward him. She didn't seem violent, and he let her approach. She took the crook of his arm, and started tugging on him. He was about to ask what was wrong, when she froze, and in her silence he could hear the slightest sound from outside the room. It was a sliding, shuffling sound.

Like a pair of dead feet being dragged up a flight of stairs.

Aurora pushed Philip behind the tapestry, hiding him under its fabric while she raced to the door and shut it. Then she scrambled back to her tube of ropes, and struggled to enter it again. She was about to lie back down when she saw the sword on the floor. Hurriedly, she hopped over to it, and nudged it to the pile of hay. She had barely regained her position in the center of the room with the sword beneath her when the door of the chamber was pushed open, and the Evil Queen entered the tower.

Philip watched in silence through a tear in the tapestry as the Queen made her way to the corner of the room that housed the spinning wheel. She stood before it for a moment, and then reached out to take the needle from the machine. It came off with such ease that Philip was sure this was a scene that had played many times before. The Queen turned back to the center of the room, facing Philip, and bent down to Aurora.

Then she took the needle, and stuck it into Aurora's shoulder. Philip fought with all his might to stand still. Aurora, for her part, didn't even flinch. A line of blood trickled from the small wound, and the Evil Queen reached inside her robe to produce a small goblet. She held it to the flow of blood, pricking the skin once more when the blood coagulated, and then brought the goblet to her dead lips. She stuck out a dry grey tongue and lapped up the fresh blood, licking up every drop until her tongue was scratching against the dry interior of the goblet. Then she stood up, replaced the needle on the spinning wheel, and slowly made her way out of the room, closing the door behind her.

Philip didn't move. He waited until he could no longer hear the Queen's footsteps, and then still didn't move. Aurora was motionless on the ground, her eyes closed, and he figured she would know better than he when it was safe to walk about. Eventually, Aurora sat up, and Philip threw aside the tapestry and came toward her.

As she struggled out, he saw now what he hadn't noticed before. What had looked like scars on her skin were in fact the calligraphy of her abuse. This was a ritual, Philip realized, the Queen taking Aurora's blood. Then he remembered the trail through the dust. It must be the reason she wanted the girl in the first place, and Philip thought he remembered hearing whispers when he was a boy, stories of the Queen bathing in the blood of virgins in an attempt to remain perpetually young. He had forgotten those tales until now.

Aurora slipped out of her ropes again, and Philip looked at her with intense pity. "I'm going to rescue you," he told her. "No one is ever going to hurt you again."

She looked at him with attention, but it was in such a way that he wasn't sure if she understood a word he was saying.

Never mind that now. He could explain later. He took up his sword from the ground, and crossed to the door. It was locked from the outside, but the gears of the lock were so rotted with time that he easily cut them away. The door swung open, and he turned to Aurora.

"Come with me," he said. "We have to leave now, before the Queen suspects anything."

Aurora raised her eyebrows and took a step back. She retreated to the back of the room, holding her arms around her chest, and shook her head no.

"I'll protect you," Philip said, crossing toward her. "I promise."

She looked up at him, and then beyond to the open doorway. He could see the temptation in her eyes. Then she looked back at him, and held up one finger. She needed a moment.

It was such a human gesture that it seemed odd coming from her in her state. Philip waited, and Aurora bent down and placed her hands on the stone of the wall. Barely discernable in the moonlight were childish drawings, like cave paintings, of a series of little women, fairies with magic wands and pointed hats. And Philip realized that Aurora was saying goodbye to these drawings, as if they were friends she had to leave behind. For all he knew, these imaginary friends were as real to Aurora as he was.

As she whispered to these images, Philip had to turn away. He looked up at the opening in the stones high above him, trying to imagine what it must have been like to spend a life in this hellish chamber. There was a dribble of dew under the window. That must have been her drinking fountain. What did she eat? he wondered. He couldn't imagine the Queen providing her with food.

She stood up and turned to him. He looked into her eyes, and wondered, Did she even remember him? Did she remember her life before this prison?

He was about to turn to leave when his eyes fell on the tapestry, and he thought it might be best to take it with them, as a way of covering Aurora once they were out in the woods. Aurora stared in amazement as he ripped it off the wall, as if he had just moved a mountain that had been on the horizon her entire life. He tried to wrap it around her, but she only pushed it off. He ended up folding it up into a bundle and tossing it over her shoulder, which she allowed. Then they went down the stairs.

He forced Aurora to hold his hand on the way down, pulling her from step to step like a stubborn mule. When they eventually landed on the bottom, he saw a look of astonishment on her face as she examined the hallway, the ceiling, the floor. It was as if she had never been out of that room, as if she were seeing all this for the first time.

She nearly screamed when they turned the corner and saw the Queen's throne room through the archway. He held his hand over her mouth until she calmed, and then she simply stared curiously at the unmoving dead. He looked up, his eyes moving to the throne—to find it empty.

Philip gave a sharp intake of breath, looking forward at the trail of dust. Ahead of him in the hallway were his footsteps from earlier. And overlaid upon them were a second set, dragged across them. The Queen must have seen his marks, she must have—

Aurora screamed. A moment later he saw it too. The Evil Queen shambled toward them from the darkness of the hallway, her mouth open in a dry rasp, and her hand extended, reaching for them.

Philip grabbed Aurora by the hand, and led her through the archway of the throne room, away from the Queen. The dead were waking under their cobwebs, their heads turning and mouths opening with a groan. Aurora's scream had broken their slumber.

They ran the length of the room, the Queen following behind. She shook the shoulders of any of the dead who were still sleeping as she passed, and their groans echoed throughout the room, undoubtedly waking more of their legion in the depths of the castle. Philip and Aurora barely made it to the second archway before the dead around them had risen to their feet enough to lunge after them.

"Down here!" Philip shouted, pulling Aurora to the second dark stairwell. They had no time to be cautious with this one, and they half ran, half fell down the steps.

The dead were rising in the courtyard as they passed. A lone man had stumbled into the middle of the hallway, blocking their path with his arms extended. He wore a shroud of cobwebs like the veil of a bride, and when he opened his mouth to groan, a torrent of spiders emerged, the black bodies crawling over the dead man's face and skittering along his shoulders and down his chest.

Losing no time, Philip raised the sword and hacked the man down, slicing him through the middle as if he were one of the briars blocking his path. The force of the blow sent the spiders flying, landing on Philip and Aurora. Hurriedly, he brushed the little things off of his clothes, shuddering as he felt them run over his fingers. He turned to Aurora to help her, only to find her with a delighted expression on her face.

She was plucking the spiders off of her bare skin, and popping them into her mouth like candies. As she crunched away, Philip had his answer for what foods constituted the girl's diet in her cell.

The moans of the dead, both in the courtyard and those shambling down the stairs, brought him back to attention. He led Aurora back to the hallway that contained his entrance, and then remembered it was still blocked. He poked desperately at the stones, trying to dislodge them, as the dead grew closer and closer. Aurora tugged on his sleeve, and he shouted at her, "This was the way I got in! It's blocked now!"

She let go, took two steps to her right, and unhooked the latch that locked the door. It opened without trouble, and she stepped through.

Philip blinked. He hadn't thought to use the door, not after having so much trouble getting through from the other side. He scrambled after Aurora, shutting the door behind him, but unable to close it completely with the dead pushing from the other side. With no time to grab his armor, he took Aurora and ran through the open mouth of the castle, back into the crisp open air, and over the drawbridge of the castle. He didn't stop until they had made it to the other side of the tunnel through the briars, and here he called out Jack's name.

"Jack! It's me: Philip. Come out *now!*"

But no one came out of the woods, and there was no time to look for anyone. With one hand holding the hilt of his sword, and the other holding Aurora's hand, he turned south. If he could make it to the southern end of the wall, he might be able to avoid the hordes he encountered on his way to the castle. Then he could follow the wall back to the gate entrance where he began.

It was such a relief to be out in the open air again after the confines of the castle that when Aurora's feet began to slip as she ran, he simply lifted her in his arms and carried her. She was so light that he barely felt the weight, and even if he had, he wouldn't have minded. He knew that for her, this flee from the castle was probably more exercise than she had gotten in over ten years.

When the trees began to thin, Philip knew they were approaching the wall. They hadn't seen a single one of the dead in the past ten minutes, and Philip was fairly confident he had outpaced the Queen's legions. Regardless, he knew they were still behind him. Even if they weren't, there were plenty of others he might come across. So when he reached the dark shadow of the wall that circled the land of the dead, he didn't stop. He simply turned to his left, toward east, and kept going through the night.

When the dawn broke ahead, Aurora began to stir in his arms. He set her down, and she rubbed her eyes, looking around her as if she had forgotten what had happened and how she had gotten here. The tapestry was sagging off her shoulder, about to fall off, when she glanced back at Philip. Dim recognition showed in her eyes, and then she looked to her right, toward the wall.

Stepping toward it, the tapestry fell from her shoulders into the dirt. Philip picked it up and followed after her. Just as she stopped before the wall, the north wind blew the curls of her hair over her shoulders. There, on her right shoulder, was the rose birthmark. Philip stared at it as if looking at the face of God.

"Oh, Aurora," he said, overcome with memories, "I've missed you so much."

She turned to him, her bleary eyes widening, and looked with fear toward the woods. Philip turned, hearing what she did: the sound of branches snapping, of something coming toward them quickly from within the trees.

"Behind me," Philip said, placing himself in front of Aurora with his sword ready.

Out from the trees galloped a horse, the horse from Philip's party, and chasing the horse was a stream of the undead.

"Whoa, boy!" Philip cried to the frantic animal. He ran

up to it, trying to ignore the wild look in its eye as he reached for its reins, and dragged it back toward the wall with Aurora. The horse, still wild, seemed to recognize that Philip was not like the creatures chasing it, and submitted to stand as Philip lifted Aurora onto its back, and then climbed up himself. Once in place, with Aurora held in front of him, he kicked his feet into the horse's side and sent it galloping along the wall.

He turned behind him, seeing a throng of the dead emerge into the open space near the wall. He couldn't tell from this distance if any of the creatures following were the men who had chased him in the palace. As they grew smaller in the distance, he turned forward, grateful to be able to so easily outrun them.

Once the panic of flight left him, Philip took in more details about the horse. There were gashes along its neck, and one in particular that was clearly a bite mark. This horse would not last long before the infection would take it, and Philip intended to push it as far as it could go on their route to the gate.

Aurora, meanwhile, became more and more disturbed by the rising sun. She whimpered, pressing her face into Philip's chest and trying to block out the light with her hands. After all those years in her dark cell, she couldn't stand the brightness of the world, not even when the sun was blocked as it was now by low-hanging clouds. Philip wrapped the tapestry over her like a cloak, and she left it on this time, shutting herself away in her own private midnight.

The horse lasted until what Philip estimated was noon. Its front legs crumpled forward, and Philip barely had time to throw himself off with Aurora bundled in his arms to avoid being crushed. He patted the poor animal on its hot neck, thanking it mentally, and then continued on foot with Aurora.

They were nearly at the town by now. He thought he could see the peak of the palace over the trees, but he couldn't be certain. Despite their proximity to the gates, Philip was now too tired to carry Aurora, and their pace was considerably slowed for this last stretch. It wasn't until late afternoon when the wall began to turn north, and Philip could see the entrance gate at a distance through the mist.

"We did it," he said to Aurora with relief. "We're going to make it!"

She grunted at him under the tapestry, but didn't bother to look out to see what he was talking about.

But as they neared, a crowd of the dead became visible, huddled directly across from the gate.

"This way," Philip whispered, drawing Aurora closer to the tree line and away from the wall. They made their way forward in the shadows of the trees, trying to walk as silently as possible, and watched the circle of the dead massed ahead. They were children, the children from town, and as Philip got nearer, he could see that none were facing him. They were all facing inward, to some center of their circle. And when he got nearer still, he could see—and hear—what that center was.

Jack was perched in a dead tree across from the gate entrance. The dead children surrounded him, reaching their arms up as Jack tried desperately to remain out of their grasp. Every now and again he'd slip, causing the children to surge forward with expectation, and Jack to scream out in terror as he shimmied back up the branch.

On top of the wall, watching the scene, was the Gatekeeper.

Philip looked from his friend, to the Gatekeeper, and back to his friend. None of the dead were watching the gate. If he and Aurora were quiet and slow—and they would have trouble being anything but slow—they might be able to make it to the door without attracting notice. Then they could wave to the Gatekeeper, and make it through without a fight.

It was a horrible plan, both in its morality and potential

for failure, but Philip couldn't think of another option. He couldn't fight that many of the dead, and even if he could, he might not want to if it meant putting Aurora in further danger. His first responsibility was to get Aurora to freedom; Jack knew what he was getting into.

There was a bitter part of Philip, too, that knew that if Jack hadn't fled before, if he had remained at Philip's side, he wouldn't be in that tree now. It was what he deserved.

He turned to Aurora, taking her by the shoulders and forcing her to look at him. "We're going to go around them," he whispered, "And we have to be very quiet as we do it, otherwise they'll hear us. Can you do that?"

She stared at him for a moment, her expression blank. Then she nodded.

"Let's go."

Together they walked through the open sunlight and through the range of ashen tree stumps to the wall. The dead were still a hundred paces in the distance, but not one had turned around. Once along the wall, Philip pressed his body against it, and with careful steps, started to work his way north. Aurora followed behind him, the tapestry around her shoulders like a shawl.

The Gatekeeper saw them when they were nearing the horde of the dead. Philip implored him with his eyes to remain silent, and the Gatekeeper's expression relaxed as he understood their plan.

Then, when they were nearing the doorway, Jack saw them.

"Philip!" he cried out. "Help me, Philip! Don't just leave me here to die!"

Philip put his fingers to his lips, but it was too late. Some of the children were turning around. A moment later, some were shuffling forward.

"Open the gate!" Philip screamed, and pounded his fist against it.

"I'm sorry," the Gatekeeper called from above, "but I can't with the dead so near."

Philip cursed, and then had Aurora move behind him. He would kill every last child if he had to, if it would save Aurora.

They stumbled toward him, their eyes glowing with hunger, and formed a line in front of him. The tallest among them, the pigtailed girl with the green-leaf cape, seemed to be their leader. She stepped out first, and twisted her features into a snarl.

"Back!" Philip yelled, raising the sword. This gesture seemed to make the children smile. The girl took another step forward.

But then Aurora pushed on Philip's shoulder, and let out a piercing, deafening scream. Her hand came out from behind the tapestry, and she pointed north, between the trees and the wall.

There, standing in the mist, was the Evil Queen. She stood tall and proud, although dead, with her grey-white skin ageless and taut on her stern face. There were no soldiers behind her, no entourage, but she marched forward imperiously as if leading all the dead of the earth. The children froze when they saw the her, and the shoulders of some shrank down in fear, like dogs cowering before their alpha.

But the girl in pigtails only snarled with more intensity than before. She ripped the cape from her back, and held it in the air like a flag of war. Then, groaning with incomprehensible rage, she charged forward, throwing herself at the Queen.

The other children watched in stunned silence as the pair connected, the girl ripping at the black cloak of the Queen. Then, as one unit, the rest charged the Queen as well.

The Queen threw the children off of her, undeterred in her progression toward Philip and Aurora. The children bit and scratched, but were unable to harm the Queen in her armor. She threw off a girl that Philip recognized as Ada, Rip

Van Winkle's daughter. The girl tumbled, picked herself up, and then reached into her pocket for a long match. Just as the Queen had come within five paces of Philip, the flame caught the back of her cloak, and sent her dry body up in flames.

She spun in a circle, unable to put out the flames as they rose on her body, burning away her cloak, scorching her armor, and blackening the well-preserved skin of her face. As the flames smoked, she reached up to her face, feeling not the fire, but the horror as her beauty turned to monstrosity.

Then, still sizzling, she brought her charred gaze toward Philip, and stampeded toward him.

"Run!" he yelled to Aurora, pushing her to his left and blocking her from the Queen's path. The Queen tried to reach past him, but Philip struck at her armor with the sword, knocking her arm down. Aurora escaped, and the Queen turned to Philip instead.

He kicked her back, the white heat of her armor searing his boots. She barely felt the kick, her boiling armor clicking together like the exoskeleton of a giant insect. There was no use trying to get it off her now; it was melted onto her skin.

She came at him again, scratching treacherously with her gnarled fingers, and he pushed her back by landing his sword in her stomach. It didn't pierce the armor, and she threw him against the gate, glaring at him with absolute maleficence.

As their eyes met, Philip knew what it meant to be face-to-face with the Devil. There was no humanity left in the Queen's gaze. Her eyes had been boiled yellow by time and fire, her skin had been blackened, and as she leaned in to snap her teeth at Philip, smoke sizzling up from her body, she looked less like a lady than a dragon.

She pressed down on him, and then reached out and caught him by the wrist, trying to dislodge his grip on the sword.

This was the end. This was how he would die, and there

was nothing more he could do about it. Still, he kept his eyes on hers, refusing to look away.

And then, suddenly, the Queen flew from his sword, and was thrown to the ground at his right. Philip looked up in surprise, and saw Aurora standing there, naked, holding a large rock with both hands and glaring at the Queen with a savage expression.

Before the Queen could get up, Philip jumped to his feet and lunged the sword through the back of the her neck. He wiggled the blade upward, cracking off her helmet and slicing through to the brain. The writhing body of the Queen collapsed underneath him, and Philip stepped back, pulling out the blade.

Behind him, Aurora stepped forward with the rock, and heaved it down on the Queen's skull, smashing it in half. She brought the rock up again, and down again three more times, decimating the Queen's brain to colorless pulp.

She turned to Philip, her chest heaving, and dead flesh falling off the rock in her hand. Then movement to their left brought both of their attention to the trees.

Jack had climbed down during the fight, and had attempted to work his way toward the gate. He stopped now, ten paces away from Philip. He realized the eyes of not only Philip and Aurora were on him, but of all the dead children as well. Jack turned to run back to the trees, but in his haste he stumbled, landing face first in the dirt.

The children turned to him, away from Philip and Aurora, and rushed toward their meal. Meanwhile, Philip lost no time in gesturing to the Gatekeeper.

"Let us pass now," he called, "while the dead are distracted."

The Gatekeeper nodded. The bolt of the doorway sounded, and Philip gratefully pulled it open. Aurora followed, stopping only for a moment to pick up her tapestry, and then stepped with him into the dark passageway. He saw a note of fear on her face as he shut the outer door, and placed his hand on her shoulder.

"Don't worry," he whispered, "we're safe now. It's all over."

The outer door bolted, and they stood in the darkness waiting, listening to the sounds of Jack's screams grow louder, and then silent. Then, outside the other door came the Gate-keeper's voice.

"Just the two of you in there?" he called.

Philip went to the door and confirmed it. Then the lock slid open, and Philip allowed Aurora to take the first steps out, her first steps of freedom in over ten years.

"There's a crowd waiting for you," the Gatekeeper said in an uninterested drone. "This way."

He went before them, walking slowly on the path back to the settlement. "They were encouraged when the other one showed up in the tree," he continued, "although I knew his case was useless. And now that there are two of you—and the *princess*, no less—they will be unable to contain themselves."

Philip was silent, the fatigue of his journey making each step an effort. He was relieved though to be back. Any amount of exhaustion was worth having Aurora at his side again. He smiled at her, and noticing the gore speckled on her shoulders, he made sure to cover her nakedness with the tapestry.

With time, he thought, she would learn how to be a lady again. And they would rule the new kingdom together, saving the people from their despair, and ending the fear of the dead once and for all.

But as he thought this, a wave of nausea passed over him, and he had to let go of Aurora's hand to cover his mouth. When he took his hand away, he noticed a scratch on his wrist where the Queen had been holding him. It wasn't more than an inch long, but it was already darkening like a bruise, and causing the blood in the veins around it to blacken.

He stumbled, and the Gatekeeper turned around.

No, he couldn't let it end like this. If he told them now, he'd be thrown back into the land of the dead. Who would take care of Aurora? Who would make sure she was crowned?

And what about him? Didn't he deserve his happy ending as well? Why ruin that for a scratch? He wouldn't become a monster. He wouldn't let it get that far.

Philip felt more tired than ever, and pulled his sleeve over his wrist. He took Aurora's hand again, and continued down the path to the settlement.

As the trees parted, the rumblings of the townspeople could be heard.

The Gatekeeper stepped forward first, presenting Aurora to the stunned onlookers. Philip watched from the shadows, his mind growing drunk from sickness.

"Your princess," the Gatekeeper said. "Safe, at last." Then he turned to Philip on the path, and motioned him forward. "And here, I present your new king and savior."

Philip could feel the energy of the crowd surge. He had rescued their long-lost princess; he had saved their town. He wouldn't let it all happen again.

He tripped out into the sunlight, and met their cheers with a smile.

THE SCREAMS OF POCAHONTAS

Pocahontas was an ugly little troll of a girl, her father's least favorite out of a hundred children.

She was short, with a pig's nose and buckteeth, and eyes that looked as dull and empty as a toad's. She had no talents, and nobody loved her. But despite her flaws, Pocahontas had a poet's soul, and yearned to experience the mysteries of life. She wanted to soar with the eagles, sail beyond the sea, and discover what lurked just around the riverbend.

But all her village would give her was a basket, and an order to fill it with corn.

It was the harvest.

The women of the tribe had been sent out at dawn into the cornfields, their faces tired but resolute. They wore deer-skin outfits that did their figures no favors, and wore their black hair in ponytails. The sky glowed pink overhead as they trudged through the morning mist, and the birds chirped and the air smelled of evergreen. It might have been a nice day, had there been a chance to enjoy it.

Pocahontas sighed, last in line to collect her basket.

"Every day like the last," she whined, pulling her skirt lower to hide her thick legs.

"No thanks to you," snapped Grandmother Willow.

Pocahontas looked up at the old medicine woman of the tribe. She didn't understand Grandmother Willow. The old woman should be kooky and fun. She practiced medicine and magic, and earned her name by living in a giant Weeping Willow tree. They should be friends.

But instead, the old woman was close-minded and strict. She had no sense of adventure.

Pocahontas took her basket and stalked into the corn-fields, catching up to her sister Nakoma.

"How is she not dead already?" she joked.

Nakoma didn't laugh. She held her head high, and said, "Everyone has to do their part."

Pocahontas rolled her eyes. The two sisters had been close when they were younger, but lately Nakoma was less concerned with friendship, and more focused with becoming a respectable woman of the tribe.

They parted ways, and Pocahontas started to pile dry husks of corn into her basket for the fourth day in a row. She heard Nakoma laugh with one of their other sisters from the next row over, and felt even more alone than usual.

She hated this place. She hated everything about it.

She was just about to trade in her basket for the third time when a great blast came from up on the hill—the bellow of the conch shell.

The conch was a warning: an alert of incoming armies or the outbreak of war. The women turned toward it, the panic rising within them.

Powhatan, their chief and Pocahontas's father, had praised the coming months of peace at last night's fire. A surprise attack at this time was extremely unusual.

Pocahontas heard the footfalls of her many brothers as they ran past the fields and then worked their way like ants up the side of the hill. With her eyes on them, her hands took another basket, and went back to the task of plucking the corn from the stalks.

Unfortunately, the conch was a warning to be answered by the men. The women had to keep working. But even though none of the women changed their actions, the energy of the field had changed. The chatter had stopped, and the women's faces grew tense.

Something was wrong, and they waited in suspense, unable to see anything from their side of the hill.

Finally, one of the tribe's warriors came back down the hill and into the field. Kocoum was a strong man, but he shook with fear.

"What's wrong?" asked Grandmother Willow.

Kocoum, his eyes wide and unblinking, could not answer. He motioned for the women to follow.

The group of women dropped their baskets on the spot, and ran as one behind Kocoum. They made their way up the hill, and when they got to the top, Pocahontas found herself at the end of a crowd of people. She heard gasps and talk of alarm, but she could not see what was the matter.

She pushed her way forward, squeezing in between those that had arrived before her, and stepped to the front of the crowd. She looked below.

From this vantage point, she could see the vast expanse of grey river before her, dimmed and hazy from the fog. Her eyes flicked down to the shore, taking in a great mass of boulders, and then moving on when something inside her stomach twisted. It was the kind of internal twisting that she would get if she found a spider crawling on her arm. Her eyes returned to the rocks, and at once she realized why they had seemed odd to her.

There had not been rocks there before.

The mist circled around the base of them, a base that seemed unusually smooth and curved. Then, as the fog flowed around the mass, she could make out great shapes floating in the air above it. These were as white and wide as clouds, and blended in with the fog to such a degree that she could only see them because they remained still while the clouds shifted around them.

An indistinct terror rose within her, and she could feel the buzz of fear in the people around her.

It wasn't a boulder. It had too distinct of a shape for that. This was something built by intelligent hands, yet so different in size and design from anything she had ever seen before that it obviously came from someplace distant and alien.

"It's a ship," said one of her brothers with a gasp. "It's a ship!"

Pocahontas shook her head; it was too big for that. What kind of monster sailed in a ship so huge? The panic rolled within her stomach again until she thought she might be sick.

There was talk behind her, and she felt her back being pushed by the shuffling of the crowd. Her father, the tall and proud Powhatan, made his way forward. He was dressed in a robe of deerskin, decorated with raccoon tails, and wore a royal headband adorned with turkey feathers. His face was lined, his black hair shaved, and his face and chest tattooed with blood-red insignias.

His face betrayed no emotion. Part of what made him a good leader was his ability to hide any and all emotion in situations like this.

He listened as the lookout relayed what little information there was: within the last hour, this massive entity had crashed against the shore. The ship had not moved, nor had any man come out. None of their people had gone any closer than they were standing now.

Powhatan nodded, taking this in. Then he pointed to two warriors holding spears. "Go down," he said, "and report back."

Pocahontas and the rest of her people—all work had ceased in the village by this time—stood on the hill and watched as the two warriors worked their way down the side of the hill, and out onto the beach. It was now apparent just how large the ship was when the men approached, their size giving context to the colossal height of the ship. It must have been taller than ten men standing on each other's shoulders. Everyone held their breath as the warriors drew near to the ship, and there were gasps as they tapped on the side with their spears.

Then they walked around to the far side of the ship, blocked to the villagers' view.

It seemed like hours before they emerged again, and made their way back up the hill, their faces looking relieved for being back in the safety of their people.

"It is unlike anything we have ever seen," they told Powhatan. They told of strange building techniques and materials they had never seen before. They discovered a ladder on the far side of the ship made of rope. When they climbed it, they found the deck bare, and everything in a state of ruin. The masts were broken and the sails ripped. But there were doors to below, with strange writing carved onto the frames above them. All of these doors were locked.

"Were there any men on board?" Powhatan asked.

The warriors shook their heads. "Nobody. Not that we could see, anyway."

Powhatan took this information in without so much as lifting an eyebrow or moving his lips.

"We will wait," he said. "A lookout will be placed at all hours to monitor any changes. Warriors will be kept at the ready. Everyone else, back to the fields. We must not starve because a curiosity has washed ashore."

Pocahontas's mouth dropped open. They had a visitor from another world, and she was supposed to go back to picking corn?

The warriors and women around her nodded, accepting the chief's pronouncement in silence. They began to work their way back down the hill, and Pocahontas lingered behind with Powhatan.

"Father," she whispered, "where does this thing come from? And who is inside?"

"That's no business of yours," he snapped. "Your job is to think of the harvest. Don't waste time thinking foolish thoughts."

With that, he turned back to the village, and Pocahontas was forced to return to the field.

As she picked up an empty basket and entered a row of corn, the ship dominated her imagination. Anything could be inside. The object was too foreign, too different, to be from another tribe. But who had sent it? What had been their purpose?

And were they still on the boat?

Lost in these thoughts, the day passed slowly for Pocahontas. By the time the sun had hidden itself in the far land, and the evening fires were lit, her shoulders ached and her soul burned with curiosity. She helped the other woman prepare the nightly meal in silence, setting out the eating tools and cleaning the sitting places. The work was done, and this time of relaxation only wound her up more.

Finally, when the food was finished, and her people were sitting around the fire, talk was allowed to center on the ship.

"It has not moved since this morning," one of the lookouts told the others. "Perhaps it has fallen from the stars."

"It is the gods," stated Grandmother Willow, the firelight creating strange shadows in the wrinkles of her face. "They have come to revel in the harvest, as in the days of old."

"Why would they come now?" Pocahontas asked. "What is different now?"

The old woman ripped the meat off her squirrel bone, and smiled. "Perhaps some people aren't working as hard as they should."

Pocahontas dismissed this, but not lightly. And the other women around her looked down nervously. She hadn't been the only one slacking at the harvest. The idea of gods arriving to offer great punishments was much less encouraging than the fantastic beasts Pocahontas had been imagining.

The night turned black, and the women started to return to their lodge to sleep. There were no more reports from the ship, and to Pocahontas's bewilderment, no one seemed to think much more about it. She held her tongue and settled into a hammock in the lodge, her mind still racing, and listened as the women around her fell asleep one by one. She stared with eyes wide open at the hammock above her, the bulk of one of her sisters weighing down its net, and thought of the ladder on the side of the ship, flapping in the breeze, practically inviting her...

She tossed and turned, but was unable to sleep. Finally, after listening to Nakoma snore for the better part of an hour, Pocahontas couldn't take it any longer. She had to see the ship.

Just one look, she told herself. No one would be harmed in that. If anyone asked what she was doing up, she could feign indigestion.

She rolled out of the hammock, setting her bare feet on the floor. Then she crept past her sisters, out the door flap, and hopped along the path through the village. The fire had been reduced to a pile of glowing embers, and three men sat around it dozing. Otherwise, she didn't see a soul.

The cool mist of the forest kissed her bare arms and ankles once she reached the trees. She instantly regretted not planning ahead enough to bring something to wrap around her shoulders, but figured the excitement of the night would have to be enough to distract her from the cold.

She tiptoed along the path through the forest, a walkway so familiar to her that she could walk it blindfolded. Which was fortunate, as she was nearly blind in the darkness of the night. She hurried on, and as the tension of being caught by the tribe lessened, she began to notice all the strange sounds that were made by the creatures of the night.

Things rustled in the branches and bushes around her. At one point, a mouse scurried across the center of the trail and tickled her feet. At another, she walked right into a thick spider web that stuck to her face and hair, and made her feel itchy all over. And all along, perhaps most unsettling of all, she could see the animals watching her in the shadows, their eyes reflecting the light of the moon.

Midway along the path there was a slight offshoot that led through tall grass to the great Weeping Willow tree that Grandmother lived in. Pocahontas crept carefully here, as the old woman was said never to sleep. She turned away as quickly as she could.

The path narrowed on the way to the beach. Most people used the path over the hill, so this way had become over-grown in the last season. She pushed her way through, branches scratching against her arms, until she finally reached the mud of the shore. She looked down, seeing her arms laced with light scratches, and knew she'd have to come up with an excuse for those in the morning.

But she would worry about that then. Right now, she had a ship to explore, a ship from another world.

She ran across the shore, for fear of one of the lookouts seeing her. She was far from his post, and there was a heavy fog in the air, but she didn't want to take any chances. She ran straight to the water's edge, and felt the icy waves lap around her ankles. She came up along the far side of the ship, ducking low as she ran, and didn't stop until she pressed herself against the cold hard wood of the vessel itself. Her chest was heaving, and, from the eerie sensation of touching the ship itself, goosebumps erupted on her scratched skin.

It was like touching something forbidden, something ancient and powerful.

She ran her hand along the wood, feeling its grain with her fingertips, and touching the metallic nails that kept the giant beams of wood tight against the ship. This was an entirely different form of construction than the canoes and sailing boats her own people built. It was larger, more sophisticated, and sturdier.

And yet... why did it crash? If it was so advanced, why did it wash up on shore the way it had?

She tilted her head to the sky and stared up at the ship. She could barely make out the high sails in the fog, but she could hear the material flapping in the breeze. The ladder itself smacked against the side of the ship. She waded waist-deep into the water, and then reached up toward the bottom rung.

The ladder was at least familiar. And as she climbed up, she realized the ladder was built for someone her size. That is, the size of a human.

So much for Grandmother's gods.

Maybe these creatures were more like her tribe than anyone expected? Maybe these beings weren't so powerful after all.

But all the confidence that thought had given her vanished as she heaved herself over the railing of the ship, and rolled herself onto the massive deck.

It was much as the warriors had described, only seeing it in person was a completely different experience. There were little rooms with windows that stuck out from the deck floor. She crept up to one of these, marveling at the material that was used in the windows. It was translucent, and divided into little squares. She pressed her hand against it.

It was as smooth and clear as ice, only not as cold. And when she touched it, it did not melt. But when she took her hand away, her fingertips removed some of the grime, so that she could see through toward the inside. She used her palm to wipe away a small circle, and then peered inside.

It was a room, elaborately furnished. There were scrolls laid out on tables, and fantastic instruments, not put away.

There was what looked to be a cup on the table. But where were the ship's sailors? How long had they been away?

She drew back from the window, and followed along the rail to the rear of the ship. From there, she saw a set of stairs leading to a raised platform. She climbed them.

At the center of the platform was a wooden wheel with spokes in a great circle. She looked at it for a moment, confused by what it represented. Was this a way to make the sun rise? Or something else?

At this point, all restraint had been replaced by curiosity, and she went toward it at once, placing her hands on it.

It spun at an axle in the center, and revolved for a quarter of a turn before it locked up. She put both hands on either side, pretending she was sailing, and she understood: it was some sort of guiding wheel used to steer the ship.

It was ingenious. Perhaps these were gods after all.

With great reluctance, she left the wheel platform. She made her way back to the center of the ship, tasting the mist on her lips, and growing used to the leather sound of the sails slapping in the night breeze. Near the middle of the deck, the flooring was replaced with a crosshatch grating made of a dense metal, like a fence placed on its side. She tested the grating with her feet, but didn't trust it enough to walk over. It looked too much like a cage.

She was about to move on, when a freezing blast of wind swept by her side.

It blew away the fog, and allowed the moon's light to cast a sharp beam directly onto the deck of the ship. It passed through the lattice of the grate, and sent silver squares down to the cavern below.

It was a room. There were sacks of what she guessed contained food, a mess of straw thrown about, and a series of metal chains that were connected at one end to a post on the wall, and at the other end, in the center of the room, to a hairy demon.

It lay on the floor, pale and fat, with a face and head covered with dark hair.

Pocahontas stumbled away from the grate, and ducked down to the edge of the deck. Her heart thundered, and her eyes scanned the deck for escape. The rope ladder was on the other side, but she was too scared to go across the grating again to reach it, not with a chance of that thing jumping up and touching her. She heard it shuffle down below, and Pocahontas gasped.

She threw her hand over her mouth to stop any future outbursts, but it was too late. At her gasp, the thing below stopped moving. Then it did something that made Pocahontas's entire body shiver, from the scalp of her head to the toes of her feet.

It spoke.

The thing below whispered in a gruff voice that she recognized as male, but in words that she had never heard before. It was a strange new language, and Pocahontas was certain that whatever was speaking to her now, whatever was making its first communication, was one of the things from another world.

It whispered again, a long slithering sound like the wispy hiss of a snake. And Pocahontas closed her eyes, wishing to wake up from this nightmare.

She sat there, huddled, until her fear had subsided enough for her to attempt to cross the grating. She crept along the deck, intending to climb down the ladder and run back home to the safety of her hammock. But as she neared the grating, her curiosity overwhelmed her. For some reason she couldn't explain, she would feel safer if she could see that the creature was still there. Maybe because if it was still down below, that meant it couldn't be on the deck with her, or waiting for her down on the shore.

She crept up to the grating on her stomach, and peeked over the side.

The creature was still there, looking down on the ground. The hair on his head was twisted and long, as well as the hair around his mouth. She was about to move on, when it looked up at her with wide, blue eyes. She stopped, and they stared at each other in the moonlight, taking in the sight of the other.

She marveled at his gaze, finding it full of melancholy and longing. Whatever his strange appearance, it was clear that he was suffering.

Then she noticed the shackles around his wrists, and suddenly the whole picture seemed incredibly sad and lonely to her. It was hard to be afraid when he looked so vulnerable, and she forgot all about leaving the ship.

Could it be a man after all? If it was a man, he was unlike any she had ever seen before.

Perhaps he was the man of the wolf, the one Grandmother Willow had told stories about? The man who lived on the moon, and would come down from the sky once a month when the wolves howled to him.

Only this man, in his strange ship, didn't seem to be someone out of *their* stories. He was from somewhere else entirely, somewhere beyond her imagination. This made him all the more interesting.

She crept closer, laying her body over the grate. The man below, his eyes never leaving hers, said something again. Only now his whispers seemed softer. He reached up his hand, and repeated his expression. She could not understand the words, but the intention was clear: he was asking for help.

"I don't know how," she said in her own language, her heart racing with the adrenaline of talking to the stranger. He stared at her a moment, obviously not understanding her words but trying to guess at the meaning. He said something else, a single word as a question, and she could do nothing more than stare back at him in response.

Then he pointed to his wrist, where a metal cuff was

attached. Its chain led to the wall. He was locked up. He pulled on his chain to show her this, and then looked up at her imploringly. His eyes looked brighter from being in the middle of his hairy face.

He was quite beautiful, in his own way.

He raised both arms to her, pantomiming that he was lifting something, and after a moment of guesswork, Pocahontas saw that he meant for her to lift the grating. Should she? But then, what was the danger if he was locked up? She crawled back from the grating, so that her weight was no longer heavy upon it, and then pulled against it. It clanked and would not give.

After some fiddling, she discovered that a cylinder had to be pulled back and another latch thrown at the same moment. Then there was a click, and she could lift the grate. She stood up, holding it as she swung it open along a hinge, and set it down carefully on the deck. Then she looked inside, and saw the man smiling at her. She smiled back, feeling ridiculous, and she could swear she heard him laugh a little. It was a laugh you share with friends. She laughed too, and his eyes were so appreciative and so welcoming, that without a moment's hesitation she hopped down below into the ship, and landed in the straw a few paces away from the man.

She stood up to her full height, and they stared at each other, neither daring to take a step toward the other. He was taller than her, and oddly dressed. While she was barefoot, wearing a light animal skin around her waist and torso, he had a number of strange fabrics molded around his body. There was a light colored billowing shirt that was open at the chest, and it looked stained from the many days within this prison. He also wore a set of leg coverings that were molded to his shape, and instead of bare feet, he wore intricately carved boots, the fashion of which Pocahontas had never seen. He was dressed so peculiarly, that his frazzled hair and beard did not seem the strangest thing about him anymore.

He moved slightly, and the moonlight sparkled on the metal shackles around his wrists.

He caught Pocahontas gazing at them. He pointed to one. Then he pointed at Pocahontas.

No, not at her. Behind her.

She turned her head and squinted into the darkness, barely able to discern the walls of this man's prison. She looked back at him, and he nodded his head, smiling again. He mumbled some words of encouragement, along with a single syllable spoken over and over.

Pocahontas took a careful step back into the darkness of his prison, and when she grew closer, she saw a metal ring hanging on a hook against the wall. On this ring were what looked to be shining metal fingers. The man repeated his word again when she looked at this thing, and urged her to take it.

She lifted it off its hook. Immediately, the man held out his hand before him, palm up, and clasped and unclasped his fingers like a hungry raccoon. He wanted this thing she held, what he kept referring to as "keys."

"Keys?" she said, testing out the word, and the man laughed a little too heartily and nodded vigorously.

"Keys," he repeated. "Keys, keys!"

And by his eagerness, and the way he had pointed to his shackles earlier, Pocahontas understood that these keys unlocked his chains. They would let him loose.

But she stayed where she was, eyeing this wild man.

As curious as she was, she also felt incredibly vulnerable. She was a young woman, and no one knew she was here. She had nothing resembling a weapon, and she was in the dark with a creature whose history she could not even imagine. Could she trust him? She wanted so much to talk to him, to understand more about him.

"Why are you locked up?" she asked in her own language. "Who put you here?"

But of course he did not understand her. He was still

chanting his one phrase again and again: "Keys, keys," something something, "keys!"

She looked again into his eyes, and the gaze that met hers was so kind, so intelligent, that she couldn't imagine him doing anything wrong. He must have been locked up here against his will—as an innocent. Maybe he was the outcast of his tribe, just like she was of hers.

She stepped forward, and put the key ring into his outstretched hand.

His whole body was shaking with excitement as he stuck one of the keys inside a hole on his shackle. There was the sound of something dislodging inside, and then the cuff split in two and fell away. The man gave a shout of glee, and then hurriedly jammed the key into his other shackle. It fell to the floor of the room with a loud clank, and he laughed, rubbing his sore wrists with pleasure.

Then he looked up at Pocahontas, as if he had forgotten she was even there, and something in his mood shifted.

His smile fell from his face, and he stood up tall, placing the keys into a pocket on the front of his garment. He stared at her from the center of the room, the moonlight casting long shadows over his eyes and nose, his expression unreadable.

Pocahontas's fear returned in a flash. She started to tremble, and backed up to the corner of the dark room. What had she done? How could she be so foolish? He was bigger than her, and his eyes—a look of feverish hunger began to shine from them, a look made all the more terrifying by the tangles of his wild mane and beard.

They weren't a team. He was a wild animal. Pocahontas chastised herself through her fear. How could she be so easily won over after a lifetime of abuse? Hadn't she learned anything about human nature?

He took a step toward her. She put her hands up to shield her face, and let out a scream that echoed into the night.

He took another step, ignoring her cries, and took hold of her hand, pulling it away from her face. She screamed with even more panic now, and watched in horror as the man sunk down below her, crouching, pulling her hand to his mouth. She was unable to pull it away.

His mouth touched her hand with a kiss.

Her scream was silenced, and she stared down at the man with wide-eyed surprise.

He kissed her hand again, his tearing eyes looking up at her with unrestrained gratitude. He whispered something that sounded reverential, apparently thanking her for releasing him. And she was so dumbfounded that she could do nothing but stare as his soft lips touched each one of her fingers. He wasn't going to hurt her. He was thanking her. Kissing her.

She had never been kissed before.

Maybe she had been right to trust her instincts after all? They locked eyes, and although she could not understand a word he said, she could listen with her heart. He did not shrink away from her appearance, and she realized that this might be the only person she'll ever meet who wouldn't be biased by her reputation in the village.

But the intimacy of the moment was broken by a shout on the beach. The lookout had heard her screams.

"Quick," Pocahontas said, taking the man by the wrist and pulling him to his feet. "We have to get you out of here."

He looked at her in dumb incomprehension, but gave no resistance when she tried to pull him back to the center of the room and out through the grating. They climbed back to the deck, closed the grate, and ran back to where the ladder hung. Pocahontas went down first, with the strange man climbing down second and jumping out into the wet waves of the river beside her.

He looked at her like a helpless child, shivering in the cold, and she was tempted to stop and hold him. But there was no time.

"Come," she said, and took him by the hand. She pulled him toward the shore, and together, water dripping from their bodies, they ran along the beach. She hid him behind the first tree she found, and then raced back to throw sand over their tracks. In the daylight it would be obvious where she had traveled, but she hoped in the darkness the lookouts would not notice. Then she went back to the tree line, and led the strange man through the dark woods, along the path through the trees, and emerged back at her village.

She had to hide him. There was no telling what the men of her village would do to this kind, strange-looking man. And she felt an overwhelming desire to protect him. She had freed him from his chains; he was now her responsibility. Plus he just seemed so defenseless.

Her eyes scanned her village for a potential hiding place. She spotted a hut used for drying animal skins, and led the man quickly inside before anyone could see. She closed the flap that acted as a door to the hut, and waited for her eyes to adjust to the darkness.

She could feel the man breathing beside her. He now seemed more afraid than her, and then she saw why:

This hut was full of supplies for skinning and stretching the flesh of animals. There were curved hooks and knives, skulls picked of flesh in piles on the floor, and animal parts strewn haphazardly along shelves. It was a place of death, and it smelled foul.

"Oh, but it's safe," Pocahontas whispered. "You can stay here."

She took the man and sat him down on a pile of furs, and tried to make him understand that he was to stay put.

"You can't leave," she said, pointing outside and then slapping her hand, to show that it was the wrong choice. She wasn't sure if he understood. So instead she kneeled down to him and pressed his head against the soft furs. He seemed to understand this, and curled up in the pile. She wanted so much to stroke the hair on his face, but she didn't want to frighten him any further. So instead she covered his body with animal skins, to keep him warm, and to hide him from view.

She began to back out of the hut when she saw him stir. He poked his head out, and then reached an arm toward her.

He said something, in a quiet voice, that expressed great yearning. As if he didn't want to be left alone.

"I have to go," she said, much as the way she might speak to a pet. "I have to go back before my sisters wake."

He pouted, and it was both unexpected and endearing to see his hairy mouth make this human expression.

Then, without warning, his entire body convulsed beneath the furs, and his face twisted in agony. He started to cough into a closed fist, his breath wheezy and phlegmatic as he struggled to breath.

It was then that she saw, by the ray of moonlight coming through the open flap of the hut, that the man's wrist was crisscrossed with blackened veins. It made Pocahontas's insides squirm just to look at it. He had touched her.

Kissed her.

The man regained himself from his coughing fit, and then saw her staring at his wrist. He quickly pulled up his sleeve to cover his arm.

But she had already seen. And looking at his sallow face, the dark circles around his eyes, she did not know how she could have missed it.

This man was sick.

She motioned for him to cover himself again with the furs, and he did so. Then, stepping lightly, Pocahontas left the hut, and made her way back to the women's lodge. A dark frown had formed on her face. She slid under the door flap, and then tiptoed her way back to her hammock.

Maybe the man wasn't sick. She couldn't know for sure. Maybe he just needed a safe, warm place to rest and a few good meals. She could provide that for him. There was also the possibility that this was simply the way he looked normally. She had no way of knowing.

She settled into her hammock, her heart racing and her body exhausted. She closed her eyes, eager for sleep yet knowing she'd be less likely to fall asleep now than before she went out.

She felt the dread of responsibility for bringing this man back to her village. She had let him out of his prison, and there was no putting him back again.

What would happen if he were a demon after all?

*   *   *

"You look dreadful," Nakoma told her the next day. Pocahontas had been dragging her tired body though the field, collecting even less of the harvest than the day before. Her mind was distracted by the man in the hut, and even more so by the fact that she hadn't had a chance to visit him in the morning, and now it was almost midday. Was he even there? What if he left? She had to check.

"Pocahontas?"

"I think I need a break," she said, turning to her sister. "Will you cover me if I take a nap?"

Nakoma looked about to say no, when Pocahontas added, "For old time's sake? I won't tell anyone."

With this, her sister relented. "I'll distract Grandmother. But you'll owe me one."

Pocahontas agreed, and snuck around the rear of the cornfield while Nakoma pretended to ask the old woman's advice on what hairstyles were best to attract a man's attention.

Pocahontas tried to walk slowly through the village so as not to attract attention to herself. Some of the older women were busy around the fire pit, preparing the meal for later in the day. She managed to snag a piece of cornbread as she passed, but almost bumped into a trio of warriors in the process. She kept her eyes to the ground, but didn't fail to notice that they carried spears and tomahawks, and that their bodies were painted for war. They walked toward the hill in the direction of the river, and Pocahontas slipped inside the hut where she had hidden the man.

She glanced at the pile of animal skins and furs in the corner of the hut, but couldn't tell if the man was still under them. He was either gone, or hiding extremely well.

Then she realized that he had no way to know it was her. He would be blind under the blankets. She bent down to the floor.

"Are you there?" she whispered, and lifted up an edge of the fur.

She almost gasped when it revealed a head looking back at her, its skin pale and eyes bleary.

It was the man. He hadn't dared move until he saw it was her. Then he let out a sigh, and pushed himself up from the floor, the furs sliding off of him.

"I brought you something," she said, and picked up the cornbread. She held it out to him.

He looked worse in the daylight, or maybe he had become worse in the intervening hours. His face was white as snow, and his forehead was crossed with dark black veins. His eyes were red and swollen, and, when he reached out for the bread, his hand almost glowed in the shadows of the hut. The back of his hand was streaked with the same blackened veins of his forehead.

The man took the bread, and began choking on it at once, the crumbs flying from his open mouth. Pocahontas tried to hush him, but it was no use. He put his hand over his mouth to muffle the sound, and kept coughing until he hacked up every last particle of the cornbread.

The cornbread, and a few sticky globs of black blood.

He tried to hide this by wiping his hand on the furs, but Pocahontas had seen it and felt her stomach grow nauseous.

THE SCREAMS OF POCAHONTAS

Still, the thought of losing her new friend this quickly made her feel even worse.

"Are you sick?" she asked him, although she knew he couldn't understand. "Are you in pain?"

He looked up at her, again as if he had forgotten she was there, and stared at her intently. He didn't say anything.

Then, with almost inhuman slowness, he raised a hand to his chest and laid his palm against his heart. He said something, and she didn't recognize the words. He repeated it again, slowly, again pointing to himself. Her mouth formed the words unconsciously as he said it again.

"John Smith," she said.

He nodded excitedly, and then took her by the hand, and pressed her palm close to his chest.

"John Smith," he said.

She answered the same, and then something clicked.

At once, she took his hand and held it to her chest. "Pocahontas," she said. "Pocahontas."

It took him a few tries, but eventually he got it. They had been introduced. The exhilaration of this filled her with so much joy that she forgot entirely about his sickness, even about their situation as a whole, and started picking up random objects in the hut and sounding off their names to him.

"Deer," she said, stroking her hand along the pelt of a deer. She laid it over his waist as he sat. "Raccoon," she said, holding up a raccoon head, the flesh still on it. She set this on a shelf behind him. "Rabbit," she continued, and in a few minutes, John Smith was covered with a pile of different parts and heads and skins. He looked so silly among them that Pocahontas giggled and sat down in front of him.

She was having so much fun that she had forgotten it wasn't safe to make noise, and a moment after she laughed, she heard a voice say, "That's where you are!"

The flap was pulled back from the hut, and Grandmother Willow stood outside, clutching Nakoma tightly by the arm.

Nakoma mouthed, "Sorry," to Pocahontas. The old woman let her go, promising to deal with her later, and then shuffled inside the hut, closing the flap behind her. She hobbled into the room, and stood over Pocahontas.

"My dear child," she said, "what are we going to do with you?"

Pocahontas froze. She had been caught. And by the worst possible person in the entire tribe. If it had been one of her sisters, she might have been able to interest her in the adventure of the situation. Or perhaps bribe her somehow. But Grandmother Willow didn't like fun, and she had no use for possessions. She already had whatever she wanted without trade.

She squinted at Pocahontas. "What's the matter with you girl?" she snapped. "Your face looks *guilty*."

The old woman's eyes scanned the room, and Pocahontas couldn't breathe as Grandmother Willow's gaze went over the raccoon heads, the deer pelts, and John Smith's head exposed among them.

The old woman went on scanning, mistaking the man for one of the animals, and then turned back to Pocahontas. "What is it then, you lazy beast? Sleeping while your sisters work themselves to death?"

Pocahontas opened her mouth, but it took a second for her body to be able to make noise again. "I—I needed a rest. But we can go back now."

Grandmother Willow let out a deep sigh. She hobbled around Pocahontas, and sat down—directly on John Smith's lap. Pocahontas gasped.

Grandmother prodded him, taking him for a chair beneath the pelts, and then she stared at Pocahontas. It was all the girl could do to keep her eyes on the old woman's face, and not John Smith's directly above it.

"You've always been a troubled thing," the old woman said. "You need to start thinking about your future. You've only got a few good years left. After that... well, they won't even be able to look at you."

Pocahontas could only nod. She didn't want to start a fight, but she couldn't very well agree with the old woman's insults without arousing suspicion.

Besides, Pocahontas already had a suitor. The old woman was sitting on him.

"I might as well be talking to a tree stump," the old woman said, giving up. Then, shuffling in her place, she began poking her "chair," trying to make it more comfortable. "I should know better at my age when to give up on a child, when they're not worth it. But I'm too kind for that. My heart is too big." She elbowed backward sharply, and John Smith let out an *oof*.

The old woman froze, and her eyes flashed to Pocahontas. The girl looked back at the old woman with a frantic expression, one that only made the old woman's surprise turn into shrill panic.

She turned around, feeling behind her as she did, until she was face-to-face with the pale hairy stranger.

"Ahhh!" cried Grandmother Willow. She fell away from John Smith onto the floor, taking the pelts with her and seeing him now as unmistakably alive. She started to scream again, and John Smith pounced on her with a quickness and violence that made Pocahontas jump. The old woman tried to squirm away, but he wrestled her to the ground. He managed to put his hand over her mouth, keeping her from screaming more, as she fought beneath him.

"Stop struggling," Pocahontas whispered to Grandmother Willow. "He won't hurt you."

The old woman turned to Pocahontas, her eyes filling with betrayal. She mumbled something under John Smith's hand, and Pocahontas answered.

"Please," she said, "he's my friend."

John Smith looked up at Pocahontas, and said something

in a tone so grim and determined, there could be no mistaking his meaning: he wanted to kill the old woman.

Grandmother Willow, for her part, seemed to understand this. But rather than play along and keep quiet, she doubled her efforts at escape. She shook her head rapidly, and managed to slide partway out from under his grasp. As his hand came to her mouth again, the old woman bit into it with her ancient teeth.

John Smith screamed out, whipping back his hand and looking at the bite. Grandmother Willow turned her wrinkled face to Pocahontas, and gave a proud smile, her lips dripping with blood.

Then, in a flash, John Smith was on her again. He picked her up by the arms and slammed her back onto the floor of the hut. She tried to scream again, and he gripped her throat with both hands and started strangling her in a fit of rage.

"Stop!" Pocahontas cried.

Just then, the hut exploded with noise. The flap was ripped off, and five warriors rushed in with spears and axes. Pocahontas was thrown to the floor, and Kocoum bashed John Smith in the chest to knock him off the old woman. Then the men pounced on him, holding him down as they tied up his wrists. Grandmother Willow groaned from the ground, bruises forming on her neck, and the blood still fresh on her lips from when she bit the man.

John Smith did not fight his capture. He allowed the men to tie him up, and when they dragged him from the hut, he looked back at Pocahontas with the oddest of smiles. It was calm and almost sinister, as if he were still in complete control.

Pocahontas climbed to her feet and left Grandmother behind on the floor. She was unable to stop the men before they dragged John Smith into the tribe's meeting lodge, shutting the doors and locking her out. Pocahontas was left standing in the center of the village, shaken and confused.

Women were returning from the field at the noise, and some ran past her to help Grandmother Willow.

As soon as she was on her feet, the old crone began shouting.

"A monster! Pocahontas was hiding a monster in the village," Grandmother Willow said. "The girl was trying to ruin us all!"

"No!" Pocahontas shouted, but already a crowd was forming, the men and women encircling her. She started to cry. "You don't understand," she said. "He was gentle."

"He attacked me!" Grandmother Willow cried, throwing up her hands and playing to the audience. "He attacked a defenseless old woman!"

There were grumbles in the crowd.

"You scared him," Pocahontas said feebly, but no one was listening to her. The crowd had already decided her guilt, and some were edging closer to the meeting lodge, trying to hear what was happening inside.

Pocahontas regained her composure and tried to work her way forward to hear as well, but she was pushed back repeatedly.

Then, much too quickly, Kocoum emerged from the lodge. "Our chief," he said, "the noble Powhatan, has decreed that we will send this white devil back to hell."

The crowd cheered, and Pocahontas's legs went weak. This was happening too fast. She had just met this man. Now they would kill him, before they had learned any of his wisdom, without knowing why he arrived in the first place.

The warrior continued. "He is to be executed immediately, and the ship to be burned."

More cheers from the crowd.

"Wait!" Pocahontas cried. "Let me see my father! I have to explain."

The warrior shook his head. "The chief does not desire any further council."

Tears formed in Pocahontas's eyes, but the expression in them was firm. "I *must* speak to my father," she said, and rose to her feet. "There is something about this man that he must know. Something that will be lost if he is killed."

Of course, Pocahontas didn't know *exactly* what would be lost. But she had to try something.

The warrior looked at her for a moment, and then disappeared into the lodge. In his absence, the crowd scrutinized Pocahontas. She heard whispers among them, but no voice was louder than Grandmother Willow's.

"Possessed," she said. "She's been possessed by a devil. Burning—that's the only cure. We have to burn it out of her."

The warrior returned just in time. The crowd was already starting to advance on Pocahontas.

"Your father will see you," he said.

Clutching her left elbow with her right hand, Pocahontas made her way forward. She stepped through the doorway of the meeting lodge.

The room was hazy with tobacco smoke, and animal heads hung from the walls. At the rear of the room, directly in front of Pocahontas, sat her father. Spears and war trophies were placed on the wall behind him, and he sat on the floor with his arms crossed, and his pipe sitting next to him untouched. A thin wisp of smoke curled up and disappeared into the ceiling.

On his left was John Smith, his entire body roped and his mouth gagged. He was lain out on the ground like the centerpiece of a feast. Next to his head was a smooth black rock. It was half the size of his head, and would be used to break through his skull.

"No," Pocahontas gasped, running forward. She threw herself in front of her father and prostrated herself. "Please," she said. "Grandmother started the fight. This man is not dangerous. He is gentle and kind, and we know nothing of the ways he can help us. Just look at his ship, and think of the wonders that might be on board."

"He attacked one of our own," was her father's response. Pocahontas lifted her head from the ground. "But that's not true! I saw the whole thing. She bit *him*, not the other way around. Grandmother was just scared because he surprised her."

"She's lying," said a voice behind her. Pocahontas turned to see Grandmother Willow smiling at her with a look of satisfaction on her face. Then she turned back to her father.

"Please," she begged. "You have to trust me."

He stared at her a moment longer, and then shook his head. "He is too dangerous."

"No!" Pocahontas shouted. Her father rose to his feet and started to walk over to John Smith, and bent down to pick up the dull rock.

He was going to kill her friend. He was going to smash his beautiful face.

"No!" Pocahontas shouted again. "I won't let you."

She ran across the room, and threw herself on top of John Smith. "If you kill him, you'll have to kill me too."

"Daughter, stand back!"

"I won't!" she shrieked. She turned and looked up at her father, careful not to take her arms away from John Smith. She met Powhatan's eyes, and then looked away with embarrassment. "I love him, Father. I choose him as my mate."

The warriors within the hut gasped. Grandmother Willow's smile grew larger and the blood sparkled on her lips. Powhatan could only look at his daughter with his mouth open, unable to speak. Finally, he started to shake his head.

"You have brought great shame upon our family," he whispered. "Great shame." Then he reached down, and took Pocahontas by the arm. He yanked her off of John Smith, and when she tried to crawl back, he took her hair in his fist and dragged her across the room.

She screamed, the pain burning her scalp, but he did not stop. He tossed her outside the hut like garbage, and then turned to go back inside.

But Pocahontas could not be suppressed. "No!" she wailed, and wrapped her arms around her father's ankles, holding his feet together so that he could not walk. "Don't! Don't!"

"Get off me!" her father snarled, and tried to kick her away. "I must kill the devil!"

He reached down and slapped her across the face, but she would not let go.

"If you don't let go," he shouted, "I will kill you too!"

"There's no need," said Grandmother Willow, stepping out from inside the hut. They both looked up, their fight interrupted. She held the stone in her hands. "The devil is already dead."

Pocahontas let go of her father and started to rush the old woman. "You murderer!" she screamed, and was stopped in her advance by a line of warriors. She was ready to beat the old woman to a bloody pulp.

Grandmother Willow laughed. "I didn't kill him," she said, handing the stone to Powhatan. "Although I would have been glad to." She pointed back into the lodge. "He was sick, my dear. He died on his own."

Pocahontas was allowed to see for herself. She ran back into the lodge and fell at John Smith's side. "It's me," she said. "John Smith?" He did not move. His open eyes, frozen in an expression of agony, did not blink. His chest did not rise and fall.

Chief Powhatan entered and pushed Pocahontas away to see for himself.

"He's dead," Grandmother Willow repeated, following them into the lodge.

Powhatan looked at John Smith's face, and then reached forward to touch his hand.

"Ah!" he said, dropping it. "He is like ice."

He wiped his hands and then stood up slowly. To his warriors, he ordered that the body be wrapped up for a quick burial.

"We must first flush the demons out, before he is in the ground," said Grandmother Willow. "The girl too. I have the tools back in my tree, the pokers and prodders. She'll be seeing all the colors of the wind before we're through, you can be sure of that. And if she tries to fight it—"

Her speech was interrupted by a horrible coughing fit. It seized her frail body, and brought her to her knees. She held up a hand to keep the warriors back, and kept her head down as she coughed fiercely.

When she rose to her feet again, the ground beneath her was pockmarked with dots of blood.

"I need my medicines," she said, her voice weak. "The demon's power is strong."

Powhatan nodded. He pointed to several warriors, and ordered them to accompany the old woman to her tree in the forest.

"I feel my throat burning," said the old woman. She rubbed her neck with her fingers, her veins darkening on her wrinkled hand. Then she caught Pocahontas looking at her, and a cruel smile formed on her lips.

"Don't think your black magic will work on me, girl," she wheezed. "I'll be fine once I'm out of your sight."

She turned to leave with the warriors, then paused with a cruel smile.

"And Powhatan? Don't forget to lock up the little demon lover. She might try to escape while I'm gone."

With that, the old woman hobbled off, leaving Pocahontas to be encircled by the guards.

* * *

KEVIN RICHEY

Pocahontas was tied to a post near the center of their tribe. She was given neither food nor water as the day turned to afternoon, and the tribe members went on with their daily routines. John Smith's body had been wrapped in a blanket and placed by the fire pit near to her, and she stared at it, feeling a mixture of pity for the man and fear for herself. Grandmother Willow had never liked her; now she had an opportunity to torture her senseless.

But Grandmother Willow didn't return, and the next morning, a second trio of men was sent into the woods to retrieve her. This group returned almost immediately, one member of their party wounded in the attempt.

"She's gone," Kocoum told the chief, holding a bloody hand. "The men as well. Not a sign of them."

Powhatan asked what had happened to Kocoum's hand, and the warrior laughed shakily.

"Just a raccoon bite. A bandage and I'll be fine."

"Strange," muttered Powhatan. "Raccoons are normally peaceful creatures."

But the raccoons weren't the only animals that seemed bewitched that day. Wild crows forced the women out of the fields early. The crazed birds swooped and attacked like no one had ever seen, and many women returned scratched and bitten, already developing fevers. The men returned from their hunt early as well. Strange rustlings and unnatural sounds in the shadows destroyed their nerves, and they were almost glad when Kocoum started vomiting blood, as it gave them an excuse to head back.

By nightfall, all work had ceased. The women retired to their lodge, and the men gathered around the fire with their chief. They dared not speak above a whisper, glancing from the dead man to Pocahontas, and back again. Pocahontas glared at them from her post, but she said nothing.

Then, after an hour when no one seemed to speak at all, the quiet of the night was broken with a scream.

548

Kocoum, who had been sitting among the others around the fire, suddenly and heavily fell forward into the dirt, his face inches from the flames. Those nearest to him pulled him back from the fire, but it was obvious in a moment that there was no need to worry about his safety: he had fallen over in death.

No one wanted to touch him, and before they could fully comprehend the tragedy, sobs were heard from the women's hut. Nakoma and two of their sisters ran out and sought the attention of Chief Powhatan.

"They're dead!" Nakoma cried. "All the women that had been scratched—their bodies are stiff and lifeless!"

Powhatan stood rigidly, trying to hide his panic. The ripples of the fire's light blazed against his blank expression as his mind tried to work out a reassuring command.

"Help us, Powhatan," Nakoma wailed. "Tell us what is causing this."

Powhatan turned uncomfortably, his eyes moving through the crowd. Then they landed on Pocahontas.

"It is her," he said. "The white man is dead; he is not the source. It is *her* that is causing this."

The entire tribe quieted and then joined in his gaze. At the sight of someone so low and defenseless, fear turned to hate in their eyes. Here was something they could handle.

Pocahontas pulled back at her restraints. Her wrists were bound, and she dropped to her knees. "Please," she whispered. "I am innocent!"

"Silence!" her father yelled, and he came toward her through the crowd. His hand went to his belt, to the holster of his tomahawk.

"But I'm your daughter!" she yelled, looking from his eyes—eyes that looked eerily calm—to the faces of her friends and family. She spotted Nakoma. "Sister!" she called. "I have done nothing!"

"Quiet, white demon!" shouted Powhatan, drawing out

his tomahawk. "You cannot fool me. I see you for what you are."

Pocahontas squeezed her eyes shut, unable to escape, and awaited her father's blow.

But instead of the tomahawk, what fell upon her were more screams.

She opened her eyes, and saw a commotion among her people. They were no longer looking at her, instead at something near the fire. She looked up, and her father was turning toward whatever had caught their attention, the tomahawk still raised above his head. The people of the tribe scrambled backward in fear, separating and revealing what had caused their alarm.

There, next to the flickering fire, was the tube of blanket that John Smith had been wrapped in after death. It was bent around the middle, perpendicular to the ground, as if the man were sitting up inside of it. Then, like a butterfly waking from within a cocoon, the blanket began to shake and loosen. It separated and fell to the ground. And there, sitting with a horrific grin on his face, was John Smith's living corpse.

Pocahontas stared in disbelief.

"She has summoned the dead!" shrieked Nakoma, pointing at her.

Before Pocahontas could object, there were shouts and screams from the women's lodge. Everyone turned to see the women streaming out, fighting each other in the doorway. The crowd bottlenecked, so that an old woman and two young girls could not get out. There were shadows behind them, and something from within the hut jumped on their backs and pulled them back inside. The women screamed, and the inhuman terror in their voices woke the men into action.

They pushed past the women that had fled the lodge and made their way to the doorway—and then backed away with a start.

A grey-skinned woman shuffled forward, her eyes blackened and lips raised in a snarl. Two more walking corpses joined her, and the three raised their arms, their sharp fingernails scratching at the air. The screams of the women inside the hut abruptly stopped, and were replaced with the sounds of flesh being torn and hacked.

The men stumbled backward, their eyes wide with horror.

"They were dead!" Nakoma screamed. "Those women were dead!" Then she turned and fled toward the trees, followed by the men and women of the village.

Pocahontas pulled at her rope desperately. She was not next to these dead women, but she was trapped, and that was dangerous. "Please," she called to her father, who had his back to her. "Please, let me go."

One of the dead women from the lodge stepped in their direction, her eyes filled with a demonic hunger.

Powhatan ran in the opposite direction, not even glancing at Pocahontas as he made his way to the tree line.

As the tribe reached the trees, Nakoma screamed. She was at the head of mob, and started to push back into the advancing crowd. A moment later there were more screams, both men's and women's. Pocahontas's panic increased, and she pulled at her ropes. She glanced back to John Smith, but the dead man hadn't moved. He simply watched the action with an amused smile.

The crowd retreated back to the center of the village, and it was then that Pocahontas could see why: stepping out from the darkness were the missing warriors, their bodies grey and lifeless, and their throats torn. They blocked any exit, and shambled forward with groans.

Nakoma, who had been at the front of the crowd, was now at the rear of the retreat. The dead warriors pinched the air in front of her face as she pressed against the backs of those nearest to her. The tribe members pushed her away in their own struggle for safety, and Nakoma lost her balance and slammed down to the ground. No one stopped to help her up.

Stunned, Nakoma struggled to push herself up as a low form crawled out from the trees behind her. It was only when the thing was right over Nakoma that Pocahontas recognized it as Grandmother Willow—only the old woman had changed. Her face was like a goblin's, twisted and deformed and pale, and her garment had been torn and soiled with blood. She pounced on Nakoma, laughing in a horrible cackle as the girl tried to escape, her young hands scraping at the dirt with no effect as the old goblin sat on her back.

Then, in one quick flash, the old woman descended, landing her jaws on the back of the girl's neck. Nakoma gave a frightened yelp, kicking her feet as the old woman bit harder into her skin.

In a moment, the old woman was ripping the girl apart. The wet sinews and tendons of Nakoma's flesh reflected in the firelight, and soon the girl's screams became a mild whimper. Pocahontas turned away, unable to look as her sister's life faded.

The dead warriors stepped forward toward the crowd. The tribe was trapped, encircled by the dead. With nowhere to run, the tribe members huddled against each other, clawing and fighting their way to the safety of the center without thought or human dignity. A child was knocked to the ground and trampled by his mother. Those at the center of the mass called out that they were being crushed, but the bodies around them only pushed harder, because all along the outside of the circle, the dead were snatching up the living.

And whoever the dead killed would rise from the ground and join their ranks, so that the numbers of the dead grew exponentially as the battle continued.

Pocahontas could only watch from her post as the earth drank up the blood of her people. She did not dare make a sound. The dead hadn't noticed her yet, except for one.

John Smith hadn't taken his eyes off of her. He watched her with a crazed amusement from his seat to her right. In ten steps, he could reach her. But he seemed content to remain a spectator at the moment.

Then something happened from inside the hoard of people at the center of the village. From within, pushing their way out, came the warriors, followed by Chief Powhatan. They ran past the grey-skinned corpses, dodging grasps and using what weapons that they had against them. Her father used his tomahawk to slice through a grey-skinned woman's shoulder, and was shocked when the blow did not seem to affect her. He the left weapon there, and followed the other men to the meeting lodge.

It was obvious to Pocahontas what they planned: the meeting lodge was the storehouse for the tribe's weapons. And surely enough, not a minute later, the warriors ran out of the lodge brandishing spears, tomahawks, bows and arrows. With a wild war cry, they ran toward their struggling people, and started to hack, slice, and pelt the dead.

When her father passed on his way to battle, Pocahontas yelled to him.

"Father!" she cried, struggling with her ropes in frustration. He couldn't possibly desert her at a time like this.

He turned toward her, seeing her out of the corner of his eye. Then, without changing his blank but deadly expression, he turned away and stepped into the middle of the battle, where the men worked to bring down the dead, but seemed unable to kill them.

Pocahontas watched her father hack down the grey-skinned demons, chopping into undying women and children, until movement at her side drew away her attention.

Grandmother Willow, walking on all fours, started to advance from the shadows toward Pocahontas. She carried something in her mouth like a dog, something dark and dripping, and her eyes blazed with an insatiable hunger.

Pocahontas tugged at her restraints without success, and as the danger neared, she grew so desperate that she began to chew on the rope. She looked up, trying to get a warrior's attention, and noticed that John Smith was struggling to free his legs from his blanket. He was still looking at her, and attempting to stand.

"Help!" she cried. "Save me!"

John Smith pushed away the last of the blanket, and wobbled onto his feet. It was obvious at once that, despite his reanimation, John Smith was still very much dead. The pallor of his skin was even more unnatural than that of the other dead, and his eyes were darkened with black circles. And when he walked, he seemed to do so only with considerable effort.

He was incredibly slow. Pocahontas turned, and saw that the old woman was only a few paces away from her. She pulled away as far as the rope would allow her. The old woman dropped what she was carrying in her mouth, and the object rolled toward Pocahontas's feet.

It was a head. It was Nakoma's head, rolling up to her bare feet.

Pocahontas cried out, and the eyes of Nakoma opened on the grey-skinned head, looking up with hatred. The head's mouth opened with a gasp, and then clacked shut again inches from Pocahontas's toes. Pocahontas gasped, and kicked the thing away from her, sending it rolling like a gourd into the tall grass.

She barely had time to look up to see Grandmother Willow jumping toward her. There was no time to react. Her teeth clenched as she anticipated the attack, when from behind her something knocked into her back, pushed past her, and flew through the air.

It was John Smith.

He crashed into the old woman, the impact of their bodies making a sickening crunch. Then they fell to the dirt, rolling and snarling, fighting each other like rabid dogs. Pocahontas stepped back as much as she could, and watched unsure if John Smith was fighting to protect her—or to protect his claim to eat her.

The old woman, weaker in life, was apparently also weaker in death. John Smith pinned her, sitting on her stomach and straddling her as he reached for her head with both hands. She snarled at him, clawing away his grasp, but he did not react as she tore at his skin. He held her firmly on each side of her skull, lifted it a few inches from the ground, and then slammed it down against the hard earth. Grandmother Willow's snarling intensified until foam bubbled out of her black lips, but John Smith did not stop. He lifted her head again, smashed it down, and repeated again and again until there was an audible crack. Her skull had been split down the back, and in the next thwack of her head to the ground, it exploded. Her brains spread like gelatinous slugs along the ground, and her body moved no more.

"You killed her," Pocahontas whispered, not realizing she was speaking out loud. She was too amazed that one of the demons had been stopped. This was the first she had seen defeated in the entire battle. "The head," she whispered. "You have to destroy the head."

John Smith let the old woman fall from his hands. He stood up. Pocahontas tensed as he turned his head slowly in her direction, but in his eyes—his blue eyes—there remained a glimmer of his human kindness. Despite all the violence, this look broke her heart.

"Why?" she asked. "Why have you done this to us? I trusted you. I ... *loved* you."

He smiled at her, his eyes glowing in his blood-splattered face. Then a grey tongue protruded from his mouth, and slid over his black lips. Pocahontas took a step back and reached the limit of the rope. He advanced on her, his hands raised like claws, and pounced.

"No!" Pocahontas cried, dodging a direct hit. John Smith's nails caught in her skirt, and he tugged at it, trying to pull her closer to his snapping jaws. Pocahontas lifted a knee and pressed it against his stomach, barely holding him back as he leaned forward, his teeth bared, trying to bite her neck. "Help!" she cried, and looked over at the melee of fighting in the center of the tribe. No one was looking.

John Smith snapped forward, and Pocahontas retreated, managing to remain one step away from him. But as she circled, her rope tethered around the post, and her range of motion became shorter and shorter.

Finally, the rope was no more than an arm's length, and she could no longer move from side to side. John Smith's smile widened. It glimmered from the middle of his tangled beard, and a husky laugh began as he realized his victory.

It must have been this laugh that finally got her father's attention. She saw him turn away from the fighting and start to close the distance between them. His tomahawk was raised, but he seemed so far, and to be moving so slowly. John Smith came close to her face, still laughing, when her father reached them. He knocked John Smith in the side with the tomahawk.

John Smith staggered to the ground, and her father brought down the tomahawk again, this time landing a blow in his stomach. He pulled it back, and chopped into his chest. None of this was having any effect on the dead man. He laughed into Powhatan's face, and Pocahontas was reminded of the smug look he had had at the end of his life, being dragged away to die.

He knew, she realized. He knew what would happen.

The dead man, undeterred by the blows, reached up his white hand to Powhatan's forearm. He gripped it, and Pocahontas saw her father try to struggle as the dead man pulled him toward his mouth.

"No!" Pocahontas screamed. "Don't hurt him!" Then

she turned up to the other warriors in battle. "Help," she cried. "Your chief needs you!"

At this call, three warriors ran from the fighting in her direction.

"There! There!" she called, and gestured down toward where her father struggled with John Smith.

"Ah!" her father cried, and Pocahontas saw blood.

The warriors arrived and kicked off John Smith, stabbing him and chopping at him, driving him away from their chief. The white man's smile didn't fade. He crawled away to the shadows, gave one last look back at Pocahontas, and then disappeared into the trees of the forest.

Meanwhile, the warriors were helping Powhatan to his feet. He was clutching his forearm, and from under his grasp blood streamed out. The warriors had started to lead him away when he stopped.

"Wait," he said. "Free her. Free Pocahontas."

The men hesitated. "But…" one said, "she is a demon."

Her father shook his head. "No. She was attacked by the white man, just like the rest of us. We have been fools, turning against each other just like he wanted. Pocahontas is one of us. Free her."

One of the men came forward, gave a tentative glance at Pocahontas's face, and then slashed through the rope: first where it connect to the post, and then sawing away at the knots around her wrists, until the girl was free.

She rubbed her tender wrists, and then ran to her father's side. "You must hit them in the head," she told him quickly. "It is the only way to kill them. A blow to the head."

He nodded, and then handed her a tomahawk from his belt. Clutching this, Pocahontas felt infinitely safer. Then, without another word, they fell back into the battle.

"Destroy the head!" her father shouted, and the warriors repeated his call. Pocahontas joined the men and hacked away at those of her tribe that had turned—those that in life had

557

ignored her; had mocked her; and had stood by as she was tied to a post and left to die. Her emotions were conflicted: she was angry with them, but even through her anger she knew they did not deserve to die. What was happening to the tribe was larger and more horrific than anything that had ever been done to her—or to any of them. And as she fought, side by side with her father and the other warriors, she felt a sense of belonging in her tribe that she had never felt before.

They had been bonded with their tragedy, all joined together against the common enemy of death.

With the knowledge she provided of how to kill the creatures, the tribe was finally making progress in the brutal fight. The dead piled up under their feet, and they stayed dead. But in the effort, more villagers were lost. The warriors were killed. The children were all but extinguished. And their home was reduced to ruins.

But at last, as the stars faded and the sky began to lighten, the fighting had ceased.

Pocahontas and the remaining villagers panted, crouching down and resting their elbows on their knees. They searched with quick eyes for any movement among the bodies on the ground, and wiped away the blood from their arms and faces. Chief Powhatan was still among them. He looked at the few that lived and the piles of the slain all around them, and his proud face crumpled in an uncharacteristic display of emotion. He looked ready to weep.

Their tribe of three hundred had been reduced to a handful of survivors.

Then his eyes searched the bodies on the ground, first casually, and then with growing panic.

"Where is he?" he yelled, kicking over the corpses. "Where is the white devil?"

The other survivors looked and started talking among themselves, the relief from the battle's end fading. Pocahontas felt her stomach turn stony with dread.

"He ran into the woods," she told him, and he turned to her. "He got away."

Chief Powhatan took her by the shoulders. "We must find him. *You* must help me find him. No one else remains that is strong enough to fight."

Pocahontas looked around at the feeble survivors: old women, little children, and young men who looked ready to collapse. Her father was right. There was no one left but them.

She nodded.

"You knew him best," he said. "Do you have any idea where he would have gone?"

Pocahontas blushed at the mention of her former love, and then closed her eyes to think.

At once the great ship appeared in her mind.

"His ship," she said, opening her eyes. "It is the best chance."

"Then that is where we must go."

They each armed themselves with a tomahawk, and then began the walk toward the hill, leaving the survivors behind and entering the shadows of the trees. They went in silence, and it was only in this quiet that Pocahontas noticed the ragged nature of her father's breathing. Each step seemed a struggle, and his face was clenched with obvious pain. As the path began to ascend, his pace slowed to a crawl.

"Let me help you, Father," Pocahontas offered, but he waved her away and tried to climb up the hill himself.

But after a few steps, he stumbled and fell.

Pocahontas kneeled at his side. "You are hurt, Father. You must rest."

He shook his head. "No," he said, "I must die." Then he brought up his right arm, and showed Pocahontas his wound.

The bite from John Smith had blackened, and the veins leading away from it were dark. "I don't have much time," he said, and looked up at Pocahontas. His forehead was dripping with sweat, and Pocahontas could feel the heat of his fever radiating from his body. "You must—" he said, and then coughed.

His shoulders heaved as he choked to breathe, coughing up blood and phlegm. When he recovered himself, he looked up at her with blood-shot eyes.

"I am sorry, daughter," he said. His voice was weak, but his tone was strong. "We have abused you, when you have shown yourself to be one of the strongest among us. Please forgive me."

She nodded.

"But you must not let your emotions cloud your sense. It is up to you to save our people. You must be strong. You must do what must be done."

Pocahontas was silent. Her father had never spoken to her like this. He was talking to her like an equal.

"A curse like this is vicious, spreading out like ripples on a still lake: small and insignificant at first; then growing wider and wider, until it is unstoppable. We must stop it before it travels outside our village, and destroys all the people of our neighboring tribes." He paused a moment to breathe, then continued, staring into her eyes. "Every instance must be stopped. *Every* instance."

She stood up, realizing his intent. "No, Father," she whispered. He was asking her to kill him.

His eyes left hers and went to something he had tied to his belt. "Here," he said. "Take this."

He held out a flat round stone. It was the same stone from the meeting lodge that had been intended to kill John Smith.

"Your heart must be hard to win this battle," he said.

"But Father—"

"*Take it.*"

Trembling, she took the heavy stone into her hands. Her father faced up at her, and she looked away toward the trees.

"Look at me," he commanded, and she was forced to turn back and meet his gaze. "Look at me as I die, and think of what caused this. *Who* caused this. Then you must go to the ship, and *end this*."

She looked down at her father, at his majestic face, calm and in command even now. His eyes glared into hers, unblinking, as she held the stone over him.

"End this," he barked at her.

Her shoulders shook, and her eyes filled with tears. Here was the acceptance she had longed for her entire life. Here was the love. Now she was supposed to let it go? After all this time? She hesitated, holding the stone.

"Now!" he shouted, his voice booming out into the air like the bellow of a conch shell's blow. *"Do it now!"* he screamed, and Pocahontas looked down at him. She met his eyes, tightened her grip on the stone. *"Do it!"*

She screamed at the top of her lungs, and brought the stone down on her father's face with all her might. It smashed into him, blocking his horrible open eyes, and cracked his forehead in two. His warm brains splashed out on her hands, and she let go of the rock as her father's body fell backward into the dirt.

Her palms stung with the blunt force of the impact, and the entire world took on a sharp, ultra-real quality that made the moment even more fantastic. She could feel his blood and brains on her bare legs, dripping down to her ankles.

She looked down at her father. He was dead now. It was difficult to comprehend, even after so much death. He would never love her again. Then she looked up toward the trees, toward the hills that blocked the view to the river's edge, and her chest began to burn with a rage she had never known.

He had taken this away from her. He had tricked her. The white man was to blame.

The unfairness of all her years ignited within her, and all at once every abuse, every name she had been called, every time she had been excluded, rejected, defeated—it all came into her at once until she was glowing with rage.

"Ahhhh!" she yelled into the mist, unable to hold it within herself anymore. She bent down, pulled a tomahawk from the belt of her father's corpse, and went running into the trees.

She did not need the warriors. She did not need her father. She would kill John Smith herself.

She climbed the hill with the most direct route—there were no more lookouts to be wary about—and stood at the top of the hill, looking down. The sky was lightening in the east with the first efforts of dawn, and down below, shrouded by mist, was the ship.

And on its cursed deck was a torch, burning like a dying star among the shadows.

The man had lit it. There was no question about that. But why, she did not know. She did not care. She would kill him by its light.

She whisked down the hill like an eagle on the wind, and dunked her bare feet into the sand of the beach. The grains stuck to the gore on her ankles, turning from white to red with the blood of her father. She continued on, and when she met the cold waves of the river, the intensity of the cold only added to her adrenaline.

She climbed up the ladder, staring at the glow of the torch reflected in the fog. Perhaps he had lit it to signal to her. She would meet his call gladly.

She reached the top of the ship, and fell over the railing and onto the deck. The sails were silent and still above her, and she looked up, surprised to see John Smith sitting on the platform, leaning against the steering wheel. He hadn't even tried to hide.

He faced away from her, out toward the water. Beyond him, at the rear of the ship, was the torch he had lit, and it made his outline black against its brightness.

At the sight of him she felt the sting of his betrayal. She had loved him, however briefly, but the memory of her love was no longer warm. Just the opposite: its residue choked her painfully, like the smoke after a strong fire.

She would not have her father's blood on her hands if she had not tried to save him. Now, she would correct her mistake.

Slowly, silently, she made her away around the little room and to the twin stairways that led to the top of the platform. With stealth she climbed the steps, not once making the wood creak, or exposing herself to the man. She would reach the top, and jump out to surprise him. One quick blow to the head, and this would all be over.

She paused near the top, looking at her shadow as it rippled from the torch's light. Even her outline looked different now. She was no longer the weak, unlovable creature she had once been. She now had the confident stance of a warrior.

She took a breath, and then thrust herself up to the platform. She landed on her feet in front of John Smith, her tomahawk raised and ready to strike.

He smiled at her.

She was startled by his joy, and stared at him in confusion. His arms were resting at his side, and his posture was decidedly relaxed. His face, illuminated by the torch's glow, was a mess of blood, tangled hair, and deadened eyes.

"Don't you care?" she asked him. "Don't you have any remorse for what you've done?"

And at her question, from deep inside his chest came a slimy gust of air. It smelled foul, and was repeated with more force, until Pocahontas realized that the dead man was laughing. He couldn't even understand her words, yet he was laughing at her. He took pleasure in her pain.

"I will kill you," she said, and raised the tomahawk higher.

He looked beyond her, and laughed some more. Then, with a lazy movement, he raised his hand and pointed behind her.

Pocahontas screamed at his gesture, imagining his claws

against her skin, and brought down the tomahawk on his skull. Its blade struck and vibrated down to her elbow. She lifted the weapon and hit the man again, widening the crack in his skull, and then lost all sense of herself as she brought down the blade again and again, chopping through his forehead, through his deceptive blue eyes, through his mouth and hair and beard, until in her wild rage she had decimated his head down to the stump of his neck. She landed a final blow into his collarbone, and then fell to her knees in exhaustion.

Her shoulders heaving, she stared ahead without seeing. There was no glory in the kill. There was no relief. Everything she had lost would remain lost.

"I'm sorry, Father," she whispered. "I'm sorry."

Then, slowly, as the deck of the ship grew brighter, her senses awoke to the scene. She was facing away from the river. Suddenly, she could hear something behind her in the water. The sound of splashing on the waves.

She turned, remembering when she did how the white man had pointed before he died. A newfound terror filled her breast as she stood to face the river.

The morning light had painted the river a dull grey. On the ship, the torch flickered at the rear, and beyond, on the river, was a line of floating lights stretching along the horizon.

In a daze, Pocahontas descended the stairs of the platform and walked to the railing at the rear of the ship, taking in the scene before her with astonishment.

Ships. There were more ships, being drawn toward the signal John Smith had placed. Each vessel was as large or larger than the one on which she stood.

And in front of these ships, splashing through the river and making their way forward, were hundreds of rowboats full of the white men. They seemed to fill every bit of space in the water. By the dawn's early light, Pocahontas could see plainly that these men were sick with a horrible plague, their jaws snapping greedily, and their groans filling the air as they set their eyes on the fresh new world before them, yearning to devour the land and everything living upon it.

It was obvious these people from another world were not just visiting; they had come to conquer. The battle that had raged in her town the night before was only a preview of the slaughter to come. John Smith was not an isolated ripple, but the first wave of a tsunami.

Pocahontas dropped to her knees.

Her people could not fight this, any more than they could fight the wind. All she could do is watch with fearful awe as the panoramic waves of death rose before her, blocking out the sun.

She trembled, the first witness to the end of the world.

ABOUT THE AUTHOR

Kevin Richey lives and writes in Spokane, Washington. When he's not working on his next book, he enjoys watching movies, reading, infrared photography, and touring the countryside of the American Northwest.

Find out more at **www.thekevinrichey.com**.

Made in the USA
San Bernardino, CA
19 March 2020

66002217R00356